BANNERS OF THE NORTHMEN

JERRY AUTIERI

1

October 885 CE

Ulfrik crouched behind the shrub willow, peering through the night at squat buildings outlined in silver moonlight. He focused on the mead hall. Orange light seeped from the edges of its doors, though no windows adorned this beggar's hall. His hands tightened on his spear, straining to listen but hearing only the purr of the sea on the nearby beach. With a grunt, he stood, the faded green tunic covering his mail hauberk catching a branch as he did. He replaced his helmet and sidled down slope to his men.

"They're in the hall, no guards at the door," he whispered to his gathered crew. Thirty men hugged the damp and cold earth, metals blackened with mud and dark wool cloaks drawn tight over their heads. Their breath rose in gray curls and their eyes flashed in the dark. They were as anxious as him to close the trap. "But there's no singing, no sounds at all."

The statement fell flat and the men traded worried glances. Toki pulled down his cowl and scratched his scalp. "They should be feasting or celebrating. Do you think they spotted us?"

Ulfrik shook his head. "If they were alerted, they'd be faking a celebration to draw us out. I don't understand the silence."

"A waste of time this was," a man muttered loud enough to demonstrate he wanted all to hear. Ulfrik did not need to see him to recognize Thrand's complaints. "We should not have listened to the gossip of traders."

"Then go back to the ship," Ulfrik hissed, instinctively tucking his head down. He mastered his tone and continued. "You'll get none of the spoils if you do. Are you with us?"

Thrand's dark shape sat like a lump of rock in the darkness. A few heads turned toward him, but most men looked aside. After a moment of chill silence, Ulfrik jabbed his spear butt into the earth to regain attention.

"Einar, you lead seven men up the east side and be in position to pick off anyone fleeing for the trees. Toki, take three men to clear out anyone on guard or wandering near the hall. The rest of you with me. We fire up the hall and kill whoever spills out."

Heads bobbed in acknowledgment. Einar and Toki selected their men and swept into the night. Waiting for them to reach their positions, Ulfrik removed his striking steel and gestured for the tinder box of dried heather branches. A ring of bodies crowded to block the sparks from enemy sight. In moments, Ulfrik breathed life into a small fire while another man unwrapped torches soaked in whale oil.

"We steal from thieves tonight," Ulfrik said to the remaining men. "A great treasure awaits us in that hall, one that will bring us honor and glory. Let's go."

Ulfrik cradled the tinder box while tucking his spear under arm. He did not lead a charge as much as a cautious jog. This was no glorious clash against enemies, no fair fight to bring glory to the victors. He consoled himself knowing these men in the hall were worse: slavers and murders who had happened upon more treasure than they deserved. He needed to raise a stronger army to defeat threats to his people, something only gold could enable.

Halfway to the hall, they touched their oil soaked brands to the tinder box, then converged on the hall. The yellow globes of fire fanned out around the building. A scream that collapsed to a gurgle broke across the field of silver grass. Toki had silenced guards and the raid had begun.

Torches spun through air to land on the roof thatch. A section fell away where a torch landed, such was the poor condition of the building. Too late to reconsider the truth of the raiders' wealth, Ulfrik kicked the hall door with a shout. He stumbled through, expecting it to have been barred but finding no resistance.

Men scrambled to their feet, having been lying close to the hearth in slumber. Ulfrik scanned for the nearest, most alert man, then hurled his spear at him. The ill-thrown shaft pierced the man's thigh and he collapsed with a howl of shock and pain. Ulfrik unslung his shield and drew his sword, blocking the door while he hoped the roof caught flame.

The raiders' leader sprung from the floor, clothed and wrapped in a bear skin, but unarmed. He kicked his drowsy men to life while the first tendrils of smoke spread along the murky ceiling. He and Ulfrik noted the smoke at the same time, and Ulfrik pulled back to seal the doors. He had only wanted to alarm and confuse them, and not burst in on them.

"Bar the door," he shouted as he backed up. His men fed spear shafts through the door handles. In the same moment those trapped inside slammed against the door, cursing and screaming.

The main force now trapped, Ulfrik spun about to face reinforcements. His crew had spread out, eyes on the surrounding buildings and weapons held low. No one came from the darkness, only Toki and his men emerging to the edge of the moonlight.

"They're all inside the hall," Ulfrik said, more to himself than anyone else. No women or villagers had been seen on the way in and none now came to the brightening glow of flaming thatch. This place was a hideout and not the home he had been told to expect. He hoped the other information was not as wrong.

The thud of axes shuddered on the hall walls, shaking off flaming bits of roof as the men inside chopped open an escape. The flames were not catching fast enough, and were dying in spots. Too much moisture was in the air and had permeated the thatch. But fear had gripped the enemy, and Ulfrik counted a frightened opponent half beaten.

Men burst through the wall with growls and oaths on their lips. Ulfrik and his crew prepared to meet them with iron. The first pair flew from the gap with axes flailing in wild arcs. Spears impaled them, and Ulfrik's crew shoved their bodies back into the gap to impede the others. But desperation won out, and more spilled through.

Another ax sundered the wall and widened the gap. Ulfrik trudged forward with his shield out, realizing the men inside were breaking free and had to be killed the hard way. "Crowd them at the wall," he ordered. "Don't let them escape in force. You three, follow me to the opposite side."

At a brisk stride, the men fell in behind. Rounding the corner, he found what he expected: another breach where an arm and leg already poked through. As the man fell out of the narrow opening, Ulfrik kicked him onto his back and stabbed down into his gut. A rush of others followed on the first, and Ulfrik wheeled to find the wall had collapsed wide enough to let through two men at once.

Now men leapt out, and Ulfrik ducked behind his shield as a poorly aimed blow struck for him. His three other men engaged those trying to flee, leaving Ulfrik to fend against two more.

The two foes ranged about him, and Ulfrik saw the rabid glint in the eye of the one he had named as the leader. Each wielded a short sword better suited for a shield wall than a fight in the open. Neither had shields. "Surrender and I will show mercy," Ulfrik said, though not softening his stance.

"By Odin's one eye! Die, you fucking dog!" The leader snarled and rushed forward.

Ulfrik named the strike before it even launched, reading the intention in the undisciplined motions of the leader. Turning to the side, Ulfrik slammed the rim of his shield into the face of the second attacker as he watched the leader's blade flash blue and orange in the night. A satisfying snap of breaking bone preceded the other attacker's scream. The fight unfolded like the slow melt of ice on a warm morning. Ulfrik merely had to watch the leader overextend his ferocious strike, wait for the armpit and ribs to slide out from behind the protective animal pelt, then ram his sword into the exposed flesh.

The blade slithered between the ribs beneath the leader's sword arm. The other opponent struggled to see through the blood and tears of his ruined face while his leader tumbled to the ground with death in his eyes. Ulfrik yanked up and back, so his sword would not snap as the man collapsed. It exited with a sucking noise and a thin trickle of blood trailed the blade.

Whirling to face his second attacker, he discovered the man crashing to the grass with a sword blade in his neck. Thorstein, one of Ulfrik's crew, had dispatched his foes and now assisted him. With all the attackers slain on his side, Ulfrik looped around the back of the hall to ensure no others had carved an exit. None had. Then he rejoined his men on their side, finding an easy victory for his crew.

The raid was over. Bodies heaped on the ground, some still half trapped in the breached walls. Blood puddled and arms twitched in the final moments of life. Over twenty raiders lay dead in a ring about their smoldering hall. The thatch fire pitifully burned out, and a section of roof collapsed as if to announce the end of hostilities.

Ulfrik surveyed the carnage with a smile. His men all stood, though some clutched wounds, and he had taken no losses in the gambit. Now he had to only count the spoils.

He called Einar out of his guarding position, and in moments all of his men had gathered around the hall. Many were already hunched over the dead and stripping away valuables.

"Not much of a fire," Toki said as he came to Ulfrik's side.

"But better off without it, honestly. No waiting for ashes to cool. Now we can be off at first light and head home." Ulfrik rubbed his hands, anticipating the treasures stacked inside the hall. The traders had described enough wealth to see his crews through winter. It only needed to be pulled from the wreckage of the raiders' hall.

"Call Snorri around with the ship. We'll have theirs to tow, and I want to get this treasure on our ships tonight. This is a glorious moment." Toki laughed as he departed to execute Ulfrik's command. Ulfrik wiped the blood from his sword and smiled.

$$\sim$$

AT FIRST ULFRIK blamed the moonlight. Later, he convinced himself the treasure lay buried under the hall. Finally, he told himself the wealth they had collected was acceptable for the effort expended. Squatting in a ring of men under the pink and yellow streaks of dawn, Ulfrik lifted a plain silver armband from the small pile of treasure before him. He rotated it through his hands, feeling the cold metal warm in his grip. Tossing it back onto the pile, the band gave a bright clink. Sea birds screeched in the distance.

"Once we hack down the rings and a few of those plates, everyone should take away a fair portion of silver." Snorri's old voice sounded like thunder in the silent cluster of disappointed men. "I don't get a share, since I didn't do any of the fighting."

"You guarded our ship, and rowed like the rest of us," Ulfrik said as rose to his feet. He grimaced as pain shot through his leg, a gift from his old enemy Hardar. "We agreed beforehand, and you'll get your due."

"Then I'll forfeit my share to you. I'm an old man, and I can't eat silver anyway."

"You can't even eat soup," Einar, his stepson, quipped. "Not with three teeth." Laughter rippled through the group, Ulfrik sensing the heaviness concealed behind it. He laughed as well, and rubbed his leg while smiling at Snorri. Age had seized him in these few years, rendering his face sunken and leathery and his motions labored and stiff. Heavy black rings circled eyes peering from behind grayish locks of hair. At least he had not gone bald, and retained an uncommon amount of hair for the old age of forty-five. Ulfrik still remembered him as a man half that age, standing with him in his father's shield wall.

Everyone gazed down to the miserable treasure gathered in the field beside the hall. Dead bodies had already attracted gulls to peck

6

and tear at the open wounds. Ulfrik experienced a wave of pity for the dead, having spent their lives for a paltry sum. Though deserving of death, as Ulfrik's informers had so vociferously proclaimed, he did not enjoy trapping and killing them inside their hall. Maybe because his Uncle Auden had burned alive in his hall and his father Orm had been poisoned, Ulfrik detested such tactics. However, he could not doubt their efficacy in battle.

"Well, I can't eat silver either, but I'm taking it." Thrand pushed his way to the front, then scooped up a ring from the grass. He thrust it at Ulfrik, blue sky reflecting in its curve. "This is what we sailed all the way to Norway to get. This fucking pile of silver that won't pay for the repairs to our ship and weapons. Great job, Lord Ulfrik."

Yanking Thrand's arm down, Ulfrik's free hand dropped to his sword hilt. "You weren't forced to join. You're drunk again, Thrand, but I won't indulge your disrespect. Do you understand?"

Ulfrik locked his gaze with Thrand, whose face had grown puffy and red with drink. He had become unpredictable since his brother Njal died three years ago. He blamed Ulfrik and Toki for it. Having learned firsthand how evil words could undermine a leader, Ulfrik brooked none of that attitude from him or any other. He would rather fight now than find a knife at his throat later.

Thrand backed down, as he always did, and twisted his arm from Ulfrik's grip. He flung the ring at the grass before Ulfrik's feet, then pushed away to be alone in his humiliation. Men parted for him, everyone familiar with his moody outbursts. Many heads shook as he stalked off, and Ulfrik let his hand fall from his sword.

"He's a drunk and a poor speaker," Ulfrik said to the others. "But he voices what all of us think. I share your disappointment. We expected much more, and bet on easy riches we did not find. I should've suspected the traders used us for revenge rather than passing on good information. No king's fortune in the hands of this crew."

"We still haven't made a proper search of the land and these other buildings," Toki said. "Maybe there's a chance they buried it nearby."

Ulfrik sighed. "True, it should be fresh enough to find if it is. This is not their home, though, but an abandoned village. If anything, they were resting here to waylay the walrus ivory trade from the north. We might consider the same idea, actually."

Walrus ivory traders made fat targets, but also employed escort ships that Ulfrik's small crew could not overtake. For that matter, neither could the raiders he had just defeated. He gave up trying to make sense of this, and accepted the traders had played him to eliminate a problem. Ulfrik never harassed traders, since his island home depended on them for survival. But the Norwegians were a different lot, and many pirates prowled the trade lanes out of Norway.

"All right, let's check the houses and search for any hint of a fresh dig. Maybe they've got buried dead that'll give up some gold. Get looking."

The men spread out under the brightening skies. Ulfrik drew in the sea air, glancing at the dark line of spruce trees and the violet and black mountain ridges pushing up behind them. He missed trees and forests. His home on the Faereyar Islands had no welcoming forests, no deer or elk to hunt nor any wolves to avoid. Many feared forests for elves and spirits dwelling within, but the trees had ever been a place of solace for him.

A voice broke his reverie. The shout came from a small byre standing near the mead hall. The door hung open and Thorstein stood framed against it. "There's a prisoner in here."

Ulfrik jogged over, his man standing beside the door and pointing inside. Ulfrik ducked within, and the sunlight filtering through cracks and holes provided a dim light his eyes momentarily fought. Tied by his wrists to a pole stood a man even older than Snorri. He wore a gray shirt of rough wool and his brown pants were cinched at his bony waist by a cord. His right pant leg had torn to the knee, revealing a thin leg covered in gray hair and bruises. The man's eyes were dark enough to be black, and were set into a regal head that titled back defiantly. Ulfrik would have laughed had the gesture not seemed so natural to the man.

"They must have recently put him here," Ulfrik said as he moved closer to inspect the man.

"How do you know?" Thorstein remained at the door, waving others over.

"No filth on the floor. I've spent a few days tied to poles, and you don't wait to shit if you have to."

Ulfrik examined the man, who returned the same scrutiny. Though thin and old, his skin was not rough. His unshod feet were scabbed from going barefoot. Ulfrik grabbed the man's face, who did not resist, and squeezed open his mouth to reveal it still held most of the man's teeth. He let go, and the prisoner pulled away with a hint of disgust that drew a smirk to Ulfrik's face. His gaze dropped to the slave collar chaffing the old man's neck, and he noted despite the rust of the collar, bright metal showed where it had been clamped shut over his throat.

Ulfrik stepped away, slipping on a deep red cloak lying on the floor. He kicked it aside, watching the man's eyes follow it. He emanated defiance and confidence; he reminded him of his wife, Runa, when he had first met her as a slave. The collar may have marked her as such, but her spirit suffered no enslavement.

"So they had a slave, and a new one at that. He's not yet ready to accept Fate's judgment. Just look at those eyes." Ulfrik playfully slapped the slave's face. "You might be the best part of the treasure we take today."

Toki entered along with a few other interested men. The slave's eyes darted between the new arrivals. "Why didn't he call for help?" Toki asked as he came in. "We might've left him here."

"Exactly," Ulfrik said, pulling on the bindings. "Better off chancing the ropes to break than giving himself over to us. Isn't that right?"

Ulfrik drew a knife and began cutting away the ropes. The slave had nowhere to escape, whether he knew it or not. The slave's hands came free, and he immediately began massaging them. Ulfrik chuckled.

"Don't get too used to freedom. I don't normally take slaves but we didn't get much for our efforts." Ulfrik grabbed his arm and started to guide him to the door when he started speaking. The words sounded familiar, as if he should understand them. He noticed Toki's

9

surprised expression, then realized the slave was speaking heavily accented Norse.

"You can understand me, slave?"

"Yeah, understanding. Humbert is still slave, no? Humbert freedom wants."

Ulfrik laughed, both from the accent and the request. "But the gods do not want freedom for you. So when they give it, I will be first among men to congratulate you. Now come with me, and be good. I won't be hard on you."

The men in the byre doorway chuckled, though Toki remained impassive. "You know Runa will not approve of taking a slave."

"He is already a slave," Ulfrik said. "Besides, he's a priest or a noble of some sort. Just look at him. We can ransom him to someone. He will be free and we will get a little richer."

"Or we'll be stuck with another mouth to feed."

"Then he'll go to the slave block," Ulfrik snapped. "What do you want me to do? He's a slave and we are free. When the gods wanted us free, they made us so. Same for this one. Runa will have to accept it, just stop worrying about it."

He pulled the slave, who called himself Humbert, which sounded Frankish to Ulfrik's ears. But Humbert pulled back, pointing at the ground. Ulfrik, his patience worn out, hissed and yanked Humbert forward. He yelped, and renewed his tug of war while still pointing at the floor.

"Please, master!" Humbert said. "On the ground, my cloak. Please!"

Ulfrik rolled his eyes and hauled Humbert out of the byre, flinging him through the door. He toppled like a child's doll, crashing into Einar who refused to step aside. The crew's laughter drowned out Humbert's pleas. He knelt in the grass, pointing at the byre with tears streaming down his face.

"Please, my father's cloak. Dear father. My father's cloak is all Humbert has. Please, just a small rag for Humbert. Please, master!"

Ulfrik's anger increased at the needless humiliation he had inflicted on the slave. He hated his sympathy for Humbert, but could not escape that weakness. He had suffered the disgrace of slavery and knew the pain this man felt. Some day slavery would bring him worse suffering, but at least Ulfrik would not be the originator of it. He felt his face growing hot as the others mocked Humbert's weeping.

"If you don't stop crying, I'll ram the fucking cloak down your throat!" Not the soothing words of a kind man, he knew. "Toki, fetch it for him. The rest of you, leave the poor bastard alone and let him have his cloak."

Toki handed Ulfrik the cloak, and he flung it on the tearful Humbert, who snatched it and rubbed his smiling face over it like a lost lover.

"I don't think he's going to be much use to us," Toki said as he watched Humbert weep with joy. "Why did you let him have the cloak?"

"I don't know. Before I met you, a hirdman of mine had lost his whole family to my brother, and after that wherever he went he carried a bearskin blanket that belonged to them. This reminds me of it. Anyway, if it shuts him up then let him keep it. We've a long journey home."

2

The blue strip of the southern island of the Faereyar grew on the horizon as Ulfrik stood in the prow of *Raven's Talon*. Gone for nearly two weeks, he anticipated reunion with his family. Sea spray wet his face and beard and the bracing air filled his lungs. Dolphins leapt through the waters as if in greeting. He stepped down from the prow, the sail full and cracking above his head. He smiled at Toki, who piloted the ship. It has been his since Ulfrik first met him, and no one else ever laid a hand on the tiller if he was aboard. He seemed equally eager to return home.

Towing the raiders' captured ship slowed the return journey to Nye Grenner. Ulfrik had taken great pains to hide along the coastal islands, realizing a towed ship was a beacon to other pirates seeking two fat prizes for one attack. Fortunately, numerous islands sprayed the northern coast of Norway with ample concealment. Once he hit the open sea, lookouts kept watch for following sails that never appeared.

Within the hour, the rolling slopes of Nye Grenner appeared. Despite strong winds, columns of white hearth smoke lifted over the green turf roofs of the village. His home and hall stood at the highest point of a slope that swept up from the beach, built on a strategic location that limited attackers' approach to the hall. The placement had saved it more than once, and Ulfrik believed it still discouraged enemies from trying its famous killing fields.

He waved from the prow along with others of his crew not busy with rigging or the sails. Everyone lined the shore in greeting. His heart beat faster, both from the excitement of returning and the anxiety of disappointing treasure. Runa's chiding words still echoed in his head. *You can't run after every promise of gold with no better proof than a stranger's say-so.* While others would see a captured ship and be mollified for a time, Ulfrik knew Runa would cut through his bluster with the keenness of a new blade.

He hated admitting she had been right. She almost always was right, and it drove him mad even if she was careful not to dwell on it. In fact, he wished she would so he could latch onto an excuse to become angry with her.

Raven's Talon glided into dock to the applause and cheers of the assembled families. He spied Runa observing from higher up the slope, his second son Hakon sleeping on her shoulder while Gunnar stood close to her side. Groups of wives, siblings, and mothers shouted the names of their men. Ulfrik appreciated their worries, since many who go *a-viking* never return. The crew threw ropes to the boys on the dock and they lashed these around poles. The towed ship, a small vessel, bumped against *Raven's Talon* and jostled everyone aboard. One man fell off the rails into the shallows to the shouts and laughter of those watching.

Ulfrik met Runa's small smile and Gunnar's placid, almost disinterested gaze. Hakon's tuft of golden hair showed beneath the wool blanket swaddling him. Spirits lifted, he drew his breath and jumped to the docks. Several people rushed forward to greet him, patting his shoulders and welcoming him home. Ulfrik made a show of what little wealth he had carried back from the raid, throwing a sack of the silver plates over his shoulder. He had padded it with rocks to make it appear bigger to the casual eye. People needed to see success.

Wading through the press of welcoming arms, he arrived before Runa and Gunnar. She cooed to Hakon, rousing him from his sleep.

Weeks away from home had refreshed his sight of her, and Runa's clear face bought a smile to his own.

"Welcome home," she said, a smile struggling to escape. She nudged Gunnar, who looked more like his mother each day. "Go on and welcome your father home."

Ulfrik dropped his sack of treasures and opened his arms for his son. Gunnar walked carefully, as if a hundred eyes followed him, then ran the last few paces and embraced Ulfrik. "Welcome home, Father."

"You've been good, lad. Protected your mother and brother while I was away?" He pulled back and ruffled Gunnar's hair, who nodded dutifully. "So let me see your mother, and ensure she is well."

Ulfrik slid to Runa's side, kissing her. "How I've missed you. It took longer than I thought."

"And you are well? No new wounds?" She leaned back, examining his face and brushing a few scabs and bruises suffered in the raid. Hakon shifted on her shoulder, raising his head a moment before sleeping again.

"Hakon sleeps for his father's return?" Ulfrik laughed as he peered into the swaddled bundle. His second son was barely a year old, ever hungry and sleepy. As much as Gunnar resembled his mother, Hakon's young face was Ulfrik's.

"He was awake all morning. You were late in returning." Runa shunted Hakon higher on her shoulder, then flashed the playful smile he had long missed.

"And we will be up late reuniting, that's a promise."

"Did you bring back great treasure, Father?" Gunnar interrupted them, standing on his toes to check on his younger brother.

"Of course," Ulfrik said, his voice so full with false confidence that Runa frowned at him. "Look at the docks. Men are unloading their treasures now."

Clusters of hugging families milled and clumped before the two ships. The captured ship bobbed next to *Raven's Talon*, where crewmen stowed the sail while others threw the few sacks of treasure onto the beach. Toki supervised the work as he had no one to greet him, his wife, Halla, still in the north with her mother. As Ulfrik and

Runa watched, Toki tugged the slave Humbert to his feet and directed him onto the dock.

"Who's that?" Runa asked, her voice tightening.

"A slave we found, probably a Frankish priest or skald, definitely not a worker or warrior." Ulfrik did not look at Runa, but studied Humbert's clumsy fall over the rails to the dock. Landing in front of a crewman securing the ship, Humbert received a derisive kick before he could regain his feet. Ulfrik winced.

"What you do when you're *a-viking* is your concern," she said, forcing evenness into her tone. "But I've told you not to take slaves into our home."

"He was already a slave when we found him."

"Don't twist words, Ulfrik. You know my meaning."

"I do, but, well, we probably shouldn't discuss this out here with everyone around."

"No one is listening to us; they're all wrapped up with family. What you want to tell me is that you didn't find the king's ransom you hoped for."

Ulfrik's vision skipped from the warm scene of reuniting families, landing on the far horizon. It tugged at his heart, beckoning him to sail to it and discover greatness and honor, a new land with opportunity. Yet he felt Runa's eyes on him, drawing his thoughts back to the far-flung island of grass he called home.

"No, we did not find what we were promised."

Their eyes remained locked above the head of their son. His head tilted in challenge, daring her to berate him for the danger and expense of the raid. Whatever showed in his eyes caused hers to falter. Instead she sighed and stroked Gunnar's head. "But you found something at least, and captured a ship. Most important is you have returned unharmed."

"Unharmed but no better off." Ulfrik nodded at Humbert as Toki led him over. "If I can find out where he's from, I'll ransom him back, and if I can't ..."

Runa gave a curt nod, but the flash of her dark eyes told Ulfrik the matter had not been settled. She understood slavery and its place in the world. Some men were born to it and could know nothing more. But she had long ago made it clear to Ulfrik she disapproved of his reducing freemen to slavery, as had been inflicted on her. Ulfrik had hoped since Humbert was an old man and a foreigner he would elicit less empathy from her.

Toki arrived with Humbert in tow. For a moment he forgot the slave and knelt to embrace Gunnar, who ran to him with a shout of excitement. Laughing with Gunnar clinging to his side, he held his arm out for Runa to slip beneath for a welcoming hug. He ruffled Hakon's hair, eliciting an irritated protest which Toki laughed off. Ulfrik studied Humbert's reaction. He clutched his cloak tight as his narrow head scanned the scene, undisguised disgust and disdain wrinkled his face. Ulfrik chuckled at the irony of the woman who he regarded with such repulsion would rather set him free than sell him.

"So we're back, and with an extra empty stomach." Toki pointed with his chin at Humbert. "Where does he go? Lock him up?"

"He'll serve us in the hall. He can grab a corner of it for himself. Just make sure he doesn't handle any knives when my family is there. Do you understand me, Humbert?"

His dark eyes snapped to Ulfrik's with a hint of annoyance, but then he smiled. "Master Alfuk sends Humbert to the hall, no?"

"Ulfrik," he repeated his name clearly, even as Gunnar snickered. "If you get one word right, make it my name. Toki will show you to your new home. Later we talk about a ransom for you."

Humbert's brows stitched together as if confused, but Ulfrik wanted him out of the way. "You'll understand soon enough. Take him, Toki."

With Humbert gone, Runa placed her hand on Ulfrik's shoulder. "He's a Christian priest, no doubt. Same arrogance of the Irish monks or my dear common-law sister."

"Whatever he is, he's probably the best I got out of this whole raid. The silver will be divided out, but I keep the ship and him. He'd better be worth something."

He watched the priest stagger after Toki, his red wool cloak dragging wearily behind him. Runa sniffed.

"His eyes are unkind," she said. "He'll not be worth the trouble he will bring us."

～

SEATED with Ulfrik at the high table, Snorri scratched his stomach beneath his shirt one more time. Ulfrik watched his old friend pick and rake, frown, then scratch again. Ulfrik laughed, looked around at Einar seated to his left and several other men dotted throughout the low light of the hall. A guttering hearth fire threw deep shadows into the creases of Ulfrik's smile.

"You'll rip a hole in your gut if you keep at it," he said, drawing chuckles from the gathered men. Snorri looked up bemused.

"It's nothing; just no one to clean my clothes since Gerdie passed last winter. These filthy clothes itch me all day."

He patted off his stomach and adjusted his shirt while Ulfrik's smile faded. The last three winters had been brutal, killing the old and weak. Mention of Gerdie's death clouded the mood, but Snorri displayed none of his usual tact. Age had roughened his polish.

"Yeah, she was a fine woman, and I miss her every day. It's Fate, after all. I'm not complaining, but wish we had more years together. My bed's so cold now. Tough winters."

Ulfrik drew his mug across the table and drained the last of the summer mead into his mouth. Finishing the summer brew had been the purpose of the gathering. Snorri's comments left the hall darker and quieter, each man reflecting on their losses.

Three nights had passed since returning from the raid. His crew still lingered at the hall before returning to their farms, only a fraction regularly quartered at the barracks as a standing guard. Most of them had returned wealthier than when they had left, but not enough to justify the risk to their lives. Ulfrik watched them now, in pairs or small groups muttering in low voices. Thrand had taken his drink and left early, to Ulfrik's relief. His drunken ravings had become increasingly intolerable.

Winters had turned harsh in recent years, and everyone counted losses in their families. Runa had delivered a daughter, a golden-haired child they called Brida. But the infant fell ill and died in her first winter. Halla had given Toki two sons, both dead within months of birth. Snorri's wife had not passed from the world alone.

A sudden movement broke Ulfrik's moody ruminations. Someone had dragged Humbert from his corner at the back of the hall, yelling at him to serve the high table. Humbert fell away, shot a deathly glare at the man, then approached the high table. Slavery did not sit well with him, and he did nothing unless forced. Now he reluctantly stood before Ulfrik, a sour expression demonstrating his distaste.

"The master needs Humbert?"

"I didn't call for you," Ulfrik said, sitting up straighter on his bench. "I think we're just sick of watching you relax all day. You need to be kissing my feet so I don't decide to make you tend flocks or harvest hay. Work in the hall is easy, but you won't even do that much."

Humbert's scowl softened and he tightened his cloak around his neck.

"Since we're all gathered, let's talk about Humbert's ransom." Ulfrik banged the table, earning the attention of his men. "Come up here and let's hear what this slave can get us."

Humbert's head tossed about, eyes wide and brows raised. Ulfrik laughed, letting the arrogant man suffer a moment's confusion. Toki joined him at the high table, slapping Ulfrik's shoulder as he sat. Others resettled closer to Humbert as Ulfrik gestured to him.

"You're a terrible slave, Humbert. You're a waste of my food and mead, and a stinking bed for lice in my hall. I'd like you better if you were a woman, and about thirty years younger." Chuckles followed and Humbert's face reddened. "So I want to get rid of you. I can sell your hide at the slave market in Dublin. But the journey would cost me more than your ancient body will earn. So tell me where I can ransom you."

Ulfrik stared into Humbert's eyes, prepared to judge his next words carefully.

"Ransom is not possible for poor old Humbert." He bowed his head, picking at the hem of his cloak.

"You're a Christian priest or a rich man, both the same as far as I know. Someone must want you back. Tell me where I can ransom you. Don't tell me it's not possible."

Humbert shook his head again. Snorri leaned forward on the table, peering through slitted eyes.

"He's a fucking liar," he announced. "Listen, slave, your eyes betray you. Look at me and tell me you can't be ransomed. Look at me!"

Humbert jumped and Ulfrik smiled at the spark of the old Snorri he remembered. Hesitantly meeting Snorri's gaze, Humbert explained himself.

"I am a priest; God forgive me for hiding it. But it is true, Humbert cannot be ransomed. Humbert is a wanted man now."

Ulfrik exchanged glances with Snorri and Toki. The deepening shadows of the dying hearth fire lent a graveness to the statement, as if the darkness conspired to hide Humbert's secret.

"Wanted is good," Toki said. "We ransom him back to whoever is after him."

"No!" Humbert's hands flew out to implore Ulfrik. "No! Humbert's from a faraway place where Northman cannot go."

The hall erupted with laughter; Humbert spun around to wave down their laughter.

"Humbert is true. Can the Northman enter Paris? That is Humbert's home, where the bishop is Humbert's enemy. He sold Humbert to the Northman so that they will take him far away and never return. The bishop will not want Humbert back, will not pay gold to see Humbert again."

His outburst silenced the men. Ulfrik folded his arms and studied the slave, who quivered and shrunk as if expecting a blow. His bearing, however frightened he appeared, belied something else, another layer to his tale not yet revealed.

"And so your story to me is you are worthless? Well, I guess I was wrong about you. There's another way you can serve me. Winter is coming and the gods have been cruel to us these years.

Since you can't bring us gold, then you can bring us favor with the gods."

Humbert grew still, his hands slowly dropping to his sides. Ulfrik relished knocking down the slave's arrogance.

"Men, secure him. At dawn we will strangle him in Odin's name by the sacred stone."

Without delay, the two closest men seized him with wicked delight. Humbert howled as if already in his death throes.

"Wait! I have a secret! Let me tell you about the gold!" Thrashing between the two laughing men, he pleaded to Ulfrik.

"Hold on, then. You have a secret? What a surprise." Ulfrik smiled at Snorri, who returned a satisfied wink.

"Yes, Humbert knows the bishop's secret treasure." He glanced around the room, nodding and eyes full of hope. "This is why the bishop betrayed Humbert. Because I caught the bishop taking heathen gold, late in the night from foreign men who want to control the bishop. He took ancient gold to make himself rich and hid it where Humbert knows. The bishop learned I discovered him. He cannot kill Humbert, not with his own hand, for God would call it a great sin to kill a priest. So he tricked Humbert with a promise to share the gold."

The men holding Humbert let him go as he gained confidence in his tale. His face fattened with delight and Ulfrik leaned forward in interest.

"He put a sack on Humbert's head." He mimicked a sack drawn over an imaginary head. "Then he hit Humbert and tied me down. To the Northmen I was given, and was made a slave for so long. Humbert does not know how long."

He surveyed the now attentive group, his mouth bent in solemn despair.

"Nice story," Ulfrik said, arms still folded and head leaned back. "But how is this helping your situation?"

"Because Humbert can show you the gold." His tone implied the words, "you fool," and his eyes flashed irritation. "You take Humbert to Paris and help me get revenge. Humbert shows you the hidden treasure. Understand?"

"I thought Northmen can't enter Paris?" Ulfrik stood, shaking his head. "You're just delaying for your life. You go to Odin at dawn."

"No! It is true!" Humbert crashed to his knees. "Humbert knows the secret ways, the ways to the abbey and the bishop. If Humbert lies, you can kill me there. Please, believe me."

Tears began to stream from his eyes and his lips quavered as he folded his hands. Ulfrik regarded him. The tale might be genuine, but the conniving of the Christian priests was famous. He could no longer verify it with Humbert's former owners, all long dead. He also did not have much heart for human sacrifice, believing instead the gods valued lives of strong men slain in fair combat over wormy slaves throttled while bound. His tongue prodded his cheek as Humbert whimpered at his feet. Eyes fell on him for a decision.

"Stop crying and stand like a man. I'll consider your story. In the meantime, be a better slave or I'll forget about Paris and your ancient gold."

Humbert stood, wiping away tears with the back of his arm. "You will not regret helping Humbert."

Ulfrik wanted to laugh, but in the dark places of Humbert's eyes he glimpsed a coldness that instead made him turn in disgust.

3

Down the slope and across the indigo dark fields, the golden lights of Nye Grenner's hall blinked. A cool breeze swished the grass in waves hardly visible in the half-light of night. Thrand leaned in the doorway of his house, a horn of dark beer in his trembling hand. The faintest traces of laughter reached him, causing his frown to deepen. A sheep bumped him from behind, the dumb animal wandering to the open door. He goaded it back inside with his foot to rejoin the six other sheep crowded into his home. With winter approaching, he needed their warmth indoors.

"If that's all the drink you have, then I'll be going." Thrand's friend, Kolbyr, spoke from within the house.

"No more for you, you leech. I used my silver to buy this cask for myself. A reward for my troubles." Thrand shoved off the door frame, spit in the direction of the hall, then turned to face Kolbyr. He fixed his friend with his good eye. Men called him Thrand the Looker for his lazy eye, and he had a habit of relying on the good eye to focus. Two fish oil lamps filled the single-room house with wan but clear light. Kolbyr sat at his table, two sheep idly chewing at hay strewn beneath his feet. He was a young man just short of being handsome.

A newcomer to Nye Grenner, he was no doubt a fugitive from trouble. He served in Ulfrik's crew with reasonable dedication, though Thrand knew Kolbyr could offer more. After the death of Thrand's brother, Njal, he had no family or friends. Kolbyr was the only man who would drink with him.

"I've got silver too," Kolbyr said, touching his belt pouch as if to ensure he had not lost it. "But it's not as much as yours. Ulfrik likes you for some reason."

"Likes me! Ha!" Thrand pulled the door shut against the night and shambled to the table, wading through his sheep. "He feels sorry for me. Takes pity on me! Like I need it."

Kolbyr raised his eyebrows and guzzled from his mug. The dismissive gesture riled Thrand.

"I risked my life for his family. My brother went to the sea grave for them. But what did it get me? Ruin! Look at this piss hole! Where are my flocks?" He pointed at his sheep. "This is no flock, not even close."

"You drank your flocks," Kolbyr said, dropping his mug on the table with a dull thud. His eyes were clear ice and his hair an enviable blond. Thrand could never exactly place what detracted from his looks, but he suspected his words made him less fair. "Are you listening to me?"

"I don't need to listen to your shit," Thrand said, draining the last of his beer. He placed the horn upside down on the table.

"But you should, since I'm the only one talking to you anymore. You've convinced everyone else to avoid you."

"Well, I'm not keeping you here, am I? Go fall off a cliff, plenty of 'em around."

Kolbyr laughed, pulling the pouch of silver off his belt. He shook the contents onto the table, sharp triangles of silver hacked into bits from plates and rings clinked together on the wood. He stirred the pile with his finger, spinning off flashes of lamplight. "How much do you think Lord Ulfrik holds out for himself? We all risked our lives the same, but he took a slave and a ship, along with a share of silver."

Drunk as he was, Kolbyr's words sobered him. His friend's chill gaze met his from under his brow, finger still pushing bits of silver.

"I know, but he is the jarl. Aren't they all the same? More for them and less for everyone else. He's no better than the rest."

"No need to get so nervous. I was just asking the question."

Thrand sat upright, shocked he had appeared nervous. Kolbyr swept his pile of silver to the table edge and then back into the pouch. Thrand scanned his cramped house, a wreck of disorganization and half-broken relics of an old life. He had fought for Nye Grenner, fought for its people and its jarl, and sacrificed his own brother in its service. Now he was alone, and Jarl Ulfrik would rather he not live here at all.

Kolbyr's pile of silver was not much larger than his own. But had Kolbyr made the same sacrifices? Had he lost family, given up his life in service? Of course he had not, and Thrand felt his stomach tighten at the thought. All he had offered up, all he had lost, and he received maybe three or four scraps of silver more than a man who had not even nicked his skin in service to the same lord. Thrand did not consider himself a great thinker, but this did not make sense to him. If treasure was tight, then Kolbyr should have received much less.

"How can he hoard more?" The question slipped out of Thrand's mouth before he could consider it. "We all saw what was taken."

"I mean, could he have more treasure from before that he's not sharing? The man is holding out, is my guess. But like you said, all jarls do." Kolbyr stood, staggered a few steps, then belched. "I'll be going."

Thrand remained at the table, his fists clenched and his mouth pulled down. Kolbyr pushed past him, bumping through the sheep to the door. When it creaked open, Thrand called him to stop.

"What if Lord Ulfrik is holding out? Do you think you deserve more?"

Staring ahead into the stone bowl of the oil lamp. The grass wick began to gutter against the decreasing oil. A sheep bleated into the silence.

"Maybe I do," Kolbyr admitted. "I came here to get rich. Isn't that why you followed Ulfrik, too?"

Thrand let Kolbyr exit, but did not move to bar the door. He slouched over the table, fists clenched, frown deepening, and the light of his lamp burning out.

4

"Hold it strong," Ulfrik said. Though Gunnar stood taller than other boys his age, he still vanished behind the round wooden shield he braced before him. Ulfrik could no longer afford the luxury of creating a shield in a boy's scale, not with the scarcity of wood. So Gunnar practiced with a grown man's shield.

Ulfrik watched his son dig in his heels and drop his waist. Snorri worked next to him, tugging him down farther and kicking Gunnar's feet wider. "That's more like it, lad. Make yourself a rock by pushing yourself into the earth. Protect yourself and the man at your side and the man behind you will hold you up. That's how the shield wall works."

Gunnar nodded understanding. At nine years, he was already training to be a warrior. Many more years would pass before he could stand in a shield wall, but Ulfrik knew the value of a long apprenticeship. For more than any other reason, he wanted Snorri to pass on his wisdom directly to the next generation. Ulfrik guessed Gunnar would be his only son to learn from the old breed, men who understood glory and honor, men like Snorri and Ulfrik's father. Hakon's illness would prevent him from standing in a shield wall, and the pain of that thought bit at Ulfrik's mind as he watched Gunnar preparing.

Clouds scudded past, carried by the wind, and the scent of Runa's cooking blew across his nose. In the distance, people wandered among buildings attending their daily chores. The happy scene should have raised Ulfrik's spirit, but instead he waited for Snorri to finish his instruction, feeling disheartened. No matter how he tried to distract himself, in idle moments his thoughts wrapped around the seidkona's derision and the worries of coming winter.

"We're ready," Snorri called across the brief distance. Hunkering behind Gunnar, he placed his hands on his back. Gunnar peered out from behind his shield.

"Let's hear your war voice," Ulfrik said as he prepared himself for the run. "Your grandfather was called the Bellower, so do him honor. A strong war shout can stop a man as good as a shield wall."

Gunnar lowered his shield and screeched his war cry. Ulfrik suppressed his laugh, and noticed people in the distance glance toward them. The shrill sound needed age to deepen and fill it out.

"Come get us, you goat turd!" Snorri added his own challenge. "Or go back to sucking your mother's tits!"

Galvanized by Snorri's taunt, he started his jog. Gunnar fearfully snapped behind his shield, and both Ulfrik and Snorri trembled at restraining their laughter. He gained speed as he approached Gunnar, then pulling before him, Ulfrik hopped up and slammed his foot on Gunnar's shield.

His son grunted and shoved into the blow, but the force drove him to the ground and Snorri stumbled backward. Catching his foot on something, he collapsed as well. Now Ulfrik's laughter exploded. "Easiest battle I ever fought, one kick to breach a shield wall."

Snorri rolled on the grass laughing, while Gunnar threw his shield aside. "Not fair! You didn't give me time to brace."

"Any more time and Snorri would've died of old age. Now stand up and we'll try again."

Gunnar sprang to his feet and retrieved his shield. Then Ulfrik heard his name shouted in the distance. His stomach tightened, and he shared a worried glance with Snorri who still sat in the grass. He faced the caller.

Running across the field, a man waved his arms overhead and shouted. As he neared, Ulfrik recognized him as Darby, a shepherd for his flock. "Lord Ulfrik, raiders! Raiders!"

"Gunnar, raise the alarm at the hall." Ulfrik removed the shield from his son's grip, who looked up at him with wide eyes. "Run, now!"

Ulfrik ran to close the gap with Darby, Snorri following fast behind. As they met, he saw Darby's face and shirt smeared with blood. A quick glance across the horizon revealed no smoke or other sign of destruction.

"Raiders," Darby said, stumbling the final distance. He leaned on his knees, fat drops of blood running from his head and plopping to the grass. "They stole your flock, about two-thirds of it."

"Are they headed over land or sailing away?" Ulfrik grabbed Darby's shoulders, then lifted his face to examine the wound. He had been gashed above his left brow. "Did you fight them?"

"No, lord," Darby's eyes fell aside. "Too many, and they struck me in the head. I was dazed for a long while. They must've thought me dead."

"Better you didn't fight, lad," Snorri said, patting Darby's shoulder. "You did well to warn us."

"Have they just gone? We could catch them, if we are swift."

"I ran as fast as I could, lord. They know the land, using the paths up the northern cliffs. It will take time to herd the sheep down to their ship. You could catch them still."

Ulfrik ran for the hall without another word. A blaring horn told him Gunnar had fulfilled his task. The paths along the northern cliffs were steep and treacherous, and hidden from anyone who did not already know where to search. This meant he had time to intercept them at sea, and also meant the raiders were locals. Hit and run foreign pirates would not bypass an unsuspecting village to steal sheep from pastureland. His northern enemies had come to pick at his weakness.

Outside the hall, men already fell into place, dragging shield and

28

spear in their rush to meet the threat. Runa waited outside the hall door with Gunnar, her face a tense picture of fear. She reached for Ulfrik as he neared, as if touching him would dismiss the threat. "What's happening? Gunnar said raiders are coming."

Pausing only long enough to offer Runa a reassuring squeeze, he moved for his men. "Gunnar, fetch my sword and shield. You men, listen! My flocks have been raided, through the north cliff paths. So it's our shit-eating neighbors come to fatten their stores for winter and empty ours."

Angry shouts met his announcement. As Snorri fell in beside him, Ulfrik handed him the wooden shield he had carried from prac-tice. "Darby said they might still be near. So get to the ship and catch these bastards!"

Gunnar emerged, shield and sword wrapped in his arms. Ulfrik accepted these, and nodded at Gunnar. "Go to your mother."

"I want to go with you."

"Go to your mother and protect your brother. Hakon needs you." He had no time to waste on Gunnar's protest or Runa's worry, but bounded downslope with his men. Fortunately, *Raven's Talon* still sat at dock and had not been carried into the boathouse for winter. The fastest men were already loosening her moorings and preparing to sail. Streaking down the slope, he dashed across the dock and leapt the rails.

Snorri barely made it aboard as the ship slipped free, men using oars to launch the ship. "Gods, lad! Did you plan on leaving me?"

Ulfrik ignored him, straining his eyes along the horizon. He guessed his thieves were relatives of his old enemy, Hardar. His cousins had slipped back north after Ulfrik's victory, but had returned often enough to be a continual threat. The raiders would have to sneak from the fjord and take a northern route along the cliffs. Ulfrik only had to follow, and if the gods loved him he could catch the raiders as they passed out of the fjord.

Men rowed as hard as they dared, conserving strength for the fight they anticipated. Though the stolen sheep belonged to Ulfrik, reduction of flocks hurt them all equally. The sheep were more valuable than jewels and gold, especially in winter.

The wind fought them, but Ulfrik roared into it as if he could blow it back. He threatened, cursed, and cajoled every back at the oars. Even Snorri rowed, muscles bulging as if he were a man twenty years younger. No one wanted the raiders to escape.

"Ship ahead!" someone shouted. Ulfrik craned to see beyond the prow, spying a wide ship in the gray distance. Over the wind and the slash and spray of the sea, he heard the bleating of captured sheep.

"Row harder, men! It's a fat ship, slower than ours. Keep at it, and bring me to those scum!"

The ship was an impractical choice for a hit and run raid, though Ulfrik understood the need for size to hold his flock. Their mistake had been in not killing Darby, for now they would be caught. Ulfrik bit his lower lip in anticipation of capturing the ship and throwing its crew into the sea.

Waves pressed both ships toward the cliffs and rocks, making progress arduous and dangerous. Both sides knew the waters, and where the major threats lay. Along the route, the looming brown cliffs were cut with deep crevasses and inlets. Waves crashed and jetted spray into the air with thunderous roars. One such inlet lay ahead, though rocks made a wave-break before it. Almost the same moment Ulfrik cast his eyes at the dark purple slit in the cliffs, a thin knife of a ship launched out of it.

He slammed on the tiller, forcing a groan from the hull as *Raven's Talon* strained to bank away from the second ship.

"Ambush!" he yelled. "Get down!"

Swearing as he collapsed to the deck, first he heard arrows plunking into the planking then heard a howl as a shaft found flesh. Covering his head with both hands, his world darkened as the arrows fell. Being attuned to his ship, he sensed the current take command of its course. Even as arrows streaked across the gap, he leapt up to seize the tiller and steer against the waves ceaselessly forcing them to the cliffs.

Men huddled against the gunwales, sheltering from the arrows.

One man squirmed on the deck, curled against his pain and gripping his pierced shoulder. Blood smeared the deck beneath him.

A second volley streaked after the first, though the wind batted many shafts into the water. Ulfrik hunkered at the tiller, forcing *Raven's Talon* to straighten her course. The cliffs glared down and their shadows brushed her hull. He glimpsed the ambushers lining the side of their ship, stringing more arrows.

"Do we have any bows?" Ulfrik's question sounded more like a plea. He had not prepared bows, thinking only to catch the raiders' ship. No one replied, but held themselves low against the next volley. Now the gap had widened and the last flight of arrows served only as a warning not to drift into range. Ulfrik ran to the prow, past his cowering men, jumping up to shake his fist at the ambushers.

"Come fight!" he challenged. The crew of the slender ship waved their bows overhead and laughter skipped across the water to Ulfrik's ears. "You won't escape me, you turds. I know who you are!"

By now the rest of his crew had recovered. Several huddled around their fallen companion, while Snorri joined Ulfrik at the prow.

"They laid a trap for us, lad. Thank the gods they were stupid enough to spring it early."

Ulfrik's fist beat the neck of the prow as he watched the ships glide farther into the distance. A black fletched arrow had sunk into it, and he snapped the shaft out of the wood. He held the broken arrow out for Snorri. "I'll put ten of these into each of those bastards. I swear it, Snorri.'"

"And so do I." He took the shaft from Ulfrik's hand, then tossed it into the water. "But we don't have enough men on this ship to take on two of theirs. We barely escaped with our lives, except for Thorstein."

Shame immediately overtook Ulfrik. Einar had grabbed the tiller and several men worked the oars to keep clear of the cliffs. The rest stood dejectedly over Thorstein. He no longer squirmed on deck and a thick puddle of black blood spread beneath him.

The men parted for Ulfrik as he knelt beside the body. Thorstein's eyes stared into the trackless skies, and his hand clenched in death on the hilt of his sword. Ulfrik stroked his eyelids closed, then bowed his head.

"Our brother has gone on to the feasting hall. His was a warrior's death, one we will not grieve but forever remember. Keep him in your hearts when we avenge his death. We will follow their ship at a safe distance. They may raid Ingrid's hall on their way home. We must discourage them from that idea. Someone help me wrap Thorstein's body, and the rest of you get on an oar."

Snorri began to shift Thorstein's corpse to retrieve his blood-soaked cloak. Ulfrik cast his gaze north from beneath a furrowed brow. His flocks would not be recovered, and yet another dead man and another defeat marked a day closer to the arrival of winter.

ULFRIK LICKED grease from his fingers, then guzzled the bitter beer from his wooden mug. The stew had lacked flavor and the meat was overcooked, but his stomach had been filled. Leaning back on the bench at the high table, he glanced past Ingrid sitting before him. Behind her, embers in the hearth throbbed and the scant light of day slanted from the smoke hole. Doors hung open to let in gauzy light and fresh air, but nothing could clear the stale mood from the men silently chewing their meals at the long trestle tables. Ingrid had fulfilled her obligations to Ulfrik, ordering a feast prepared in welcome and surrendering her hall while he visited. However, burying Thorstein earlier in the day had soured everyone's mood.

Ingrid hid her age well enough, but Ulfrik spotted the gray in her platinum hair and the lines clustered at her eyes. Her half-smile irked him, as if she enjoyed his defeat, though his suffering was hers as well. Their fortunes were tied through marriage and sacred oaths. She rubbed her chin, then looked back to her bowl.

"Do you think they'll return?" Toki, who lived here with his wife, Halla, offered to take Ulfrik's mug for a refill.

"And why not?" Ulfrik said, handing over the mug. "I would come back until I'd taken everything I could."

His gloomy comment drew sidelong glances from the men at the lower tables. Forgetting himself, Ulfrik straightened his posture and tried to brighten his voice.

"But if we are united, and take this fight north, we will be victorious. We are the men of Nye Grenner, and we defend our own."

Ingrid smiled and glanced sideways. Halla sat beside her, and shared a fleeting smile with her mother. Ulfrik mistrusted the two of them, because Halla looked more like her father every year than for any other reason. Now that she had married, her hair was pulled into bun and hid under a covering. It was unflattering, and strengthened her resemblance to Hardar. But Toki was her husband, and he trusted him above anyone else. Still, his mood on this day was easily ruined.

"Do you not believe it, Ingrid? We cannot defeat those northern scum?"

"Why doubt my belief, Lord Ulfrik?" Her wide eyes sparkled and she put a blue-veined hand to her chest. "Of course we can defeat any enemy we choose. For some reason, we have not chosen to destroy them yet."

Toki returned to the bench with a filled mug running over with thin foam. "We've been merciful," he said as he sat between Ulfrik and Snorri. "But now they've gone too far. Almost a whole flock gone! They'll pay in blood."

Ulfrik's flaring temper cooled at Toki's timely interjection. Both he and Snorri shared happily surprised looks, since Toki's words historically worsened matters rather than smooth them over. Attacking his refilled beer with relish, Ingrid jumped into the gap.

"Mercy is a fine quality. But I fear it is wasted on Skard and Thorod. They have never understood mercy, mistaking it for weakness."

"Christ taught us to be merciful just as our Father is merciful." Halla's face beamed as if her statement was more profound than anything ever spoken. Ulfrik grimaced.

"My father would've cut the balls off the lot of them, then nailed their heads to his mast. I'll take my own father's counsel in this."

Laughter circulated around the room, which Ulfrik welcomed; it masked over the insult Ingrid had slipped at him. Disregarding Halla's sullen frown, he met Ingrid's cold eyes. She had appeared dutiful and loyal, despite fears she would side with her dead husband's family. Yet at the same time, her former family took no revenge on her and left her lands alone. He wondered at this luck.

"Those are all fine words, Lord Ulfrik. But the fact remains Skard and Thorod sail freely along our coasts. They've refilled their crews and now test your armor. Today they found a gap in your mail."

Silence settled over the hall, and Ingrid gently tilted her chin forward. Halla gasped then studied her lap, while others turned on their benches to watch. Ulfrik's stomach tightened and he felt his lip curling, but he bridled his anger and reminded himself to be firm and confident for his men.

"What they found was the path up the northern cliffs. Call it a gap in my mail, if it pleases you. But those two fools have gone beyond what I'm willing to tolerate from them. I've conserved my strength, ignoring those scavengers to focus on better things. Now they've invited me to war, which I will not give them. Instead, they'll get slaughter."

The hall erupted with shouts of agreement and oaths of vengeance. Toki patted Ulfrik's shoulder and added his own curse on the two cousins, Skard and Thorod. However, Ingrid did not waver in holding Ulfrik's eyes.

"Their strength matches our own, and soon will outnumber us. You couldn't even follow them today." Her voice came thin but confident over the roars of the men. "How will you bring this slaughter?"

"I have no fears of those two cowards." Ulfrik shoved away from the table, and stood. He threw back his cloak, so his gold and silver armbands gleamed in the shadowy light. "Your men and my own are more than a match for the bandits and scum those two recruit."

Ingrid's brow raised and a wry smile twisted her lips. Ulfrik knew he had accused the cousins of the very thing he did to fill his ranks. Her smirk further tested his control, and he balled his fists.

"What they've done today is murder. It's more than Thorstein, many more. Without our flocks, what do we eat in winter? How do we

34

keep warm? What do we have when the traders come for wool? They're killing our people, and so they must die!"

"I did not ask why we should destroy them." Ingrid now stood, which gave Ulfrik and the others pause. "I asked how you plan to do it."

"Do not challenge me, woman." Ulfrik's voice lowered. "That I've vowed to destroy them is good enough for you. Your oath requires you and your men to obey me. So obey!"

His command broke across the hall like thunder, and many eyes turned to the floor or looked aside. Ingrid's haughty confidence melted and she slowly took her seat as Ulfrik glared at her. Not satisfied, he continued.

"You've suffered nothing from these two, so don't complain. Don't question me, and don't speak about defeat and loss. If we all sailed north and died in battle it would still be glorious. Only if we hide in our homes do we die in shame. I don't know what you are hinting at, but let me clear your mind. We will regroup and we will bring down these cousins. Your hirdmen will stand in the shield wall with mine, and fight for our homes. Anything less makes you and your men oath-breakers."

Only the intermittent snap from the dwindling hearth interrupted the silence. Ulfrik scanned the room, and met every eye that dared to raise to his own. He nodded at each man, assuring them in his confidence and testing their strength. Satisfied, he retook his seat in front of Ingrid, whose eyes fluttered and turned away.

"I did not mean to anger you, Lord Ulfrik. I am merely a worried, old lady. The tidings you brought me today are the worst I've heard in many years. My lands are closer to theirs, and I fear they could return for me one night."

"Be vigilant," Ulfrik offered, glad to be done with conflict. His temples throbbed and his eyes hurt. "I must return home for a short while, but Toki will come to represent your lands. We will devise a plan to keep you and everyone safe through winter. When spring arrives, we will welcome it with a blood sacrifice such that the gods will remember us for all time."

Ingrid inclined her head, then excused herself and Halla to help in cleaning the remains of the meal. As she stepped down, Ulfrik whispered to Toki. "Can I trust her?"

"Yes, but with a wary eye. She's an opportunist."

Ulfrik nodded and watched as people turned back to muted conversation. His own closest hirdmen, Snorri and Einar, along with Ander and several others, continued to watch him. He waved his hand as if shooing a fly. "We'll discuss her later. For now, we rest before returning home."

5

Runa hefted the sword overhead and tightened her grip on the wooden shield. Across the grass, Ulfrik circled with his own blade drawn and shield held in guard to his left. Behind him the usual line of women who came to shake their heads and gossip appeared as a dark blur. This time, she decided, she would tag Ulfrik if it meant cutting him. Sweat rolled into her eyes and down her nose. Ulfrik no longer teased her, instead appeared half-focused on her and looking into another place. *You'll learn to pay attention to me*, she thought.

Her short sword struck down at Ulfrik's face. He recognized the flashing iron, pulling his shield to defend. A smile played on Runa's face, and she pulled her strike to slash at his exposed leg.

Ulfrik recovered with practiced ease, stepping back from the blade and sweeping his own sword at Runa's head. Reflex took over and she raised her shield to intercept. The thud of the impact shuddered up her arm. A flash of anger bit her, and she saw his exposed forearm. Her heart raced, finally the opening she had been seeking. Yet her cut passed through air, and suddenly Ulfrik had wheeled to her right side with his shield out. He shoved it into her sword arm, the force of it driving her sword onto her own shield and pinning it. A cold pinch at her inner thigh informed her of defeat.

The tip of Ulfrik's blade pushed into her deerskin pants. She cursed and stepped back, dropping her sword and shield to her sides. Ulfrik laughed, pulling away.

"That was a well-done bit of swordplay, Wife." A few claps came from the distant onlookers, and Runa's face grew warm.

"What good is it if you lamed me?"

"Not lamed," Ulfrik corrected as he sheathed his blade. "Such a cut would bleed you to death before you could curse Fate. But don't let it discourage you. You fight against the best. The worms you're likely to face would fight like the farmers they are."

Runa threw her shield in the grass and sheathed her blade. Though she had been practicing with real swords and shields for over a year, the effort still left her shoulders sore and her back aching. She rubbed her shield arm which still tingled from the force of Ulfrik's blow. He drew her close and rubbed it as well, kissing her forehead as he did.

"We have to do this regularly if you expect me to meet farmers in battle. It's not enough to practice every time you fear a raid is coming."

He stopped rubbing and drew her tighter. "Then we will make more time. It's important for you to defend yourself."

They stood in a quiet embrace long enough for Runa to feel shame for chiding him. If anything, she had cajoled him into teaching her proper sword fighting, and he desired assurance she could stand on her own.

"Ulfrik, I am sorry. Finding time to practice is not easy with all the real work I have." She turned to face him, then wrapped her arms around his waist. "And you want more children, yes? We must stay busy with that plan."

He laughed and the two began to walk toward the cliffs. Runa watched him as they strolled, and she read the worry in his face. He had not been himself since his visit to the seidkona. Meeting with Ingrid no doubt worsened matters. The Hag-Queen and Witch-

Daughter were Runa's private names for Ingrid and Halla. Unfortunately, after Gerdie's passing, she had only Gunnar to share her bitter complaints. Ulfrik had not revealed what happened at Ingrid's hall, but she surmised the old hag had tested her limits. Runa figured Ingrid should have followed her husband in death and all her lands pass to Ulfrik, but for some reason she was spared. *Show a little mercy*, she thought, *and the world takes you for a fool.*

"I must have more gold to raise more men." Ulfrik spoke flatly, searching the rolling hills before them. "We must take revenge and end this threat once and for all."

Runa could not control her sigh, and she pulled away from him. "You've said as much before, and now we have nothing. You spent everything on rebuilding your ships and weapons. Worse yet, you spent gold on rebuilding Ingrid's hall."

"Can we not discuss that again? I told you then, she is sworn to me and that hall is my own."

"Try taking it from her, and you'll see what she thinks. Her men are loyal to her, and somehow think she's a charmed little elf."

Now Ulfrik sighed, and he rubbed the back of his neck. A smile bordering on a grimace stretched across his face, and Runa recognized his effort at restraint. They walked a short distance farther, the salty air cool on her sweat-beaded face. She heard the dull throb of waves crashing on the cliff faces as she drew nearer to them.

"My father would have done more on this island than I have done." He stopped, placing his hands on his hips. He continued to stare into the distance, beyond the edge of the cliffs and fjord. "If he lived today, he would be ashamed that I have not done more for our family."

"You don't know what he would do, so stop raising his ghost to chide you constantly. You have as much success as him, even more." She brushed his arm, hesitant to offer too much comfort. She had learned over the years that he needed to speak his troubles through before clearing his mind. Comforting words tended to slow down the process.

"After the war with Hardar, my progress has stalled. I've not climbed beyond this." He waved a hand over a swath of the horizon. "We deserve better. I am a jarl's son, and you a jarl's daughter. But what do we rule over, except sheep and poor farmers living on a rock at the edge of the world?"

"You sound as if we came from grand estates. I remember Grenner, Ulfrik, and it was not a mighty kingdom."

"My father commanded over a hundred men and three ships. The people respected him, honored him, and his name was known everywhere!" He threw his hands into the air as he proclaimed the greatness of his home. Runa bit her lip, fighting the urge to remind him Grenner was a far more humble land than he remembered. He resumed walking, his stride agitated.

"Grenner's standard should fly over a great hall, not hang limp from a battered mast on a ship that sails nowhere. My sons deserve to inherit more. Men who have served me since Norway deserve wealth and glory."

"And they have received both from you, or they would not remain in your service. Now stop and listen to me." Folding her arms across her chest, she planted herself and determined not to move. "We have survived all that Fate has designed for us, and we have lived to see our sons grow. They are happy, and so am I. So we live as farmers. Better to live as freemen and not as slaves, and better still to be alive. That is success enough. In this life, with cruel gods laughing at us, living is the greatest success of all."

Her neck pulsed with her emotion, and she studied Ulfrik for his response. His eyes searched hers, and though she expected his answer, she still hoped for his agreement.

"It's not enough, Wife. Living is no more than what animals do. We were born to more, and that is why the gods have kept us alive." He dropped his head and shook it. "I can't believe we are under threat from those two scum, Thorod and Skard. Between the two of them they've not enough wits to piss a straight line. And yet, they're crushing me, undoing me. Can I let that pass?"

Runa waited, touching her finger to her lips. His head continued to droop, the wind blowing his hair across his face. The lines of his body drew defeat for all to see. Such weakness rankled her, but she kept her voice even. "Why even fight with fools? We could leave this place as easily as we came."

"God of Storms, this idea of yours will never go away." He tilted his head back to the sky and raked the hair from his face. "It is not like there are lands waiting for us beyond the horizon. We've already been everywhere, and everywhere another lord has claimed the land."

Runa rolled her eyes but let him continue. If she could be accused of suggesting the same ideas, Ulfrik could be accused of fashioning the same excuses.

"Ships that sail north never return. I don't care what men say; there's nothing but sea monsters and ice to be found there. Norway is fouled with a high king, and I'll never pay his taxes. Same for your home of Denmark, so please don't tire me with that suggestion again."

"Gods know I would not want to tire you."

"And the Svear and Baltic people would war on us until death." Ulfrik began to pace, oblivious. Runa tucked her head down to forestall a laugh. "So where does a man create a kingdom, when kings have already taken everything?"

"Odd how kings do that."

"Respect, Wife! Respect! I am serious. There's nowhere to go, but to build a kingdom here." He stamped the earth with his foot to emphasize his words. "Made from Ymir's last rotten tooth, this fucking island is the only place."

Runa waited, watching him stare at his foot. She realized her own foot tapped, and she halted it. "We can go to Hrolf the Strider. He is your sworn lord and oath-bound to provide safety and justice for you and your people."

He lifted his face to hers. Hrolf had been the unspoken threat for the last three years. More than anything the two cousins could do to ruin Ulfrik's dreams, a single word from Hrolf could ruin more. Runa understood this, and eschewed his name. Yet undeniably, Hrolf owned Nye Grenner. Ulfrik had sworn loyalty to him in exchange for his aid in defeating Hardar. Hrolf now controlled their lives, though he had never visited nor asked anything of them.

"Have you no shame?" Ulfrik said, his voice low. "Can I crawl a second time to him, and beg his aid?"

"Now you respect me. You know I'd not mention him lightly. I don't want to go upon my knees any more than you. But if the cousins are breaking your nuts like you say they are, then visit him. Ask him to lend you gold or men, or both."

Ulfrik spun away and considered her words. She unfolded her arms, then entwined them around his waist. She whispered to his ear.

"Just think on that idea, which I'll remind you is a new one of mine. You've tried to raise the gold on your own, but a loan could work just as well. Pay it back out of the spoils. Men do that all the time, don't they? They loan you their lives, and you repay them with gold. There's no shame in it."

Ulfrik clasped his arm over her hands, and rubbed them gently as he thought. "A loan might work. I could raise more men at least."

She hushed him, tightening her hold. "Just think for now. Winter will arrive and keep the cousins busy with survival. But we can plan and prepare for spring."

She felt his posture relax, then he sighed. "Let's get home before Gunnar wears out Toki. The boy not only has your looks, but has your energy."

Runa laughed, allowing herself a moment of satisfaction. War was at hand, she did not doubt, but for a short moment she had controlled a small portion of her destiny. Arm in arm with Ulfrik, she walked home and hoped she would never have to abandon it. Yet intuition told her she would not die on these lands, and that crowded her satisfaction with fear.

6

Two of the high-sided ships floated at sea as the third glided for the shore. Ulfrik and his men had assembled in haste, but with enough time to don mail and helmets. His guts roiled along with the ocean waves ramming onto the stony beach. Two ships were bad enough, but a third ship meant his doom.

"They're waving a hazel branch," Snorri said, craning his neck forward and squinting.

"Just spotting that now?" Ulfrik asked, hitching his shield up his arm. "They've come far if it's real hazel."

Snorri spit on the grass and grunted. Ulfrik observed the ship skipping across the dull green waters; a hulking figure standing in the prow cut boldly against a stone gray sky. Animal pelts wrapped his shoulders, giving him the look of a hulking bear. His long, thin hair streamed off his high forehead as he waved the branch.

"Hazel branch or no, it could be a trick," Toki said, flanking Ulfrik's other side. "How many times have we done the same?"

As men leapt into the crashing surf to guide the ship ashore, the air rushed from Ulfrik's lungs and his body slumped. Both Toki and Snorri stared at him in surprise, but Ulfrik clacked his sword back into its wooden scabbard. "My wife has a power to summon men with her words. Only two days ago did she mention Jarl Hrolf."

"Ulfrik Ormsson," called the fur-clad man as he steadied himself on the prow. "Put away your weapons. Your old friend has returned!"

"Gunther One-Eye," he explained. "One of Jarl Hrolf's closest men. Snorri, you remember him."

"Course I do. The man can drink a lake of mead and walk away from the table."

Ordering his men down and to break formation, Ulfrik laid his own shield in the grass. He started down the slope, relief pulsing through his body. Had the ships been filled with enemies, the fight would have been bitter. He arrived at the edge of the grass and waited.

Gunther One-Eye stomped ashore with both arms out as if greeting a lost son, a ragged smile on his scarred face. He had not changed in the three years since they last met. His face remained a horrid mass of scars, with a thick worm of white flesh tangled into the socket of where his left eye had been. Gray streaks flowed into his hair from his temples and from his chin into his beard. The only difference Ulfrik noted was Gunther had grown out his beard and gathered it at the bottom with a gold ring.

"You look fat and happy, Gunther." He strode forward, meeting Gunther at the edge of the surf. They clasped arms, then clapped each other's backs in greeting. Gunther's cloudy eye glinted, and his yellow teeth showed in his smile.

"And you look like you've missed me. May the rest of my ships come ashore? We've sailed far, as you know."

"Without delay, friend. And you'll come to my hall to eat and drink, and wash the sea salt out of your face."

Horns blared on both sides, to signal Gunther's other ships and to signal Nye Grenner's hall that danger had passed. Ulfrik waited in awkward silence as Gunther's crew disembarked. He glanced at the hall, seeing Runa the first to emerge with a sword and shield in hand. He smiled at the sight.

As the other ships pulled ashore, Ulfrik left Toki to greet these men while he and Gunther proceeded to the hall. He tried to hide his anxiousness, noting how Gunther's single eye managed to appraise every building and person in Nye Grenner. He was grateful for Gunther's silence, who instead turned his attention to Runa as they arrived at the hall doors.

"As beautiful as ever, your wife. Now with a sword to match her temper." Runa's eyes widened and her mouth gaped. Gunnar, who had clung to her side, suddenly stood before her as if in challenge. Both Ulfrik and Gunther laughed. "And your son has grown fierce and strong!" He growled at Gunnar, who flinched but remained before his mother. "Braver than his father, too!"

"And another son in the hall as well," Ulfrik said.

"You've not been idle with your success, I see!"

Laughter eased both Runa's and Gunnar's stances. Ulfrik introduced Gunther again, both to Runa and to the other men. Most had never met Gunther, though Thrand the Looker had. His greeting to Gunther bordered on disdain, and Ulfrik glared him into a better welcome. Others who remembered him were warmer and Gunther shocked many of them with specific memories of their details. "You've got a sharp memory for a drunk," Ulfrik said.

"Mead sharpens the mind. Now let's go sample some of that famous drink of yours!"

Ulfrik welcomed them into the hall with a wan smile. He let them pass inside, each man laying his weapons at the door as custom demanded. Runa followed Ulfrik inside, and whispered over his shoulder, "I'm worried about this."

"That you summoned him out of the past?" he whispered over his shoulder.

"No! That he's here with three ships. Are we in trouble?"

"We'll find out."

He shepherded Gunnar along with Runa into the darkness of the hall. Moments of embarrassing confusion ensued as the villagers who had sheltered against a possible raid filed out and Gunther and his warriors entered. Runa assumed command of the transition, and held several girls back to assist her in the hall. Gunther chuckled, and his men stood in patient attention. Ulfrik caught Humbert leaving with the others, but barred him with his arm.

"Master will need Humbert?"

"You stay where I can see you. Forget any plans for taking advantage of the confusion. Go see my wife for instructions."

Moving from battle readiness to hosting guests proved a jarring and complicated transition, one that frustrated and embarrassed Ulfrik. Fortunately, Gunther One-Eye smoothed everything over with easy laughter and wry comments. One of his crew had a horn pipe, and played a tune while the hall settled. "He's a lot happier than I remember," Snorri quipped at one point. Ulfrik agreed, but wondered as much as Runa did at the meaning of his arrival.

ULFRIK HAD PASSED a wearisome afternoon entertaining nearly one hundred guests, and now sat at the high table with Gunther and his bodyguards. Toki, Snorri, Einar, Ander, and others of Ulfrik's men had joined them. The hall reverberated with loud talk and laughter, and despite the chill night, sweat beaded on many faces. Doors and windows hung open and stars winked in the indigo squares.

Gunther's arrival had forced Ulfrik to slaughter two lambs and open a cask of winter ale. Runa had prepared a sumptuous stew from the fresh goat meat and blood, and the thick aroma filled the hall. She leaned over the iron pot with a ladle, and caught Ulfrik starring at her. He smiled, but she looked away. Later, once the feast had ended, in bed, he feared her anger. He had no doubts how strongly she opposed draining winter stocks for an extravagant feast. A glance at her bearing and he heard every complaint ringing in his mind.

Gunnar stood behind Ulfrik and he felt his son leaning close. Gunther drained his horn, dropping it across the table then wiped his thick mustache with the back of his hand. He fixed his single eye on Gunnar, then leaned toward him.

"Does my eye scare you, boy?"

Gunnar shook his head, but Ulfrik felt him press closer.

"He thinks you're Odin," said a hirdman seated beside Gunther, who exploded in laughter. Ulfrik put a comforting arm over Gunnar, and drew him forward.

"That right, boy? Do you think I'm Odin? Sitting with your Da and drinking his ale?"

"No, lord," Gunnar ducked out from Ulfrik's arm, his face reddening. "I wondered how you lost your eye, lord."

"Your manners are a compliment to your father." Gunther raised his brow at Ulfrik. "He calls me 'lord' and not 'a drunk.' Did you hear?"

"I did, but he'll learn soon enough."

More laughter lightened the mood, and Gunther wiped his face with a paw-like hand. He leaned down to Gunnar's height and met him eye to eye. "Odin sacrificed his eye to Mimir for a drink from the Well of Wisdom. But old Gunther got his plucked out against his will."

"How did it happen, lord?" Gunnar's eyes widened, and his fingers drifted to his own eye.

"With a spear. One moment's distraction in a shield wall, and an enemy spear plucked away my eye. Just like that!" Gunther jabbed at Gunnar's eye with a gnarled finger, causing him to jump in surprise and drawing laughter around the table.

"Did it hurt, lord?"

"Hurt?" Gunther leaned back, a bemused smile twisting his lips. He glanced around the table before answering. "No, it didn't hurt. At the time I was too drunk to notice."

Men hurled backwards in an uproar, even Ulfrik burst out laughing. Gunnar's blush deepened as he smiled, and Ulfrik guessed he missed the humor.

Soon the meal was served and Runa and her women circulated through the crowd with steaming bowls. Humbert had been pressed into reluctant service, filling mugs and drinking horns. He distributed them with an expression that made it seem he handled urine rather than ale. He spilled a horn over someone's head, Ulfrik guessed intentionally, and he received a reflexive punch that sprawled him on the dirt floor. Another was following, but Gunther stopped the man with a shout.

As the feast proceeded and men ate and drank, then sang songs or told riddles, Ulfrik's mood lightened. Even Runa, now seated beside him with Hakon on her lap, smiled and laughed. For a short time, he forgot his worries and reveled in celebration. However, each time he met Gunther's toasts with a raised mug or answered one of his simplistic riddles, dread smoldered in the pit of his gut. He still did not know Gunther's purpose.

At last, late in the night when most of his men were face down on tables or fallen beneath them, he lifted his one eye to Ulfrik's. True to memory, he had consumed copious volumes of ale but remained sitting straight and clear-faced. Ulfrik had paced himself, knowing the moment for real talk would require his full wits. Gunther's single eye drifted to Runa, who sat defiantly for a moment before rising from the bench.

"A good night to you, then," and Runa strode toward their room where Gunnar and Hakon had already gone to bed. Ulfrik watched her go, then turned to Gunther.

"You didn't just come to sample my hospitality." He gestured Snorri to slide closer while Toki, Einar, and Ulfrik's other trusted men leaned in to listen.

"Your hospitality is as great as it ever was, nor has much changed in three years." Gunther's single eye squinted, while the ruined flesh of his other eye wriggled. "I expected you'd have expanded since defeating Hardar."

Ulfrik sighed, while his men bowed their heads or turned away. "After you left, winter was hard. Every winter has been hard. It took all my wealth to rebuild, and to rebuild Ingrid's lands. And ships and weapons cost, as you know."

"That they do," Gunther agreed. "But I thought you wealthier."

"I was, but I had lands to the north that now need tending, and blood prices to pay after the war with Hardar." Ulfrik found himself glancing at the red-faced and frowning Thrand the Looker, who sat at the farthest end of the high table. "Summer raids have not been good. We're just returned from one that barely paid for itself."

"Why not raid farther south? What's wrong with Mercia or Ireland?" Gunther belched, then raised his horn for another drink. Humbert emerged from the darkness to fetch the horn.

"We can't be gone so long. Hardar's cousins harry us. They just robbed me of half my flock. Imagine what they could do if I were gone an entire summer."

Now Gunther turned away and a few of his men smirked. Realization sparked for Ulfrik.

"You've come to summon me, haven't you? Jarl Hrolf has not forgotten me after all."

Gunther sighed, nodding his head. "Jarl Hrolf the Strider is summoning all bondsmen to attend him with as many men and ships they can muster. You have a month to prepare and travel to the meeting place in Denmark."

Ulfrik straightened, then steadied himself before speaking. He projected confidence into his voice, though his mind raced through the depressing implications. "Hrolf makes war on the Danes, then?"

"Not at all; he has allied with them. Jarl Sigfrid is a mighty Dane, much like Jarl Hrolf. He had led an army to Frankia and demanded payment from their king. He refused, and now Sigfrid plans to plunder Frankia as a show of strength. He spoke with Jarl Hrolf, and the two made a plan to assemble a great army."

"Like the great army in England?" Ulfrik had heard stories of the great army's victories against the Saxons, but considered them overblown.

"A greater army," Gunther spread his arms as his voice rose with excitement. "This army will swallow the Franks. We are going to sail up their rivers and destroy everything in our path. Sigfrid is demanding seven hundred pounds of silver!"

Ulfrik sucked his breath at the enormous sum, as did others gathered to listen. "Even a king would struggle to raise that much silver."

Gunther and his men laughed. "Now I know you've been on these islands too long. The kings of Frankia are wealthy beyond imagining.

But wealthy and weak. Their fat bastard of a king couldn't even hold a knife in battle. The king is a reflection of the people. We'll stomp the Franks into the earth if they find guts enough to oppose us."

Gunther's men grumbled and nodded in agreement. Humbert, hovering at the periphery with Hrolf's refilled horn, used the moment to present it to him. Ulfrik watched the slave, who trembled as he handed over the horn. He recalled the promise of hidden gold inside the walls of Paris.

"Tell me this, do Hrolf and Sigfrid plan on attacking Paris?"

"More than plan on it. The fortress town is on an island in the middle of the river that gives access to the richer cities beyond."

"The Seine," said Humbert, who lingered at the table. His dark eyes flashed and he glanced hopefully at Ulfrik.

"He speaks Norse?" Gunther asked.

"A little," Ulfrik said. "He is a Frankish priest I've taken as a slave."

"He'll be useful to you then. But yeah, it's called the Seine or something like that. It's a big river with plenty of ripe towns along the way, waiting for us to beat the gold out of their churches. How do like that, slave-priest?"

Men laughed, but Humbert did not flinch. Instead Ulfrik saw a wave of irritation pass across his face.

"So you've come to summon me and my crew, but find us under attack. I'm afraid I can offer only two ships at best." Ulfrik looked to Toki and Snorri for support, and both nodded. Gunther's laughter died.

"Then it's two ships you bring. I ensured Hrolf remembered your name, and came to ensure you didn't miss this chance."

"Gunther, I appreciate your troubles. Yet being away over winter will invite disaster come summer. If word of my absence travels north, my enemies might even dare a winter attack. I am bound to protect my people."

Leaning back on his bench, Gunther's expression flattened and his men looked to him for a reaction. Ulfrik held his gaze steady. The two regarded each other for long moments before Gunther replied.

"First, we will be returned before summer. The Franks cannot withstand an army of Danes and Norsemen. We'll rip them apart and leave rich as lords. Second, you are bound to serve Jarl Hrolf, and that comes before anything else. But third, and this is most important, I want you there."

"Why? I'd bring eighty more men to share in the spoils. It's better if you had less."

Gunther waved his hand between them, wrinkling his nose. "Jarl Hrolf sees to me, no worries there. You must go because Jarl Hrolf sees farther than Sigfrid. There's potential in Frankia to not only demand wealth but land as well."

He let the words resonate with his listeners, Ulfrik catching himself leaning forward. "Land is a great thing, but I am surely a small and unknown jarl. When land is handed out, I might get a scrap to farm if I am lucky."

"But you are lucky."

Gunther's seriousness drew a dismissive snort from Ulfrik. "I'm holding onto this land by my fingernails."

"Bah! You are the right man for this. Hrolf needs leaders, strong war leaders, and you are one. Remember what I told you? I find a man like you once every ten years, if that. Were you truly so poor, truly so unlucky, you would be alone at this table. But men still follow you, and that's a sign to me. I'll put you near Hrolf in the battle line and you will do the rest."

Snorri clapped Ulfrik's back and other men banged the table in support. The loyalty of his men warmed his chest, and he nodded to each of them, even Thrand who merely scowled.

"Your praise does me honor, but why do you care for my fate? Let's be honest, there must be a benefit for you or you would not have undertaken the journey. Tell us, Gunther, why would you help me so?"

Gunther winked, then guzzled his horn of ale until it spilled out the sides of his mouth. Finishing, he slammed the horn on the table. "Because I like to win. Hrolf is breaking with his father. He had troubles with Harald Finehair, as you can imagine. Losing his father's support means losing some capable warriors. Whether or not Hrolf wants to admit it, he needs men like us to realize his vision."

"So it's just plain loyalty that drives you, nothing more?"

"Aye, plain loyalty to the winning side. I will be high on that winning side, and I want my own friends beside me. Do you take my meaning?"

Ulfrik stroked his beard, his eyes darting among the faces of his friends. Each man searched him for a sign of his thoughts, which he made no attempt to hide. A bold plan was forming: a promise of glory, land, and position in a new kingdom and a chance at Humbert's treasure to fund his estates. Yet he was time-bound by the seasons to complete everything before summer returned enemies to his home. Such a daring plan would entertain the gods, and they favored men who bring them entertainment. His smile widened as he twisted the tip of his beard.

"I take your meaning, Gunther, and I like what I hear. I am glad you sought me out, but I will have to discuss with my men before giving a final answer."

"We have talked much tonight, and I'm finally beginning to feel that ale. I'm going to curl up in a corner and let you sleep on the matter." He stood, stripping the wolf pelt off his shoulders and folding it over a thick arm. "Think carefully. If you refuse, I'll take my ships and never return, but you'll never be free to sail from these islands again. You'll be an oath-breaker, and a wanted man. So decide if you really love this land of sheep that much."

Despite the threat, Ulfrik laughed and stood with Gunther. "You've given me much to think upon. Rest well, Gunther One-Eye."

Men drifted from the tables, though Humbert approached Ulfrik. He said nothing, but gave a knowing stare and a slight smile alighted on his face. Ulfrik provided a subtle nod, his pulse quickening to the promise of glory and adventure.

～

"DUTY AND HONOR require me to answer the summons of my lord."

Ulfrik surveyed the faces of his ten closest men, those who had followed him from Norway or those who had earned their seats, like Thrand. Toki and Snorri flanked him and the others sat around the high table in the empty hall, a wan light of a gray afternoon streaming in from the open smoke hole. Ulfrik heard Gunther's men loitering outside, gruff voices vibrating through the walls. "I don't plan to disobey, but you are my closest companions, and I desire your counsel."

The gathered men nodded, though Thrand, sitting at the furthest end and still drunk from the prior night, spoke first.

"What counsel can we give you? I don't want to be named an outlaw. So we go to Frankia, and maybe find treasure worth the risk to our lives."

Others grumbled in agreement, and Ulfrik inclined his head to concede the point. "True words, but is everyone willing to risk being gone for all of winter? What if word of our absence travels north? Could you live with yourself if your families were butchered because we were not here to defend them?"

"It's the risk they take for a better life," answered a square-faced hirdman, Gran Redbeard. "No great deed is without danger."

"I agree," Ulfrik said. "And my family will share the same danger. But think on this, what awaits us in Paris? A long fight for the glory of a foreign lord, then a small share of the ransom and whatever else we can carry away. Then even that will be divided with Hrolf."

"You heard Gunther, lad," Snorri said, rapping the table with his knuckles. "It's more than money, but glory and land. He's letting you in on something grand. Don't piss your pants wondering about your sheep and hall. More is at stake."

"You know me too well to think I worry for sheep over my wife and son. Make your words useful."

"Take family with us," Snorri countered, unperturbed at Ulfrik's irritation. "Abandon this place and start anew."

The suggestion caused Ulfrik to sit straighter. "After all the men who bled for this land, I won't abandon it for a vague promise. Our flocks would die in winter, and we'd have nowhere to return if Hrolf's adventure failed."

"Then make sure he doesn't fail. It's why Gunther wants you there, said so himself."

The men chuckled and a few slapped the table. Ulfrik glared at Snorri, but his old friend's stern face melted to a smile and he began to laugh as well. Finally, Ulfrik waved his hand in defeat.

"Your confidence honors me, but I remain firm on that point. Our families hold the flocks together while we are gone. I will follow the will of my oath-lord. Does anyone object?"

Each man drew still and solemn. Toki put his hand on Ulfrik's shoulder. "None would hinder you, and the honor of all our people are at stake if you refuse. Know I would serve you and share your dangers equally."

"I'm commanded to fill my ships, but any man who wishes to remain behind may do so without shame." He searched the hard faces, finding only grim resolve. Thrand shifted on his bench, and scratched his head.

"The rewards better be as good as One-Eye promised."

"Shut up, you drunk," Snorri said. "We follow to honor our oaths to a fair lord, and rewards are a secondary concern."

Thrand opened his mouth to protest, but Ulfrik intervened.

"There is one more matter to discuss, and I must swear all of you to secrecy." He waited for their attention to return, and leaned forward to speak in a near-whisper. "Humbert's treasure is now a possibility."

"By the gods!" Thrand exclaimed, falling back from the table as if he had been struck. "You don't believe that lice-ridden liar, do you? He just wants to slip his bonds."

"The drunk is right," Snorri added. "I don't trust Christians or their dead god, liars all."

Expecting the criticism, Ulfrik smiled patiently. "But think on this. At last the gods have given us a sign of favor. They sent us Humbert, then Gunther with orders for us to attend Hrolf in Frankia. Paris, no less! It's the gods' work."

"It's a coincidence." Snorri turned on his bench and met Ulfrik's eyes. "Think no more on it."

"Fate rules us all. What is coincidence? That's when you need a comb and find it by your hand. But this is destiny." Ulfrik stood, excitement animating his face. He leaned on the table with both hands, meeting each man's gaze. "A treasure of gold lies hidden in Paris, and the man who has suffered for that secret is in our possession. Do you think Humbert lies? Maybe so, but without Gunther's arrival how could he have benefited from it?"

"By staying alive while you wondered if his tale might be true," Snorri answered the question, frustration coloring his voice. A few men nodded in agreement, but Ulfrik did not care.

"A good point. But I believe him. I did not at first, but now I've seen the work of Fate here. If any of you are undecided, then let us consult the futhark. I am confident we will have our answer."

Heads turned to a pinch-faced man with a dark red beard and ruddy cheeks. He wore a headband to contain his bushy hair. The mention of his rune sticks, the futhark, seemed to alarm him. Though long in Ulfrik's service, he only recently discovered Ander read futhark. Ulfrik extended his hand to him.

"Ander, you have your rune sticks? Cast them now and tell us if we should believe the priest."

"The futhark is my power, lord. I bear them always." He stood, feeling for a pouch strapped to his belt. Ulfrik pulled the table away from the north wall, where Ander would cast his sticks. Snorri helped, and murmured to him.

"The futhark, lad? Do you think Ander has the guts to tell you anything more than what you desire?"

"I cannot read them," he said, then added in a louder voice, "but if the futhark say I should ignore the priest, then I will heed that wisdom. Ander, are you ready?"

Ander nodded, facing north toward the seat of the gods' power. He held his sack of sticks in both hands and closed his eyes. Men gathered close, always eager to see the working of magic. Ulfrik smiled, confident that he understood the gods' message. He had no need to influence Ander, and so he remained behind the gathering.

After long moments of silence, Ander flung the sticks from his bag onto the dirt of the floor. Clattering over each other, he knelt to read the runes, seeking those that had landed faceup. Mumbling as he pointed to each rune, he also traced the crisscrossed patterns with his finger. At last he stood, a smile on his face.

"Lord Ulfrik, the priest is true. The gods show he possesses great treasure. I cannot be clearer, lord."

"So now we know the truth," Ulfrik said, taking his seat at the table while Ander and several men admired his rune casting.

"What an amazing surprise," Snorri grumbled, sitting next to Ulfrik and rolling his eyes.

"The futhark do not lie, lord." Ander glared at Snorri as he returned to his seat. "And I would not dare mislead you."

Ulfrik waved Ander to his seat, then squinted at Snorri. "Humbert told the truth, and now we have a means to act on that knowledge. Before we could not hope for access to Paris, and now we are called to join an army that will sack it. Humbert must be protected, and kept safe at least long enough to show us his hidden ways into the city and the location of the gold. He asks for vengeance in trade, and so would I were the situation reversed. We will provide it for him. I've no trouble killing his traitorous bishop if it means we claim his gold."

He paused, finding more appreciative faces. Only Snorri frowned, and Ulfrik lightly punched his shoulder. "Combined with our shares of the plunder, you will all be wealthy men. But here is where I need your solemn oath, from each of you. You'll swear it before the gods. No one beyond our circle may know of this plan, especially Gunther One-Eye and Hrolf the Strider. Were either to know, they would claim the gold for themselves, leaving only a share for us. So everything will require secrecy. I don't like deceit, especially to a worthy lord like Hrolf, but the gods have sent Humbert to us for a purpose. I don't believe the purpose was to put more gold into Hrolf's hands. Do you all agree?"

Everyone, including Snorri, agreed. Ulfrik rose and unclasped his silver armband, holding the dully gleaming ring over the table. "Everyone place your hands upon this ring." Hands reached in and touched the ring. Ulfrik turned to Toki, who gave a sheepish smile. He had once broken an oath sworn on this ring, but Ulfrik trusted the gods had punished him for that sin. "You swear to reveal our plan to no one, and to do your part in this undertaking in return for a fair share of the spoils. Each man so sworn is bound to me and to the gods to keep his oath under pain of banishment."

Each man in turn gave his oath, including Snorri whose skepticism Ulfrik appreciated. Few men dared counter a jarl's words, and those who did so with good intentions were more valuable than any treasure. He acknowledged each man's oath with a nod, and paid special attention to Thrand the Looker, who gave his oath with a snarl but also without hesitation. Satisfied, he withdrew the ring and replaced it on his arm.

"The specifics of the plan will have to be made in the field, where we can observe the situation. While I'd like the rest of the crew to share in this, for the sake of preserving secrecy, they must not know. I will find a way for them to benefit as well. Now, we've made our decisions and our oaths. I'll give Gunther the news."

7

"And if I disagree, it means nothing to you?"

Runa plunged the bucket into the barrel, avoiding Ulfrik's eyes. Her lips and limbs trembled, and hauling the filled bucket of water from the rain barrels behind the hall consumed more strength than usual. Precious fresh water, collected from daily showers, sloshed and spilled to the grass. The earthy scent of rain still hung in the air and cold wetness seeped through her hide shoes. She stared at the half-filled bucket, listening to those damned foreigners chatter and laugh in the distance.

"Humbert should be fetching water for you." She heard the waver in his voice, and anger flared.

"Like I haven't done this for years before that cursed man turned up? And you'll be taking him away to chase your treasures."

He shushed her, eyes wide and searching for eavesdroppers. The urgency further maddened her, and she slapped down his fluttering hands. "Not to worry, since you'll not find anything for your troubles. You wouldn't know the lie if it was rammed down your throat."

A frown creased his face and he opened his mouth, but Runa turned up her chin in defiance. He was wrong, and Runa was convinced both understood it. He lowered his head, then rubbed his face. "Even if you think the treasure a lie, can you not shout about it? Just the talk of treasure could cause me troubles."

"I'll agree to that. The talk has already caused troubles, it seems to me." She folded her arms, self-conscious of her trembling. Again she was being left behind to run a household and guard their children. Again, her husband was leaving her surrounded by enemies.

"Put aside the treasure." Ulfrik smiled, the thin smile he relied on to calm her and signal acquiescence. "I gave my oath to Hrolf years ago, and I cannot break it."

"Oaths are broken all the time. Be realistic."

"Mine are not. Be reasonable."

He glared at her, and the two remained locked. She searched his eyes, a strangeness creeping over her as she did. His determination and pride was not unusual, but something fluttered behind his eyes —belief and hope.

"All right, I will be reasonable." She broke their stare, turning aside to fix on the purple shadows of mountains lost in rain-bloated clouds. "But you know what I meant, and don't pretend otherwise. No games with me."

"No games," he said with surprising gentleness. She still looked away, but his warm hand gripped her shoulder. "If I was willing to remain trapped on these lands forever, I could decline. Gunther gave me that choice."

"Then why not decline?" Her head snapped back to him, and her lip trembled harder and her eyes grew hot. She hated this weakness. Was not every other wife suffering the loss of her man as well? Did they all weep and beg like she did?

"The gods have given me this chance. Ander cast the rune sticks, and the gods say Humbert is true. We are destined for more than life on a treeless rock at the edge of the world." His grip pressed into her flesh and his speech quickened. "Fighting beside Hrolf will win fame and glory for me and all our men. Claiming Humbert's treasure will gain us wealth. All good in life comes from those three things. The Fates have put their eyes upon Frankia, and I need to be there. Great things will happen, I know it."

She smiled, not from humor but from her husband's pitiful understanding of what motivated her. He stood smiling, his eyes bright with excitement. More laughter of the foreign men tumbled out of the distance, distracting her thoughts with anger at their intrusion. If only she could roll them back into the trackless ocean, none of this fruitless conversation would happen. She placed her hand over Ulfrik's at her shoulder, the warm roughness emphasizing the chill in hers. She intertwined her fingers with his, drawing them to her lips to kiss, scenting the saltiness of them. He was lost to her, she knew, but she was compelled to dissuade him.

"I know you want to benefit our family, but do all good things in life come from gold and glory? Did Gunnar and Hakon come from it? Did I? Did gold and glory keep our daughter alive in winter? All I want is a peaceful life and a happy family. There is glory in that, too."

"A woman's glory," he said, pulling his hand away. He barely concealed the curl of his lip. "A man is called to carve his will on the world, and to entertain the gods with the spectacle of his bravery. Hiding under my bed while an army sails to battle and spoils is the worst shame I can bring on our family and people."

Runa closed her eyes, neck pulsing as she bridled her response. Once composed, she spoke with labored evenness. "So who will protect us when you are gone? How many men will remain while you sail to battle and spoils?"

Eyes still closed, she waited on his answer. Nothing but distant laughter and rush of wind-stirred grass met her ears. Her eyes opened, and Ulfrik was peering into the distance, his lips tight and closed.

"You are leaving me with no one?" She abandoned any effort to restrain herself. A cold line of tears ran over her cheeks. "All winter I must cower in fear with the women and old men, begging the gods to wreck our enemies' ships. This is how you care for your family and home!"

"Everyone must go." He remained fixed on the distance, his voice rough. "To leave my trusted men behind would shame them. To leave the new, untested men behind is as much a risk as leaving you with my enemies. Shame and idleness would provoke them to evil."

"So take us with you!" As soon as the words escaped, she regretted them. This argument had become stale even to her. "No, instead you stay. You stay and take the responsibility for protecting all your people, not just the honor of some men. You selfish bastard!"

Her fist shot out for his face, and he jerked aside moments before it connected. Yet her training had built her agility and speed, and her other fist landed in his gut. Her knuckles collided with the hard muscle, but her wrist bent and the power drained from the punch. Ulfrik exhaled with a grunt, then grasped her arm and yanked her close. She tipped the bucket over, and the water rushed uselessly into the ground. Her sobbing erupted like the toppled bucket, and she collapsed against the scratchy softness of his wool cloak.

He spoke to her and stroked her hair, but the words made no sense. Again she would be defenseless and alone, and enemies would encircle her. Nye Grenner would look to her for strength where she had little, and protection where she could offer even less. Nothing could change this. Fate, the Three Norns, had woven their threads and created the pattern of her life.

"When must you leave?" Her question was interjected with sniffles, and salty tears flowed over her lips. She could feel his heart pounding beneath his shirt. She placed her hand over it, wondering how long she had to feel it throb before he sailed off to find his destiny.

"We have a month to make the journey. I've already given Gunther my word, and he sails today with our news. We go to Denmark first, to meet the main fleet. We will set out in two weeks."

She nodded, and more tears pressed from her closed eyes. He rested his chin atop her head, and squeezed tighter. "I have not forgotten the treasure of my family, Wife. I do this for us. I promise to return by summer, and bring two hundred men at my back to finish off those northern turds. Do not fear."

Runa shivered in the final throes of her sobs. Gunther's men continued to shout and laugh in the distance, and rain began to peck wetness onto her face as a new storm cloud floated overhead. She drew in a deep breath of salt air and the comforting scent of her husband. No matter what he said, she did fear. She feared to the core of her heart.

~

GUNTHER'S two ships already lurched and rocked on the foamy water of the fjord. Ulfrik faced the huge war leader, hard rocks of the beach poking his feet as if urging him away. Extending an arm to Gunther, the two men clasped arms. A sureness was set in Gunther's good eye, and his rough hand squeezed Ulfrik's forearm.

"Was good to see you again, Ulfrik. I'll carry word to Hrolf, and he will be pleased that you've answered his call."

Gulls screeched overhead as waves broke and hissed behind Gunther. Ulfrik smiled and returned the squeeze. The malty taste of ale guzzled in a final round of good-byes only an hour ago still clung to his mouth. Runa had left him more conflicted on his choice, and words fled him at this parting. He could still choose not to go, even after Gunther departed. No one would seek him out again, and his life would forever be tied to these islands.

Withdrawing his arm, Gunther turned to his men and with a wave of his hand they started boarding his ship. The rest of Ulfrik's hirdmen had escorted their guests to the shore, and now stood in awkward silence behind him. Snorri spoke, filling the unseemly gap.

"We'll meet you in Denmark, no worries for that. But Frankia better be all you've promised."

Gunther put a hand over his gut and bent back in laughter. "I love to tell tales, old friend, but I promise you I've not exaggerated the riches. Christians are strong there, and where their priests go so goes the wealth. We'll peel back their city walls like scales off a salmon, and the flesh inside will be just as delicious. Believe me, even with one eye I can see that much!"

Polite laughter met Gunther's claims, though he doubled over laughing at his own words. The gregariousness of such a fearsome warrior drew a smile to Ulfrik's face, and he shook his head to clear it.

"Fair winds for you, One-Eye. We will drink together in Frankia, atop a pile of gold."

"So we will, and that reminds me." He patted around his waist until he plucked a leather pouch from his belt. "I've been a poor guest. I drank your ale and ate your meat, but brought no gift. I am a shameful man, too focused on this adventure to remember my manners. Take this instead."

He extended the pouch; brown and care-worn, it bulged with sharp points. Ulfrik knew it was packed with hack-silver and probably some gold. Gunther dangled it by its tie.

"I did no more than the honor due you, One-Eye. Such generosity is unnecessary." He spoke the words but his eyes never left the pouch. He needed silver enough to practically taste its metallic tang. The bag twisted in the cold autumn breeze.

"A guest must bring his host a gift, especially when he invites a hundred other friends along."

Jiggling the pouch by the tie, Ulfrik still hesitated. The gift was one more bind to Gunther and Hrolf, one more knot tied in the connection. When he did not grasp it, Gunther seized his limp arm and yanked it out. He crushed the heavy pouch into Ulfrik's palm. Then he folded up Ulfrik's fingers, drawing close enough for his sweaty musk to fill Ulfrik's nose.

"You hesitate when you should not." Gunther's voice was a low grumble. "This is a gift from me, for what I took during my stay. Nothing more. Take what I offer, and use it however you wish. Resupply for the winter; fix your armor; buy women for your crew."

Men nearby laughed at Gunther's final comment as he stepped back. Ulfrik's face heated and he accepted the pouch. He glanced at Snorri and Toki, then to his other men. He glimpsed Runa as a dark shape lingering at the hall behind all of them.

"Your generosity is almost as deep as your stomach. My thanks, One-Eye."

Gunther roared laughter again, then turned to join his men as they pushed his ship out to sea. His hair flowed over the gray wolf pelt draping his shoulders as he trudged into the surf. Men helped him aboard, and he returned to the rails to shout over the breaking waves.

"We meet one month hence. Toki knows the way. Gods keep your hall safe."

Ulfrik raised his fist, and Gunther returned the sign of strength. He and his men watched the three ships gather and then steer east out of the fjord for the open sea. His own ships would soon follow the same path.

"You won't break your word," Toki's statement sounded like a question to Ulfrik.

"Of course not. The gods are with us. We will return before summer, our hulls brimming with treasure."

Gunther's ships faded to smudges in the misty horizon. Ulfrik turned to regard his crew, but everyone had drifted back toward the hall leaving him alone at the edge of the surf.

8

Rain battered Thrand's house, and distant thunder rattled the walls. Water spattered onto the floor and furniture from a dozen spots in the roof. The smoke hole cover sagged with gathering water, and a constant stream splashed into a bucket beneath it. The rainwater intensified the rank scent of the sheep packed inside the home. Thrand shouted at their constant bleating, and they clustered tightly at the center of the room. He had been watching the door, listening to the rain, and drinking sour ale from his horn. Finally, it broke open and Kolbyr tumbled in.

The sheep spun in a circle, startled at the sudden entrance. Kolbyr huddled under a sealskin cloak, and as he tore it away gouts of rainwater dumped to the floor. Thrand laughed at his bedraggled friend.

"You look like a drowned cat."

"Where do these storms come from?" Kolbyr plopped his cloak over an empty stool, then wiped the water out of his face. "The night looked clear enough when I set out for your house."

"Live here a while and you'll learn how fast storms appear. The gods hate this place, Kolbyr, and whenever they notice it they lash it with rain and lightning. Now, warm yourself with good ale." Thrand trained his clear eye on Kolbyr. The ale was the worst he had tasted in years, but he filled a mug for his guest and smacked his lips. "We've got much to discuss tonight, my only friend in this world."

Kolbyr settled onto his stool, the oil lamp between them painted deep shadows into his face. He accepted the mug and tipped it into his mouth. He pulled it away with a grimace and swallowed hard. "Is it sheep piss?"

"It'd taste better if it was, but it's not. Now drink up. We have to be quick."

"You've got a woman sneaking out here in the rain, do you?"

"With your pretty face, you'd be good enough. Now are you ready to listen or do you have more shit to drop from that hole under your nose?"

Kolbyr flung his full mug onto Thrand's bed in the corner, then sneered at him. "Sleep in your sheep piss, if you love it so much. Now what have you called me out here to discuss?"

Thrand dropped his head and scratched his scalp, fighting the urge to strike back at Kolbyr. Yet he needed help, and no one besides Kolbyr could offer it.

"The bed is a nest of lice anyway. I'm better off on the floor." Thunder cracked close enough for the table to vibrate under Thrand's arms; the sheep panicked again but had nowhere to run but in a circle. "We sail for Frankia next week. What do you think of that?"

"I hear it's warmer, and filled with beautiful women. We'll get to kill and loot the bastards until we're rich. Sounds great."

"Sounds great until you consider we've heard this from Ulfrik before." He raised his head to regard Kolbyr. Confused lines drew over his face, and Thrand continued. "A few weeks ago, you were sitting on that stool and complaining about your poor share of spoils. Now you've got another one of Ulfrik's stories, and you're feeling great. Does that make sense?"

"Don't it?" Thrand shrugged. "That one-eyed giant sailed into the fjord with an army and promised us riches if we followed him."

"No! He promised Ulfrik riches, and he gifted Ulfrik with a bag of gold. I saw it myself!"

"Which eye saw it?"

"I'll pull your fucking eyes out, you turd, and teach you some manners!" Thrand squelched the impulse to fight by draining his horn and throwing it aside. "Now think again. Whatever you and I take in loot, he'll be sure to claim a share as his own, and whatever his lord awards him won't pass to our hands. But we'll be in the shield walls, our lives at risk just as his, even more so since no one will defend us if we stumble. Does that sound fair?"

"It's that way everywhere," Kolbyr spread his hands wide. "It's a rare jarl who splits evenly with all. Never heard of one, actually."

Thrand covered his face with both hands, the scent of dirt and sour ale trapped over his nose. Had he misunderstood Kolbyr's intentions, or was he being cautious? He let his hands fall to the table, the air cool and refreshing where he had covered himself. Rain continued to pelt the house, and the constant splash of water running out of the smoke hole made him feel like urinating.

"Listen to me, Kolbyr; I've got a secret to share with you." Lightning flashed white through the cracks in the walls and openings, but thunder did not follow. "There's more happening during this adventure than you know. Ulfrik has a secret plan."

Thunder finally pealed; a warm and distant growl of a retreating storm. Kolbyr sat straighter and leaned across the table. "I'll keep your secret, friend. You know I am trustworthy."

Thrand smiled, but wondered at the self-proclaimed trustworthiness. Yet he had no one else. "You know that Frankish slave we captured, the priest? He claims to know of treasure hidden in Paris, and if we help him take revenge on his enemies then he'll lead us to it."

"Why not cut off one finger at a time until he reveals the treasure and skip helping him?"

"And it may come to that, but it's not the important part. The treasure is a huge cross of ancient gold, hidden in one of the Frank's holy places. Ulfrik plans to follow the slave into Paris, using secret paths, and to steal that cross without his lord knowing." Thrand held his breath, ensuring Kolbyr looked him in the eye. "Nor anyone else."

Kolbyr leaned back, shadow flowing about his face like black water. The oil lamp guttered and the room twisted in long shadows. Dripping rain water filled the silence until Kolbyr spoke.

"You're drunk, as usual. Just a moment ago you told me Ulfrik's plans were a waste of time and now you talk about a plot to steal treasure from Paris."

"I thought the same as you, but Ander cast his rune sticks. The gods have shown us the truth. The slave's story is genuine and the gods favor us with its secret. Ulfrik swore ten of us to secrecy, his closest men. He only did that because he couldn't get the gold alone. Otherwise, he'd tell no one, not for all that treasure."

"And you're betraying his secret to me for the same reason."

Thrand stiffened, blinking at Kolbyr who sneered at him. His ale-loosened tongue gave a ready reply. "I underestimated you. You know what I'm asking of you?"

Kolbyr nodded with a smirk. "But why don't you tell me, in case I'm mistaken. You're in Lord Ulfrik's inner circle, after all, and not me."

"It's not a test," he said with more anger than intended, though it only made Kolbyr smile wider. "I'm offering you a chance at a treasure that your lord planned to hide from you. He won't even allow you to participate. Splitting it ten ways is hard enough for him, never mind among everyone."

"And how will you get me into Lord Ulfrik's circle so that I can get a share?"

"Let me be clearer. Ulfrik has failed me. On every count, total failure. My home collapses over my head. I call five sheep a flock. My brother gave his life so that Ulfrik and Toki could have everything they desired, while I got nothing but a share of pitiful treasure. Now he plans to enrich himself, and spend that treasure on building ships and weapons. And if I even live through this, I'll get an armband and a share not worthy of all I've done for the man.

"You and I are going to relieve Ulfrik of that treasure. We will split the gold, and each of us will be free to go our own ways. No more will I follow a stingy and short-sighted lord. No more will I have to endure life in a barren land without women or people to call friends. That treasure, we will have it."

His head throbbed from his anger, and Thrand's vision filled with images of Ulfrik laughing and drinking with his friends while he sat unwelcome in a corner. Swimming throughout were other thoughts, where Ulfrik wept for his brother and promised to honor him. Yet the memory vanished and he saw Ulfrik scowling and calling him a drunk. He shook his head. Once cleared, he again saw Kolbyr with arms folded across his chest.

"Do you have a plan to get away with this? Before I agree, I want to know what I'm getting into."

"Of course, the details aren't clear, but I have an idea. The two of us cannot do this alone, but no one will aid us from this place. There will be other jarls with their men at Paris. If we can cause trouble between one of them and Ulfrik, we will have a distraction. Then we either get the slave to take us to the treasure or use the distraction to steal off with it."

"That's another way to tell me you're relying on luck."

"Not at all! I cannot plan until I see the landscape. Right now I need to know you are with me on this." Thrand waited, his hand sliding beneath the table to grasp the cool, sharkskin-covered handle of the short sword he had laid against the table leg. The rough sharkskin bit into his grip, and he watched Kolbyr's eyes follow his hand down. If he declined, Thrand decided, he could not live.

Thunder boomed in the distance, and the rain had decreased to a patter. Kolbyr held still, and Thrand's pulse throbbed in his grip. He tasted salty sweat rolling off his lip into his mouth.

"Put your hand back on the table. I'm in."

Thrand exhaled with a smile, letting go of his sword and reaching out to shake Kolbyr's hand. "Then we've decided. I knew I had not misjudged you."

They shook, Thrand impressed at the strong grasp of his young partner. The relief was exuberant, though in his heart he knew Kolbyr would eventually try to kill him for a chance at all the gold. It was the way of such alliances, and Thrand expected he also understood it. For now, they were unified in purpose.

"There's one final thing we should be clear about," Thrand said. "To be successful, we might have to kill Ulfrik."

"If he fights, he will die."

"No, I mean that our plans may be best served if we kill him in his sleep or at another time. You won't have trouble with that, will you?"

"Not if we are getting all that gold for ourselves. I'll slit his throat myself."

Both men laughed, and thunder rolled in the distance to seal their pact.

9

November, 885 CE

"Finding Gunther among so many people will take all night." Ulfrik and his eighty warriors had waded ashore and now stood on a sandy beach at the meeting place designated a month ago. Locating the fjord had been simple, since Ulfrik guessed every longship in the circle of the world headed to the same place. He had only to follow the others.

Toki plodded past him, drawing a deep breath through his nose. "Smell the pines? This is Denmark, home!"

"Smells like fish and sweat," Snorri quipped. "Gunther will be where the ale flows freest."

Ulfrik shook his head and ordered his men to follow up the shallow slope. They hefted bags, folded tents, blankets, and war gear and trudged out of the cold wetness of the surf. The scene spreading before Ulfrik summoned memories of the markets in Kaupang. His father had taken him to trade in the market every summer, and each time he had marveled at the throngs of people, the strange languages and accents, the goods and money changing hands, the games and brawls in every corner. It was a spectacle to never be surpassed —until now.

The fjord was choked with anchored ships, and the beaches were thick with dark hulled vessels of every size. The cloudless purple sky of twilight revealed an array of stars, mirrored by a pinpoint web of orange campfires and bonfires along the shore. Shadows of men formed clusters and lines that rippled and writhed in the firelight. Boisterous voices, laughter, shouts, off-key music, bleating sheep, and even the squeals of children rivaled the breaking waves for rhythm and volume.

Thousands upon thousands of warriors and many more of their families camped here, and ships still slipped into the fjord as darkness pulled down to the jagged horizon of pine treetops. Surrendering to the futility of locating anyone in such a gathering, Ulfrik dropped his pack into the grass.

"Let's set our camp here. Einar, take some men and find firewood. Toki, fly my standard and leave it for Gunther to find us."

Their tasks assigned, Ulfrik settled to the grass and leaned on his pack. One of his men dragged Humbert forward, and roughly shoved him before Ulfrik. His ragged clothing was soaked from wading to the beach, but he had held his red cloak out of the water. Righting himself, casting a hateful glare at his handler, he gathered the dry cloak tighter.

"Sit with me, Humbert. We have not spoken in a long time."

Humbert looked about at the rest of the crew throwing down their burdens and stretching on the grass. Only after satisfying himself of safety, he sat a respectful distance away. Ulfrik chuckled at his caution, but understood it. Men often treated their tools better than a slave.

"Tell me, Humbert, what do you think of this gathering?"

"It smells like a dead whale and sounds like a dying moose."

Ulfrik rocked back in laughter, both from the apt comparison and the heavily accented Norse. "Are there moose in Frankia?" Humbert shook his head, and Ulfrik laughed again. Snorri settled beside him, and others dropped their packs close. Thrand and his blond-haired friend, Kolbyr, joined as well. Thrand offered him a rare smile.

"I was more interested in what you think of all these men. Do we have enough to conquer Paris, and the cities beyond?"

Humbert scowled and threw a cursory glance at the crowds of warriors. "Maybe enough."

Laughter met Humbert's mumbled assessment. Toki, who had just fastened Nye Grenner's standard of black elk antlers on a green field to its pole, stood over Humbert. "Maybe? There are enough warriors here to conquer the whole country, maybe the whole world."

"Who would be king of the world?" asked Darby, whose head still bore the scars from the sheep raid. "Would it be you, Toki?"

"And why not? A fool like you would spend all his days counting the sheep in his kingdom. But I would count the women, and sample each one!"

Someone playfully tossed a clod of dirt at Toki and all laughed. Ulfrik's mirth was tempered by a strangeness he sensed from Toki. The closer they had come to Denmark, the more carefree he had become, but it seemed tinged with something Ulfrik could not place. Ignoring the sensation, he returned to Humbert.

"You don't think an army this size will prevail? You still doubt, or are you too proud of your people?"

"This is no army," Humbert's dark eyes glittered in the darkness. "No one leads them. Loyal only to yourselves, you will not last when trouble begins. Humbert thinks the master has never seen Paris before. When master sees, he will know Humbert's meaning."

Ulfrik was about to probe Humbert's meaning, but then his slave looked up with surprise. Ulfrik turned and found a dark shape wavering behind him. The outline of the wolf-pelt across the shoulders and the massive body defined Gunther in an instant.

"No trouble finding the gathering spot, I bet!" Gunther's voice boomed over the cacophony, and he extended a hand to help Ulfrik to his feet.

"None, but finding a coin at the bottom of the sea felt easier than finding you here." Gunther's rough hand was hot with sweat as it wrapped onto Ulfrik's forearm. Groaning, he hoisted Ulfrik to his feet and the two clasped together in greeting. Gunther's stiff wolf pelt pushed into Ulfrik's face, smelling like ale and coppery blood. They drew back, and Ulfrik swept his arm across his camp. "All eighty warriors answered Jarl Hrolf's summons. We are here for gold and victory."

"Can't be gold without victory!" Gunther softened his expression, a genuine gladness drawn into the lines and scars on his face. "I'm glad you chose to answer the call. You will never regret it."

Ulfrik nodded, and Einar and his chosen men returned with armfuls of firewood. "We haven't even built a fire yet. How did you find us so fast?"

"You're as late as can be, and we sail tomorrow. So I've had boys watching every open landing spot for you. Not too many new arrivals now, so you were easy to find. In fact, leave your gear here but go see Hrolf. He'll be heartened to greet you and your eighty warriors."

Ulfrik waved his men to their feet, instructing them to leave their packs. Humbert stood, nervously clutching his cloak to his throat. Thrand stood beside him, dusting down his pants. Ulfrik pointed at him. "Keep an eye on Humbert and don't let him wander."

He shot Thrand a knowing look, and he replied with a solemn nod. Humbert meant too much to his plans, and though Ulfrik did not fear his fleeing, he worried for theft. Anyone looking closely would notice his bearing and intelligence, and might be tempted to steal him as one would steal unattended silver. The red cloak marked him out as well. Relieved once Thrand grabbed Humbert's arm, he followed Gunther.

As they worked through the press of men, he heard the Danish accents spoken everywhere. He glanced at Toki, who as a native of Denmark blended with the local language. Norwegian accents drew glances, most indifferent but some disdainful.

"None of these people know how to talk," he said to Toki, who followed at his side like a child at a festival.

"It's music. If my sister were here, she'd tell you the same."

The mention of Runa hit him harder than he expected. The day he had sailed, he had offered her a kiss and a sword. Pressing his short blade into her hand, she allowed him a single kiss before pulling away. "Go with the gods, and find victory. I will pray to them for your safety."

"Practice with the big sword, but use this one if you must fight. It will be a goose feather in your hand. It is mine, and has served me well. I pray you will have no need of it."

"A prayer you share with me. Now, go and return in spring as a jarl rich in gold and glory. And if you don't return, I'll pass this sword to Gunnar."

"Don't say it, Wife! Have I not always returned?" He reached for her but she stepped away. They traded stares, and her eyes warned him to silence. He left her at the doors of his hall, and did not look back. Now, he regretted his reticence.

A man tumbled at his feet, drawing him back from his thoughts. Gunther side-stepped, but Ulfrik nearly tripped. Two more men followed, and pummeled the man on the ground who barred his face with his arms. Ulfrik and his crew flowed around the brawl, Gunther never pausing as he pushed deeper into the fire-bright welter of sweating, stinking men.

"We've been idle too long," he called back over his shoulder. "Many have been here a week with nothing to do but drink and grow bored. Lots of fighting, even some killed. Time to move on, I say."

Slipping out of the throng, Ulfrik greeted the cool air with an exaggerated sigh that drew a knowing chuckle from Gunther. They had arrived at a wide clearing populated by numerous tents, two of which stood higher and wider than the others. A bonfire blazed at the center and clusters of spearmen idled around it. Banners flipped around poles at the entrances to the tents, but did not fly true enough to see the markings.

"Hrolf dwells in that tent." Gunther pointed to the leftmost tent, brown with dirt from long years of use. It was not as large as the center tent, nor as bright.

"And Sigfrid is at the center," Ulfrik finished for him.

Two men guarded the worn tent, but Gunther ignored them and

stood outside the flap, addressing Hrolf. "Lord, more warriors join your band. Ulfrik Ormsson has arrived with hirdmen, and they will present themselves."

A response came that Ulfrik could not hear, but One-Eye backed away. In the next moment, the flap opened and Jarl Hrolf the Strider ducked out of the tent. Three years had passed, but Ulfrik could hardly forget the tallest man he had ever met. Clad in shining mail and a heavy cape rimmed with fox fur, he appeared ready to leap into battle. Gold rings caught points of bonfire and gold and silver armbands sparkled with the dancing flames. Thor's hammer hung across his chest, the polished silver reflecting so powerfully the talisman seemed on fire.

He threw his arms wide; clear, fierce eyes set in a regal face meeting Ulfrik's. His presence had not diminished over the years, and the gray forming at his temples and in his pointed beard contributed to his kingly appearance. "One-Eye said you would come. Be welcomed!"

Ulfrik inclined his head. "My lord, I would not miss the opportunity to join you in such a great undertaking. I bring three ships and eighty men to the glory of your banner."

Snorri grunted beside him, and Ulfrik smiled. Flattery was not his strongest talent, but he understood its value to men like Hrolf. The grunt was Snorri's critique of his awkward delivery, but Hrolf appeared unconcerned as he surveyed the men arrayed behind Ulfrik with an appreciative nod.

"Eighty men! One-Eye, how many warriors under my banner now?"

"I can't count that high, lord."

"Find someone who can, then tell me I have more than Sigfrid."

Both men laughed, but Ulfrik noted the rivalry with a sly smile to Snorri. Hrolf put his hands on his hips, scanning the crew, then stopped and pointed at Humbert. "You took no women with you but brought an old man? I thought I knew you better, Ulfrik."

Humbert crumbled back like he had been struck with an arrow, casting his gaze to the ground. Thrand grabbed his shoulders and shoved him to his knees before Hrolf. Ulfrik laughed at Hrolf's jest. "He is a slave and a captive, a priest from Frankia I hope to ransom. He speaks our language, too, and so might be of use."

Hanging forward enough to nearly prostrate himself, he croaked his greeting, "Lord Hrolf."

"Did he just die?" Gunther joked, then slapped his leg as he cackled. Humbert was immediately forgotten when a horn began to blast.

"Sigfrid is ready to address the men," Hrolf said, pointing to the center tent. "I will join him. You are all lucky to be in the front, where you can be seen with the great jarls."

Hrolf left with his bodyguards, and Gunther went to summon his crew. Ulfrik gathered his men close, keeping Snorri and Toki to either side. Overturned carts made for a makeshift stage. The crowds of warriors gathered around the bonfire to hear their lord's address. Many drunken calls filled the night as the crowd formed.

Emerging from his tent, Sigfrid greeted his allies with nods curt enough to be insults. His pale eyes glittered in the firelight and his wide face was written with lust for attention. Leaping onto the wagon with a single jump, he landed easily and drew approving shouts for his agility.

"Bastard practiced that for weeks," Snorri's rough voice whispered in Ulfrik's ear, and he put the back of his hand to his mouth to cover his laugh.

Sigfrid raised his hand to the crowd, and men began to stomp the ground or beat their shields. Soon all joined in, Ulfrik pounding the earth with his foot. Sigfrid circled to face every man, his freshly scoured mail orange bright and his rings and chains sparkling. Shadows filled the curvatures of his muscles, making him appear stronger and larger than reality. Waving down the crowd, he shouted for silence. It took a long while, but he finally captured the massive throng's attention. Ulfrik craned his neck to look behind, seeing no end to the men gathered.

"This summer I offered the Frankish Emperor of the Holy Roman Empire, Charles the Fat, terms for his safety. Seven hundred pounds of silver would satisfy me enough to leave him alone. But the fool refused, and now he will pay. We'll have that silver, plus whatever we can carry away. We'll remind the Franks why they should fear us. We sail at dawn!"

Sigfrid threw his arms overhead again and roared, soliciting his audience to join him. Many were drunk and many were impatient, and so shouts followed. However, Ulfrik frowned and hollered to Toki over the din.

"What is this? We're going to remind the Franks? He makes it sound like an errand."

"Not much of a speaker," Toki agreed.

Sigfrid shouted a while longer, promised death to any Frank standing in his way, then abruptly returned to his tent. Confusion rippled through the crowd, which did not appear to understand the gathering had finished. At last, Hrolf mounted the wagon and dismissed everyone.

"How many women do you think wait for him in that tent?" Snorri asked as they turned to leave.

The tight clusters of bodies slowed their return to camp. Weary and hungry, he anticipated a meal and sleep. As the crowd broke apart, they moved faster until they found Nye Grenner's standard again. As his crew settled onto the grass, Gunther One-Eye reappeared.

"I've got a favor to ask of you," he said without preamble. He rested his heavy hands on the shoulders of a young man dressed in mail and draped with a wolf pelt. He hefted a bag, which he let drop, and carried a new shield of iron-rimmed wood that was painted red and gold. A short, blond beard hid his face well enough for his age and his features looked nothing like Gunther's. However, his mannerisms and expressions were drawn directly from him.

"I did not know you had a son," Ulfrik replied, gambling that he was correct. Gunther patted the man's shoulder and pushed him forward.

"My name is Mord Guntherson." He glanced at his father, who kept his eyes on Ulfrik while his hands pushed his son down. Mord dropped to his knee and bowed his head. "I would be honored if you allowed me to serve under you."

Ulfrik blinked at Mord, not comprehending. Snorri, Toki, Einar, Ander, and several others who stood nearby paused and watched with guarded expressions.

"I want him to learn from you," Gunther explained. "Keep him close, and teach him how to lead men in battle. If I had him with me, I'd always be worried. That'll just get us both killed. What do you say?"

Blinking again, he regarded Mord kneeling in the grass. Teaching Gunther's son was not a difficulty, but keeping him close would imperil his plans for Humbert's treasure. However, to refuse would not only be groundless, but would also ruin an important relationship. Worries and arguments passed through his mind, until Mord raised a quizzical eye to him while still kneeling.

"Sorry, but of course I would be gladdened to have Mord join my crew." Gunther's skeptical expression melted to a smile. Ulfrik raised Mord to his feet. "Be welcomed and find a place for your pack."

Mord flashed his father's carefree smile and thanked him.

"You'll not worry for him in the shield wall," Gunther said. "I've trained him and drilled him. He knows what he's doing."

"I'll keep him close, but I can't guarantee any man's life in battle."

"Understood, and I won't hold you to it."

Ulfrik watched father and son hug each other in parting, Gunther thumping him on the head and admonishing him to do well. Yet all Ulfrik could think is somehow Gunther learned about the treasure and planted his son to spy on him. Shaking his head at the stupidity of the thought, he returned to settling into camp and tried to forget his worries.

10

Prowling among trees again brought a joy to Ulfrik's heart not experienced since fleeing Norway. Winter had stripped branches bare, and these dueled overhead in the cold breeze. The dead leaves crunched beneath his goatskin boats as he led his scouting party of fifteen men. The Frankish wilderness was colder than promised, and far more wet than expected. Mud seeped into his boots, chilling his toes. However, the clear and earthy scent of the woods summoned fond memories that warmed his spirit. He and his men huddled beneath green and gray wool cloaks, any exposed metal smeared with dirt to prevent reflections. Ulfrik stood at the head of the group, with Einar hulking beside him. Young Einar, whose stepfather Snorri remained at camp with the remainder of the crew, had grown tall and strong. Ulfrik was glad to have his blade in his service.

"Toki has been gone too long," he whispered.

"How long is too long? He takes whatever time needed to find a sign of the enemy. Haven't heard a sound yet, so he's not been discovered nor has he discovered anything."

Einar nodded, and Ulfrik returned to squinting through the sparse trees. A milky haze clung to the wet ground, and patches of slushy snow emphasized the whiteness. Far down the hill, the walled fortress called Pontoise brooded like a block of gray stone streaked with brown. The fortress had halted the progress of Sigfrid's fleet, positioned on the confluence of the Oise and Seine Rivers. Curls of smoke rose over the brown rooftops, giving it a false look of peace and comfort. Arrayed on the opposite side of the fortress were hordes of Danes and a river choked with their ships. The fortress commander had defied Sigfrid's demands to surrender, and now Sigfrid prepared to raze the fortress to rubble and ash.

Hrolf had persuaded Sigfrid to delay the attack, hoping to find another way into or around Pontoise. Ulfrik, as eager as his lord to move on to the real fight at Paris, had volunteered to lead a scouting party. He sought a weakness in the fortress or a portage to avoid it completely. A siege of an unimportant castle delayed his ultimate goal of a quick success in Paris and a return home before spring. He was unwilling to dally, and if needed would push all of the 30,000 men Sigfrid claimed he commanded to Paris.

Something flitted between trees, and Ulfrik instinctively dropped to a crouch. He heard the crunch and creak of mail and leather as the men behind him did the same. He grasped his sword hilt, cold and rough in his hand, but did not draw it. He held his breath so the fog of it would not give him away.

Toki's dark, curly hair identified him as he strode the last distance to their position. Ulfrik relaxed as Toki arrived, and Mord loped behind him. Toki smiled, rushing to Ulfrik and whispering excitedly.

"We've found something! Come and see."

Ulfrik's pulse quickened and he could not help smiling as well. "Is it another way in?"

"Yes, but it's easier to explain if I show you. There's no one about, but men watch from the walls. Be careful."

They followed Toki and Mord, Ulfrik and his scouting party clinging to whatever cover was at hand. The slope dropped precipitously and slowed their advance. One man fell in the mud to the hisses of his companions, and Ulfrik glanced at the fortress as if it might rise from its foundations and attack them. Yet it remained quaint and at rest, though as he neared he spotted pennants on the towers and black dots of men on the ramparts. He had to remain undetected for fear of either being killed outright or taken as a captive and tortured for information.

Toki led them to a large stream, then turned toward the fortress until they came to the edge of the sparse woods. Clinging behind trees, he motioned Ulfrik to him. "Follow the stream down, it flows into their fortress. Can you see the grate where it enters the wall?"

Ulfrik squinted, his vision blurry at the distance, but could see where the stream disappeared beneath the walls. "Their water source!"

"Exactly, the weakest part of their walls. The only trouble is leading a force to attack from back here. I don't know how we'd get around without facing their arrows and worse."

"And that's why we're all fortunate you're not leading this army." Ulfrik rapped Toki's head with his knuckles. "We don't attack. This stream is not so wide nor so deep that it can't be blocked. Gods know the Franks can't get to the Seine. Cut off the water, and their gates will open in a few days."

Ulfrik flushed with the excitement of finding the defenders' weakness. He had never seen anything so large and so seemingly permanent as a stone fort, and the prospect of attacking it was madness to him. Now those high stone walls meant nothing.

"By Odin's eye, you're right!" Toki rubbed his head where Ulfrik hit him. He pointed at Einar. "Get some men to begin filling this stream ..."

"No one do anything," Ulfrik countered. "First, we can't do it ourselves. Second, unless it's done quickly the defenders will sally out to stop us. So we return to Hrolf, explain what we found, then lead a strong group back to do the job. We don't need all of our men to guard the blockage we'll create, just enough to deter the defenders. We can get ten ships' worth of men back here without trouble."

Satisfied with the plan, Ulfrik scouted the terrain farther up the stream. He found a large tree-fall that would make a good start to blocking the stream. As long as they worked far back in the woods, the defenders would not know the threat until too late. Rubbing his cold hands together both for warmth and in anticipation, he ordered his men to return to camp.

～

"FOR A WET STONE FORTRESS, it burns fiercely." Ulfrik spoke to no one in particular, though crowds of cheering Danes crowded around him on the marshy shore of the Seine. Yellow fire splashed toward the winter gray skies, and the sounds of collapsing roofs and crumbling buildings rumbled like distant thunder. The scent of burning wood filled the air.

"I still can't believe how easy this was." Toki pressed through the cheering group, slapping Ulfrik's back as he joined him. "We carried away everything in three days. Maybe Paris will only take five, and the other cities seven. We could be home before Yule!"

"If the Franks build all their fortresses like this, you may be right." Ulfrik searched the sparsely wooded hills behind the black clouds of smoke. The last of the line of retreating defenders, leading their horses through the trees, paused to watch the roof of the highest tower catch flame, then resumed their trek. He wondered if they traveled to warn Paris, or if they would return to their farms until their lords summoned them again.

As Ulfrik had expected, the blocked stream did its work. Cut off from the Seine and from its alternate water supply, the defenders of the fortress called Pontoise pleaded for terms. They had held out for three days, and each day Hrolf struggled to prevent Sigfrid from attacking. "Waiting is for women," Sigfrid had proclaimed one night when Ulfrik sat with Hrolf and the other leaders. However, Sigfrid stayed his sword and won victory. The defenders negotiated safe passage out of the fortress as long as they took nothing but their horses and weapons. Sigfrid demanded hostages, taking the commander's children as assurance the Franks would not turn on them. It was a practical arrangement, but one that made Ulfrik wince when thinking of his own sons. He might return home and discover Gunnar and Hakon prisoners of one of his enemies, Skard or Thorod.

"Find any spoils in the castle?" Toki's question broke into his thoughts. "Not much left once we got in there, which isn't fair since we came up with the plan. Still, look at this knife. Brand new and forgotten under a bed."

Toki drew a length of the long knife from its tooled leather scabbard. The blade gleamed in the dull sun. Frankish weapons were prized throughout the world for their craftsmanship.

"Actually, I stayed behind with Humbert and Snorri. This isn't what we're here for. It's wasting time." The words came out angrier than intended, and Toki tucked his prize into his belt and moved off. He called behind him. "It's a fine blade. Don't gamble it away."

A shift in wind rolled black smoke toward the Danes and encouraged many to return to their ships. Ulfrik's crew had scattered into the throng seeking spoils in the abandoned fortress. He spied Einar returning with a sack over his shoulder. Others would soon return, and he wanted to be ready to sail. He joined Snorri and Humbert at the shore, both standing by his beached ships.

"Still think we can't take Paris?" Ulfrik teased Humbert, who scowled and looked away. Now that they had arrived in Frankia, Ulfrik ensured Humbert had a guard at all times. Snorri took that duty this day, leaning against the hull of *Raven's Talon*.

"Looks like someone wants you, lad." Snorri did not move, but nodded past Ulfrik.

He turned and Hrolf and Gunther were approaching, both men at least a head taller than anyone surrounding them.

"This is a great day," Hrolf said as he arrived. "A castle sacked and an enemy defeated. The commander surrendered his treasury too! The gods love us!"

"You saved us a lot of trouble," Gunther added, swatting Ulfrik's back with a chuckle. "A little patience worked better than stone-throwers, and probably faster."

"No man can live without water. Victory was guaranteed." Ulfrik drew a deep, satisfied breath. "Now we apply the same leverage to Paris, and taste a sweeter victory."

Both men laughed, and Hrolf worked a silver armband off his bicep. "This is for your service. Take it with my gratitude."

The silver glinted in the light, nicks and scratches reflecting the diffuse light. Ulfrik straightened himself, a smile alighting on his face. "It was not much service, Jarl Hrolf."

"Mord told me how fast you acted on what you found," Gunther said. "You knew what to do, how to do it, and another man might have made a mess of the chance. Because of you, we acted before the Franks could protect their weak spot."

"You've shown you can fight with your head as well as your heart," Hrolf added, proffering the armband. "I need men like that in my command, men who can see far and not just hack off a head in one blow. Wear this arm ring with pride."

Ulfrik took it with both hands, then clasped it around his arm, squeezing it to a snug fit. People nearby clapped or offered congratulations, and he nodded to them. Both Gunther and Hrolf patted his back in congratulations, and Ulfrik's smile widened. How long had it been since anyone had recognized him like this? Pride and accomplishment were sensations he had nearly forgotten, so seldom had he occasion to experience them.

The gathered crowd parted as two brawny men in mail coats shoved people aside with their shields. Striding between them was Sigfrid, his bleached hair unmoving in the breeze and his face streaked with soot. His eyes bored into Ulfrik's as he approached. The group joined Hrolf, and onlookers backed away a respectable distance.

Sigfrid searched Ulfrik up and down, as if waiting for a sign of obeisance. Ulfrik snorted then swallowed. *Until you break my knees I won't kneel, so stop staring, you fool,* he thought, and a smile trembled at his lips.

"I have you to thank for today's victory," Sigfrid said, more questioning than stating.

"I suggested cutting the water supply, lord." Ulfrik at last offered a slight nod, careful not to overtly insult the greatest jarl in their army.

Grunting and nodding back, Sigfrid glanced at Ulfrik's new armband. "What's your name again?"

Ulfrik answered, and Sigfrid, mouth closed and pulled down, twisted off a ring from his left hand.

"Good work." He tossed the ring, and it plunked into Ulfrik's hands. It was a plain band of gold, flattened at the bottom from years or wear. The metal was warm and smooth.

"I am honored, Lord Sigfrid." Now he bowed and again onlookers clapped. Then he displayed his prize to the crowd as if it were a more generous reward than it was.

"I don't like waiting," Sigfrid said. Ulfrik simply bowed a second time, restraining the urge to reply. If he had chanced words, they would have been mocking. With a curt nod to Hrolf, Sigfrid and his two bodyguards twisted away and marched back into the crowds.

Ulfrik squeezed the ring in his hand, and watched him shove against the flow of men heading for their ships.

"Enough royal visitors for one day, eh?" Hrolf tapped Ulfrik's hand, and he held it open to show Sigfrid's ring. Hrolf rolled it between two fingers. "Better than what he awards most people, believe it or not." He replaced the ring in Ulfrik's palm. "But Paris is close, and greater riches await us. If the Franks are foolish enough to fight, I want you close in my battle line. Your advice would be welcomed."

Hrolf winked then left to find his own ship. Gunther followed, but paused to squeeze Ulfrik's shoulder. "You already have a name with the great jarls. Didn't I say you would do well here?"

"That you did, One-Eye."

Ulfrik stepped back to *Raven's Talon*, more of his crew gathering before it and reviewing each other's loot. Einar and Ander went through each other's bags, while Thrand and Kolbyr taunted Humbert with a wooden crucifix held over his head. Others were tossing their bags onto the deck.

"How does fame sit with you now?" Snorri asked as he joined him. Ulfrik glanced back at the castle in time to see the roof of the highest tower collapse with a spray of sparks.

"It has come too early, considering all we need to do."

Snorri gave him a knowing look. "Do you really still believe the slave? His jabbering has stopped since we arrived here, like he's afraid of something. Being found a liar, maybe."

Ulfrik wiped his face with his hand, dirt and soot rubbing off. He observed Humbert holding himself aloof from Thrand's crude teasing. "He is probably waiting for his chance to run, or maybe he's surprised at making it this far."

"I don't think you're going to find what he promised."

Thrand began hitting Humbert's head with the cross, and he remained unflinching. Ulfrik waited for him to buckle, but he merely gathered beneath his mud-spattered red cloak. After a while, he called off Thrand. "That's enough. Get him aboard and keep him in one piece. You heard me!"

Sulking like a child, Thrand stopped and flung the cross on the ground, stamping it into the mud. Ulfrik waited in silence until all of his ships were prepared to shove back into the Seine. Just as Snorri began to leave, he grabbed his friend's arm. "Ander read the rune sticks, and saw the truth in Humbert's tale. The more I watch Humbert, the more I believe he spoke honestly. I think he fears revealing the treasure to us."

"You've grown into your father's stubbornness."

"That'd be a compliment."

"Not always." Snorri continued on his way, and Ulfrik fell in behind. Paris lay ahead, and within its walls lay riches and destiny.

11

Flames roared and roof timbers collapsed in a pile before Runa. The fresh air tore the blaze upward in an explosion of bright heat. Tears flooded her eyes and smoke choked her. Barely discernible in the fire and swirling ash were the murdered bodies of women, old men, and children. Their blood flowed like an orange and black stream.

Gunnar clung behind and Hakon wailed at her feet as she ranged her short sword before all of them. Picking effortlessly through the blaze came the dark shape of a gigantic man. She could only see the brightness of his iron blade. He hulked over her, his shoulders covered in a wolf pelt that smoldered with embers from the collapsing hall.

Striking with a low feint, Runa reversed her thrust up to the giant's belly. His sword swept aside the strike while his huge hand punched her in the head. She sprawled out and Gunnar screamed. The giant man loomed over her, his blade reflecting the fire consuming the hall. The point of it hovered at the base of her throat, and she shrieked as he rammed down.

She awoke to her own screaming, then sprang upright in bed. The bear-hide covers slipped from her, revealing Hakon curled beside her.

He frowned and shimmied to her side. Darkness filled the room, but she could hear Gunnar's rhythmic breathing emanating from his bed. No signs of a fire or an attacker. She slumped forward, dropping her face into her hands. *How many more of these dreams will the gods send me?* she wondered. Ever since Ulfrik sailed a month ago, terrifying dreams stalked her nights. They followed the same themes every time: invaders trapping her, killing her family. In sleep, Runa's mind was free to envision all the fears she suppressed during the day.

Thunder exploded close to the hall, rattling the walls and shaking the bed. Only now did she hear the blasting wind and rain. Water dripped from the roof somewhere in the blackness of the room. *If Ulfrik were here, he'd fix it, but now I will have to beg someone or do it myself.* She hit the bed in frustration, in time with another boom of thunder followed quickly by a flash of white from the lone window set high on the opposite wall. The lamb skin cover sucked against the hole, threatening to fly outside into the storm.

Hakon mumbled in his sleep, and she lay down beside him again. The fierce storm lashed the hall, but she knew it would be done by morning. If the hall blew down with her inside, then it was Fate. She did not worry for things beyond her control. She could not, for her sake and for her children's.

RUNA AWAKENED to the cheerless morning, a slow drip of water from the roof leak pattering on the floor. Gunnar had left an empty in his bed, and she swept her hands across the feather stuffed mattress to Hakon. He smiled a gurgled laughter at her touch. Raising herself to the edge of the bed, she pulled the bearskin about her and slumped on her knees. Beyond the door, the faint clack of wooden plates and murmur of voices informed her that she had overslept. The savory notes of a stew floated into her room.

As she nursed Hakon, she listened to the vague conversations from the hall. She yearned to hear the deep tones of Ulfrik's voice, but only heard women chattering and children laughing. Something toppled and a female voice shouted in irritation. Finished, she let Hakon to the floor and went to the sword Ulfrik had left for her.

It was his short blade; a sax is what he called it. The blade was sharp and well made, but it lacked a cross-guard. As promised, the sax was like a feather in her hand after practicing with a long sword. She hung it on Ulfrik's armor rack, and each morning fit the belt around her waist so the blade hung at her lap. A weapon was useless leaned against a bed or racked on a wall. Wearing it drew looks and snide remarks, but she cared little what others thought. They would hide behind her when trouble arrived, she did not doubt. Feeling its weight slapping her thighs as she walked comforted her.

Hakon stumbled a few steps then fell, preferring to crawl. Runa scooped him up after she finished dressing and combing her hair.

Morning light streamed into the hall as women in red and white linen hair covers flitted about their duties. The hall doors hung open and bright sunlight sparkled in the water dripping from the roof. She entered the hall in time to see Gunnar dash out of the hall with several other children following. With the hirdmen gone, the hall remained empty most of the time, though families whose men had left with Ulfrik gathered to share meals in the hall. Several young men sat at the trestle tables while their mothers and sisters gossiped and minded the cooking pot.

Runa smiled at the women, who paused and inclined their heads as she wandered into the hall. She spoke each of their names in greeting as she passed. Elin, Ander's wife, was the only one she considered an honest friend. After Gerdie's death, precious few friends remained with her. The other women distanced themselves, afraid of the jarl's wife and her odd behavior.

"Quite a storm last night," Elin remarked as she dropped dried heather branches into the hearth while a young girl worked a billows to build heat.

"Is there any damage?" She leaned over the cooking pot, letting the pungent smell of simmering whale meat fill her nose. She passed Hakon to Thora, a young woman who cared for Hakon while Runa tended chores and duties.

"None I know of, but I haven't heard from the outlying farms. I'm sure all is well."

"I'll take a look around anyway." Runa excused herself and stepped out to the wet grass as a girl hauling water passed her.

Scanning the rooftops, she saw no damage to her untrained eyes. The roofs would have to be gone for her to notice. Her breath fogged on the cold morning air, and she folded her arms tight. Gunnar was running with a group of boys, all clashing together with wooden swords or leather-tipped poles for spears. Their laugher was thin on the crisp morning air.

Her wandering led her across the fields and parallel to the verdant mountains in the distance. The hem of her dress became soaked and flocked with blades of grass as she approached the cliffs where she and Ulfrik often visited. Nothing led her to this place, but she smiled without humor as she found herself there. Gulls soared in the distance, as if they too had come out to survey the results of the night's storm. One seemed to screech at her.

Standing a safe distance back from the edge, she peered into the distance. Fog rolled on the waters, obscuring the land across the fjord. Facing north, she wondered how long before square red sails emerged from that fog. Ships full of enemies confident of victory, knowing only one woman with a sax stood against them. Certainly everyone would fight, but anyone with a talent for it had long sailed south. For now, as winter clenched its grip around the islands, men would remain with their farms. Yet winter would not last, and the inevitable raids would renew.

"Ulfrik, you had better return in time or you will have nothing to return to."

Speaking the words relieved the burden of carrying them in her heart. Worse than feeling defenseless was having no one to talk to. Elin was not close enough; she would not trouble Gunnar with her fears; Ingrid and Halla were witches. With the men gone, she found no one to share her mind. It surprised her to realize she related better to men than her fellow women. None of them had experienced the hardships she had, but the men understood better.

Lingering at the cliffs, she decided, would foul her mood, and a twinge of guilt followed her for not assisting with the morning meal. She had taken to sleeping later since Ulfrik had left. Being the nominal ruler in his absence, it set a bad example. So she picked up a stone and decided to toss it into the sea before leaving. The distance of the fall fascinated her, but Ulfrik would never let her get close enough to drop a rock. She giggled at the childishness of it.

Carefully sliding to the edge, slimy rock in her hand, she peered over. The sheer drop made her feel like it was dragging her down. Catching herself, she stepped back, heart thudding. Now she understood why Ulfrik forbid her from looking over the cliff, but was still determined to watch her rock plunge into the water below. Revising the plan, she got on hands and knees, the cold dampness seeping through her clothes, and crawled to the edge. Being grounded on all fours cured the vertigo, and she was able to look straight down.

Releasing the rock, she watched it fall but was disappointed that it was too small to see it hit the water. The rock disappeared into the background of waves breaking at the base of the cliffs.

"Well, now you've fulfilled your dreams, Runa. Congratulations." She laughed at the whole exercise, and began to crawl back from the edge.

Then she saw the man.

He was sprawled on a flat rock, debris floating on the water around him. While the sea battered sections of the cliff faces, clumps of large rocks formed natural wave-breaks, and the man rested within one now. Runa called down to him, but realized her voice would be lost in the roar of the sea. He lay face down to the rock, a tattered white shirt brilliant even in the shadows of the cliff. She suspected he might be dead, then he turned his head to another side.

Backing away from the edge, Runa knelt in the grass and considered what to do. He could be an enemy whose ship was wrecked in the storm. From the distance she could not determine the man's age, but he appeared young. That would rule him out as belonging in these waters.

In any case, she ran back to the hall, holding the sax steady as she did, drawing comfort from the feel of the leather wrap in her palm. Finding Gunnar outside, she called him over. "Gather the strongest boys, and meet me in the hall."

Gunnar and his friends lowered their toy swords to the grass. "Enemies?"

"Hurry," was all she said as she continued to the hall. Stopping at the entrance, she leaned inside. "I found a man washed up on the rocks by the northern cliffs. I'm taking the boys to help me rescue him." She scanned the blank faces, all stopped in the midst of whatever they had been doing, and found the man she sought. "Ornolf, I need your boat. Come with me."

Ornolf, a man with shaky hands and white beard, stood with the care of the elderly, but he smiled. "Glad to finally have something to do."

By this time Gunnar had arrived with three other boys. Together with Ornolf they ran for the shore where Ornolf's son left behind a small fishing boat. The rest of the hall emptied out behind them, women fluttering with speculation and worry. At the boat, Runa ensured they had rope, and tied it around all of them in case any one fell overboard.

Ornolf steered his ship while Runa and the boys worked the short oars. Gunnar sat beside his mother, his young arms straining at the work and a determined scowl on his face. The gods favored them with calm waters, and Runa was further relieved to see no other ship in the foggy distance. They held a tense silence as they navigated to where she had spotted the man. Gunnar was the first to see him. "On the rocks over there! A man with a white shirt!"

"Careful now," warned Ornolf. "Getting to him is another thing than seeing him. The tide wants to push us into the cliff."

Warned, the boys refocused on their rowing. Runa moved to the prows of the small boat. Only two people could sit on a bench, shoulder to shoulder if they were men, Fortunately, her crew were slighter and the vessel could accommodate another passenger.

Ornolf, despite his decrepit appearance, nosed the boat closer to the rocks with confidence and skill. He snapped at the boys to cease rowing and let the natural tide take over. As they closed, she first saw the man's bare feet, then his calf which had been cut. Entering the calmer waters, Runa gathered up the slack in her rope and leaned forward to call to the man. She saw a halo of disheveled yellow hair as the man barely raised his head, and she called him again.

Bumping into planks of wood and sea weed, Ornolf guided the boat to the side of the rock. "Told my boy I could still do this," he said, and clapped his hands. "They should've taken me too."

"I'm glad you stayed," Runa said, focusing on the man. She carefully stood, and Gunnar steadied her. "I need you boys to help me get him aboard. Ornolf, can you keep the boat against this rock?"

"Not without a tie-off or anchor. Be swift, Lady Runa."

"You there, can you hear me?" The man on the rock raised his head again, rolling to face Runa. He nodded. "You must help us get you on board. Can you move?"

The man seemed unsure, but both his legs moved in reply. The boat bounced against the rock, and while the water was still, she put her foot on the rock. Her skirt restricted her and she had to immediately return to the boat. "You boys will fetch him. Gunnar, stay with me to steady the boat."

"No, I will lead my friends," and he jumped onto the rock with his two friends following. She bit her lip, hearing Ulfrik's words in her son's voice.

The rope had enough slack, but Runa tugged forward as they worked. They propped the man on his elbows and he shook his head. Gunnar hooked the man's arm over his shoulder while another boy did the same. The third boy steadied the boat as the man got to his knees to crawl forward.

"Here's the difficult part," noted Ornolf. "Don't let them fall or we're all going to the bottom."

"I'm aware of that," she snapped.

The man shuffled on his bloodied knees. He was young and strong, though bruised and cut in a hundred different places. He wore tatters of what appeared to be fine clothes, and a gold torc clung to his neck still. She scanned him for weapons, and found none. At the side of the boat, Gunnar ducked from beneath the man's arm and helped him to the boat. Rather than assist, Runa found herself drawing the sax and pointing it at the man.

"A Valkyrie? I am dead, then?" The man managed to smile, revealing teeth reddened with blood.

"I am here to help, but I don't know you. I have many enemies."

His head lolled and he muttered words Runa could not understand over the growling of the waves against the cliffs. The boys managed to roll him into the boat, and it rocked and pushed back. Ornolf steered it close to the rocks and all the boys rejoined. Gunnar gave her a sheepish smile. She pursed her lips, but patted his shoulder. His smile widened and his cheeks reddened.

They began to row back, the man lying uncomfortably between benches.

"Thank you for your kindness and bravery," he said. His bottom lip was split and his eye blacked, but confidence filled his exhausted voice. "You will not regret this, I promise."

Runa nodded, squeezing the hilt of her short sword. Glancing again at the milky horizon, she saw nothing but the black dots of sea birds weaving over the ocean. The gods made no sign for her, good or ill, but her other hand sought the hammer of Thor beneath her robe. Fate had woven a new thread into her life, and winter was at hand.

12

November 25, 885 CE

Ulfrik watched Paris rise from the middle of the Seine River. He and his men gathered in the prow and strained for their first glimpses of the city between the hundreds of other striped sails obstructing the view. Silence spread from ship to ship in the great Danish fleet, and as Paris revealed itself to the crew, their excited voices stilled. The fire in Ulfrik's blood cooled. The fort called Pontoise now seemed like a fisherman's shack.

As winds pushed the ship ever closer, the size of Paris grew. Its walls consumed nearly the entire island and were made of gray rock stained brown with age. The walls stood beyond a height rocks should be lifted. Towers rose above the walls, fat and round, and pennants fluttered from them. Worse than the walled city were the two bridges that barred passage deeper into Frankia. To Ulfrik's eyes, they were low, dense lines of black spreading across the river like the two arms of a giant. Each bridge was anchored to a mighty tower of stone, both square but with protruded round corners.

"Now you see Paris," Humbert said, a note of triumph in his voice. "And you wonder how to get through those walls."

Ulfrik frowned, then stepped out of the prow to face his slave. He held his head back, one hand pulling his beloved red cloak tight against the chill morning air. Despite Humbert's defiance, he had to agree that Paris was formidable, though he dared not voice it before his crew.

"If men built it, then men can tear it down."

"Not if God protects it." Humbert's free hand made a strange sign, touching his head, chest, and both shoulders. He had seen Toki's wife, Halla, make the same signs in her prayers to the dead god. Several of the crew eyed Humbert suspiciously, though Ulfrik shook his head and returned to the tiller. Toki waved and shouted across the waters.

"I hope the Franks pay the ransom."

Ulfrik waved agreement, and the two ships continued forward with the main fleet. Ulfrik had managed a position close to Hrolf's and Gunther's ships, which were behind the front of the formation. Sigfrid led the way to Paris, and though nominally all ships were under his command, his personal count was still higher than any single jarl. Additionally, his ships towed massive war engines and siege supplies stored on crewless vessels. During the journey south, Ulfrik had seen them disassembled, tied down, and covered against the weather, and wondered how they would be used. Gunther One-Eye told him Sigfrid had experienced men to work them, and in one day the machines would turn any city into rubble. He trusted Gunther's assessment, and spit on the deck to dismiss his worries.

Following Sigfrid's lead, the massive fleet pulled onto the shore northwest of Paris. While plans had been shared, not everyone remembered or followed them. Some ships continued forward while others dropped anchor, and others collided amid shouts and the cracking of broken oars. Being close to Hrolf guaranteed he understood the plan. Sigfrid would allow Paris to buy their lives at a dear price before he attacked.

"By Odin's one eye, can you smell that?" Snorri asked as he assisted with taking in the sail. "Did all of Paris shit their trousers at once?"

"It's the smell of big cities," said a flat-nosed man called Thorkel. "London is the same. I visited there with my uncle as a boy. They smell worse inside."

Thrand glared with his good eye at Humbert, who still leaned over the railings and watched Paris like it was his lover. "So is shit what you've got waiting for you, slave? Is that your treasure?"

Humbert ignored Thrand, but Ulfrik hissed through his teeth. He fell silent and returned to his task. Thrand's carelessness with their secret began to grate on Ulfrik. Had he not been a better man before drinking consumed his wits, Ulfrik would have dismissed him. Yet Thrand had once risked his life to save his wife and son, and he could not put aside that debt. Thrand, for all his careless bluster, deserved respect.

Ulfrik and his crew disembarked, taking their shields off the racks but leaving their mail aboard. The bank of the Seine was muddy and soft, and the forest grew nearly to the river's edge. Sigfrid had found a cleared section for enough of the fleet to gather. Masses of excited men clustered and pointed at Paris, many hurled curses and insults at the fat block of stone plunked into the heart of the river. Ulfrik arranged his men in loose groups and waited for orders. Soon, Gunther One-Eye shoved through the crowd.

"Hrolf wants you at the parley," Gunther proclaimed without preamble. He stood as if he had just awarded Ulfrik the kingdom of Frankia. "Meet at Sigfrid's ship."

"And why me and not one of his other boot-lickers?"

"He needs men thinking men. That'd be you and me."

"I'll bring my slave to translate." He pointed at Humbert, who suddenly became wide-eyed and pale.

"No." Gunther pushed Ulfrik's arm to his side. "Just you. Besides, we've got Franks who speak Norse on our side. Now get into your war gear and be fast."

Gunther slipped away into the crowd, and Ulfrik gave bemused looks to his crew. Toki congratulated him.

"It's an honor to go. You bring glory to all of us."

Nodding, he clapped Toki's back and boarded his ship to wear his mail hauberk. He ensured his silver armbands showed beneath the short mail sleeves. The lack of silver and gold adornments fed his self-consciousness. The entire time he wore his mail and traveled to Sigfrid's ship, he fretted over his status. No matter how close he stood to Hrolf, he would look like a farmer playing at a lord.

Before he had left, Snorri had surmised his thoughts and grabbed him close to growl confidence into him. "You're every bit their equal. What you wear on your arm is not as important as what you carry in your heart."

The words buoyed him, but now standing in the ring of men attending the parley, his confidence fell out. Sigfrid was his usual self, a glittering mound of iron and gold. He took three bodyguards who wore mail and helmets scoured to unusual brightness. One shouldered an ax engraved with coiling dragons. The wealth of his three men glistened like scales of a fish. Only Hrolf, Gunther, and himself wore more practical gear.

Sigfrid snorted and spit, then frowned at all of them. "If you've got a message for the Franks, let's hear it now. When we get up there, I do the talking."

"You'll do well to remember we're all equals here," Hrolf chided, though Ulfrik knew he bridled the power of his voice.

"And you'll remember I invited you to the feast, and that I dumped my fortune into the machines that'll tear up their walls. So I do the talking. Clear?"

Muscles twitched about Hrolf's jaw, though he remained silent.

They boarded Sigfrid's high-sided ship and a crew of thirty men rowed them up the current to where the mighty tower brooded in front of the bridge. Each jarl gathered his own men, Hrolf herding them to the prow where no one else stood. "Sigfrid places himself over us," he said to Ulfrik and Gunther. "He is like clear ice on a pond. I can see to the bottom of what he desires. But know this, I bend a knee to no one and you two only bend a knee to me. We decide whether to listen to Sigfrid. Remember that."

As the distance closed, Ulfrik observed the bridge, which was constructed of stone. Sitting low to the water, no ship could pass beneath. The sides of the bridge provided cover for defenders and prevented scaling. Ulfrik admired the clever construction and anticipated crossing it in victory. Parisians already lined it, the tops of their conical helmets glinting. Many of the crew began to joke about children wearing their father's armor, but Ulfrik was more interested in the walls of Paris itself. From this distance, he could see no way inside. Humbert, if he had been honest, promised a secret entrance. While he did not expect to see it at a glance, he could not imagine where it existed. Every approach to the walls was observed from multiple angles. He wiped his face and shoved the worry aside for another day.

Sigfrid pulled ashore a safe distance from the tower, then gathered them on the banks. His crew remained with the ship, but one man joined the group. He was a head shorter than all of them, dressed in plain clothes of green and gray but bearing a shield with Sigfrid's colors of black and yellow. He looked at no one, and went directly to Sigfrid's side. Curiously, he unfurled a white flag and held it aloft.

"What is that standard?" Ulfrik whispered to Gunther.

"Not a standard. It shows the Franks we come in peace."

Ulfrik swallowed his laughter. "The bright white blinds them to the thousands of berserks waiting behind us?"

Gunther and Ulfrik followed behind Hrolf, and all of them watched as the gates of the tower popped open and a party of armed men emerged.

"They're like children," remarked one of the men, and Sigfrid laughed.

"Makes it easier to crack open their heads," he replied. "Don't have to swing too high."

Nervous laughter filled the moments it took for the Frankish party to cross the grass. Ulfrik's eyes flicked between the parley group and the Franks of the tower and bridge, expecting treachery from men who he did not expect to understand honor. The foul odor of the city hung in his nostrils, and that repulsiveness transferred to the Franks who arrived before them.

Up close, Ulfrik found they were not as short as children, but their prideful and disdainful faces were immediate aversions. Two men went before, dressed in mail and wearing fine linen surcoats of blue and white. One had a round head with thin brown hair that clung to it as if soaked. Dark circles ringed his hooded eyes, and a barely contained snarl trembled on this thin lips. The other man was older, with a long and narrow head and curly gray beard. His motions were crisp and lively, and despite his obvious years, he held a posture like a man half his age. Ulfrik guessed him a fighting man. A heavy wooden crucifix hung about his neck. Behind these two were eight men-at-arms in helmets and mail, gripping spears. Ulfrik noted their knuckles were white and their eyes wide behind their noseguards. He held the gaze of one man until the Frank's eyes darted aside.

Both parties sized up each other, sounds of the river current rushing by filling the awkward quiet. Ulfrik noted a crow passing overhead. Hrolf and Sigfrid noted it too, and like himself, Ulfrik guessed they surely took it for a sign of the gods' favor. Sigfrid watched the bird glide toward the city, another good sign, and he nearly laughed. This drew a frown from the Franks, who finally decided to speak.

Their language sounded like the twisted speech of an animal. Ulfrik thought of geese. The round-headed man spilled them like beer, and once finished looked to another man Ulfrik had not noticed. The man had been obscured from Ulfrik's sight, and he was no more than fifteen years old. His beard had not yet formed on his soft jaw. He spoke fluidly, with a Danish accent.

"My lord is the glorious Count Odo, defender of Paris. With him is the esteemed Joscelin, abbot of Saint Germain-des-Pres and bishop of Paris." Ulfrik heard the name of the priest as one long slur of weak sounds. "He knows of the great Sigfrid, but does not recognize his companions."

"Tell your goat-fucking lord that Sigfrid and Hrolf, stand before them."

"Courtesy, please." The abbot spoke Norse fluently enough to fool Sigfrid to searching his own men for the source of the admonition. When he realized Abbot Joscelin spoke, Sigfrid howled laughter. Ulfrik raised a brow, and thought of Humbert's pained rendition of the language. He also wondered if this priest was Humbert's enemy, and so studied him carefully.

After Sigfrid recovered and the boy translated, he continued. "Some of you are clever men. That is excellent, since I'm certain clever men must also be reasonable men. You see the ships filling your river. There are thirty thousand warriors at my back. Go ahead and tell them. I want to see their faces."

The boy rushed his translation, emphasizing parts of his babble. Ulfrik admired the young boy's pliant mind, for he doubted his own ability to learn foreign tongues. Odo and Joscelin both nodded, but betrayed nothing. Ulfrik instead studied the guards, whose expression told more. Fear and terror passed across their faces. They attempted to mask them, but widened eyes, hard swallows, and tight lips betrayed them. Hearing of their enemies, the guards took furtive glances to the distance where ships bobbed at anchor. Ulfrik sneered and turned his chin up at them, letting them know he feared nothing.

"Count Odo wishes to understand what Lord Sigfrid desires."

"Is he getting this right?" Sigfrid turned to his own interpreter, who nodded. Assured, Sigfrid raised his voice and spoke at a level of courtesy Ulfrik could never imagine possible from such a brute. He bowed his head low, and spoke directly to Abbot Joscelin.

"Have compassion on yourself and on your people. We beg you to listen to us, in order that you may escape death. Allow us freedom of the city. We will do no harm and we will assure that whatever belongs either to you or to Odo shall be strictly respected."

The boy translated into Odo's ear, while Abbot Joscelin required no assistance. Instead, he bowed his head, and used the same respectful language. "Merely freedom of the city? When the great Jarl Sigfrid last visited us, he demanded a large tribute."

"Of course," Sigfrid said, as if just recalling a trifling point. "The tribute still stands. Seven hundred pounds of silver will see to the safety of Paris. I give you my word, which is worth more than silver or gold."

Count Odo deepened his snarl as the boy fed him the translated words, though Joscelin stood composed. He smiled and inclined his head as he replied, placing a firm hand on the ever-angering Count Odo's arm.

"The Emperor Charles, who, after God, is king and ruler of nearly all the world, has entrusted Paris to us. He has put it in our care, not that the kingdom may be ruined by our misconduct, but that he may keep it and be assured of its peace. If you had been given the same duty of defending this city, and if you were to do that which you ask of us, what treatment do you suppose we would deserve?"

The clear notes of the abbot's warm and deep voice gripped Ulfrik's attention. Such a voice and manner of language was seldom heard beyond the skalds of the great jarls. The abbot's words had even stilled Sigfrid to a thoughtful silence. As if waking to his senses, he shook his head and glanced at Hrolf before answering.

"I'd deserve to have my head cut off and thrown to the dogs. Nevertheless, if you do not listen to my demands, by tomorrow my war machines will destroy your walls and my men will raze your city. Your wives and daughters will pleasure us, and your boys will be slaves to row our ships. All others will die. I promise there will be no end to this, for every day that a Dane breathes, your people will suffer."

The veneer of politeness shattered, Sigfrid's posture tightened and he drew himself taller. The Frankish guards began to lower their spears at the threat, but the abbot held up his hand. "Then you have your answer. God protects us and God will drive your ships back to the lands of ice and snow in sorrow and despair."

The groups stared at each other, Ulfrik searching the resolve of Abbot Joscelin. Humbert had not named his enemy, but Ulfrik held no doubt this fierce and intelligent man was the one. He turned with the confident finality of a king leaving a beggar to grovel for mercy and shoved through his guards. Odo lingered and cursed them in his language, which Sigfrid's Frankish traitor translated, "By tomorrow you will suck the devil's prick in hell."

As both parties pulled away, Sigfrid began to laugh and rubbed his hands together. "At last! It'll feel better taking the silver out of their hides anyway. Tomorrow, it's war!"

13

Thrand's temples pounded as he drained his skin of ale while idling on the deck of *Raven's Talon*. Ulfrik had disappeared beyond his sight, gone to glorify himself with the mighty jarls. *Raven's Talon* bobbed placidly in the shallows of the river bank. Surrounding her on the river and on the shore were enough ships to make it appear as if the Seine had disappeared beneath them, their masts like black spines on the back of a river-sized dragon. Thrand did not care if Paris would be a tough fight. He was not planning to remain for it. He did worry that Humbert and his treasures would slip through his hands, dooming him to a life of servitude and poverty under Ulfrik.

He decided to ensure that would not happen.

Most of the *Raven's Talon* crew had drained away. Humbert sat against the gunwales with his head down and tethered to the mast by a rope long enough to span the deck but no farther. He could untie or cut the rope, of course, but his guards would prevent it. By now, sitting idly on benches and consumed in their thoughts, only Snorri and Einar remained. Mord, Gunther's son, had left to find old friends.

Einar picked his nose, examined the results, then flicked it away.

Snorri appeared about to doze off. Both men pitied Thrand, and though pity offended him, he knew it could also be a useful tool. If he could get them off the ship, even for a short time, he could work on Humbert.

"So we are the last three men to listen to Toki's orders," he grumbled as he sauntered over to Einar's bench. "Even he didn't follow his own command, but left the ship."

Einar grumbled but otherwise stared ahead at nothing. Thrand sat on the bench beside him, glancing at Humbert who appeared as listless as everyone else.

With Snorri half asleep, Einar was the natural choice. He had sailed with Thrand and witnessed his brother's death. He barely had his beard then, but over the intervening years he had grown a head taller than everyone and developed incredible strength. Unlike most other strong men, he was not dim but in fact a quick thinker. However, Thrand knew how to work him.

"Toki's been strange, don't you think? The little half-jarl has been eager to find himself elsewhere," Thrand said. Einar raised a brow and Snorri opened an eye to glare at him. "You know what I think? He's fucking a slave girl or some whore."

"Any more shit falls out of that mouth and I'm going to slam it shut." Snorri did not move, and closed his eye as if his threat had settled matters.

"Then where's he going all the time? And what is he so happy about? I have a right to know. My brother didn't die so he could plow any cunt he wants. Toki defied the gods for his wife, and we paid the price to help him do it."

The words delivered the sting he had hoped. Both of the men knew they had a part in the shame Toki's actions brought them. He saw it in Einar's averted eyes, and Snorri's exaggerated indifference.

"You shouldn't speak of what you don't know," Einar said, too softly to mean it. Thrand felt the smile tremble on his lips. These fools were too easy.

"Then maybe I should go find out. I'll go right now and no doubt

I'll catch him with his naked ass in the air, somewhere in the woods."
He waved generally at the dark line of bare trees, then stood as if to
leave. As expected, Snorri barred him with his leg.

"Sit down and don't make trouble. Tomorrow we may all be dead
at the foot of those walls, so let him have his fun today."

"So even you think it's true. Well, for any other man I agree with
you, but not Toki. It's not just my brother's blood for Toki's lusts, but
my friend Bork. And it doesn't stop with him; what about all the
others dead in the war with Hardar? And still his cousins attack us.
Maybe Skard and Thorod are burning our homes now. All because
Toki wanted to fuck a jarl's daughter. Maybe he's found the wife of a
jarl now, and is ..."

Snorri's hair was gray, his cheeks hollowed, and skin hung lose
under his neck, but he pounced with the speed of a young man.
Thrand hurled back as Snorri's fist plowed into his gut, squeezing all
the air from his lungs. He stumbled over the bench and thudded to
the deck. Snorri followed, straddling him with his fist extended in
challenge.

"Warned you that I'd break your shit-spilling mouth if you kept at
it. Now shut up and keep your ale-fogged thoughts to yourself. Gods,
man! We could be going to war any moment, and men need confidence in their leaders. Don't bring doubt to battle, you oaf."

Were it not for being breathless, Thrand would have laughed at
the ease of manipulating the two men. Einar now stood beside his
stepfather, a frown tight over his face.

"All right," Thrand said, holding out his hands as if to defend
against another blow. "But just let me go see for myself. And you
should know these words are not just mine. The others have said
as much."

"And who fed them those words?" Snorri asked.

"This is the first I've spoke of it. Do you think all the others are
fools? Toki certainly does."

Snorri paused, then softened his stance. He stepped back, and
Einar extended his thick arm to help Thrand stand. He dusted

himself off, then waited for what he knew would come next. He was not disappointed.

"I'll check on him," Snorri said, rubbing is face. "If he's fooling around, I'll ask him to at least be more careful about it."

"I'll go too," Einar said. "Better chances to catch him if we split up."

"Then who will stay with Humbert?" Thrand tried not to overact his frustration. "I want to see this with my own eyes."

"And you don't trust mine? You'll only worsen matters if you catch him, and if you find out he's innocent you'll try to make trouble. So stay with Humbert. We won't be long." Snorri nodded to Einar that they should leave. Thrand made as if to protest, but Snorri rounded on him. "Just stay here and I'll tell you what we learn."

He watched as they leapt into the shallows and waded to the shore teeming with people. Once they slipped into the crowd, he turned to Humbert, who still slouched in the shadows of the gunwales. He wore a sardonic smile, and his dark eyes followed Thrand with keen interest. Sitting on the deck before Humbert, Thrand slipped his sax from its sheath. Humbert's eyes did not waver.

"Well, priest, it's just us two now." He let the point of his sax thunk into the deck, palming the hilt so sunlight flashed off the blade. "No one else around, and I think it's time you shared your secrets with me."

The ship rocked and a splash of water came from behind. Thrand turned to see Kolbyr hauling himself aboard the ship. His cheery countenance was at odds with Thrand's frown. He joined Thrand, dripping water across the deck. "I thought you might be talking to our friend, and didn't want to miss out."

"Or were you planning on finding Humbert alone?"

"Of course not!" Kolbyr's face widened in a smile. "We are partners."

Humbert watched the exchange and his smile widened. With a growl, Thrand flicked his blade to Humbert's throat. "No more laughing now. A shame to die in the shadow of your freedom."

Humbert's laughter jarred Thrand, and he reflexively lessened the pressure on his sax.

"If you kill me, you lose everything. You can't kill me yet."

"But I can hurt you!" Pushing again, the blade drew a bead of blood that made Humbert flinch but failed to eliminate his smirk. "Let's be clear. Kolbyr and I intend to get your treasure. Before this day is done, Ulfrik will return to tell us your friends in Paris all shit themselves when we arrived. We'll be inside your walls tomorrow. But Ulfrik is Hrolf's dog now, and One-Eye's son is spying on him. If you think he'll help you take revenge, forget it. He wants to keep your gold secret, and so he'll hold you close. You'll have to wait. Maybe for years."

He tapped Humbert's head with the flat of his blade, failing to draw more than an irritated shake of his head.

Kolbyr laughed and added his own threats. "And you'll have us around all the time. We won't miss a chance to remind you of your position. You'd love that, wouldn't you, little priest?"

Humbert's smug expression flattened and Thrand's chest grew warm at the sight. At last, he was kicking through this ignorant Frank's pride. Glancing over his shoulder to be sure no one was near, he pressed his point.

"But there is a way out. We can release you, right now even. Kolbyr and I will kill your enemy in exchange for the treasure. It's that simple, really. You watch, Hrolf and Sigfrid want to get past this dung heap and ransom the cities to the east. Hrolf will take Ulfrik, and he will take you. But if we cut you free, your life will be your own."

Thrand could not determine if Humbert considered the offer. His dark eyes clouded and his thin lips were tightly drawn. He seemed to struggle focusing on Thrand, which his lazy eye tended to inflict upon others. Yet he suspected the priest was deep in calculation. After long moments, the priest's dry lips parted.

"Humbert thinks you are wrong. Paris will fight. Count Odo and Bishop Joscelin would rather die than surrender."

Kolbyr snorted. "They'd be killing everyone in their city. I thought you Christians don't like innocents to die?"

"They will listen to God's will, and He will demand faith. Paris will not fall, not with His hands upon its walls." Humbert closed his eyes and spoke with a reverence that made Thrand want to ram his sax through Humbert's neck.

"You'd better hope your god puts his hands over your throat before I slice it open." Snapping the sax to Humbert's neck again, the priest tilted his head back to avoid being cut. "If you won't agree to work with us, we can always force you. We can skip your revenge, and get right to the treasure. I know plenty of ways to make you reveal it, trust me."

Humbert grew still, and Thrand now stood while keeping the sax at the slave's neck

Kolbyr stood as well, chuckling. "I say you give him a demonstration. Maybe hold his head under the river water for a while, just to see how he likes it."

"Yes, we don't have to leave marks for Ulfrik's eyes, do we." Thrand traced his sax down to where Humbert's red cloak was held with a button of deer antler. He hooked the tip beneath it, as if to pop it off. "I could choke you with this rag you love so much. Would you like that? If you cooperate, you can escape all of this."

Humbert scuttled away and pushed the blade aside.

The sound of the commotion reached Thrand and he stepped back. Turning around, the crowds on the shore were like angry bees and making as much noise. Thrusting his sax back into its sheath, he spared a snarl for Humbert before running to the prow. He called to the other crewmen boarding a neighboring ship.

"What is happening? Paris is surrendering?"

Men shook their heads and called back. "They want a fight."

Thrand and Kolbyr looked at each other in surprise. After a few moments of the news sinking in, Kolbyr broke their silence. "War complicates things. Ulfrik will try to move on this treasure during the fighting."

Nodding in agreement, Thrand stroked his beard. "It's not so bad yet. Many will die in battle, and not many know of the treasure. Sounds encouraging, doesn't it?"

Kolbyr's brow furrowed, then realization showed as a wicked smile. "I didn't expect that even from you. Still, sounds challenging."

"In the madness of battle, young Kolbyr, no one knows who kills what. We only need aid Fate a little; wherever one of Ulfrik's inner circle survives, we correct the mistake."

14

November 26, 885 CE

"There are only two hundred men to defend all of Paris, so take heart." Ulfrik stood on the northern banks of the Seine, his forty warriors arrayed into two blocks. Dressed in mail and helmets, bearing spears and shields, they arrayed for battle. Behind them, in the dull morning sun, a vast fleet of dark ships crawled past. The shouts and war cries of their crews filled the air, where dark birds circled in anticipation of the killing to come.

"Lord, Humbert claims his god protects them from our arrows and blades." One of his crew, an older man with a white scar over the bridge of his nose, raised the concern. He glanced nervously at his peers. "Is it possible?"

"Our people have been sacking the new god's churches for generations. The new god is a dead god, and his hands and feet are nailed to wood. Did you notice? The man promising his god will save the Franks is lashed to a mast." Ulfrik joined his men in laughter. Having drawn duty for land assault, Ulfrik had to leave his ships behind, and tied Humbert to the mast to prevent his escape. "Both god and slave are unable to move, and so the Franks are doomed."

Toki arrived with two other men, each of them carrying skins tight with ale. They began distributing the skins into the ranks of men. In his youth, Ulfrik let his fury carry him into battle, and scorned drink. Now, older and with more to lose, he needed the courage found in the skins. Men guzzled ale as Ulfrik paced before them. A hot tightness filled his stomach, and his eyes flitted to the dark gray tower looming to the east. Once the skins were in circulation, he reviewed the plan a final time.

"When the horns blow, each block picks up their ladders." He pointed to the two huge siege ladders stacked between him and the warriors. Gunther and his men delivered them in early morning, along with instructions. They were longer than both of his ships lined up, and wide enough for one man to climb at a time. Two rough-hewn timbers accompanied each ladder, to steady it.

"Don't draw your weapons, but hold your shields against arrows. If our fellows are doing their work, the Franks won't dare come to their battlements from all our own bow fire. We lay the ladders at the tower base like we practiced. Then it's up and in. Sigfrid is offering a reward for the first men up a ladder. Hrolf will match it, as will I. But you have to live to collect it, so nothing passes to your families. Until the city is breached, accept no surrender and take no prisoners."

He commanded the men to wheel toward the east, and prepare for the order. The army of Danes and Norwegians converged on the banks behind Ulfrik's position. Jutting from blocks of troops were banners of the northmen in every size and color, waving in the gentle breeze. Ulfrik gestured for Toki to raise Nye Grenner's standard. As he hoisted the pole overhead, the green banner unfurled with a snap. Ulfrik pumped his fist in the air and roared. The throaty cheers of his men joined his. All across the banks and spilling out into the water the ceremony repeated.

The great army was waking, roaring like a beast of war. The land shuddered with the furious shouts.

At the fore of the army stood Sigfrid's forces, and his white standard of a boar's head with bloody tusks flew over scores of warriors in glinting mail. Hrolf's forces were anchored to the river bank, and would support a direct assault. His red banner embroidered with a golden dragon bobbed as he drove his ranks of men to join Ulfrik's position. Gunther followed with his men on Hrolf's left flank.

Lumbering ahead through the crisp, clear morning air went Sigfrid's war machines and their crews. Settling into positions along the banks, the massive wooden arms cocked back as their crews worked heavy cranks. Ulfrik strained to see the workers, who had been busy throughout the night moving and arming the giants. He heard wood groan as boulders were loaded into the slings of the machines.

"A few good hits and the tower will fall." Mord, who Ulfrik had placed in his block, waved dismissively at the fat tower in the distance.

Snorri spit on the ground, then grunted. "They'll have to hit the tower to do that. Not sure these things will."

Ulfrik reserved his opinion, studying the pantomime of the siege engineers. Men from the distant south with olive skin and brown eyes commanded these machines, and if the rumors were true, demanded a jarl's take of the spoils for their knowledge. He held his breath in anticipation. The war machines, dark against the morning sun, dipped back and quivered.

Silence swept out over the horde of Danes. A thin and lonely voice shouted. Then the great arms released.

The explosive violence of the machines made Ulfrik twitch in surprise. The sound reminded him of the grating, rocky crash of a collapsing iceberg. The arms struck bars with deep thuds and the slings lobbed rocks over incredible distances.

The boulders aimed at the tower missed, falling short or sailing past. The defenders jeered, their voices faint and weak. The boulders aimed at the city fared better. Many plopped into the river with enormous splashes, but others sailed over the walls to careen into the building beyond. One boulder hit the wall and exploded in a cloud of dust and stone fragments.

"Ranging shots. It will be better this time," Hrolf called down the front of his line. Ulfrik realized Hrolf positioned himself only ten files down from his own. He had no time to relish the honor the proximity gave him, for the next volley of stones released.

Boulders hurtled and tumbled through the air, and one crashed into the tower. The hit exploded into a bloom of rock dust. Ulfrik found himself stepping forward to cheer. All of the Danish army joined him. Men on land and on the water banged their shields and screamed victory, as if the single rock had destroyed all of Paris. As the glittering dust poured to the ground, the point of impact showed. The tower wall had been cratered, but little more.

The machines fired in alternating ranks, so a steady flight of boulders streaked through the air. Ulfrik laughed at the ease with which the machines flung rocks that took four men to lift. It was like watching giants at play. The Danes did not cease in their cheering and shouting. Ulfrik and his men added to the din, delighting in the massive wave of noise they shot at the Franks.

The last machine slammed forward and ejected its boulder, which skimmed the stone bridge and bit off a section of its guarding walls. Then silence and stillness descended, like the passing of a furious storm. A horn blew three times from the lead ship on the river. Oars extended and dipped into the water, and the fleet was on the move.

"Ready yourselves," Ulfrik called to his men. "The ships will cover our approach with bow fire, so the order to attack is coming."

Ulfrik looked to Mord, whose eyes were wide with childlike amazement. Then he turned to Snorri, who simply nodded his grim determination. Others in his block included Thrand, Ander, and several other of his trusted crew. Toki led the other block, along with Einar. None of them had stormed a wall before. None of them knew what waited at the tower. Yet all of them trusted and protected each other. All of them were brothers in war, and their lives were bound together. Ulfrik swallowed hard, knowing many of them would die. He could only pray death would come swiftly for those so fated.

Sigfrid's banner waved, and the deep bass note of his horn sounded.

"Pick up your ladders and move!" Ulfrik shouted the command

and grabbed a rung of the ladder. Despite its size, it felt weightless as he lifted it along with the others. Rough wood bit his sweating palms. He looped his right arm into his shield and joined the march.

After the first dozen yards, Ulfrik began to jog to keep pace with the line converging on the tower. Then the jog increased to a run. Men shouted, and the tower drew ever closer, higher than anything he had ever seen. Solid as a mountain. Still as forest glade.

He bellowed, an animal shout from the pit of his gut. He released his fear and fury, spilling it to the tower, and his spirit rose. His men added their voices to his. Their feet thumped into the soft earth, shaking the ground with the thousands of others pounding for the tower.

The sound of a linen sheet tearing came from the right flank and a shadow passed over him. Arrows fired from the ships choking the river. More arrows than Ulfrik could conceive being shot at once. A black cloud of death arcing to the tower.

"We're almost there." His breath was labored, his heart pounded. The fat gray stones of the tower drew up before him. "Get your shields up. Don't wait."

Arrows clattered down the sides of the walls, missing their marks and piling at the foot of the tower. Sigfrid's line was already setting up their ladders while Knut led his force to sweep to the north face of the tower and still nothing from the defenders.

Another black wave of arrows screamed overhead, and Ulfrik pulled his shield up from reflex.

"They're going to surrender!" Mord screeched triumphantly. "They're afraid to fight!"

Distant but clear notes of a horn sounded.

"Shield wall!"

The Franks answered the call to battle, leaping to the battlements with bows ready. Their arrows sliced down into the rich field of enemy targets. Ulfrik spotted a column of men stutter and collapse as white-fletched arrows fell among them, then he ducked behind his shield.

Their run slowed to a jog. Arrows stitched the earth around

Ulfrik's feet, then a few thumped his shield. He further slowed his run, but those behind crashed into him.

"We don't want to be the first. Let others take the brunt of the defense."

"What? We should be first in glory!" Mord pulled at the ladder in protest, huddling in the darkness of the shield wall.

"I lead to win and to live. Do as I say." Ulfrik peeked out from his shield to see Toki had mimicked his pace. Whatever his faults, Ulfrik could always depend on Toki to be smart in battle.

"That was the brunt," Mord continued. "Let's not miss the fight."

The Franks answered for Ulfrik. Arrows clattered on their shields like hail. Their pace became as men in a blizzard. They pulled their shields tight, and the arrows streamed without end. Bodkins pierced the wood. One popped through a thumb's width from Ulfrik's face. The tip lodged in the cheek plate of his helmet.

The sound of arrows hissing and screaming back and forth overhead was unearthly, like a windstorm from the cold plains of Nifleheim. His mouth had become so dry he feared his tongue would split. Screams of dying and wounded men encircled them. He knew they were at the final approach to the tower by the number of corpses they had to dance over. Under the shield wall smelled like ale and urine. Someone retched on himself, and further fouled the air.

"We're here! Run the ladder up. Hurry!"

Ulfrik forgot every instruction on using the ladder. The moment the shield wall parted, he looked skyward to a wall that must reach the clouds. Hundreds of battles had not prepared him for this.

An arrow clipped his helmet with enough force to knock it over his face. Shoving it back, he roared again, and pulled the ladder forward. "Keep the angle shallow! Move!"

Ladders were already placed and men were clambering toward the defenders atop the tower. Some had placed their ladders too steep, and the defenders waited for men to get halfway up before shoving the ladders back with long poles. He watched one shove away, balance vertically as men screamed, then collapse back into the crowd. Howls of agony combined with the thud and crunch of the bodies slamming into the ground.

Holding his shield overhead, he guided the ladder with one hand. Two of his men came forward with support beams to brace it. Before he could order them, one spun away with an arrow shaft through his eye. He collapsed atop the beam just as the ladder came to rest.

"Get up as fast as you can!" Ulfrik grabbed Mord by his mail sleeve and all but threw him on the ladder. "The more men on it, the harder for them to push it back. Go!"

He scurried to retrieve the brace. He refused to look at his man's face as he twitched in the grass. Instead, he grabbed the man's hand and forced it from gripping the arrow shaft and onto his sword hilt. At least he would go to Valhalla. As the body slumped in death, Ulfrik struggled to roll it aside, but holding his arrow-studded shield overhead made the work twice as hard. Glancing to check Mord's progress, he was not far along and the ladder already tilted to the unbraced side.

Dumping his shield, he took both hands to roll the corpse aside. The sky darkened, and he looked up to find Snorri holding a shield over him.

"You'll get yourself killed, you old fool!"

"Hurry up," was all Snorri said, and huddled closer to Ulfrik while trying to cover both of them with his shield.

Ulfrik shook his head and dragged the dead man off the beam. Despite the weight of his mail coat, he flopped aside like a child's doll. Ulfrik's arms trembled with fighting rage, and anger at his own fear. He scooped up the heavy timber beam and dragged it to the ladder. Wedging it in place with Snorri's aid, the ladder straightened. Mord continued his climb, awkwardly trying to hold his shield before the pelting arrows. Men lined behind him, moving at a steady crawl.

Retrieving his own shield, he surveyed the field. Toki was leading his ladder, and nearly traversed half the distance to the top. To his left, Hrolf strode from ladder to ladder, shouting encouragement and threats. His shield bristled with arrows, but his sword was drawn and pointing to the top. Ulfrik's gaze followed it up.

Arrows slid down the walls; missed shots from the ranks of Danish archers. Dust and debris washed down the sides, combining with the broken arrows to form a waterfall of shattered junk. Helmets plummeted, lost weapons clanged against the stone as they fell. Worst of all, men tumbled from the walls shrieking and wailing through the long fall.

His shield seemed to rise on its own, then he realized Snorri had pushed it up for him.

"Stop gawking and let's move!"

Turning to follow Snorri, he heard screaming drawing closer. Looking up, a Dane clutching a Frank plunged out of the sky. He had seen death and gore, good men hacked to bits and charred bones buried under rubble. Nothing compared to the two men slamming into the earth. They exploded into a pink mist, bones piercing through flattened bodies. The sound was horrid, like a barrel of ale shattering. Nothing was left to define the two men beyond a mush of flesh and blood and fragmented bone.

The whole world seemed to be screaming as he gagged and staggered after Snorri. His mail hauberk tugged from behind, and he felt a line of searing pain at the back of his arm. An arrow had caught in his mail, cutting him. Snarling, he joined Snorri at the foot of the ladder, behind the last men of his block.

Screams came from the right and he whirled toward them, knowing what he would see.

Toki's ladder had been shoved away from the wall. They had set the angle too shallow, and the bracers had been hastily set. Rather than push back, the Franks shoved the ladder down. The effect was the same.

He watched in horror as twenty of his men collapsed straight down half the height of the tower. Arrows chased them to the ground, seeking the unprotected bodies. Many sank into flesh, quivering from the pile of victims.

Grabbing Snorri by the collar of his mail, Ulfrik dashed toward the wreck. Despite the crashing noise enveloping him, their moans were like thunder in his ears. Bodies moved, likely those toward the end of the ladder. Two men were already rushing to the fallen, looking into their faces.

A rock thumped into the ground a hand's breadth before him. It had nearly buried itself in the ground, such was the force. Ulfrik pulled up short, Snorri crashing into him, and looked up. Silhouettes of men hefting large objects overhead lined the tower top. They flung their loads down on the Danes.

"They're going to crush us with rocks!" Snorri yelled in his ear, his old voice cracking.

"Help me find Toki."

Dancing amid falling rocks and the rain of arrows, he reached the line. His shield weighed heavy from the scores of arrow shafts embedded in it. A rock clipped the edge and flipped the shield around. Flinging it to the side, he began searching faces. Bloodied men looked skyward, many with dull eyes full of death. Ander mumbled and blinked, but his eyes were unfocused and blood flowed from his ear. Scuttling to the front where Toki had led, he saw Thrand leaning over a man.

His shield was slung across his back, and he held and arrow in a white-knuckled grip. His face was sprayed with blood. Seeing Ulfrik, he recoiled.

"Toki is alive," Thrand said, barely audible over the noise.

His heart pounding, Ulfrik forgot his safety and rushed to Toki's side. He had lost his helmet but seemed unhurt.

"Toki, can you hear me? I'm getting us out of this mess. Snorri!"

He cupped Toki's head, and glared at Snorri to move faster. He came with Kolbyr, another survivor of the crashed ladder. Toki's grip was firm on his arm.

"We can't lie here, or arrows will slay us." To emphasize his words, a stone crashed down an arm's length distant while more arrows drizzled after it. "I think my leg is broken, but I survived. The gods love me after all."

Toki chuckled, and Ulfrik laid his head down. Snorri arrived beside him.

"Get him off the field, and take whoever else you can. I'm calling a retreat."

He did not wait, but sprinted to his other ladder, where Mord was stalled two-thirds up. The ladder was well-set and the hooks arrayed against it could not prevail. The Franks, however, had decided to shoot straight down the ladder. Mord and the men near him had formed a pitiful shield wall against the assault. One man hung dead on the ladder, his blood running like a tap. Ulfrik dashed up the rungs, easily reaching the rear man.

"We're retreating. Take whoever you can carry and go. Send word up to Mord."

The man thumped Ulfrik's helmet in acknowledgment, and pulled the hauberk of the man above him. Ulfrik scrabbled down the ladder, noting Snorri retreating with Toki limping beside him. Other survivors fled past them.

Satisfied he could save enough of his men from the madness of taking the tower with ladders, he started to run. The Danes were in full retreat and scattering everywhere. He saw Gunther One-Eye, his wolf pelt pierced with arrows, charging away with his arrow-pierced standard dragging behind. He searched for Hrolf, and found the giant man easily.

Standing at the foot of his ladder, he shouted curses at the Franks. His men filed down the ladder, slipping away into the mass of fleeing Danes. Hrolf, however, held up his sword in challenge.

A rock the size of a fist clanged off his helmet, denting it and pounding him to his knees. One look up and Ulfrik spotted a cluster of dark shapes reaching their bows over the battlements.

Hrolf lay sprawled faceup when Ulfrik reached his side. Instinctively, he threw himself over Hrolf. Two arrows struck his back, but failed to penetrate the mail. Still, the blows reverberated deep into his body. Another arrow tore his shoulder and a fourth deflected off his helmet.

"Lord Hrolf, stand up and flee. We are finished here."

Blood seeped from Hrolf's nose and Ulfrik read the confusion in his unfocused eyes. Wasting no time for the archers to take a second shot, he hauled Hrolf upright. Another rock landed in the grass where his head had been moments ago.

"You again?" Hrolf mumbled, as he staggered to his feet.

"Faster, lord. The Franks are running out of targets."

The arrows stopped falling and cheers now flowed from the tower rather than missiles. Glancing back as he aided a wobbly Hrolf from the battlefield, he saw men holding bows overhead and one man standing in their midst holding aloft a staff topped with the cross of the new god.

"We had them," Hrolf said, his voice slurred. "Just another moment was all we needed."

Ulfrik made no reply. His body burned with every motion. The Franks began to chant in victory, and Ulfrik bit his lip as he fled the defeat and carnage that lay thick at the base of the tower.

15

R una entered the hall, two baskets of wool in each arm for the girls working the looms. Two other women tended chores, one of whom was Elin. Seeing Runa enter, she put down the bellows she had been using on the hearth and rushed to help. The cold still clung to Runa's robes, and her face immediately warmed as she met Elin halfway. Relieving one basket from her, she drew close and spoke in a low voice.

"He's awake now, but is still resting. He has been asking for the Valkyrie who saved him." Runa thought Elin's smile was almost chiding.

Stopping and handing the other basket to Elin, she wiped her hands on her legs. She touched the sax at her lap, barely aware it calmed her. "So he's making sense now. Let me check him. Where's Gunnar?"

"Collecting branches for the fire." Elin paused, her face growing red. "He is harmless, lady Runa?" Elin's question stopped the three other women at their chores, and their eyes gathered on her. Runa shrugged.

"No man is harmless, but he is weak." The girls at the loom stole worried glances at each other, and Runa waved her hands at them. "Do not fret. He spoke gratefully enough when we rescued him."

Patting Elin's arm, she then checked Thora and Hakon, who both enjoyed a game of catch with a ball of wool. Hakon smiled at the sight of his mother's return, and she held him briefly before deciding to address the stranger. "You want to play longer? Here, back to Thora you go."

With winter drawing nearer every day, the sun lingered in twilight. Despite the years spent here, she had never accustomed herself to the midnight sun of summer and the endless half-light of winter. A thin blue light filtered into the hall from the open smoke hole, combining with the hearth fire and oil lamps fluttering in their bowls around the hall. The fishy scent of the oil filled her nose, but would soon disappear after she accustomed to it. Rather than unpin her cloak, she gathered it at her neck and stared at the cleared section of the hall where the man she had rescued now lay by the wall.

His bright yellow hair stood out against the dark wool blankets piled on him. Since his rescue he had shivered from the cold and slept night and day, crying out in his nightmares of a ship going down at sea. The heartfelt terror in his voice elicited Runa's sympathy. She had endured a storm at sea once, and she and Gunnar had nearly been washed overboard. It was that dreadful trip to find help for Ulfrik, where Toki had nearly been killed and Njall, Thrand's brother, had drowned. She shuddered and put the thought aside.

Kneeling beside the man, she placed her cool hand on his forehead. Sweat moistened her palm and she smiled. "You are no longer cold, nor too hot. You are awake?"

The man's hazel eyes blinked open and struggled to focus, but finally fixed on her. The swelling on his lip had decreased, but they had become as black as coal. Cuts and bruises marred his skin, and lumps disfigured the strong shape of his face. Yet Runa recognized the youthful handsomeness beneath the damage. Even in his disheveled state, he had the face of man accustomed to command. Something in the lines between his brows and the clean trim of his beard marked him for a leader. Forming a weak smile, he spoke in a hoarse voice.

"My Valkyrie has come for me at last. I am thirsty."

Runa smiled. He certainly was used to command, but she wanted him to understand who ruled this hall. "Wait a little longer. Drink may not be what you need yet. The healer must see you first and decide."

He frowned, but it faded as if holding it consumed too much energy. "I am Konal Ketilsson, from Ireland. Your name is Runa?"

"So Konal Ketilsson, you have been awake longer than we thought. And what else have you learned in that time?"

"That you don't take me for an enemy, and your son Gunnar shares your kind heart."

Runa stood, disliking the deception and the intimacy this man seemed to presume. She struggled to keep the irritation out of her voice, though she heard a rise in its pitch. "My son felt it was his duty to sit with you during your recovery. Tell me, Konal Ketilsson, where is your real home? Irish monks live in these islands, and they sound nothing like you."

"I went to Ireland as a boy, but my family is from Rogaland in Norway." He raised his head slightly, his brow cocked. "Are you calling for the healer? I am thirsty."

Folding her arms, she sighed. "Elin, bring a mug of water."

After gulping the water, he lay back down and thanked Runa. "My ship was swamped at sea and overturned. A storm from nowhere overtook us. Two other ships sailed with mine. The winds blew us apart into the darkness. The gods sent me a broken section of deck, and I clung to it even as the splintered wood tore my hands. The water was terribly cold. So cold."

Konal drifted into silence and closed his eyes. Runa relaxed her stance, imaging the dark waters foaming madly in the blackness. She had seen it herself, and dreaded the ocean ever since. Konal had suffered her worst fears, but Fate had spared him. She knelt to retrieve the mug. "Rest now, and don't think more on it. You are under a roof now."

"The gods may have allowed me life, but in my sleep they show me the faces of my crew and fill my dreams with their screams. I wonder if rest will ever be possible again."

Patting his shoulder gently, she stood up. "I have seen my share of terrors, and can tell you the horror fades. The gods will eventually tire of tormenting your sleep."

"There are no men in this hall." His eyes flicked open, so sudden and accusatory that Runa put a hand to her neck in surprise.

"My husband is the jarl, and took the men on raids." Recovering from the surprise of his keen observation, she straightened herself and forced confidence into the volume of her voice. "They will return soon."

Konal stared at her, a slight smile on his blackened lips confusing Runa. Did he suspect the lie? She began to leave, but he called her name again.

"Your husband left his sax with you, and you wear it always. I fear the gods have placed me in a different kind of stormy sea."

"You've a lot of questions for a man who should be asking little and thanking more. Have you never seen a woman wear a sword before?" He shook his head. "Then get used to it; I won't be removing it."

Averting his eyes, he swallowed. "I apologize. I behave like an ungrateful child."

"You behave like a man who has no trust in the people who saved his life."

Konal's bruised face reddened, but his smile remained undiminished. Runa understood his mistrust, yet his openness of it bordered on arrogance.

"I have seen men saved only to be taken into slavery."

"And you would be trussed up by now had that been my desire."

Elin stumbled and pushed a bench over. The sudden crash made Runa and Konal jump. She recovered and apologized to both before returning to her work hauling empty casks outside to be returned to storage. Konal and Runa exchanged glances and laughed.

"Please sit with me a while longer. I've been on my back for days and want to sit up. Besides, I wish to amend my ill manners, and tell you more of my circumstances."

Drawing a bench to his side, she sat while Konal struggled to prop himself against the wall. Despite his pain, Runa allowed him to rise on his own. He had a face that did not hide danger, but she did not trust him enough to get too near. After several moments of adjusting position, he settled in and licked his lips. Runa called Elin for more water, which she delivered.

"My brother's name is Kell and he is my twin. See me and you see him. My sister's husband, Hrut, traveled with us from Ireland. We each commanded a ship with forty-man crews."

"Large ships," Runa said, adjusting the sax across her lap so it hung at her side. "You are wealthy, then?"

"My father is wealthy, and he is generous with his sons." He winked, but Runa held her expression flat. Clearing his throat, he continued. "In the storm that wrecked me, even ships so large were like the dry twigs fed to your hearth. Thor saw us on the water, and his anger was fierce. From nowhere clouds gathered and winds roared. You know what happened then."

Runa nodded. As Konal recounted the storm, he seemed to be looking inside himself, seeing the disaster repeat. How well she knew that torment, though Konal had not told her more than she already knew. "Where were you sailing and why were you risking these waters during the start of winter? You must know Thor detests our winters and rages unexpectedly."

He shrugged, then sucked his breath as he reacted to a pain in his side. "We were sailing for home, for the reasons you stated. No one wants to be at sea during the winter in these waters."

"You are in the Faereyar Islands. Did you know that?" Konal paused, a moment of shock showing on his face. "Why would you be here?"

"Our route took us past these islands, but the storm must have pushed me farther north to your land." He rubbed his side again and fell silent.

"Konal Ketilsson, you want me to trust you but you fail to answer my questions. Why are you in these waters? Only traders or pirates come this far north. Which are you?"

He laughed, but his smile faded when he saw Runa did not share the humor. "Some of my father's men had betrayed him and stolen an item of great value. We learned these men had fled to Norway and hunted them there. But we found their hall burned and all the men slain."

Heat spread through Runa's guts and her breath caught. Konal stared ahead and did not notice her shift in mood. She tried to smooth her voice as she spoke. "And I suppose your treasure was nowhere to be found?" He nodded. "What was the treasure?"

"A slave," Konal said absently. He appeared to grow tired and he shimmied down until he lay flat on the floor. "I am more tired than I thought. You were right; I need more rest."

"Do you think the slave was killed and you did not find him?"

"No, a battle had taken place and footprints were left behind. Some other raiders got to them and sailed off. I doubt we can find the slave again, though my father will want us to continue the search."

"That's much effort for a slave."

Konal grunted and closed his eyes. "My brother is alive. I feel his life as he must feel my own. So he will search for me, and find me. Then the hunt for our treasure will start anew. Forgive me, but recounting all of this has tired me."

"Then rest," she stood, pushing the bench back to the table. "Your brother would be a fool to seek you in winter, not unless Thor loves him above all others. You will be well cared for while you wait for him."

Konal chuckled at the joke. "The gods would not love my brother more than me. Thank you for your kindness. I owe my life to you, and will repay you. For now, I fear I can only be a burden."

Runa left him to his sleep, excusing herself from the hall to see what delayed Gunnar's return. Outside in the cold air of the twilight sky, she thought of Humbert with Ulfrik and a strange sensation of joy and dread overcame her. "Be careful, Husband," she muttered. "The gods are at play with you once more."

16

November 27, 885 C.E

Ulfrik had covered the decks of his ships with their sails, forming a makeshift tent. The sun appeared as a bright spot of yellow as it peeked through the clouds. Beneath the sailcloth, the air was rank with blood and sweat. Ulfrik sat on the deck, still in his mail from the day before. A bit of broken arrow shaft remained snared in the sleeve of his mail. Toki stirred beside him, having slept the night unlike Ulfrik. The wounded moaned, and though the sailcloth muted their voices, to Ulfrik each groan was like a shout. He had led these men on a pointless charge with no chance of glory or dignity in death. Instead, they were pounded with stones, pierced with arrows, or shoved off walls.

"Is it morning so soon?" Toki murmured, then yelped at the pain in his leg. "Gods, that's painful."

"I'm not sure it's broken," Ulfrik offered him. "At least it will keep you from scaling that wall again today."

Toki lay quiet, and Ulfrik glanced at him. His gaze was far away, and doubtlessly his mind's eye replayed the horrors of the day before.

Ulfrik could not close his own eyes without seeing two men explode like barrels of ale dropped from a wall.

"How many did we lose?" Toki's voice was small, fearful.

"Nearly half."

"Dead?"

"Many dead, others wish they were. There are still men at the foot of the walls." Ulfrik lowered his head and closed his eyes. Screams echoed in his mind, and he saw the ladder falling straight down with his men clinging to it. "As soon as I can, I will lead a group to find our people. They don't deserve to lie alone out there, unremembered."

"Snorri is alive?"

"He carried you away. You don't remember?" Toki shook his head. "It's a blessing you don't remember. Rest a while longer. I've been waiting for you to awaken, to be sure you would. Now I must see Hrolf and learn what happens next."

Ulfrik scrabbled away, but stopped short by the mast where Humbert was bound. Their eyes met, and a smile flickered on Humbert's lips.

"Master now understands, yes? Paris is strong. Release Humbert and let him show the secret way before you are killed. A cross of gold as thick as master's leg is hidden not far."

"Can an army fit through your secret way?" He stared at the slave, and his eyes faltered. Ulfrik snorted at it. "I thought not. I lost half my men yesterday, and I don't know if I have enough left to help you get revenge."

"The bishop is an old man." Humbert strained against his bonds, emphasizing his words. "Master will kill him easily. Only you need to go."

"Joscelin fought beside the men on the wall. He will die there, and not likely from my hand. So instead you will trade your secret gold as the price of your freedom. You tell me where it is, and you will be free after I retrieve it. Until then, I will let you off this mast only to eat and shit, but for nothing else." Ulfrik pushed his face into Humbert's, whose smile had vanished. "You better pray I find your gold as thick as my leg. I led good men to their deaths on your

130

promise of wealth. If it's a lie, you will suffer before I send you to your god."

Without waiting for Humbert's response, he ducked out of the covered ship and into the shallows. The cold water braced him as he sloshed ashore where men were already gathering. The noise of their activity had not ceased all night, and now he saw their handiwork. A giant tower of wood, shielded with leather covers and wooden scaffolding, sat on a base of four wheels next to the catapults. The height was staggering, for it seemed at least as tall as the tower.

Snorri, Einar, Mord, and Gunther were also admiring the colossal construction. A fire began to fill Ulfrik's belly, and a stream of curses flowed out of him. He drew the attention of his friends, and Gunther called out to him.

"That's right! We're going to give it to them now that we've got our tower."

"Now? What about yesterday? We had this fucking beast and didn't use it? Are our lives worth less than a tower of wood?"

"Sigfrid doesn't like to wait." The voice came from behind, and all wheeled to find Hrolf approaching with two bodyguards flanking him. He wore a bent smile and his deep voice rasped with annoyance. "With so many bodies to throw at the Franks, why wait to build a siege tower?"

For a moment Ulfrik was appalled, then realized the irony. "Does Sigfrid know what he's doing? We can't repeat yesterday's failure."

"No, we cannot." Hrolf stopped, nodded to the others, then held open his arms to Ulfrik. "Thanks to you I survived it. Again you have snatched me away from death. My gratitude is endless. Come."

He gestured that Ulfrik should embrace him. A quick look to his friends revealed Gunther studying his feet while Snorri and Einar beamed. Stepping into Hrolf's embrace, the giant jarl crushed him tightly and slapped his back. A faint stench of vomit emanated from his clothing, probably from all the heaving Hrolf must have suffered after being struck on the head. He pulled back, releasing Ulfrik to fresher air.

"I know who you are now."

"Lord?"

"You are the one the gods have sent to protect me. No one has ever done so much to ensure my life, even while other men fled the field." Ulfrik noted a barely perceptible turn of Hrolf's head toward Gunther. From the periphery of his vision, Ulfrik saw him shift in embarrassment. "It is my fate to achieve greatness, so the futhark have shown me. Each time I have thrown those rune sticks it is the same. There is always the sword of the gods crossing me, protecting me from harm. That sword is you."

Ulfrik's mouth hung open, and words collided in his mind. He stammered out a lame protest. "It can hardly be me. I live on an island at the top of the world. I am no one, lord."

"Which further proves to me you are the protecting sword of the gods. My life has been in true peril but a handful of times, yet twice you have been there to save me the final blow. There is no such thing as chance. Fate rules all."

Exasperated, Ulfrik had no words. He searched for support, but only Mord spoke. "You are a great leader, jarl Ulfrik. I am honored to serve you."

"Listen to the boy," Hrolf said with a chuckle. "You are a great leader, and I reward greatness. One is for your bravery in holding out to the last, the other is for saving my life." He reached to his arm, searching beneath the sleeve of his mail, then pulled free two gold armbands. One was a plain band while the other was crafted to resemble a serpent biting its tail. Holding them forward, an errant ray of morning sun blazed off the serpent's head. "You will be rich in my service."

Ulfrik accepted them into his hands like they were delicate pottery. Still warm from Hrolf's arm, he fitted one to each of his biceps as his friends watched. Emotions long held back gurgled up inside. The wealth he desired, the glory, the honor he brought to his family and men were to be found here in Frankia. Even without Humbert's gold, this adventure would allow him to provide a better life for all his people. Lost in his thoughts, he did not hear Hrolf's first words.

"Are you listening? I said that I name you Hersir. When we are finished here, you will hold part of my lands and the jarls there will be sworn to you."

"Hersir?" Ulfrik's face warmed at his inarticulate response. Fortunately, Hrolf roared laughter and slapped him on the shoulder.

"It's much to absorb, and there are details to work out. But for now you have one important duty, and that is to be at my side in battle. Remain with me at all times."

"As you say, lord." He spoke the promise even as he understood Nye Grenner was now finished. The people would follow him, and benefit from his future wealth and power. However, his simple acceptance of Hrolf's terms had shattered his independence.

"There are many men without lords after yesterday. I will be sending some to you. You will lead these men in battle today, and those who survive can choose to serve you or find a different lord. In any case, there is much to do yet. I will summon you before the assault so we can discuss strategy." Hrolf gathered his bodyguard and strode off toward the men gathering around Sigfrid's standard flying in the distance. Ulfrik watched him go.

"Congratulations," Gunther patted Ulfrik's shoulder, though his voice was flat and expression dull. "I told you joining us was the right thing for you. Fate is at work."

Ulfrik nodded, then met Gunther's eye in surprise. He understood now that the two of them were of equal rank, or at least much closer. Gunther had shamed himself for fleeing, and now he suffered Hrolf's scorn. He wondered if Hrolf's generosity was not inspired by a desire to humble Gunther. Being a tool, even in a roundabout way, sullied the exhilaration Ulfrik experienced at his change in fortunes.

As Gunther turned away, Snorri and Einar surrounded him, both speaking in a rush of praise. Mord, however, first tried to speak to his father, but was shoved away. He lingered a moment before joining the others.

"How does it feel, lad?" Snorri asked, his eyes creased from his smile. "Lands and title are as good as gold, even better."

"I don't know what to think." Ulfrik laughed, a foreign nervousness suffusing him. "Everything is changed now."

"Soon the world will know your name," Einar said.

"My father was right to praise you," Mord added.

Ulfrik stepped back, touching his head. "This has been a strange morning. I need time to consider things."

Snorri laughed. "All right. But don't think I'm going to call you 'sword of the gods.'"

Ulfrik left them laughing among themselves. Falling into the crowds of people hustling to prepare for the next attack, he let his mind drift. Bouncing through the groups, he could not concentrate. Eventually he wandered toward the trees. In his youth the forests provided a place for him to think as well as play. Deprived of that luxury in the barren Faereyar Islands, he looked forward to a short walk beneath the bare branches. He had to make sense of the changed landscape, and what it meant for his future.

17

"**D**on't do that where everyone can see!" Thrand hissed through clenched teeth. "For the love of the gods, I can't believe you slit their throats!"

Kolbyr and Thrand strolled among the frenetic crowds running along the banks of the Seine. They leaned together so their words were kept from others, though no one had any concern for them. A second attack on the tower was planned and everyone had a task assigned, but Thrand and Kolbyr had slipped theirs.

"Well I couldn't throttle them, and smashing their skulls would be obvious." Thrand looked aside from Kolbyr's angered retort, and smiled at a sour-faced man carrying sheaves of arrows under his arms who passed close to them.

Wiping his face in frustration, he halted and grabbed Kolbyr's cloak. "And slitting their throats was not obvious?"

"Course not. Just a quick jab and cut." Again Kolbyr demonstrated how he had slit the throats of Ulfrik's men as they lay dazed after their ladder had crashed.

"I just told you not to do that!" Thrand slapped Kolbyr's hands down.

"You're drunk again," he said, pulling out of Thrand's grip. "Plenty of cutting went on yesterday. Who's to know what I did from me slicing the air?" He slashed the air with his phantom knife in front of Thrand's face.

Batting the hand away, he snapped back. "Any fool can tell a throat pierced with an arrow from one slit with a knife. Did you think of that? I stuck arrows into their necks, which is more reasonable."

"And all of Ulfrik's favorites getting an arrow in the neck isn't obvious either?" Kolbyr stopped again and frowned. "You are drunk. Your breath is half beer and half fog. You're getting worried, Thrand, and that worries me. No one could tell what happened in that mess other than who lived or died. Neither Ulfrik nor anyone else suspected us. We reduced our worries yesterday, not increased them."

Thrand searched Kolbyr's hard face. His clear eyes showed no fear, no concern that his undisguised murder would reveal their treachery. People swarmed around them, shouting and shoving, but they faced each other like two rocks in a swift flowing river. Deciding that Kolbyr could not be swayed, he refocused on the goal. Tugging Kolbyr's cloak, he asked him to follow as he set out toward the woods.

"Listen carefully and decide now if you're with me on this. A second attack is planned this afternoon. Even if our side wins, I think we stand a good chance of dying. I can't get rich if I'm dead." A large man shoved between them, nearly bowling him over. With a curse, he continued to move through the crowds for the trees. "So there's a change in plans. We take Humbert now, and force him to guide us through his secret paths to the treasure."

"And your plan for dealing with Ulfrik? I doubt he is willing to stand aside. Maybe we should wait until the attack begins, then slip back here to get the slave."

Shaking his head, Thrand grunted. "We'd stand out like two cowards, and everyone would see us. Besides, I've got something better planned."

Exiting the crowd and now only a spear-throw from the woods, he stopped and leaned in to Kolbyr. "While I was out this morning, I spotted Ulfrik headed into these woods. Alone."

He let the words hang, waiting until realization glittered in Kolbyr's eyes. "But there are only two of us."

"You distract him and I will put my sword through his liver. He trusts us and won't expect a thing. Alone in the woods, with all this noise to cover us, the timing is perfect. In fact, you might say the gods have given us this chance."

Kolbyr's face darkened and he stroked his beard. A fire kindled in Thrand's guts, but he clamped his mouth shut against the angry words. Kolbyr had to help him, as Thrand knew he could not overcome Ulfrik alone.

"He is a great warrior. I've seen him fight three men at once."

"Three enemies. We are two of his friends and he won't be prepared. Think on it. He dies in the woods and when he doesn't show for battle men will search for him. During that time we escape with Humbert and before anyone realizes, we're gone from their reach. I told you at the beginning we might have to kill Ulfrik to ensure we get the treasure."

Kolbyr nodded, tentatively, but then with vigor. "All right. It's true; this is our best chance."

Thrand unhooked the loop holding his sword in its scabbard, and Kolbyr did the same. "By tonight we will have a fortune in heathen gold."

Laughing, he led Kolbyr into the woods where Ulfrik awaited his doom.

18

Runa froze in her steps outside the hall, buckets in both hands swaying from the sudden stop. For a moment it was Ulfrik's voice she heard, the deep tones vibrating through the walls to her, but the laughter was wrong—neither strong nor joyous enough to be him. She flushed at her foolishness, then resumed lugging the filled buckets of water to the hall. Rain had refilled the barrels over night, and the wet grass licked her ankles as she rounded the corner into the hall.

Elin and another woman relieved her of the buckets as she entered. Wiping her hands on her skirt, she caught sight of Gunnar seated with Konal and several of the older boys. Despite his bruises, he narrated his shipwreck to his audience with exaggerated gestures, describing steep waves and crashing ships with wide swings of his arms.

"One night of sleep seems to have restored our guest," Elin said as Runa followed her to the hearth. She upended the bucket into the cooking pot, swirling up the pitiful remains of the prior night's soup.

"A man of surprises," Runa said. She swished a spoon through the thin soup, sniffed its pungent odor, and determined it could be served, then turned to Konal.

Something about the way Gunnar responded to Konal's story irritated her. She could not decide the exact reason, other than the familiarity with her son felt presumptuous. *Is he attempting to manipulate me?* she thought. *Gods, Runa, why are you seeing danger everywhere?*

Sitting on the bench beside Gunnar, she arrived in time for Konal to conclude his tale. "And then I was saved by you three brave men. An amazing tale, is it not? My skalds will make it a poem one day."

"You have a skald?" The oldest boy leaned forward, a fourteen-year-old who had begged to go with Ulfrik but instead remained with his mother and sisters.

"We have two, and many more visit us." Konal smiled at Runa. "They sing of my adventures, and those of my father and brothers."

"Now they will sing of your black lips and blue face," Runa said. "And how you could scare a troll."

Gunnar and his friends erupted with laughter, but Konal sat back with a raised brow. "When I'm recovered, I can do more than scare a troll. I can kill him, with one hand!"

Again the boys rollicked in laughter, and even Runa could not deny a smile to Konal's ridiculous claims. "Don't exert yourself yet. Helga, the healer woman, will visit you today, and until she says you are recovered, rest is what you need. Now you boys have chores to do with the men gone." Gunnar moaned, and Runa clucked her tongue at him. "Off to them. Go! Bitter cold out there and the clouds are dark. Rain last night but snow today. So get the sheep indoors."

The boys filed away. The oldest one wore a sax like Runa, and he thumbed it as he paused. "When you are well, will you practice with me? My Da used to before he went a-viking, and he wanted me to protect our home. So, well, practice is important."

Konal nodded. "True words, and I would be pleased to help when my nursemaid releases me."

Runa watched Gunnar leave with his friends. He carried himself with a posture so much older than a boy of nine. She took relief in his courage, but regretted how fast youth slipped away.

"It feels good to be up and talking again." Konal rotated his shoulder, holding his ribs with a grimace. "They are fine boys, disciplined. Not like my children."

"You have children?" She detested the question the moment it slipped from her mouth, but she was further angered at the wry smile drawn through Konal's swollen face.

"Two boys and three girls. My youngest girl is my favorite, the rest are a sword in my side."

"I'm sure their mother feels otherwise."

"Mothers. And I don't know what they feel, since I stay at sea mostly."

Runa stiffened at his correction, not wanting to know more than she already did. She beckoned Elin to bring the soup, and changed the direction of their conversation. Elin swept in with two steaming bowls of soup. Runa clasped her cold hands around the bowl to warm them.

"It's a poor meal," she said. "But we are poor people. You will not be getting fat this winter, unless your brother finds you earlier."

Regardless of the steam, Konal slurped from his bowl. He put it down, speaking with a mouthful of fish. "I haven't eaten in days, and haven't eat anything hot in weeks. This is a feast."

The word hit Runa, knocking free memories of the great feasts Ulfrik had thrown in the past. She had chided him for the wastefulness, but secretly she enjoyed organizing them and cooking for so many. It was a joy lost to her, and regret mingled with her memories. Had Ulfrik been here, he would find a way to feast Konal even if he spent his last bit of silver to do it. Now, scraps of the prior night's meal were the best she could offer.

"I'm glad you're enjoying the feast. Since you are recovered enough to talk about adventures and family, I have matters to discuss."

Konal looked expectantly over the top of his bowl, but did not slow down in dumping soup into his gullet.

"We are barely provisioned to care for ourselves, and your arrival is a further burden. The gods have been harsh, and winter is when they cull our numbers. I've lost a child to the winters, and more friends than I want to count. You are welcome here, but you are also stuck here. So you will have duties to carry out and earn your place with the rest of us."

"Duties?"

Now the wry smile appeared on Runa's lips. "Were you thinking of lying back until your brother finds you, if he ever does? While you recover, your duties will be light, but I expect you to do more. You are taking from us, so give back. It is fair."

Konal's brow furrowed and he thoughtfully placed his bowl on the table. Runa scrutinized him, her hand idly plucking a lose wrap on the hilt of her sax. His surprise gave her pleasure. "What sort of duties? I am a lord, you know."

"I don't know, in fact. That gold torc on your neck is meaningless here. People can't eat gold and winter does not care for titles. We must eat, stay warm, guard our flocks, and survive until the sun rises again."

"I can help with the eating." He smiled at his own joke, but Runa blinked and carried on as if he had merely coughed.

"Be reminded I am the jarl's wife, and I rule this island and all the people on it." *I just can't enforce my rule,* she thought. "I will expect your obedience while you are here."

His mouth hung open in a half-formed laugh, but Runa stood before he could voice it.

"I don't wear this sword for show. Your first duty, once you are well enough, is to practice with me daily."

"Surely I hit my head on a rock and I'm dreaming. I'm stranded on an island of women and children and the jarl's wife wears a sax and wants to practice swordplay with me." He spread his hands wide. "No one would believe such a thing."

"Start believing." She shoved away from the bench and started for the hall door. "Your skalds will turn it into a poem one day."

19

Thrand and Kolbyr picked through the woods, stepping over fungus-laden logs and skirting the bare trees. Thrand's plan was simple: get close, distract and surprise Ulfrik, then flee. Since stealth mattered little, they crushed dead leaves and cracked branches beneath their feet and spoke to each other in normal voices. If anything, he hoped it would attract Ulfrik and spare them the search.

"Gods, did he walk back to Nye Grenner?" Kolbyr shoved aside a low branch with a curse.

"It's not a bad thing," Thrand answered in a lowered voice.

They had progressed deep enough into the gray and brown murk of the woods to lose sight of the army by the Seine, though the riot of noise echoed through the trees. Thrand drew a deep breath, his nose full of wet, earthy scents. Halting, he glimpsed a shape sweep across the side of his vision. Kolbyr stopped with him. They waited, and now a clear figure in a green cloak moved, head down and hands clasped behind.

"Remember the plan," he whispered to Kolbyr. Glancing at him, he discovered beads of sweat on Kolbyr's forehead and his eyes had grown round. "Are you still with me?"

Kolbyr swallowed, then nodded and licked his lips.

Thrand called Ulfrik's name, and the figure stopped, faced them. "Lord Ulfrik, we've been searching for you."

"You've found me. What's the matter?"

Trading looks with Kolbyr, they began to pick a path to Ulfrik. Thrand's pulse quickened and his neck tightened. Kolbyr's breathing became ragged and loud enough for Thrand to notice.

Trees crowded them and restricted fighting space. He watched Ulfrik study their approach, and a frown began to draw down his face.

"Well, what is the matter?"

Thrand's nervousness blanked his mind, and the demand stopped him as good as being bashed with a shield. Kolbyr continued, looping out to the left.

Suddenly Ulfrik stood straighter. Kolbyr began moving faster.

This is out of control. Kolbyr! Slow down!

Kolbyr burst into a sprint. Not only did he strike too early, but the rough ground impeded running. As he drew his sword, stiff-armed and artless, he stumbled.

No one made such a mistake with Ulfrik and lived to regret it. Thrand changed his plans.

"Look out, Lord Ulfrik!" Drawing his own blade, he plunged after Kolbyr.

Ulfrik had no shield, but all his weapons. Thrand dashed, catching his foot on a root and tumbling ahead. Kolbyr's blade caught an errant shaft of light.

With no effort, Ulfrik had unclasped his cloak and flung it at Kolbyr. In the next instant, he had ripped his sax from the sheath at his waist.

The cloak entangled Kolbyr's sword, but Thrand was already at his back. He rammed the blade into Kolbyr's kidney, piercing the mail links and driving deep into the flesh. Blood poured and Kolbyr screamed. It was cut short as Ulfrik's sword plunged into his belly with a metallic crunch.

Kolbyr danced as both men yanked out their swords, and gouts of blood pattered to the ground. His wide eyes held Thrand's as he toppled into the leaves and mud. Blood flew from his mouth as he landed and he seemed to about to raise his hand.

Thrand gave him no time. He saw the accusation in Kolbyr's eyes. *It was going to come to this at some point,* he thought, then he thrust his sword into Kolbyr's throat with a hollow crack and a gurgle of blood.

Next he was looking up through the branches at the gray sky. Pain bloomed at the back of his head where he had struck a rock. His sword arm felt heavy, and then realization came. In one deft motion, Ulfrik had toppled him and now pinned his sword arm by stamping on it. His sax drizzled Kolbyr's blood onto his neck as its tip hovered a hair's width away.

"Explain yourself," he snarled. "Or die."

"Lord, we were sent to fetch you back. The attack is coming soon, and Hrolf wants you ready."

"Hrolf sent you to find me?"

"Yes, lord." The words made his stomach burn. He lied, and Ulfrik would know it soon enough. He only had to live through to when the attack started, and then escape.

The blade dangled, beyond it Ulfrik's face a ball of furrows and scars that pulled into his beard. Hot blood rolled around Thrand's neck to pool behind his head. His hand still gripped his sword, and he released it, trying to force the blade away from his grip. Ulfrik's eyes searched his, darting up and down the length of his body. "You've served my family admirably, Thrand. I don't want to doubt you."

"Please don't, my lord." His voice trembled with genuine fear. Ulfrik's eyes blazed with killing lust, and once ignited in him never left easily.

"This has happened to me before, almost exactly like this." The blaze dimmed, and Ulfrik seemed to review a scene in his head. Thrand felt the foot lift from his arm, his hand tingling as blood rushed back into it. "I fear it is my fate to never enjoy the solitude of the trees."

The bloody sword lifted from his throat, and Thrand closed his eye in relief with a long slithering breath flowing from his nostrils.

"My eyes tell me you moved like a man on the hunt, but my heart wants to believe otherwise." Opening his eyes, Thrand found Ulfrik still had the short sword pointed at him, and he knew the lightning flash strike could pierce his neck in an instant. "Convince me the hirdman who defended my family with his life is not a traitor."

Moving with deliberate openness, Thrand sat up with his hands raised. Ulfrik's grip tightened on the hilt of his blade and did not waver in his defensive posture. "It is all as you say, lord. I am your man and my oath is true. I saw Kolbyr move to strike, and I defended you."

"Or you changed your mind."

"No! I could scarcely believe it. He followed through on his boasts."

Ulfrik raised his brow at the comment, and the sword blade tipped—barely perceptible but enough to indicate Thrand had found his opening.

"He was jealous of the silver I received from you. Always cursing your name, lord, and calling you a miser. Said you were a terrible jarl and a fake. He wanted to be paid like a hero, but didn't ever do anything for it. I tried to correct him many times."

"All that anger, and yet I never saw it." Ulfrik's voice sounded unconvinced, and the blade remained pointed at him.

"Only when he drank, lord. And then only around me. After yesterday's attack, he blamed you for leading us into death. Swore he'd make you pay for it. That's what he said."

"And he was drunk today?"

"Must be, lord."

"But not you?"

"No more than usual, lord."

Staring past the tip of the blade, Ulfrik's face remained impassive. If he did not convince Ulfrik, he might be forced to fight. He regretted keeping his hands out, since he could not reach his own sax in time to strike.

"Where would he get those thoughts, Thrand? Why would a man

who sought to serve me become bitter enough to seek my death? Who taught him to hate me?"

Tears came with sudden and frightening ease. His breath grew hot and the wetness flowed over his cheeks into his beard. Thrand did not understand their origin, maybe for his brother, his failure, the fear of death, or even Kolbyr's murder. However they came, they were a blessing. He flung himself to the ground, balling up as if in pain and wailing and intent on riding the sorrow until Ulfrik was convinced of his sincerity.

"It was me, lord. Forgive me, but it was me!" He spasmed with sobs, and he found he could not stop. Something dammed up had broken free and he shuddered with cries like a little girl. His words were barely coherent. "W-when I am drunk ... I ... my words are evil. My mind burns with anger. I miss my brother, my only family. I blamed you, lord. It was wrong! My drunk raving, it poisoned him against you. Forgive me!"

Waves of sorrow crashed through him, and he sprawled out in his pitiful state for longer than he knew. Soon, he marshaled himself and he felt Ulfrik's boot prodding him.

"Get up and stop weeping."

Having never experienced such a powerful emotion, he lay drained, stirring only when Ulfrik's foot kicked him more forcefully. He sat up again, his face wet with tears, snot, and mud. Dead leaves clung to his hair and beard, and he batted them out with a trembling hand.

"Help me get him out of his mail." Ulfrik had already flipped Kolbyr and was hoisting the mail hauberk over the corpse's head. The scene sobered him. He had wiped the bloodied sax on Kolbyr's cloak and sheathed it.

If I struck now, I could surprise him, he thought. *A solid thrust to his gut and he'd be finished. It's possible; he's not a god.*

"Get up and help me," he repeated, glancing at him.

Thrand's hand itched for the hilt of the sax hanging at his side. His own bloodied blade lay partially covered by forest debris only an arm's length away.

Flipping belt straps aside, Ulfrik began to work the mail up Kolbyr's body, being careful not to tangle the chain links.

Thrand's arm stretched for the sword.

Ulfrik stood and dropped Kolbyr. "Your sword?"

The two men stared at each other, and Thrand could not read Ulfrik's face. He had no expression: no anger, fear, confusion, nothing. Such blankness was more frightening than anything else.

"Yes, my sword is in the mud, lord. Rust, I don't want it to rust."

"It won't rust so fast. Help me with the mail first."

He was relieved at being caught; now he had an excuse to assuage any shame for not carrying through. He joined Ulfrik in removing Kolbyr's mail.

"What about his body?" Thrand refused to look at Kolbyr's face, though he imagined his clear dead eyes staring at him.

"Food for the ravens." He snapped off Kolbyr's purse, his silver Thor's hammer, and took his weapons, tossing them into a pile next to the folded mail.

"So you're leaving him here?"

"Gods, man! You are drunk. I've got unburied men piled at the foot of that Frankish tower. You think I'd spare a moment to honor a man who tried to murder me? I curse his soul to Nifleheim. Now, you can serve me by carrying all of this back."

Thrand regarded the pile, more than both his arms could handle. Ulfrik kicked Kolbyr's corpse, and his head lolled to the side. The dead eyes locked with Thrand's and he jumped in shock. Ulfrik laughed, and pushed him at the pile.

Laugh now, he thought as he gathered the mail hauberk and weapons. *Tonight I will be gone with your slave and enjoying your treasure. Maybe I'll buy an army to carve that smirk off your face.*

Stumbling through the woods as Ulfrik walked behind, Thrand consoled himself with thoughts of vengeance.

20

Ulfrik emerged from the woods to chaos. Men streamed toward the tower and the war machines lobbed rocks at the walls of Paris or the tower itself. War cries and weapons banged on shields combined with the crack of bowstrings and the snap of the catapults. Banners bobbed and spun above the heads of the Danes. Thrand looked back at him, his bloodied face pale and frightened.

"They started without us," Ulfrik said. He suspected Thrand might not be as innocent as his tears made him seem. However, with the battle started, he set aside his doubts. "Where did Hrolf say to meet?"

"He was just shouting for someone to find you, and I volunteered to go." Thrand's eyes were wide with terror, and he kept glancing at the distant tower.

Scanning the banners at the fore of the attack, none were familiar. As he worked back, he located the three jarls stationed at the rear, Sigrid, Knut, and Hrolf. Pushing past Thrand, he went to gather his crew and join Hrolf's standard. He collided with men rushing to the attack, shoving horizontally through to the shore. His men were already gathered beneath his banner, waiting at the riverbank. Einar held it in Toki's stead. As he approached, Snorri noticed him first.

"You've already been to the battle? It just began." Snorri's eyes darted past him to Thrand and his brow furrowed.

"No time to explain. Thrand, drop your burden here. Snorri, how many men are fit for battle?"

"Enough," Snorri answered, but he butted against him and whispered. "What has happened?"

"Later. Focus on the battle." Ulfrik saw the worry in his friend's face, and reassured him with a thump on the shield. Men needed confidence and belief in order to march into battle, especially after a defeat. He refused to shake the men's morale with news of betrayals. He stood before them, arms folded across his chest. Grim faces looked back at him. Behind them on the Seine, ships glided past with their crews of archers.

"Do you men still serve me? Do you still believe in victory?" Exchanging glances, they nodded and then voices joined. Soon they roared back their belief, and Ulfrik smiled. "Good! For I believe in victory and glory. But most of all, I believe in honor. And there is no higher honor than to bravely serve our oath-holders. No matter your fate today, you will be heroes in Valhalla. If I join you there, I will be glad. Someone give me a shield and follow me!"

With cheers and shouts, they fell in with him as he merged into the tide flowing toward the tower, keeping Hrolf's dragon standard in view. Before them, the siege tower began rolling ahead. He doubled their speed, fearful Hrolf would follow the tower. However, he soon brought his force alongside Hrolf's. The giant jarl and Gunther were conferring beneath his standard, and Ulfrik lined up his men then joined them.

"You're covered in blood." Hrolf glanced up and down his length, but then turned to observe the siege tower trundling toward the Franks. Ulfrik's face must have registered his surprise at the casual dismissal, for Gunther laughed.

"Worried we thought you ran?" Gunther's mood had recovered

from the morning and he waved Ulfrik closer. "To be honest, I thought about it myself."

All around them Hrolf's warriors formed into loose ranks. Their faces were grave and their voices remarkably silent. To the front, helmets and weapons spun off stars of sunlight as Danes converged on the Franks. Black clouds of arrows wove over the heads of the men, shot from the rear ranks or from the top of the tower. Death screams and war cries flowed back to them, weak and pitiful beneath the arrow-storm.

"I was delayed," Ulfrik finally explained. "Why are we not at the fore of the attack?"

"Because we were there yesterday and learned a good lesson, don't you think?"

"We're allowing others a chance at glory." Hrolf remained observing the progress of the siege tower. "The crafty Franks built another two levels overnight. Now our tower and ladders are too short. A perfect opportunity for men craving glory."

Looking again, Ulfrik saw the hastily constructed fortifications crowning the tower. "How did I not see it?"

"The real question is how the Franks built it so fast." Hrolf placed his hands on his hips, the sleeves of his mail glittering. "No matter. Our war machines will dismantle it."

The words went straight to Loki's ears, and the trickster god of mischief delighted in them.

An explosion as deafening as a clap of thunder rolled over Ulfrik, and one of the catapults flipped forward. The arm splintered and cracked while the body of the machine lurched into the air, wheels spinning off into the crowds and the high tension rope lashing the catapult crew. The rock it was launching skittered off at a wild angle, plunking into a ship passing beneath the normal arc of the shot. The crewmen splashed out of their ship as the vessel broke and sunk as if the thumb of a god had pushed it underwater.

Men screamed as the explosive power sprawled them to the ground and the uncoiling rope tore open men's flesh like a honed blade. The wheels landed among archers, scattering most and crushing others. The broken catapult landed atop another just as it launched its rock. The arm snapped off and the machine tipped to its side. In an instant two of the five catapults were destroyed and the crews of the others had fled. The remaining arms stood half-raised, dumbfounded giants staring at the river.

"Too much tension," Hrolf remarked, never having flinched at the spectacle. Ulfrik and everyone around him had instinctively cowered at the violence, and only now recovered. "I can't work those machines, but even I know you mustn't wind them too tight. It's just like working the rigging of a ship. Tie off too tight and you're bound to break a rope."

Ulfrik exchanged amazed smiles with Gunther, who elbowed him and chuckled. "If he's not worried then I'm not worried. And we've still got three left, plus the siege tower."

However, the tower now leaned at a steep angle and progress had halted. Men surrounded it, milling and crawling over each other to get the tower into motion. Ulfrik watched in silence, his brows tight and his temples throbbing. Nothing budged the tower, its wheels fallen into a steep ditch. His eyes flicked from the tower to the desperate men on the walls whose ladders held in places and fell away in others. Men tumbled from the heights, the dark shapes of their flailing bodies clear against gray stone background. He could not watch them hit the ground, but his mind echoed with the sickening sounds of bodies rupturing like broken barrels. Rubbing his face, he doubted he could witness that terror again.

"We're going in." Hrolf announced the decision, not turning from the disaster unfolding before him. "They'll never clear the siege tower in time to be useful. Knut's men will lead a battering ram. Let's help him try the tower gates."

Returning to his own crew, they looked expectantly at him. When he explained their orders, some faces showed relief and some fear. Ulfrik bridled his own terror, forcing himself to stand straighter and appear firmer than he felt. A veteran of scores of battles, he had never experienced such a horrific chance of an ignominious death. As he led his square of men to join Hrolf's right wing, he thought of Runa and Gunnar. If they had ever angered him, ever showed him a displeased face, he could not remember it now. He only saw them in happiness and safety. He would carry them in his heart to the tower, and resolve to survive for them. Gold and glory would be meaningless as a lump of broken flesh beneath a Frankish tower. He would live, and return to them with all he promised and more.

Closing in on the tower, the shrill sounds and putrid smells of death drew over Ulfrik. Overall the Danes attacked like voracious wolves, but groups of men fled white-eyed and screaming. Hrolf cursed them as they shoved past, and other men tripped or hindered them. Ulfrik ignored them, trying to deny he would soon be following their path.

The battering ram was nothing more than a huge log chained inside a housing of wood that was topped with a slanted roof. Water-soaked hides lined the sides and protected the men carrying the housing on their shoulders. At least twenty men manned each side and Ulfrik envied the protection they received. His job was to wait for a breach and exploit it, which meant standing beneath falling rocks and arrows while waiting for his chance.

Hrolf halted his line and raised shields. Ulfrik, bearing a new and wider shield, ordered his men lock shields. Snorri leaned down next to him.

"We're going to stand here and be shot? This is madness!"

Ulfrik's answer disappeared beneath a booming thud. The battering ram crew shouted in unison, swinging the enormous timber a second time. His shield shuddered as arrows rained down, but wide and thick wood held better than his normal shield. Huddling beneath it, he shouted comfort to his men.

"Only a few more hits and the gates are coming down. Hold steady."

A grating crash followed the next boom, and a cheer went up at the top of the tower. Daring to peek through a gap in the shield wall, Ulfrik's hands went cold at what he saw.

The Franks had dropped timbers fashioned into a fork shape

from the tower. The massive fork pinned the battering ram log to the ground, ripping the housing from the bearers. Death followed.

Gray-fletched arrows laced into the men and they crumbled in a screaming, bloody heap. Even more horrible, streaming tongues of fire poured from the top of the tower. The infernal mixture of oil and wax drizzled in burning ribbons onto the men at the base of the tower. In an instant, men danced in fiery pools, spinning and waving their arms as they burned. One man had lost his helmet and fire splashed onto his head, removing his hair and face down to the bone. Engulfed in flames, men threw themselves into the Seine, preferring to drown rather than burn.

"Back!" Hrolf gave the order and Ulfrik repeated it. They backed up behind their shields, arrows pelting them in retreat. They stumbled over bodies or into ruts and ditches, but at a safe distance they turned and ran. Behind him the Franks sang in victory as all but the most tenacious or crazed Danes fled.

Many continued to run in horror. Ulfrik joined with him, allowing his men to melt away in the disordered retreat. Snorri had stayed with him, and his breath was heavy and labored.

"I don't think I can do that again." Sweat poured over his heavy face, and his gray hair was matted to his brow.

"Nor I. This is work for a madman."

"We won't attack the tower again, at least not while they're so fresh." Hrolf rose his full height, a head taller than anyone near him. He squinted at the tower, shadowing his eyes with his hand as men fled around him. "If they want to remain in behind their walls, then so be it. We will surround the city and starve them out. I can be patient, particularly when the vengeance will be sweet."

Ulfrik felt his stomach drop. A siege of such a vast fortress would last much longer than winter. Again he summoned memories of Runa and his boys, and closed his eyes, whispering to himself. "Be safe, my family. I will return to you soon, I swear."

He opened his eyes again, and Paris and its walls spread out before him larger than anything he could have ever imagined.

21

The milling confusion covered Thrand's escape. Men worried for their own lives, plodding forward with eyes open but seeing nothing. The flow of people traveled both toward and away from the tower. He allowed his pace to flag until he fell to the back of Ulfrik's line, and then melted into the flow heading toward the camps and ships.

His first difficulty lay in contacting Humbert while the wounded surrounded him in the ships. He planned to cut Humbert free, flee with him, then seek the treasure. Most of the wounded would be in no condition to prevent it.

Behind him sounds of battle shook the earth. Men swarmed at his sides, shoving past him in their panic to escape death. The tide of cowards delivered him to Ulfrik's ships, both decks covered with sail cloth to shelter the wounded. At this distance, the battle faded and terror ebbed away. Wounded men who could stand strained to view the carnage, their faces impassive but their eyes unable to watch for long. All around them broken bits of war gear poked above the grass. Shields bristling with arrows, bent swords, dented helmets, shattered spears. Defeat dragged back by haggard men.

The scene renewed Thrand's desire to escape. This was not his battle, and Paris was not his goal. A fortune in gold waited for him, and now only a few steps separated him from it. A new life awaited, one of wealth and the glory it could buy.

Women flitted about the scene, tending the wounded and receiving fresh casualties from the battle. At Ulfrik's ship, a woman emerged from beneath the sail cover. Her head cover fell as she exited and she scrambled to catch it. Losing her balance, she plunged into the water.

Thrand leapt to her as she thrashed in the shallow water. Hoisting her up, the woman sputtered and flapped her arms.

"Are you hurt, girl?" Thrand helped her from the shallows, and the girl nodded as she gasped.

"I can't swim." She looked at him and smiled. "I don't know what I would've done."

"The water is not deep; just stand up."

Her face reddened and she squeezed the water out of her skirt. Thrand noted the whiteness of her leg, and nearly forgot his true purpose. "Do you know the men on this ship?"

She blushed deeper, and Thrand realized he had stumbled upon Toki's secret lover. A smile creased his face. "Is Toki aboard, or anyone else? I am one of Ulfrik's crew and I have an urgent message for him."

"He is sleeping now; his wounds make him groggy. There is a slave aboard. The rest are on the other ship."

Thrand chuckled, and the girl gave him a quizzical look. She could not decide which of his eyes to meet. *So Toki fucks and naps while his friends risk death,* he thought. *You threw out all the injured to keep your secret. I'd be doing Ulfrik a favor to cut your throat before I leave.*

"The men are on the other ship now. Will they be all right?"

"I don't know," her gaze faltered. She was a thin woman with milk-white skin and fair hair. Freckles splattered her face and her expression wavered between vulnerability and sadness. Certain men would find her appealing, though Thrand disliked her girlishness.

"Be on your way. And I won't mention any of this, I promise."

Her face brightened and she thanked him several times before flitting off. He watched her go, then let himself aboard.

Sunlight turned the sail canopy to bright yellow. His eyes adjusted to the dim and his nostrils filled with the tangy scent of blood. Toki, his leg wrapped and braced, slumbered on his side and tucked into the gunwales. Humbert slumped against ropes binding him to the mast, head down and gray-streaked hair falling forward. For a moment, Thrand feared he had died, but then he stirred as Thrand approached.

He drew a knife, and crept up to Toki. Humbert suddenly spasmed, shaking his head violently but keeping strict silence. Thrand did not want to kill Toki, but felt the precaution had to be taken. Humbert's dark eyes glittered and wordlessly pleaded for Thrand to stay his hand.

With a frown he acquiesced, padding with exaggerated care to Humbert's side. He put his mouth directly to Humbert's ear, so close he could feel the roughness of his beard brush his cheek.

"I am releasing you now. We are going to Paris, where you will show me your treasure." He moved to Thrand's back and grabbed the ropes biting into his wrists, but Humbert struggled against the bonds and hissed in his ear.

"Wait! I have a better plan. Please, listen to me."

"No time for that." He began to saw at the ropes.

"You will get us both killed. Then what of your treasure?" His voice cracked and Thrand shot a glance to Toki, who replied with a snore.

"Keep your voice down."

"If you don't listen to me I'll scream." Not only the challenge but the sudden power and clarity of Humbert's voice stilled Thrand. Nearly nose to nose with the priest, Thrand backed away and shrugged. Humbert glared at him, then spoke.

"Where is your friend?" Thrand mimicked a cut across this throat, and Humbert's smile deepened the lines on this bony face. "Better it's just you and me. So much easier to enter Paris. Your Lord Ulfrik doesn't want to help, and will force me to tell him the secret hiding place. But Humbert never will. God willing, Humbert will die first. Many days can Humbert live and not speak. God protects me."

"I'm not sure about that." Thrand put the tip of his knife to the slave's throat. "If you're wasting time so I get caught here, your god better act fast."

"The secret way is not open. Humbert knows this because my countrymen are guarding the walls. To go that way is to die. But Humbert is smart. We will enter through the front gate as friends."

"You are wasting my time." Sawing anew at Humbert's binds, the priest's words rushed out of his mouth.

"Do you hear my countrymen? They celebrate victory. Listen!" Thrand paused and heard vague sounds of chanting. Sitting back on the deck, he concentrated as Humbert began to smile.

"They are praising God and Saint Denis. Your cowardly friends will be rushing back any moment. You will never get away fast enough. Listen to Humbert's plan. Your Danish friends won't leave Paris, and will stay for the winter. So when your friends settle in, you and Humbert will go to Paris. You will bring a disguise for us. From the dead or prisoners, take Frankish coats, shields, and helmets. We will look like Franks. At the gates, Humbert will speak and they will know Humbert is true. The doors will open for us, and we will enter. Simple!"

"So simple I don't believe it. Won't your enemy know you have entered his city?"

"But he now has much to attend to. Ulfrik told me he fights on the walls. He believes Humbert is lost or dead, and will not think of me."

"And why so sure the gates will open?"

"Humbert is a priest, and I know what to say to make them open for us. It will just be two of us, yes? No threat from two men wanting to join the city."

Thrand dropped into silence as he considered the plan. The cheering of the victorious Franks was overtaken by the footfalls of men running back to their ships. If Ulfrik lived, he would return soon. He had to slip away to make it seem he was lost in the fighting. Shooting a hard look at Humbert, he turned his good eye toward him.

"Then you will take me to the treasure, and show me how to escape after?"

"Yes," he said. "Trust Humbert. I want to return to my city, and the gold is for you. Ulfrik's plan will make Humbert a slave forever, but we can help each other."

"And no revenge? I thought that was your goal."

A derisive snort shot from Humbert's nose. "That was before Ulfrik treated me so poorly. Look at these ropes tying me to this mast. Freedom is enough."

"We'll destroy Paris. You might end up here again."

"God will not allow it. Help Humbert, and he will help you. I swear this to God."

Muffled voices came from outside the ship and Toki rolled over in his sleep with a grumble. Thrand stood, sheathing his knife. "I will find us disguises. We will leave soon."

Slipping out of the ship, he jogged toward a confused group of men stumbling back from the failed attack. Joining them, he began to plan how to acquire and hide Frankish gear until the time for escape. The promised gold, the treasure Ulfrik had risked all their lives to obtain, would soon be his.

~

December 4, 886 C.E

THRAND'S BREATH clouded before him as he crouched low. Two drunk men staggered past, their shapes outlined by moonlight. One stumbled while his companion laughed, and Thrand thought they would never move on. Beyond them the southern tower guarding entrance to Paris loomed huge and white, crowned with points of orange light from the sentries patrolling its battlements. Unsullied by attacks, it appeared solid and strong, as impenetrable as the northeastern tower had been. According to Humbert, its huge iron doors would swing open at his word.

The two men ambled away, their breath like chugging smoke from a fire. Thrand cursed them to fall into one of the trenches dug around the city. In one week, the Danish army had sacked a Christian abbey and made it their base, then dug in around both towers and riverbanks. Ulfrik had followed Hrolf to the southern bank, and participated in seizing the abbey. Thrand was glad for the easy fight, but less satisfied at digging in the mud for the remainder of the week. His hands still throbbed with blisters.

Confident he remained unobserved, he glided through the dead grass to the stand of trees and the boulder where he had hidden their Frankish disguises. Many Franks had been captured as they dug their own trenches around their towers. Their distinctive helmets and shields, plus their bright colored surcoats had been easy to obtain. He only had to wait for the right time to execute his plan.

Tonight.

While Ulfrik's men slept on land in tents pitched closed to their beached ships, Thrand had stole away with a silent nod to Humbert. He remained bound by the feet and hands, but no longer tied to a mast. Ulfrik's closest men guarded him, though on this night they had all been summoned away to attend Hrolf at the abbey, even Toki still lame with his injured leg. Ulfrik had left Thrand in charge of Humbert, providing the perfect night for escape.

He pulled up a mat of grass he had cut to hide the hole where surcoats and helmets were buried. The shields lay nearby under cloaks covered in branches. He wore the surcoat, but hid it beneath his cloak, and clutched the rest of the gear to his chest, then scurried back toward camp.

The tents billowed in the night breeze, and sentries dozed around dying fires. Shadows of men flickered as they passed from moonlight to darkness. For now, Thrand still looked like a Dane and no one challenged him. Arriving at Ulfrik's camp, the green standard of Nye Grenner flipped petulantly around its pole. Thrand halted as he drew nearer, watching the banner twist overhead.

Within moments he would break all his oaths, betray his lord, and become an outlaw. The green standard appeared dark gray in the night. Ulfrik had once been a jarl worth following, but no longer. His experiences had changed him, made him less generous and more careless with his men's lives. This entire camp was a testimony to his callous greed. All of them would die trying to climb over the walls of Paris while he accrued wealth and glory. He did not care what happened to those who served him, like his brother, Njal. His body rotted at the bottom of the ocean, and his name was hardly mentioned nor his brave deeds ever recounted.

Leaving Ulfrik and taking his treasure was more than right; it was justice.

Slipping into the tent, Humbert shuffled forward to greet him. Moonlight filtered into the tent from the open flap, and Thrand saw two shining points from Humbert's wide eyes.

"You have what we need?" he whispered in a hoarse but strong voice. The past week Ulfrik had been treating him to better food and more freedom, and his body grew straighter and stronger. Thrand considered the slave took heart from knowing his freedom was imminent.

Without a word, Thrand placed the shields and helmets on the ground, then shook out the surcoats. Humbert snatched one from his hand, holding it up.

"No blood stains on them, if that's what you're looking for. I'm not that dumb."

"And you did not drink too much today? Good. You will need a clear mind." Humbert moved with uncharacteristic confidence, nothing like the bound and beaten priest of days before. He unpinned his favorite red cloak in order to wear the surcoat. "Hurry, and get into your disguise."

In moments, Thrand and Humbert were dressed as Franks. Humbert fixed his red cloak over his shoulder while Thrand snatched two skins from the bedding in the tent. They each huddled into their furs, tucking their distinctive helmets underarm. Thrand handed a shield to Humbert. "I doubt Ulfrik will return tonight, but let's move quickly."

His neck throbbed and his breath came in ragged drags. Stepping outside the tent was his first step to a new life. His legs itched to run, but he and Humbert ducked their heads into their furs and walked as slowly and carelessly as they could contrive. At such a late hour, no one expected trouble and so the few alert sentries either ignored them or failed to spot them. Nevertheless, gaining the outer edge of the encampments felt like half a night's work. Now they turned north and strode toward the trenches.

"When do we drop the Danish disguise?" he asked Humbert. "Will the Franks see us in this light?"

"Hurry."

Humbert made no other reply, and instead began to jog. In the weak light, they located boards that crossed the trenches into the no-man's land before the tower. Bounding across these planks, Humbert dropped his fur and placed the conical helmet on his head. Then he flipped the long and pointed Frankish shield so it read easily against his silhouette. Thrand did the same. He could hear his heart beat. His head grew warm and the rush of blood thundered in his ears. If the Franks mistook Humbert, they would die. The thought repeated to the exclusion of everything else.

The tower loomed ahead. Humbert's jog increased, then skidded to a halt. Steams of foreign curses flowed and Thrand crashed into him from behind.

"A couple of Franks escaping to the tower?"

Ulfrik barred their path. Arrayed with him were Snorri, Einar, and Ander. Though they had left camp in normal clothing, all of them now wore mail that shimmered in the moonlight.

Thrand's mouth fell open, and for the first time in his life he had no words. Ulfrik's smile was that of a cat cornering a rat.

"We've been watching you, Thrand. Since that time in the woods, I've wondered what you've been about. Kolbyr looked like he had something to tell me, until you put a sword through his neck."

"Toki heard part of your talk with Humbert," Ander said. Darkness filled the creases of his frown, making him look like a troll on the hunt. "We didn't want to believe it. We all wanted to think he was still dreaming."

"You and Kolbyr were going to kill me that day, isn't it true?" Ulfrik's hand dropped to his sword hilt. "But you are a coward. Isn't that also true?"

"Why would you do this?" Snorri asked, his voice rich with anger. "If there's a treasure, we'd have shared it with you. No reason to steal it from us."

Thrand shook his head. If he fled, Ulfrik might kill him, but if he begged for mercy he might live. Ulfrik was soft enough to allow it. "Share? You think yourself a generous lord? How many of your men are prepared to die to for you, and you have no intention to share the treasure with them."

"It's a fair question." Ulfrik's hand did not stray from his sword hilt. Snorri and Einar began to move to either side, starting an encirclement Thrand doubted he could slip. "If that was in your heart, you should've asked me. All my men will benefit from whatever treasures I take, including this conniving priest's fabled gold. I will repair their homes, buy them weapons and armor, restock their flocks, and slip them gold as I can. But what would you do? Waste gold on drink and gambling, like all the other gold I've given to you. You've no thought for how I've carried you since your brother's death. Your drinking floods away all the generosity I've shown you."

Snorri and Einar moved ever wider while Ulfrik stood still. Thrand's hand flexed for his sword hilt, then Humbert shouted.

"Stop!" The command struck all of them like a slap. He threw his arms wide and looked up to the skies. He shouted something in his native language, long and tortured words. He repeated it again, and Thrand saw points of orange light gathering to one spot on the tower. Then Thrand dropped his head and slumped his shoulders.

"It is done, Lord Ulfrik. You have caught us, and we submit to you. Poor Humbert and his foolish dreams. Thrand, stay your hand and surrender to your lord. Let there be no more bloodshed, in God's name I ask this of you."

Ulfrik folded his arms and leaned back. "Such a fine speech, Humbert. Maybe your god inspires you to wisdom after all." Ulfrik and the others laughed. Humbert turned to Thrand, and nodded him forward.

Weak with defeat, Thrand agreed with Humbert and joined him

at his right side. Both bowed their heads as Snorri produced a rope and Ander came forward to seize Humbert.

"Drop your shields and weapons," Einar commanded as he reached out to grab Humbert's arm. The slave nodded.

Then chaos erupted.

Humbert jerked his shield up, slamming the rim into Ander's throat. In an instant, Humbert ripped the sax from its sheath across Thrand's lap. In one smooth motion, the blade plunged to the hilt into Ander's stomach.

Ander stumbled back, blood pouring in sheets from his mouth. No one, Thrand included, moved, but Humbert sprinted ahead.

Snorri and Einar both leapt for Ander, who collapsed at their feet. Ulfrik sprang forward, his blade half from his sheath, roaring for death. His face was etched with murderous rage, and galvanized Thrand into a run. Toki, his leg rendering him helpless, stumbled forward to Einar.

Humbert ran straight for Ulfrik, his shield braced in front of him. Ulfrik screamed and slashed with his sword. But Humbert was not there.

He ducked beneath the blow, then slung his shield into Ulfrik's unprotected shins. He let the shield fall, creating uneven footing for Ulfrik so that he careened forward. He snatched Humbert's red cloak, tearing it from the fleeing priest, but could not catch him. Humbert bolted away like a deer fleeing a hunter.

Thrand pounded after him. Ulfrik's roar made his neck hairs stand on end. His battle fury was legendary, and Thrand had seen enough of it to know he never wanted to be the target. So his legs pumped and he held close to Humbert.

The priest waved both hands in the air, screaming in Frankish. The Frankish trenches drew near, and now men threw torches down to illuminate the ground by the tower. Humbert's barrage of Frankish never ceased. Brave Danes had laid boards across the trenches, and some still remained. Humbert raced over one, and Thrand followed. Ulfrik's cries grew fainter. Clad in mail, he could not match their speed.

Humbert now banged on the iron doors. Men shouted to him, and his voice registered desperation, fear, and anger. Still the door did not open.

"You whoreson! Your head will hang from my mast. Humbert, you pig-fucking bastard, do you hear me?" Ulfrik's shape emerged from the dark, following his curses.

At last, Thrand heard the bolt drawn and the metallic clank of a door opening. Humbert shoved himself inside, and Thrand followed. He trusted the Franks more than his own people at this point.

He tumbled into a wide stone room, glowing orange with torchlight. Humbert chattered away in Frankish to six men in full mail, spears leveled. Their confused faces darted from Humbert to Thrand over and over as he rattled on in a language that sounded like a man speaking underwater. Finally, he seemed to be influencing them. The men backed away, and Humbert looked at Thrand with a face alight with victory. He raised his arm, extending a trembling finger at Thrand.

"Are we going to be safe? Did you convince them, Humbert?"

Humbert's smile threatened to split his face. He shouted one word that Thrand did not understand. "Norman!"

Six spear points jabbed into Thrand's stomach, threatening to puncture into his guts. He froze in place, careful not to help the Franks impale him.

"At last, I am home. Thanks to you and your utterly stupid companions." Humbert's Norse flowed clearly, with a command and arrogance Thrand only heard from jarls. "My name is Humbert no longer. I am Anscharic, a noble of the Ile de France. And you, swine, are my prisoner."

22

The long walk back from Ander's burial mound passed in silence. His death replayed constantly in Ulfrik's mind: him crashing to his knees, blood flowing over his chest, all his strength draining into the dirt as he flopped to his side. Ulfrik stumbled on a rock hidden in the brown grass as the small procession shambled back to camp. *Like that rock, I never saw the attack coming,* he chided himself. *I underestimated the foe and a good man paid for it with his life.*

The mass of white tents were cheerful in the cold, clear morning sun. Smoke from cooking fires billowed up across the sprawling camps, and men tended their duties uncaring and unknowing of the death of the night before. So many fine men like Ander had died that one more made no difference to anyone but close companions.

Ulfrik's new men were scattered throughout the camp, sharpening weapons, checking belts, carrying water back from the river, and all other manner of chores. They hardly knew each other, but were united in their loss of lords and friends and the need for a new leader. No one spoke as the procession of Ander's friends, with Ulfrik at the lead, joined them. The men of Nye Grenner had dwindled to nearly half their number, and Ander's loss pained them. Yet none suffered the pain more than Ulfrik.

"Do you need anything?" Toki asked Ulfrik, hobbling up with his crutch.

"Leave me to my thoughts. I'll be in my tent." He turned toward Paris, clouds of smoke rising where fires had started from the constant barrages of the remaining catapults. "I am counting the days to those walls come down."

Ducking inside the tent, the air was warm on his face. He threw his helmet onto the floor and stripped off his mail, having worn it to Ander's burial. Sitting on the pile of skins that made his bed, he put his hands over his head. The names and faces of all his lost men, not just Ander, jumbled in his thoughts. So many had died in a lightning flash of violence, only now could he count the cost. Tears began to bead at his eyes for those he led to death.

The flap of his tent opened and Snorri ducked inside. His face was slack and tired as he lowered himself opposite Ulfrik. The two stared at each other long moments, then Ulfrik dropped his head and clasped his hands behind his neck.

"If Ander could read the futhark, then why did he not see this? Why did he have to die at the hands of a slave?"

"Maybe he did see it." Snorri's gruff voice was low and thoughtful. "No true warrior wants to die in his bed anyway."

"I have led too many men to death here. Thrand's treachery was enough, but then to couple it with murder. And Humbert. That turd will pay for this. We are here because of him."

"We're here because this is our chance at being more than farmers."

"No!" Ulfrik snapped, staring into Snorri's eyes. "Ander came here on the promise of gold. Thrand betrayed me for the same gold. Humbert lured us to our deaths. My men are rotting at the feet of Paris because of him! What glory is to be had here, falling from high ladders or being burned to death by an enemy out of reach?"

Ulfrik's temples throbbed and his eyes grew hot. Snorri's gaze faltered and the two sat in tense silence.

"A good leader grieves for his men," Snorri said. "It is a hard thing to bear, knowing you've ordered them to death. But your oath-holder has asked this task of you, no matter what else motivated us. Do not shoulder a burden you don't need, lad. We're in for a long wait yet, and you have to hold up."

Turning his head aside from Snorri, whose words rang true but seemed impossible to heed, his eyes fell on the ball of Humbert's cloak. He had retained it as a reminder of the slave's treachery.

"This is Humbert's cloak," he said as he gathered it into his fist, holding it before Snorri's sweating face. "It belonged to his father and he held it dear. It will be my new standard. I will fly it beneath my banner and will not remove it until Humbert is dead."

"He deserves death." Snorri grabbed a hank of the cloak and held it up. "Fly it from the banner pole, let the worm see it flying so he knows we come for him."

Ulfrik nodded, blinking away the wetness from his eyes. "For Ander and all who have wasted their lives for his treachery, Humbert will die. Let's go tie this rag to the banner pole."

The two of them exited from the tent, and crashed into Hrolf who was about to enter. Gunther and Mord accompanied him. Stepping back from the tent, Hrolf's expression was grave. "I heard what happened, and I came as soon as I could."

His appearance was so unexpected and uncommon that both Ulfrik and Snorri cooled. They exchanged confused glances, Snorri finding words sooner than Ulfrik. "Thank you for coming, Jarl Hrolf. You bring honor and glory to Ander's memory."

"I cannot admit I knew him well, but he served loyally and so dies with honor. We will revel together in the feasting hall one day." His expression shifted, the contrived sorrow slipping enough for Ulfrik to notice. He addressed him in a lowered voice. "I want to speak with you a moment."

The two walked off a short distance, leaving Snorri with Gunther and Mord. "There is celebration in Paris this morning," Hrolf said as they walked toward the edge of camp. "Do you know why?"

Ulfrik shook his head. Hrolf nodded and gave a slight laugh.

"A great nobleman has returned to them. Anscharic is his name, though you might know him as Humbert."

An ember dropped into his stomach. "My slave? He was a noble? Is that why they opened the gates at his command?"

Hrolf nodded, smiling without humor. "The Franks are shouting the news from their walls. A valuable ransom was in your hands, and he has escaped to give the Franks hope. They say Anscharic's brother will send his army to aid Paris."

Ulfrik stopped walking, his mouth open but no words forming. Hrolf stared at him, appraising him with a shrewd eye.

"You didn't know this already?" Ulfrik shook his head. "Though you only brought one slave with you, who happened to be a noble worth a mighty ransom. Are you certain? Be honest with me."

"Of course I didn't know." Ulfrik blinked several times, his mind grappling with this impossible news. "How can this be true? I found him in Norway, almost at the edge of the world. Why would a Frankish lord be there?"

"Fate," Hrolf snapped, then turned back toward Gunther. "Fate had a plan for him and wove you into it. Anyway, once we crack Paris's walls, realize that you no longer have a claim on him. His ransom will be mine, if anyone sworn to me captures him. I want that to be clear, though I will be generous with you for your part in this."

"I've sworn to kill him."

"That's not a problem. Just kill him after I collect his ransom." Hrolf left Ulfrik standing alone among the bobbing white tents.

Fate had struck him a blow, and he wondered if the Three Norns who wove the destinies of all men were truly done with this thread. He suspected they had only begun.

23

December 21, 885 CE

Runa sprawled out on her back, cold and damp mud seeping through her cloak and clothes. Sweat steamed on her forehead, and she stared vacantly at the star-flecked indigo sky overhead. Her sword and shield remained in her hands, but the grip was weak. She closed her eyes and sighed.

"Get up, Mother!" Gunnar called, while his two friends laughed. "You can still beat him."

"Whatever light touches these islands will soon be gone." Konal's smiling face moved into her view of the sky. "Let's end today's practice. Besides, it's Yuletide."

Thrusting his sword into its sheath, Konal extended his hand to her. He defeated her nine times out of ten, but it never discouraged her. It angered her. Ulfrik had shown her all she needed to know, and she only lacked strength and practice. She accepted Konal's hand, letting her long sword and shield drop away as he hoisted her.

"Thank you," she said with a smile, looking into his eyes. He raised his brow at the sudden closeness and opened his mouth to speak.

Runa stepped on his foot and shoved him back. He tumbled like a falling tree, and Runa pulled her sax from the sheath and touched it to the inside of his thigh. "I never said I yielded."

The three boys observing their practice cheered and clapped. Konal's face reddened, but his frown vanished beneath his own laughter. Then he pulled his leg away from the blade, and swept Runa's feet with his other foot. She again found herself laid out in the grass, the boys' cheering turning to angry shouts.

"I never yielded either," he said, and groaned as he stood.

"You cheated!" Gunnar came to Runa's side, and put his arms around her shoulders. "He's a cheater."

Runa laughed, then sat up. "There is no cheating where there is no rule. Konal's a good fighter, and we are all learning from him."

They collected their weapons and swords, old gear that Ulfrik had not considered useful enough to take. Konal knew how to maintain them, and had restored their edges and worked off the rust. He picked Runa's long sword from the grass and wiped the damp from it with his cloak.

"Your mother would best most men I know," he said as he worked out the last of the dirt from the blade. "They rely on luck and a good war cry to carry them. Only the best train every day like your mother."

"I'm practicing every day, too." Gunnar extended his arm to his two friends. "We all are."

"And getting better with each drill." Konal sheathed the blade and presented both his sword and the other to Runa.

"You may wear yours into the hall, you know. You have earned my trust as well as the others'. We might even feel better if you did."

Konal stepped back, his brows knitting together. "Only the jarl wears weapons in the hall. If your husband returned to find me wearing a sword in his home, what would happen?"

"I would tell him I allowed it."

Leaving him to consider his choices, she gathered Gunnar under her arm and started for the hall. Yellow light leaked from the small windows covered with hides. Wearing pants, carrying shield and sword, she felt uncomfortable facing the rest of the community. People indulged her, a few like Elin even encouraged her, but it went against her upbringing. She knew who gossiped in her absence. Not everyone could accept such actions, even if done for the good of the community.

Heat warmed her face as she entered the hall. Gunnar split from under her arm to greet a group of his friends who had gathered for the Yuletide feast. Elin had organized the entire meal, and now stood by the hearth directing the younger women. She noticed Runa, eyes shooting to the mud stains on her clothes, and gave a disapproving scowl. "You can't wear muddy clothes to Yuletide."

"I am getting better every day," Runa said, passing through the hall for her room. "Don't let Konal know I've gone easy on him. I don't want the poor boy to feel weak."

Elin laughed as Runa left the warm glow of the hearth for the cool darkness of her room. A girl carried a lamp to her, looked at her pants, then left with a giggle. *Not much of an example for the girls*, she thought, closing the door. Outside, voices of people gathering for the feast grew louder, and she changed out of her soiled clothing. Yuletide had come, and with it a poor feast and a humble celebration. She sat on her bed, and drew her scabbarded sax to her lap. She fingered the hilt, wondering if she should wear it.

No word had come from Ulfrik on the last trading ship to visit them before winter made ocean travel too deadly. She had not expected any, but did get word that Ingrid and Halla who governed the north of the island fared well. No direct news from them was even more disconcerting. *Ulfrik would visit them*, she thought, *and remind them of his rule. It's much easier for a man, especially one with warriors at his back.*

She strapped on the sword and rejoined the main hall. Fewer people joined each year, but this Yuletide was nearly all women and children with gray-haired people speckled in between. A Yule log sat along a wall by the high table, decorated with candles. She had paid good silver to the traders so her hall could have a log for the celebration. In days past, she would have scoffed at the cost in such lean times, but Ulfrik would have insisted. He would tell her the people need to celebrate more than ever, and she did not disagree. A figure of the winter ram sat on the stand beside it, cleverly woven from branches and dried grasses.

Thora delivered Hakon to Runa, and she greeted him with kisses on the head and sat him on her lap. Happy voices filled the room with a comfortable, warm buzz. Elin and her girls were ready to serve and so Runa sat at the high table with Gunnar and the families of his friends. Ulfrik's spot on the bench always remained empty. Gunnar pressed to her side, and she patted his head.

Konal stood by the door, chatting with some of the older boys who followed him everywhere. He had become a hero to the boys left behind who longed to join their brothers and fathers in adventure. His stories were exaggerations of the greatest sort, but they eased tensions and so Runa tolerated them. She noticed he wore the sword she had given him, and placed the other beside the door. If it offended anyone, all appeared absorbed in quiet conversation and unconcerned.

Gunnar tugged her sleeve, drawing her out of her thoughts. "Allow Konal to sit with us. I want to hear his story about Old Man Winter again."

The space beside her remained empty, and it felt wrong at Yule-tide. Her palm stroked the smooth wood, and she smiled at Gunnar. "Very well."

She caught his eye and beckoned him to the table. Picking his way through the tables, he wore a sheepish smile. "I see you've changed your clothes to something more befitting the jarl's wife."

"And though you're still covered in mud, I've been asked to invite you to my table."

"We want to hear about Old Man Winter again." Gunnar stood, and stepped from his bench. "Take my seat."

"There's room here." Runa could not look directly at Konal. "Sit beside me for the feast."

Konal approached as if he feared the charge of a hidden boar. He paused before the open seat. Runa noted Elin and a few other heads turn toward them. "Are you sure?"

"My son has asked for you, and I spoil him. Sit and celebrate Yuletide with us as you would with your own family."

The warmth of him next to her was comforting. He was big, solid, and confident. She was tired of trying to be all of those things for her people. Even if it was foolishness, a man's presence beside her gave her freedom to enjoy the celebrations.

Meager bowls of salted whale meat and onions in soup and half mugs of beer comprised their feast. Her stomach rumbled, having only eaten a little at breakfast. Even still, she scooped out portions of meat into Gunnar's bowl. Konal watched this, blushed, and began eating. A few moments later, he spooned chunks of meat into Runa's bowl.

"I'm used to eating much less. Being at sea, you know."

The celebration stretched on. Ornolf, the old man who had helped rescue Konal, played songs on a cow horn pipe. The older men recounted brave fights and outrageous legends. Riddles were asked and answered. Konal shared his stories of Old Man Winter and of his mystifying homeland, Ireland. Such a place with such people seemed impossible to Runa, but then neither would she have believed in the Faereyar Islands were they not her home. The celebration lacked the drunken raucousness and levity the men always added. From the heavy sighs and faraway looks of the other women, she knew she was not alone.

By the end of the celebration, Konal remained with her on the bench, though many others had returned home or found a place to sleep on the floor. Gunnar had curled up under the bench with his cloak covering all but the top of his head. Thora had long since taken Hakon to his bed.

"This is the greatest Yuletide I can remember," Konal said, turning on the bench to face her.

"I've had a few worse, but many better. It was not much of a feast, not even a proper meal."

"It is a difficult time for your people. But it seems odd that no one exchanged gifts. You don't have such a custom here?"

Runa laughed. "Food and health are gifts enough. With the men gone, and threats from the north, no one thinks of gifts."

Konal nodded and stroked his beard in thought. Then he sat up straighter and smiled. "As your guest, it is shameless of me to have no gift."

"You were wrecked at sea. No one expects you to have prepared a gift."

"Ah, but I have!" He reached to his neck and pulled open his gold torc. Holding it in both hands, he offered it to her. "Gold. Only the slightest bit that I owe you for saving my life."

Runa leaned back as if he waved fire at her. Glancing about, no one else observed them. "That is a heavy gift, and I cannot accept it."

"Do not insult me, but take it." He smiled wider, and slid closer on the bench. "This is a trifle to me, no matter how valuable you think it is. Would you not exchange gold for your life and think it a worthy trade?"

The gold sparkled in the low light, winking orange points playing on its coiled edges. Up close it looked smaller than it did on Konal's neck.

"Your people would benefit from such a gift."

"Food is better than gold."

"But you will take this anyway. With my gratitude."

He slid closer, gesturing to clasp the torc to her neck. Her breath became shorter and her heart pounded. His rough hands brushed aside her hair, then gently pulled the torc onto her neck. The cool metal made her skin tingle, weaving from the base of her neck down to her toes. Pulling the pliant metal together, he leaned ever closer. Runa felt herself falling toward him, his smiling face and bright eyes filling her vision. His hands slid to her shoulders.

Jolting back, she nearly tumbled from the bench. Konal fell away, his face flushed. She stared at him, horrified.

"Your presumption is staggering." Her voice fluttered with

emotion, but she did not want attention and held it low. "You cannot buy me with gifts of gold."

"That was not my intention," he said, voice loud enough to cause Gunnar to stir and head lowered in sleep to rise.

"Your intentions are clear enough." She stooped to rouse Gunnar, who moaned but sat up squinting in the low light. "Good night to you, Konal."

Dragging Gunnar to her bedroom, she left Konal on the bench with his head lowered in shame. She closed the door, flung the gold torc into a corner, and went to bed. Within moments, she rose again and drew the bar lock across the door, unsheathed her short sword, and rested it against the bed.

24

January 29, 886 CE

Thin ice clung to the banks of the Seine where Ulfrik stared at the smoke from the roofs of Paris curling into the smudgy winter sky. The walls were chipped and cracked, stained with age and streaked with burns, but still encircled the island city. The air smelled of burning wood and mud, which sucked at his boots and seeped into his toes as he paced the banks. Mord and Toki joined him in his daily routine of glaring at the city and its stubborn towers. If angry stares and mumbled curses could break stone walls, Paris would have long been turned to rubble.

The catapult on the opposite bank snapped forward, launching a dead cow over the walls. Ulfrik could not help laughing at the ridiculous shape of a cow flying through the air, something he never expected possible. After all these idle months, catapult ammunition had been depleted and now only shot carcasses or trash. Two of the remaining three had broken beyond repair, and the strange olive-skinned men who mastered them had either died or fled. Only one remained with a lonely crew who barely knew their machine. In the mist beyond, the silhouette of the mired siege tower threatened to fall over. Men gambled on the day it would crash in final defeat.

Ships without crews drifted at anchor along the Seine. They tugged at their ropes, as if wanting to flee the city and sail north again. The others gathered next to him.

"How many of those ships have been emptied of their crews?" Toki asked.

"Dozens of ships have been orphaned," Mord answered. He kicked a rock out of the mud, then tossed it at Paris. "Hundreds died on those walls, and others have disappeared into the countryside. We might soon have only ghosts to sail those ships."

"The new men mix well with ours," Ulfrik said, aiming for a more positive conversation. "They're eager to prove themselves, and get rich."

"No one came here for any other purpose." Toki stood aside Ulfrik and Mord, all three men squinting at the gray tableau before them. "Raiding hasn't been too much profit, not with all the nearby churches sacked."

"We'll have to take them farther afield to fresh lands," Ulfrik said. "They've fought well enough beside our Nye Grenner men. A few I've been glad to see leave us, but most are good men. It's a shame to waste them sitting in trenches and staring at walls that never change."

"Lord Ulfrik," Mord said. "My father believes these Franks cannot last much longer and their will to fight is thin. Their emperor is in a far off land I've never heard of before, and he cannot protect them."

"Humbert claimed the Christian god protects this city, and I wonder if it's true." Ulfrik glanced at both men, whose frowns deepened."Maybe our gods cannot fight the Christian god in his lands. If Ander were alive, I'd ask him to cast his rune sticks and tell us."

The sober thought silenced the group. Ulfrik bit his lip, wishing he could find a way through the walls. The bridges and their towers had halted all progress. Any attempt to move past them, even on foot, was impossible. Days earlier, Sigfrid had filled the shallows by the southern tower with debris and felled trees and tried to march men past it. Arrows and fire rebuffed them, and the garbage now clung to the pilings of the wooden bridge. As long as the bridges held, Paris could not be bypassed or surrounded. With only two hundred men to defend it, Paris could not stand if surrounded by all the Danes at once.

"Curse those bridges," Ulfrik muttered.

"Maybe ghost crews could sail ghost ships over the bridges," Mord said with a laugh. "It might be the only way to get through them."

"Ghost ships ..." The words slipped from Ulfrik's mouth as a plan formed in a flash. It was daring plan, and a bold plan, entertainment for the gods, and it was bobbing on the waters before him every day since they had dug into their trenches. "Mord, that is what we are going to use. Ghost ships!"

"I told you not to eat the eels from this river. They're no good for your head." Toki guffawed but Mord understood immediately.

"The abandoned ships, your want to use them to defeat the bridges."

Ulfrik was already stomping through the mud to find Hrolf. "We're going to send those ships up the river and through the wooden bridge. It's coming down before this day is over."

Heart racing, he had found a way through this stalemate. His thoughts turned to family, *Runa, I might yet be home by summer!*

"YOU ARE either a brave man or a fool." Hrolf looped his arm around Ulfrik's shoulders as they stood facing the river, far downstream from Paris. "But if this succeeds, your name will live forever."

"It is my desire and plan that more than my name lives on."

Hrolf laughed, but Ulfrik studied the three ships lashed together in the middle of the river. Ghost ships was the name Mord gave them that morning, a fitting description. The men who had widowed these ships would now take revenge on the city, if only as ghosts sailing with Ulfrik. Behind him, scores of men came to watch the start of the spectacle. Many more had gathered closer to the wooden bridge, ready to follow on the collision of the ships with the bridge. Loud voices proclaimed victory and celebrated the vengeance awaiting them in Paris. Ulfrik shared their lusts, but did not share their confidence in utter victory.

Men who had completed loading barrels of oil on the ships now pulled away in small, flat-bottomed boats. Wind bent the tops of distant trees, their bare branches like skeletal hands pointing towards Paris.

"It is time," Ulfrik said to Hrolf. Gunther stood at his right, his single eye squinting at him.

"Your son wanted to join me, but I forbade it. Then he told me he could swim, and that might be useful."

Gunther nodded, but did not reply. Hrolf guided Ulfrik by his arm. "Go to meet Sigfrid before you begin. He will steal your glory if this scheme works, but scorn you if it fails. You are certain of your plan?"

Ulfrik glanced at Mord who waited with Toki and Snorri by the small boat that would ferry them to the ships. "I am. But Sigfrid has been as useful as a twig in a sword fight. Everyone will know what I did for this siege before the sun sets."

Hrolf hissed but kept a smile as they neared Sigfrid and his circle of jarls and hirdmen. "Be more respectful of Sigfrid, even if you're not off the mark. Don't bring me troubles, Ulfrik."

"Another great plan from your clever man!" Sigfrid wore his mail and sword, a shield slung cross his back and a dented helmet tucked under arm. His clear eyes gleamed with excitement as he strode forward to clasp Ulfrik's arm. "You are a brave one too. If you succeed, I will cover your arms in gold bands."

Not even meeting Ulfrik's eyes, he turned to the gathered crowd and sought their admiration for generosity. The sycophantic group cheered or stomped their feet.

"You are a generous lord," Ulfrik said, inclining his head.

"I am here to offer you my aid," he said with a sudden and feigned gravity.

By drowning in your armor? he thought, and the vision of Sigfrid toppling from the ship in his armor made him smile. "Granting me three ships is aid enough."

Sigfrid had claimed all the widowed ships that he could, which Ulfrik heard had caused friction with Hrolf. Few things were more valuable than a good ship. Sigfrid hugged Ulfrik, then pushed him toward the others as the crowd shouted encouragement.

"You are all brave men," he said when they arrived at the banks. Toki had already boarded the boat, and stood when Sigfrid addressed them. "Destroy that bridge, and show these Franks they are not so cunning as they think."

Ulfrik sat with his three companions as Sigfrid and another man helped launch their boat. Toki began to row as they slipped into deeper waters, and the crowd at the river bank began to move upstream for a better view of the attack.

"Sigfrid will cover my arms in gold bands if we succeed."

Snorri rolled his eyes and Toki chuckled. Mord spit into the river, a sour twist on his face. "Aye, and then he'll cut them off your dead body when no one suspects. My father doesn't trust him, at least where gold is concerned."

Ulfrik raised his brow at Mord, but then they arrived at the ships. They were not high-sided ships which was likely why Sigfrid parted with them. Once on the deck of the first ship, Ulfrik patted the rails. "Unless the wind gusts, these ships aren't going to be strong enough to take down the bridge."

"Aren't we supposed to burn it down?" Toki asked as he and the others worked to set the sail.

"I wanted bigger ships to burn longer and brighter, and do more structural damage." Running his hand along the rail, he walked to the stern and placed the rudder into the water. "But it seems Sigfrid wants all the best ships and all of Paris."

"Typical of his kind," Snorri said. "And the rest of us suffer for his gain."

The gods blessed Ulfrik's gambit with an advantageous wind. The sail of the first ship filled and already it struggled against the current. They spread out to the other ships, and once all sails had been hoisted, the vessels strained to race forward in the wind. They tied the tillers in place, bound their small boat for their escape, and each man took position on a ship with Ulfrik and Toki together. Their knives ready to cut free from the anchor stones. All three looked to Ulfrik for the signal. He cast one glance at the gray walls of Paris, seeking for another sign of the gods' favor. Nothing but smoke and gray skies lifted above it. Spitting on the deck, he raised his arm. "Cut us free!"

All three men sawed furiously until the ropes snapped. Snorri's ship, which towed their escape boat, lurched forward and the other ships jerked in response. Ulfrik grabbed the rail, then Toki's rope snapped away. The extra force broke Mord's middle ship free and he stumbled backwards and landed on the deck. The ships moved as one, and all laughed at Mord's fall.

The wind on Ulfrik's face made him miss the open sea. Sailing on a river, even one as wide as the Seine, was a pale comparison. For a short time, they only had to make minor adjustments as the bridge came into view. Its low profile of interlaced supports and beams was a formidable barrier. But it was wood, and therefore vulnerable.

"Set this ship afire," he said.

"We are not close enough yet."

"If it is not well aflame by the time it strikes the bridge, the Franks might douse the fire. You've seen their tricks."

The ships sliced across the waters, sails fat and masts creaking. Already Franks were scurrying along the tops of Paris's walls. Men filed onto the bridge.

Toki dug into a bag containing touchwood and striking steel, while Ulfrik used a hand ax to smash open kegs of oil. Both Mord and Snorri followed, and began splashing oil on the decks.

Toki was already crossing to Mord's ship. Ulfrik bounded after him. Holding a smoldering strip of the velvety touchwood, he tore off a piece and flung it into the oil. Fire caught in a breathless rush as Ulfrik landed on the deck. Streamers of flame sprouted wherever oil had splashed, running up the mast and rigging. The bridge was still distant, but archers were attempting to fire on them. The wind frustrated their shots, slapping the arrows into the water prematurely. Soon the range would close and the three ships would be strafed stem to stern.

They all backed into Snorri's ship, who had already let himself down into the escape boat. Toki repeated his steps, throwing a bit of smoldering touchwood strip into the oil. The first ship blazed like a god of fire, black smoke flowing off it in wind-flattened clouds.

"The last one and then over the side," Ulfrik said. Through the smoke he saw archers lining up their bows, pointed at the decks. Toki straddled the rail, prepared to start the fire and drop into Snorri's boat. Mord hurried toward him.

Then fire bloomed everywhere.

Toki screamed, ribbons of fire on his arm, and he fell overboard. Mord disappeared behind a wall of flame.

Ulfrik's hands and pants had been splashed with oil.

The world slowed. His thoughts were measured, too calm to be any use. *The wind blew a spark to this ship. How could I have been so stupid? And I've made myself a torch with this oil.*

As slow as if it were all a dream, black shafts arced down and sank into the burning deck. Flames ringed him, and his pants were on fire. He was alone on the ship. It was as though he had endless time to contemplate the situation. Looking up, the burning sail threatened to enfold him in fire as it sagged and snapped from the spar.

I'd rather drown than burn. I wish I had learned to swim. Though he ran for the bow where no fire had yet bit the wood, it felt as if he walked. The dive into the water took long enough for him to remember Runa, his boys, all of his life. Even his mother, a face long forgotten, came to his thoughts.

As cold and dark water enveloped him, turning the world to blurry darkness and muffled noises of cracking wood, time snapped back to reality. Panic seized him and he nearly opened his mouth to scream.

He scrabbled at the water as if he could climb out of it, but his hands found nothing to grab. He was going to drown, his body drawn down into the river muck to rot at the foot of the walls of Paris.

25

Thrand's head lolled in the darkness. Weak from scant food and drink, he lacked strength to hold up his head. The cell smelled of his waste, and in the dark he often rolled through it or placed his hand in it. Lice and fleas devoured his flesh. Loneliness and silence devoured his heart. He saw a guard once daily, or so he assumed, but it was only to have food shoved through the bottom of the door. Hard bread and gritty water were all he received, and he supplemented with cockroaches or rats if he could catch them. He feared rats would soon nibble at his feet, and then his face. He often awoke from dreams where rats tore his flesh with sharp yellow teeth.

Kolbyr began to visit him, sitting in the darkness in silence until Thrand begged him to leave. He could not see him, but knew it was him from the ragged gasping and scent of blood. Other times, someone sat beside him in the darkness. Whoever it was listened to Thrand speak until the figure stood and disappeared. These must have been ghosts of former prisoners. At first he complained to the ghosts for his treatment, but their silence defeated him. As weeks passed, he began to explain why he betrayed Ulfrik and even sought to kill him. Yet the spirits reminded him that much of his memories were not true. Ulfrik had not mistreated him, but carried him when others might have let him drown in mead. Many long arguments with the ghosts ended with Thrand unable to remember what had driven his spite. Was it truly drink? The ghosts never answered and Kolbyr only wheezed and bled in the impenetrable dark.

Time meant nothing now. He hung his head and drool seeped onto his chest as he waited for death. Humbert, or whatever his name was, had thrown him into this pit to die by slow starvation.

The heavy sound of a wooden bar being drawn roused him. He thought food had already been delivered, but time made no more sense in the unremitting blackness. Yellow light flickered through the small window, and like a trained dog Thrand crawled forward to the door slot to receive his bread and water.

He heard a strange sound, like metal tumbling, then another bar drawn. The door swept inward, batting Thrand away like a dried husk. The torchlight blazed and he threw his arms over his eyes. Franks began shouting at him, as at least two entered into the room. A sharp point jabbed his thigh and he cried out. Strong hands drew him up and yanked him out of the cell.

A bag of scratchy cloth slipped over his head and his arms were yanked to his back and tied. More Frankish babble followed, and the point at his back prodded him forward. He stumbled until he crashed on a stone step, the pain in his knees jolting through him like darts. The Franks cursed and picked him up, a man on each side guiding him up the stairs.

The air became fresher and cooler. Sounds of a tolling bell reached him as he struggled to keep pace with his captors. More Franks joined them, and they exchanged words before Thrand heard another door open. The light penetrating the sack was bright and yellow. His captors shoved him outside of a building. A bracing cold enveloped him and no air ever smelled or tasted so clean, even inside a dirty cloth bag. The bell tolled like thunder and foreign voices swarmed from all around.

The men hustled him along, and Thrand sensed a crowd forming. Then curses came, followed by objects that struck Thrand by surprise. A woman's voice shouted tearful curses in his face, until his guards shoved her back. He endured the swears and projectiles, smiling. Anything was better than the dark cell of rats and ghosts.

Entering another building, the angry cacophony muted as a door slammed behind. Many more Franks surrounded him, and a strong hand grasped his arm. A short walk delivered him to another room, where the hand forced him to his knees. A spear tip touched the dry skin of his neck.

"I'm not going to move, I swear it." He doubted anyone understood, but hearing his own language, even from his own mouth, calmed him.

The bag ripped away and cool air and strong light dazzled him. His eyes pulsed white, then adjusted. He sat on a floor of flagstone in a room with narrow windows up high, blue daylight pouring down. The place was as large as a hall, but decorated unlike anything he had ever seen. He only had a scant moment to take in the tapestries, candle stands, shields, and furniture lining the walls. The spear tip returned to his neck, and at the end of it was a leering Frank with curling blond hair and only three teeth in his mouth. He was dressed in mail, pierced and stained with blood and rust. He barked at him in his strange language.

"He wants you to know death is only as far away as the point of his spear." The clear Norse echoed around the room, coming from directly ahead.

Thrand peered into the shadows, seeing the forms of several men, one who was seated in a large chair of dark wood. His weak eyes adjusted and the forms became clearer.

"You may stand and approach, but stop on my order." The words repeated in Frankish, and the toothless Frank retracted his spear enough for Thrand to rise. He stepped carefully until the seated man raised his hand to stop him.

"Humbert!" Thrand could scarcely believe the transformation. They had traded bodies, it seemed. Thrand looked at his trembling, wasted arms and then at Humbert. He remained thin, but his face was full of vigor and his posture straight and strong. Dark circles ringed his eyes, but they flashed with intelligence and delight. His gray hair was neatly combed and his beard trimmed. He wore fine linen clothes and a golden cross. Tears welled in Thrand's eyes. "What have you done to me?"

"No more than what you deserved, and probably less than that." Humbert stood, and the two armed men beside him straightened as he did. "For a long time I planned to let the rats take you. I still may, but it depends on what you say and what Brocard thinks." He pointed at the gap-toothed Frank, who smiled at the mention of his name.

Thrand glanced at Brocard, but his vision was captured by the riches surrounding him. His eyes widened as he realized the candle holders were gold, and plates of silver sat on tables covered in finely embroidered cloth. The riches of Paris were true after all, just beyond his reach. Humbert laughed at Thrand's gawking.

"You must learn my proper name: Anscharic. Knowing it might save your life one day." He stepped closer to Thrand, though he leaned away and waved the air before his nose. "By God, I didn't think it possible for your kind to smell worse."

"You left me to die in a pit. What should I smell like?"

Humbert's explosive laughter passed to the men-at-arms. "Your defiance remains intact, typical of men whose last possession is pride. Let me correct that misplaced confidence. The ignorant barbarians that took you to Paris have been trying to get around two towers for the last three months. Even with their numbers and war machines, they've failed. Yesterday they tried to burn down the Little Bridge by setting three ships aflame and ramming it. Do you know what happened?"

Thrand shook his head.

"The ships burned so fast that they sank before the Little Bridge caught a spark. Your people can't even manage to start a fire without a mistake." Anscharic laughed again, puncturing it with bits of Frankish to bring his men into the joke. The room vibrated with their laughter.

Thrand's mind raced over the news. Nothing had gone right since coming to Paris. If the Franks would be victorious, he wanted to be in their good graces.

"Oh, Anscharic! I am sorry!" He crashed to his knees, the suddenness of it drawing Brocard's spear to his neck. "Ulfrik told me to mistreat you. He wanted your secrets and thought I could pry them from you with violence. He wanted me to push you closer to him, so you would confide the truth. I swear it."

Fleshy bags obscured Anscharic's eyes as he smiled. "You're a creative liar, Thrand. Remain on your knees and hear what I say. This rendezvous has already cost me more time than I wanted. You have a choice. The first is the easiest to answer. Do you want to return to the donjon, the pit as you called it?"

"Never!" He threw himself flat, shuddering as tears began to flow. "The pit is haunted. Please, I will do anything you ask if it means I can stay free of that place."

Anscharic nodded, stepping around Thrand, who remained prostrate. "Then you will take my second choice: freedom."

Thrand grew still, unsure of what he had heard. He remained facedown, waiting for Anscharic to elaborate. He heard feet shuffle a few more steps before stopping. He raised his head slowly, bumping the spear aimed at the back of his neck. He turned to the side, looking at Anscharic's clean boots. "Did you offer me freedom?"

"Freedom with a duty, but freedom nonetheless." He muttered a few Frankish words and Brocard's spear lifted. "Stand up. In return for your freedom, you will lead a party of men through the surrounding enemy. Six men, including you, will dress as Danes and leave the city during the night. My people travel on important business, which does not concern you. Your only duty, which will secure your freedom, is to be the face of your group when meeting others of your kind. You speak to them, give them names to soothe suspicions, ensure the details of your barbaric traditions are observed. You go where the group leads, and once arrived at that place you are free."

Thrand put his hand to his heart, feeling it thunder. A smile cracked his face, an expression he had nearly forgotten. Anscharic's eyes drew to slits as he regarded him, and he continued.

"If you think of running off or alerting the Danes to the truth of your disguises, you will die. I suppose you might sacrifice yourself to help your former friends, but I don't see you doing so. That's one reason I selected you for this task. Know that all the men with you understand Norse and speak it, though not fluently enough to pass as a true barbarian. But if you alert anyone, your five companions' first priority will be to kill you. That is my will, and they are loyal men. The swords I will provide you are rusted in their sheaths, and have blunted cutting edges. Don't count on them in a fight. Can I trust this to you?"

"Humb ... Anscharic, I will be as loyal as any of your men! Your mercy, it's unexpected. You are a true lord."

"Dear God, Thrand, you are a worm. Then it is settled. You will be fed well, and then released tonight."

Thrand burned to smash Anscharic's smug expression; his hands tensed with the urge. The gold of his cross sparked in the light from above, and Thrand wanted to rip it from his chest. Despite all of his fury, his voice was servile. "I will do as you say, and will ever be grateful for your help. But what do I do after my freedom?"

"A good question, one that I'm glad you mentioned." Anscharic snapped orders to Brocard, who argued with him before being silenced with an up-turned hand. Brocard and his men moved to leave the room, but he pushed his face into Thrand's before exiting.

"We go outside. Be good, or die."

"He will be one of your group," Anscharic said. Thrand watched in shock as the three men left and closed the door. "He's worried that you will do something foolish, like grab the dagger in my belt. Would you do that?"

He had not noticed the dagger with jewels in its sheath and pommel until Anscharic patted it. Hands trembling again, he forced a smile. "I would be a fool. You are a much better fighter than you seem."

Seemingly pleased, he clasped his hands behind his back and began to circle Thrand. "My family has fought your kind for generations. We kept your people as slaves. I learned my Norse from them, so I would never be ignorant of what my sworn enemies planned. My father, who has gone to God's kingdom, taught me my Latin and my swordsmanship."

"What has this to do with my freedom, lord?" He added the title, if only to soften the words.

Rather than snap at him, Anscharic paused and touched his cross. "It has everything to do with it. My father died fighting your kind, dragged into the mud by a berserker's ax. His men could not recover his body, but carried away but one possession of my father's."

"His robe."

"Yes, you remember." His eyes shimmered with tears and his mouth quivered as he held Thrand's gaze. "That robe is all that is left of my father. Yes, lands and possessions passed to me and my brother. But that cloak, he wore it to battle and died in it. It is more important to me than any of his inheritance, a mere rag to others but a treasure to me. Surely, as a warrior, you understand this. It was his battle cloak, a talisman."

"You lost it the night we fled here."

Anscharic closed his eyes, and a tear streaked from beneath his lid. "Yes. Ulfrik snatched it from me, and I could not turn back for it. Once you are freed, if you can find my father's cloak and deliver it to me, I will pay you the fortune you expected to find here."

Heart pounding again, he stammered his reply. "Of course, lord! Yes, I will get it for you."

"You can tell Ulfrik you escaped, then steal the cloak. Before you leave I will show you how to signal my men, and you will be let in. Not only would you have a fortune, but my gratitude and forgiveness. Would you be willing to accept baptism, you may even serve me. Do not fear the defeat of this city, for God will not let these walls crumble to your heathen kind."

"Of course I will accept baspism ... bapim, er, yes! A fortune and forgiveness and a place in your city." He only wanted the treasure, and the other promises were suspect at best. However, he was eager to make Anscharic happy enough to let him out of the city and perhaps trade that rag for gold. Then he remembered, and his face fell.

"What is it? Do you think I make empty promises?"

"No, Hum ... lord. Ulfrik will not take me back. He knows I planned to kill him once."

Anscharic stared at Thrand as if he no longer recognized him. His jaw twitched and he began to pace again. "I did not know this, but if you tried to kill Ulfrik, why are you alive?"

"I shifted blame to Kolbyr, then killed him. Ulfrik knows the truth now."

Anscharic gave a vague laugh. "Ruthless cunning, I had not seen that in you. Still, my offer stands. You are sly enough to come up with your own methods. My father's cloak is easy to find. I have learned that he flies it from his banner pole, so that I will know he comes for me."

"What if I can't recover it?"

Shrugging, Anscharic sighed. "Then it is not God's will for me to have it, or another may return it to me. In any case, do not return to me without it. I will know if you have it, for you will tie it to the highest branch of a tree I will show you. When my men see it, they will alert me and you will deliver it."

Thrand nodded, his pulse finally subsiding. Anscharic offered him freedom and a chance at wealth.

All he needed to do was to finish what he started with Ulfrik, and a new life awaited.

26

February 6, 886 CE

The ruins of the Christian abbey offered fortunate men shelter from the unremitting rain. Ulfrik lay buried beneath piles of blankets and furs by the hearth, listening to the rain lash the roof and leaks spatter onto the stone floor. His eyes throbbed with fever and his body ached as if he had been twisted like a wet cloth. Voices murmured and restless footfalls sent echoes playing off the fire-scorched stone walls. He pulled a wool blanket over his head.

"It seems the gods want to drown us one way or the other." Snorri's rough voice grumbled close by. He too stretched out, suffering with fever that had spread among the crowded Danish army.

"Don't remind me." Ulfrik rolled onto his side. Though he had changed clothes since his failure on the Seine, his nose still filled with the mucky scent of river water.

Snorri's quip returned the horrid memory of scrambling for something to hold beneath the water. Every instinct had told him to breathe, but he had clamped his mouth shut. The cold water had sapped his strength, and the current shunted him toward the river bottom. Yet he opened his eyes and saw a length of ship rigging waving like a slow writhing snake in the murk. He had seized it, and knew he would live. Hauling himself up to the burning wreck, he exploded from a world of cold and muted sound to a screaming blaze of crumbling debris. The rope snapped from his weight, but he latched onto a floating plank. Snorri and the others then picked him from the water and escaped to the shore. The Franks conserved their arrows against their small party, and thus spared their lives.

Toki's burns were not serious, quickly doused when he had fallen into the river. Mord had dove for safety and rescued Toki. They all made it to shore and watched the ships burn so fast that they sank without catching a spark to the bridge. Less charitable men derided the failure, though both Hrolf and Sigfrid admitted the bridge had been damaged. No gold bands covered Ulfrik's arms, and he and his men crawled back to the abbey to recover.

Then illness settled upon them, and they had slept for days.

"Bera will bring us hot venison stew," Toki said. He also sat with them, though the illness had not attacked him like others.

"Good, I'm tired of river eels," Snorri said.

Ulfrik folded the blanket from his face, cool air splashing it like water. "Are you still laying with that woman? All right a roll or two, but she's becoming more like a wife."

Toki smiled and shrugged. "She is a skilled cook and knows medicine. Should I send her away?"

Ulfrik struggled to sit up, his head heavy with snot. He blew his nose onto the floor, and studied the slime he ejected. It was mostly clear, which he knew to be a good sign. "I guess if we are going to set ourselves on fire and drown in the river, we better keep a healer at hand."

A sudden stir of excited voices came from the front of the room. The double doors hung open, a gray square of light where men gestured wildly, pointing to the north. Two figures broke from the group, heading straight for Ulfrik. They were Einar and Mord, and each one rushed to deliver the same news.

"Hold on!" Ulfrik struggled to his feet as their words collided. "You may as well be speaking Frankish. Only one of you talk."

Mord cut off Einar, physically stepping in front of the stouter man. "The Seine is rising and the bridge is sagging. They think it's going to collapse!"

All fatigue and fever lifted in that instant, and Ulfrik was already bounding for the exit before anyone could react. He stumbled into the shrieking rain, the ground dancing with fat drops that pounded the grass to mud. He paused only long enough to sight the tower, and then slogged toward it through the mud. Men streamed along with him like run-off down the slopes. Horns sounded and shouts filled the air. The mud grew thicker as he came to the river and it sucked at his feet. He did not need to go farther. His position showed him all he needed to see.

His attack on the bridge had weakened it. It bowed out at the precise spot of impact. The river had risen almost to the bridge itself, which was purposefully low to the water from the start. Ulfrik's damage coupled with the mass of debris clogged between the pilings was more stress than it could take. The first of the lattice-work braces snapped. Men cheered as more cracked and broke, snapping off and plunging into the brown water.

A seal-skin cloak slapped to his shoulders from behind, but he was so absorbed in the progressing collapse that he did nothing more than tighten it and pull up the hood. Rain now sounded loud and deep in his hood, and Toki's voice fought over the song of rain, cheers, and the groaning of the bridge. "You should keep dry while you're sick. By the gods, look at that! We did it, didn't we? It's coming down!"

Franks lined the walls. Ulfrik make out a Christian cross held toward the bridge. Though he could not see the face, it must be their holy man, Joscelin. He set his god's power against Thor's, the lord of storms. His god failed.

With a plaintive screech, the bridge shattered and all of it collapsed into shattered wood. What has stood so solid and impassible now washed down the bloated river. Boards and beams plopped into the water. Spans of bridge remained intact like small rafts. Franks who tried to cross the bridge to the tower had backed up into their gateway. A wail went up from the walls of Paris, and Ulfrik watched Joscelin's arm waver and then withdraw.

In that moment, the rain slowed, and then reduced to a drizzle. The bridge was no more than pilings poking above water like the fingers of a drowning giant.

Ulfrik recognized the sign.

"Thor has won! It is a sign of his favor. The gods love us! Destroy the tower now!"

His exhortations caught and men began to chant for blood, surging toward the tower. Franks appeared atop the tower and began to fire at the converging Danes. Though they had not come prepared with war gear, Sigfrid had gathered a prepared force of men. They crashed through the raging crowd, Sigfrid at the fore with a massive shield raised against the tower. He soon took over the rabble, and organized a team to pound the front gates with a log.

Only a dozen men remained in the tower, and they rained arrows down with imprecise fury. Several men fell, but most of the Frankish attack went wide or were blocked by the many shields sheltering the ram team.

Initially caught up with all the others, Ulfrik cooled as the arrows sailed toward unarmored targets. He was not prepared to help, and could only watch. Toki and his other men stood with him, silently observing the outcome stemming from their attack on the bridge.

"Sigfrid will claim the victory today." The smooth voice beside Ulfrik broke his concentration. He pulled back his hood, rainwater pouring down his back, and found Hrolf beside him.

"But it was my attack on the bridge that weakened it. This couldn't have happened without it."

"Agreed, but that is not something every man will see."

"Do you see it?"

Hrolf nodded, but his eyes never left the tower. The Franks had stopped firing, apparently their arrows spent. A man yelled in Frankish to the defenders in the tower.

"He's asking them to surrender." Hrolf stroked his beard and chuckled. "They're better jumping to their deaths."

Sigfrid had stopped ramming and now shouted orders, his face red and his eyes wild. The ram had split on the gates, achieving nothing. What he planned was unclear, but made no difference.

The gates fell inward and the Franks rushed out screaming, swords flashing white.

In the same moment, a cheer roared from the walls of Paris and the throng of Danes convulsed toward the enemy. Ulfrik admired their fighting spirit. "They die as warriors. I hope their god welcomes them as such."

Hrolf shook his head. "They go to the clouds and sing to their god until the end of days. A warrior has no place there."

"No wonder we crush these Christians in battle." Ulfrik's remark was countered by the deed of one heroic Frank. His sword wove and slashed, carving his enemy's flesh and pouring blood into the mud. He fended off three Danes, wounding one and killing another. The third faltered and paid for his hesitation with the loss of a hand. At last Sigfrid and another warrior bracketed the Frank, and only a stab in the back halted his relentless attack.

"Don't underestimate the Franks," Hrolf chided as the Danes cheered the death of the final defender. "We will tear down this foul tower and piss into the hole that remains. Then we go up the Seine. You will come with me, and taste the riches of Chartres and LeMans. Finally, we will have some action. What do you say to that?"

Ulfrik watched as Sigfrid and his men hacked up the bodies and flung bloody hunks into the river. On the walls of Paris, Franks melted away in silence until a small group remained. The holy man lingered, his white hair clear even at this distance. Another white-haired man stood with him, and Ulfrik's gut burned.

Is that you, Humbert? By Odin's one eye, I will have justice from you. Yet Hrolf had commanded him to leave Paris and go deeper into Frankia, spoiling the chance to fulfill his oath.

Worse still, he doubted a return home by summer, and Thorod and Skard, enemies of Nye Grenner both, would swoop down on his family during raiding season. All he had achieved in Frankia would have to be abandoned to reach them in time, and breaking with Hrolf would make him an outlaw.

He sighed and met Hrolf's inquiring gaze. "Yes, action would be good."

27

Runa sat in the hall, enjoying the warm hearth fire and the companionable silence of Elin and three other girls busy with knitting wool socks. The repetition calmed her, focusing her mind on the work and not on thoughts of winter or of her husband. Daylight grew ever longer and everyone used the time to check on herds or make repairs. For the women, they enjoyed a cold blue light to illuminate their work rather than lamps or the hearth.

She looked up at the smoke curling along the ceiling and feeling for the bright hole in the roof. The sky beyond was already tinted purple and the winter night would resume. Konal had gone to repair a storage shed damaged in a storm, taking several of his boy followers to assist. Gunnar had been sent with another to collect heather branches for the firewood. Hakon was taking his afternoon nap. It was a rare moment for her to enjoy being herself.

Placing her knitting to the side, she stood. Her short sword, the sax, had been set against the hearth where she sat and now slid to the floor as she rose.

"Sun is almost down and the men must return soon. We should start a meal."

"No sword practice today?" Elin laughed and the girls giggled. Runa had long accepted their teasing.

"Likely not. The storage shed needed repairs more than I need sword practice. Though I think the boys won't let Konal miss it, even if it means practice in the dark."

"Do you think Konal's brother is really coming?" one of the girls asked, her eyes wide. "He is so handsome, and he claims his brother looks just like him."

Elin clucked her tongue. "Your father has a man picked for you already."

"If both my father and the man return." Her voice trailed off, and suddenly everyone found a task to occupy them. Runa collected the wool into a basket and placed it by the loom.

She turned to console the girl, trying to summon a positive thought to buoy her faith.

But she froze, words stuck in her throat.

Standing in the open hall doors was a strange man. He was clad in heavy furs and a wool cap, greasy yellow hair hanging lank on the sides of his narrow head. In front of him stood Gunnar, and the man held a long, gray knife to his throat. Tears beaded at Gunnar's eyes but his mouth was bent in a defiant scowl.

The girls screamed, finally comprehending what they saw. The man walked Gunnar into the hall, and four others flowed in behind them with drawn swords. Their predatory smiles left shadow-filled lines on their faces, turning them into masks of evil.

"Shut up, woman!" the leader snapped.

The leader, who held Gunnar, was hardly a man. His beard was scraggly and his jaw still soft with youth. None of the strangers appeared older than sixteen or seventeen years. With her training, she noted the awkward way they held their drawn swords and the careless guard they assumed entering the hall. They believed no one would oppose them.

With every pounding beat of her racing heart, she resolved to make all five of these boys pay for their arrogance.

"Do as he says," Runa announced as evenly as her trembling voice allowed. "Remain silent."

The five strangers spread in from the doorway. The leader lifted Gunnar to his tiptoes by driving the knife at his throat. He started laughing. "What did I say to you? The men are gone and this place is all for us."

The group cackled and the women whimpered in terror. Elin sat where Runa had just been. Slowly, though no one paid much attention, she reached down to draw the sax upright. Runa reacted. "Elin, stand up when we have guests."

The command made little sense, but she had feared Elin planned to use the weapon. Instead, she left if upright and shot Runa a frustrated look.

"Guests! Yeah, guests all right!" The leader leaned back in laughter, his knife tightening on Gunnar's neck so that a trickle of blood sprouted. Gunnar grimaced but did not cry out.

She had to delay. Konal and the other boys would return soon. They might be able to aid her, but Gunnar had to be separated first.

"You're holding my son hostage. Let him go and you can have whatever you want."

"I'll have whatever I want, that is certain. But your whelp bit me, and he should be punished." The leader stepped closer with the knife cutting deeper into Gunnar's soft flesh. A tear rolled down his eye and he trembled. Runa tried not to look at him, instead searching for a gap to exploit.

One of the young men upturned a table with a roar. The women screamed anew, but Runa used the distraction to move closer to the hearth. The sax leaned on the opposite side, but an iron poker remained in the low fire closer at hand.

"You promised riches and women," said the one who had flipped the table. "But we've got two old bitches and three little girls. Where's the fucking gold?"

"Nye Grenner is famous for gold, isn't it?" The leader winked at Runa. "You're Ulfrik's wife; you've got gold on your neck."

She touched Konal's torc in surprise, having forgotten she wore it.

Then a shadow flitted at the doorway, and when no one followed on it she knew Konal and his boys had returned. She had to free Gunnar before he acted.

"You're local boys?" She edged closer to the poker, trying not to look at it. "Which one sent you, Skard or Thorod?"

"Loki sent us," answered another and all laughed again.

"Did you just call me a boy?" The leader's face pulled into a frown and Gunnar squealed as the knife bit deeper. Runa closed her eyes. "Before you give us everything your husband has been hiding in this hall, I'm going to show you how much of a man I am."

"Wouldn't you like to try?" Runa's lip curled. "You wouldn't even know where to point your little prick."

The insult inflamed the leader's rage, snorting and shoving Gunnar toward one of his cohort as he stalked toward her.

"Konal!"

He charged through door, his sword held low in two hands. The invaders whirled toward him, the one closest to the door crumpling into a bleeding pile before turning.

The girls screamed and Runa snatched the poker from the hearth. Konal's blade was already hacking into the leg of another attacker as another figure entered the hall. Runa had no time to see more.

Knife already in hand, the leader sprang away from Runa's strike with only a moment to spare. The poker was heavier than her sax but lighter than the sword she used for practice. Her fury carried her, reversing the poker's strike so the heated metal slammed into the leader's arm. The cloth sleeve burned away and the man screamed.

She rammed him with her shoulder, folding up his sword arm as Ulfrik had done to her in practice many times before, then slipped her foot behind his heel. He crashed to the ground with a screech and Runa took the poker in both hands and hammered it across his face. She roared all her frustration and anger, all her hatred for the man who had threatened her son, and a blindness overcame her. She only stopped when Konal's voice pierced through her madness.

"Stop! Gunnar is still hostage!"

The pulpy mass at her feet made no sense, then she realized it was the shell of the leader's head with the face beaten out of it. She had seen many gory sights in her life, but this was the worst. Bloody flesh chunks clung to her skirt and the poker's heat cause the blood on it to bubble and hiss.

"I'll kill him!" The desperate voice drew her around. Elin stood white and wide-eyed before the girls. Konal and his follower stood amid three corpses, brilliant red splatters over their faces. Then she found the source of the voice: the surviving invader had Gunnar held just the same as the leader had. He struggled against the knife, blood smearing his neck and shirt, and both cheeks shined with tears.

Seeing her son again cooled the fury. The blade rested over the throbbing vein in Gunnar's neck, and even an accidental reflex from the invader could kill her son. So she willed the intense urge to strike to drain from her limbs, no small task. The entire hall stood in frozen silence, though Runa heard voices outside drawing closer.

"I'll kill him if you don't let me go!" The man was as young as the others, not yet a full grown man but just as dangerous as one. His hands trembled, and the knife edge wobbled at Gunnar's throat.

"Don't be afraid, Gunnar. He will release you unharmed." Forcing her voice to be calm and confident took as much strength as wielding the poker.

"I'm not letting him go until I get to my ship."

"You're backed against the wall." Runa threw the poker at the man's feet. The thud made him jump and she winced as his startled reaction cut the blade into Gunnar's skin, causing him to whimper. She turned away from the man, glancing at Konal who remained still and fixed on the invader. Finding the sax by the hearth, she drew the blade from its sheath.

"What are you doing? Do you want me to kill him?"

"You are dead either way," Runa said, pointing the sax at him. "Your only choice now is to die a clean death or to suffer. Kill my son and I will make death linger for weeks. Release him, and I promise you a swift death. You will go to Valhalla where you can feast and fight eternally."

The man searched for an escape, but found none. Konal and his follower blocked the exit and Runa's blade remained two hand lengths away. Tears began to form at his eyes and his mouth trembled. "I don't want to die."

"Then you should've stayed home. It is fine for me to die, my son to die, but not you?" Runa spit at his feet. "Even with a clean death Odin would not take a crying baby into his hall! Release my son. Do it!"

Konal slipped closer and the man tightened his blade as Gunnar struggled anew. "We came for the treasure you keep. We heard all the men were gone. In summer, Jarls Thorod and Skard will come and take it, but we planned to get it ourselves. With no men around, we thought it'd be a simple thing and no one had to die."

"So you sailed in the winter darkness and risked Thor's storms? Then discovered Nye Grenner is not for men to pick over like a corpse. I should let you return with a warning to your jarls."

"I will tell them to stay away, that there's nothing here worth taking." The man nodded eagerly, and Runa smiled.

"Release my son and I will consider it."

"You promise to allow me to leave?"

"I swear it."

A tense moment passed as the man considered the offer, then he lowered his knife. Gunnar slipped free, but rather than run for his mother he turned and punched the man in his crotch. He doubled over and Runa struck.

Her blade pierced the meat of his sword arm, causing him to drop the knife. She shoved the sax to the bone and drove the man against the wall. The women screamed again but all her fury flooded back into her head. Her vision thrummed with rage. Grabbing his knife, she held it before the man's face.

"You threatened to kill my son, planned to rape me and my women, then steal my gold. You expect to walk away?"

She rammed the knife into the soft flesh of the man's crotch, nailing the dagger to the hilt. He lifted up with a scream that threatened to shatter his throat.

"You may leave now, and if you survive then you can give Thorod my message. No one threatens me in my own hall." She ripped the sax out of the man's arm, and more blood pooled at his crotch than she thought a body could contain.

"You ... promised." The man slouched to his side, his uninjured arm clawing at the dirt as if to drag himself away. Runa crouched beside him, lowering her face to his.

"Men live by their oaths. But I am a woman, and I live for revenge. Take that with you to Nifleheim."

She stood, no more thought for the dying man, and faced Gunnar. The fear she saw as she opened her arms to receive him gave her pause. Glancing around, the others stared at her with horror and shock. Looking at the blood-slicked sax, she tossed it to the floor where it clanged atop the poker. The pooling blood ebbed to her feet, and as it touched her Runa realized her life was never going to be the same.

28

March 18, 886 CE

R una and Konal dueled in the fields as they did every day, but now they had relocated to the slope that overlooked the sea. One month had passed since the invaders had been defeated, and their five severed heads now overlooked the collapsed docks where they had left their small boat. Sea birds had picked them clean, leaving the skulls on their pole and with bits of hair streaming in the breeze. The grass waved as Runa wiped sweat from her brow and lowered her sword, her shoulder burning from the morning of practice.

"Enough," Konal said, sliding his sword into its sheath. "You're even tiring me now. I don't know that I can teach you anymore."

Runa smiled at the compliment. His respect for her had risen since the attack, while others handled her with more caution. Even Elin could not meet her gaze for long. Konal, Gunnar, and his band of boy warriors seemed to be the only ones to understand what she had done.

"And then I suppose the boys will want more of me today too."

Konal groaned as he settled into the grass. "This is the hardest I've worked in a long time."

"Then rest." Runa placed herself on the grass, a careful distance away. She knew Konal lusted for her; his eyes were not as good at lying as was his tongue. Every time she beat him in practice, she saw him struggle to control his desire. Today was no different, and his red face was more from just the exertion of practice.

Runa's hands pulsed from sword practice. She rubbed the tough ridge of flesh at the base of her fingers of her sword hand and drifted into thought. Winter had been kinder than years past, and summer was soon to come. In better days, Ulfrik would have been planning a spring festival. She shook her head in dismissal, for Ulfrik would be gone at least two more months and thinking of him would only worsen her loneliness. Ever since the raid on her hall, his absence dug at her. Konal provided a strong presence but he was nothing like Ulfrik. He had neither his confident leadership nor his quick mind. More than anything, she missed his wit and humor. Nye Grenner needed laughter as much as it needed food and drink.

Konal shot to his feet. Runa startled from her thoughts.

"Two sails," he said, pointing to the sparkling stretch of gray ocean.

"Thorod and Skard!" Standing, her hand fell to the sword at her side, as if drawing it could wave away the enemy.

"They come from the wrong direction."

"How can you tell?" Runa was a poor judge of direction, but the two ships seemed to sail directly toward them. Konal ignored her question, shading his eyes with his hand. He began to laugh.

"I recognize those sails. My brother has found me." He turned to her, a wide smile on his face, and grabbed both her shoulders. "He has come at the first good sailing weather, as I foretold!"

Releasing her, he ran yelling down the slope while waving both hands overhead. Runa watched in dumbfounded stillness. Strange feelings welled up, a sudden sadness. Though the ships were not even at the shore, she knew Konal was not mistaken. Fate now worked to remove Konal from the thread of Runa's life. She touched her cheek at the thought, and her breathing grew heavier.

Konal was dancing in the surf, splashing water into the air like a child. His shouting had drawn people from the hall. Gunnar appeared at her side, and tugged her sleeve. "Is everything all right, Mother?"

Blinking several times, she patted Gunnar's head. "Of course. Konal's brother has come." Her voice weakened. "Just as he foretold."

They stared at him waving and shouting, then Gunnar remarked, "That's how I'm going to greet Father when he returns. I'm going to dance in the water like Konal."

Even as the ships slid onto the rocky beach, one man had leapt from the prow and stumbled through the water to Konal. The two men crashed together in the shallows, both of them screaming and wailing in joy. Others leapt the rails into the shallows, some to drag their ships onto the beach and others to slog through the water for Konal. In moments, the men were swarming him and reaching out to touch him. The pile of laughing men looked like boys to Runa. The clump staggered onto the beach where they finally collapsed in a pile. Gunnar laughed. "They're so happy!"

Runa smiled as an afterthought, then guided Gunnar to her side. "Let's greet our guests."

At the edge of the surf, Konal stood arm in arm with his twin. Only Konal's poor clothing distinguished him from his better dressed brother. The two shared the same smile, though the brother's seemed more open. Konal pulled out and grabbed Runa's arm, yanking her forward.

"Here's the woman who saved my life." His arm slipped easily about her shoulder, and she did not resist. "She plucked me from a rock under a cliff, where I surely would've died. Without her, you'd be fetching my bones instead."

The brother, whose name she knew was Kell, looked her up and down. His eyes widened at the pants she wore and the sword at her side, but he met her eyes and held them. "My brother is one-half my life, and so you have rescued me as well. I cannot repay you for keeping Konal well for all this time."

He bowed low and many of the dark men in salt-stained clothing behind him did as well. Several shouted their thanks while others simply looked her in the eye and nodded. A few even wiped away tears.

"I am Runa, ruler of Nye Grenner. I welcome you, Kell, to my lands and home."

Kell snapped up at his name, a wry smile on his face. "Konal's been talking about me, I see. All the good is a lie and all the bad is true, I'm afraid to admit."

Konal roared laughter, unhooked his arm from Runa, then thumped Kell on his shoulder. "How I've missed you, Brother! We've much to discuss. Let's get to the hall. But wait, where's ...?"

As his voice drifted off, a dark cloud formed over the men. Heads lowered and eyes darted away. Kell's own voice was solemn as he touched the silver hammer of Thor at his throat. "Down to Ran's Bed at the bottom of the sea. Were our blood not one in the same, I'd have guessed you'd followed them as well."

The somber air lasted only moments as Konal lowered his head and wiped his face. He exhaled and then gave a calm smile. "They were a fine crew, the best of any I'd ever known. Let's share a drink to their memories. Come."

Runa followed along as the gathering of warriors converged on her hall. Only now did she realize how naturally Konal has assumed control, as if the hall were his own. Gunnar joined Konal and Kell, receiving a greeting that Runa again felt overstepped boundaries of a guest. It was as if Konal was taking Kell to his home, inviting him into his hall. Her turbid thoughts settled and she realized that with nearly eighty men pouring off these ships, Konal had the force to settle Nye Grenner as his home. Her heart raced as she realized the real invaders might be walking aside her with smiles and songs rather than war cries and swords.

~

Runa sat at the high table, Gunnar at her side and Konal where Ulfrik had formerly sat. Male voices filled the hall, happy and vibrant conversations that reminded her of better times. As she closed her eyes, the scene transformed into the festivals of years past. The deep chuckle at her left became Ulfrik's. The sudden shout and crash became Toki's drunken stumbling. The resultant laughter came from the hirdmen. Yet when her eyes opened the scene was filled with unfamiliar actors, though no one was less happy.

Kell had fallen off the table, and his men threw scraps and laughed as he struggled to his feet. In the short few weeks Kell had stayed in Nye Grenner, he had done much good. Seeing the poor state of the buildings and the low stores of food, he had dispatched his ships to buy food and supplies from the Shetland and Orkney Islands. With the larders restocked, he then set his men to restoring the damage wrought over half a decade of disrepair. As the weather warmed into spring, Kell ensured Nye Grenner's people shook off the vestiges of winter. To Runa's embarrassment, Kell had paid for and organized the feast everyone now enjoyed.

The day of celebration drew all the community, comprised mostly women and girls. Though many were married, with husbands long gone and the prospect that many were dead, Kell's crew found plenty of accommodating women. Runa could not condemn them, but neither could she bring herself to join them.

Night still arrived early, and as the sun collapsed, so did many who had drank to excess. Others found the opportunity to slip away with a partner. The hall grew tired and quiet, and the amber light of the hearth fire cast flickering light around those who remained. Konal had reversed himself on the bench so his back rested against the table and legs stretched out. Gunnar and his friends sought mischief among the crowd below the high table and Thora had taken Hakon to free Runa to lead the celebration.

"The people of Nye Grenner are charming," Kell announced as he joined Runa and his brother. He clutched three mugs of beer, froth splashing over his hands as he offered them to Konal and Runa.

"The women of Nye Grenner are lonely and frightened." Runa

sipped the bitter beer, a fresh and malty tang she had long missed. "They're glad to see friendly men in their hall."

"What's to be frightened of with Runa the Bloody leading them?" Konal said, raising his mug to toast her. He had given her the name after the attack. She disliked it but realized having a fearful reputation had its uses. "To the might of your sword arm, which I'm proud to have trained."

Flipping a lock of hair from her face, she frowned at the statement. "We fear once the mighty Konal and his more humble and better mannered brother leave, our enemies will have revenge for the five we killed."

"But we're not leaving!" Konal rollicked with laughter, though Kell smiled and looked at the floor.

"So it seems. But there is the matter of the one you seek, yes? You will search for him, then return to Ireland?"

Kell choked on his beer, coughing wildly enough to raise a few weary heads from the tables below. His face flushed red when he recovered. "You know about him?"

"I told her a wee bit of the story, Brother. Do not concern yourself."

Runa smiled as Kell settled back on the bench. She withheld a wee bit of the story as well, and it was a warm, satisfying secret that she could use for bargaining. "All I know is you seek a slave, and from this exchange I assume you have not found him still."

Kell shook his head. "The trail has vanished into the sea. No man will find him, but we must search. There is no reason to return to Father with news of failure."

"No reason to ever return," Konal grumbled.

"What about your wife and children?" Runa enjoyed the scowl that overcame him. Kell interjected, steering talk away from him and his brother.

"You fear an attack? What kind of enemy do you expect?"

"Two kinds," Runa said, pausing to drink. "Traitors and fools. The first kind are easily handled. Ingrid holds the north of the island for me, but she is a relative of my enemies. I've heard nothing from her since my husband left. My enemies learned about our condition from someone."

"So you want to discipline your bondsmen?" Konal glanced at his brother, then looked at Runa.

"And after I do that, I want to carry the battle to the lands of my enemies. Nye Grenner has seen enough blood in its years. I'll tolerate no more enemy feet upon its fields. Let the fools of the north die in their halls, with their women and children watching. That has been Nye Grenner's lot, but no more."

A lump clogged her throat and her voice trembled as she shared her plans. Pausing to marshal her rising emotion, she filled the silence with another sip from her mug.

"My husband promised to return before summer, but he must be delayed." She stared at Konal, who over recent weeks had hinted that Ulfrik might be dead. "I cannot wait for his return to take action. He will be too late."

Konal and Kell stared at each other. A strange impression of silent communication passed between them. Runa studied their expressions, hoping to read agreement. Both turned to her in tandem, though only Konal spoke. His voice was more studied, as if he were bargaining with a trader.

"You hope my brother and I will lead our men against your enemies?"

"That is correct in but one detail. I will lead the men."

Kell's eyes widened and cheeks puffed as if to laugh, but Konal's flat reaction instead led him to drain his breath with a long sigh. Runa met Konal's eyes, seeing his anger flash but also suspecting he approved. His pride, she knew, would interfere.

"Impossible. You can wear pants and carry a sword, but it does not make you a man."

"I rule this community in the absence of my husband, the jarl. I speak for them, care for them, and I fight for them."

"Men will not follow a woman to battle. It's unnatural."

"Glory is glory, whether a woman stands before or behind them. Isn't that what your men crave, glory in battle?"

"Riches is more like it, and that can't be had here."

"Then you misunderstand me, Konal. I don't want to kill a few of their levy. I want to water the earth with the blood of every person who has persecuted us all these years. I want your men to carry away slaves and property, the gold buried in halls, the ships at rest by their docks."

The blood-thirsty request stunned the brothers into silence. Runa could devise no other way to phrase her desires, for what she described would be the same plans her enemies made for her. She had to act first and with finality, no matter how horrible.

"So you are promising all spoils to my men," Konal looked at Kell as he spoke. "And you want to lead them in battle, though you've never before led men."

"There are a thousand fools living among these islands, and every one of them must know Runa the Bloody from Nye Grenner will destroy her enemies and not chance attacking me in the future. You can organize your men, but I will inspire them and stand before them."

"You will be killed." Konal brushed imaginary dirt from his pants. "You're too small and not strong enough to push through a shield wall."

"Then we don't fight in shield wall." Her patience ended, she slammed her mug onto the table and stood. Gunnar appeared beneath the table, and others gazed up at her sudden action. "You owe me your life, Konal. To repay your debt, lend me your men to end the threat against my people. All the spoils will be theirs and all the vengeance will be mine. Don't concern yourself with my life. Fate decides what to do with it."

The already quiet hall stilled to complete silence. Runa did not flinch from Konal's hard gaze, and the two remained locked. It was a different type of duel than one fought with swords, the type Runa was accustomed to winning. She gave a twitch of a smile when Konal glanced away and stood.

"You will have my men and my word to serve you. But once it is done, all debts are paid. I risk my life to repay you, after all."

Happiness and fear eddied through her, and she blinked slowly to keep the emotion out of her eyes. "Do this and you owe me no more. I will need no more."

Konal smiled, then sat, slapping Kell's knee. "She's a tough woman, eh, Brother? Can you see her in mail and helmet at the front of our men?"

Looking over Runa, he tugged at his beard. "In fact, I can."

29

April 5, 886 CE

Paris looked no different to Ulfrik as his ship approached it from the other side. It remained the same squat, foul-smelling, smoking mass jammed into the middle of the river. It was like a fist that had punched the Danish army in the crotch, hobbling and weakening it into ineffectiveness. The ship glided across the water with the dozens of other vessels returning to the despair. Trees once bare of leaves now waved boughs of fresh green at the Danes as they sped past. White and gold flowers bloomed and birds hunted at the water's edge. The cold and wet winter had yielded to spring.

Seeing Paris again renewed all the conflicts he had set aside. The people of Nye Grenner had no walls to protect them, no bridges to bar ships from approaching. The days would be growing longer and the weather more predictable, and Thorod and Skard would soon discover an undefended hall. He had to act now or his family would suffer.

Across the water, Toki stood at the tiller of *Raven's Talon*. Beside him raced five more ships Ulfrik had accrued since joining Hrolf. As lords and oath-holders died, men swore new oaths to new jarls. Hrolf had attracted more than any other, and he doled out these followers to both Ulfrik and Gunther One-Eye to command and organize. He now had more fighting men than ever before. The raiding they had conducted in Frankia's interior had tested the new men, and demonstrated Ulfrik's leadership. The resistance had been light, but with enough skirmishes for the new war band to learn how to function together. Despite carrying away little tangible wealth, he had welcomed the chance to shape his force and do something other than huddle in a trench or in the ruins of an abbey.

Reunion with the Danish holding force was a tepid affair. Ulfrik guided his ships to a stretch of beach, set guards, and returned to the camp. Men who had stayed behind bore defeat like a stone lashed to their backs. They shuffled past and through their returning comrades as if they did not exist. One man had even bumped Ulfrik's shoulder, pushing forward without even turning his head. Mord grabbed the man to force an apology, but when he wrested free, Ulfrik dropped the matter.

"Home again," Ulfrik said to no one as he looked at the old campground. Many of the tents had been left behind, and a number had fallen or blown away. His returning crews moaned at seeing the state of their old shelters. Along the north bank, construction that had begun in winter of temporary barracks and halls were now complete. Their fresh, white wood faces beckoned from across the water, appearing as palaces in comparison to the ruined abbey and camps of the south bank.

"Nothing has changed but the weather," remarked Toki as he joined Ulfrik. Both walked toward the ruined abbey where Hrolf and his ranking men slept. The fire-scorched walls and collapsed roof provided more protection from the elements than simple tents.

"The gods have grown bored with us, and turned their eyes elsewhere." Entering the abbey, the enclosed space pressed Ulfrik, having become accustomed to long months living under open skies. Sounds were louder and the air stale. A pitiful hearth fire crackled with a sprinkling of listless men in attendance. He glanced behind to summon Snorri, who followed him inside with his nose wrinkled in disgust.

"Well, lad, back to scratching our asses while we wait for Paris to fall over." Snorri hefted a sack filled with his mail and other items. The seams had ripped in spots and the contents threatened to spill.

"Gather all the Nye Grenner men in the fields behind the abbey. Keep it away from Hrolf's eyes and be fast." Ulfrik glanced over his shoulder, spotting Mord lingering at the door in conversation with friends. "Word of my actions will travel fast enough, but I want to be done before Hrolf visits me."

Snorri paused, his brow furrowed but his lips clamped tight. He tossed his sack into a pile of others and began leaning into men to whisper Ulfrik's command.

The Nye Grenner men assembled in the appointed field, arriving in small clusters as Snorri dispatched them. Gram Redbeard, Darby the Shepherd, and Thorkel Flat-Nose were the last surviving hirdmen to have followed him from Norway and the first to arrive behind the abbey ruins. Others joined them, speculating in low voices and worried glances stealing over their shoulders. Snorri and Toki arrived with the final group, and Ulfrik cleared his throat for the group's attention.

"We don't have much time, so let me come to the point. You have served with such honor that I cannot think of better men to stand with me in the shield wall. None of you have complained for all the long months we've been here. None of you flinched when I ordered you up ladders and into the arrow storm. You are the men skalds choose for their songs. So it weighs heavy on my heart to send you home."

Confused looks circled the group, now less than half of the eighty who had followed Ulfrik to Frankia. Ulfrik's heart beat in his throat, and his eyes grew hot. He had been preparing this talk for a week, but in the moment of delivery weakness and sorrow overcame him. In this land of hostile strangers, these men were his sole family.

"But we have not defeated Paris." Einar, who stood a head taller than any other man, still raised his hand to catch Ulfrik's attention. The gesture drew a small smile to Ulfrik's lips.

"You are done with Paris, but I am not. I promised you would be home by the end of winter. I need not remind you that Skard and Thorod will be rousing from their winter dreams and filling their ships with hungry men. You have a battle to fight, one more important to you than Paris. Go defend your homes."

Faces fell and eyes averted. Ulfrik understood their struggle. Each man was oath-bound to stay with Ulfrik, yet each feared for his family and flocks. None dared shame himself with admitting his thoughts to another.

"We are at half strength," Gram Redbeard said, addressing the others around him. "Before Paris we were barely an even match for Skard."

Eyes fell back to Ulfrik, who nodded and began to pace. "I have considered this, and already have a plan. Hundreds of new men have come to my banner either by choice or the deaths of their jarls. Many wish they were elsewhere. Those I will dispatch to Nye Grenner, where the glory of a real fight awaits them and young widows will be seeking husbands. I do not doubt I can refill our ranks with good men. You've been fighting alongside them and know their quality. Only the best will return with you."

A grudging murmur of acceptance rippled through the ranks. "Who will lead if you do not accompany us?" Ulfrik did not see the questioner but soon all were repeating the same concern.

"Toki," Ulfrik pointed at his friend, whose face whitened in surprise. "And Snorri will advise him."

Snorri snapped his head to Ulfrik, as shocked as the others. "You're sending me away?"

"I'm sending you to aid my family, and share your wisdom with my friend and brother. I must remain behind to lead the men Hrolf has entrusted to me and to honor my oath to him. Is there anyone here who cannot accept this arrangement? Speak now."

Men shared cautious glances, but Darby the Shepherd spoke first.

"I agree. I've been with Toki for many a battle, and he's true in a fight. I'll stand with him any day."

Murmurs turned to cheers that Ulfrik had to silence for fear of drawing attention. "Then all is settled. It's a long journey home, and dangerous. Be prepared to leave at dawn tomorrow. Your portion of the spoils I take here will be shared with you, or your families if you should fall in battle, once we are rejoined. I swear this before the gods."

Men spoke in hushed but excited tones as the group disbanded, and Ulfrik knew he had given them what they truly wanted. Toki and Snorri lingered, along with Einar and several others.

"Why didn't you talk to me about this first?" Toki asked. "I'm not the right one to lead Nye Grenner."

"Then it is time to conquer your doubts. Nye Grenner is as much yours as it is mine. You settled the land, built the hall with me, defended our homes as bravely as any. I am counting on you. Listen to Snorri, but lead with your heart. I don't know what you will find back home, but I trust you will know what to do."

Toki opened his mouth to protest, but then turned away. Ulfrik patted his back, understanding Toki's confusion but believing he would rise to the challenge. Ulfrik had seen maturity in his friend's thoughts, despite his foolishness with women. He needed freedom to realize his ability, and Ulfrik knew leadership would be the forge to shape him. Ulfrik required capable leaders he could trust, especially if Hrolf's promises of territory and riches were true.

As Toki thought, Snorri took Ulfrik aside. "I've never left your side, lad. Don't send me away before the walls come down here."

"I'm not sending you away. You are acting on my behalf, protecting my family and my people. Go, and judge what must be done, then do it. I can no longer fulfill every obligation by my own hand. I must work through those I trust, and I trust few more than you."

"When your father died, I served your brother. After I realized my horrible mistake, I swore I would never falter in my duty to protect you. I've been your right-side shield in every battle. I can't imagine you fighting without me while I still live."

"Think of my sons in Thorod's or Skard's vile hands." He patted Snorri's shoulder. "Will you do as I've asked?"

"That I will, lad." He faced Ulfrik and the two embraced. "No one will harm your boys, I swear it." Ulfrik nodded and started to leave, when Snorri grabbed his arm. "But you do one thing for me. Let Einar remain with you. I can't show him anything more, and he should earn his place with you. Will you do this?"

He bit back protest, then reconsidered. "He has great promise. All right, Einar will remain with me, if he agrees."

Everyone satisfied, they drifted away to their own tasks. Ulfrik began considering the men to augment the Nye Grenner force, but each thought summoned Hrolf's face. Once Ulfrik's plan reached him, Hrolf would be in his rights to name Ulfrik an oath-breaker. If he did, Ulfrik was glad his closest companions would not see his shame, or his execution.

ULFRIK PULLED his cloak tighter as he strode the final distance across the wet grass. The newly constructed longhouses on the northern bank were clustered into a tight camp, haphazardly arranged with a poor eye for defense. Though drier than the ruined abbey, Ulfrik considered the camp more vulnerable. Men crisscrossed the spaces between buildings on various errands. Voices joking or cursing mingled with the singing of birds in the trees. Smoke fluttered from holes in the ceilings as evening sucked light from the sky and poured chill into the air. Hrolf's red and yellow dragon standard flew from his banner pole outside his temporary hall. He sighed and approached the two guards posted at the doors.

One smiled sheepishly as he opened the door, while the other relieved Ulfrik of his swords and throwing axes. "Jarl Hrolf is waiting. Good luck, Jarl Ulfrik."

This was Ulfrik's first visit to Hrolf's new hall. Stepping inside, the scent of fresh-cut wood, smoke, and stale beer assailed his nostrils. The hearth blazed orange heat, and two Frankish girls tended it with billows and iron pokers. Hrolf sat in a huge chair he had constructed to hold his giant body. He leaned to one side in it, head supported by his hand glistening with gold rings. No one but the girls remained in the hall, making the space seem enormous though it was not much larger than the hall constructed for Ulfrik.

"Attend me." His deep voice echoed in the emptied hall.

Yet another sigh, then Ulfrik approached Hrolf and went on one knee before him. The gesture pained him, for never had he nor his father before him taken a knee to another man. Fate had chosen otherwise for him, but he still bridled against servitude. "At your service, Jarl Hrolf."

"At my service? Get off your knee and look at me."

Hrolf had not shifted his position, his face resting slack in his hand as if enduring a dull performance. For his own part, Ulfrik feigned earnestness while containing his frustration and worry. He searched Hrolf's eyes for a clue to his success, but the jarl remained inscrutable.

"I've cleared the hall of everyone but two slaves. Normally I'd fill it with as many people as I could find. Do you know why I wanted privacy?"

"That we may speak freely," Ulfrik guessed, and the frown from Hrolf informed him of his error.

"To contain your shame, you fool! You know why I summoned you?"

"Because I sent three ships of men back to Nye Grenner without your leave."

"Because you sent them at the worst possible moment!" Hrolf snapped forward on his chair, hand slapping the armrest. "You must have known Sigfrid had already quit the fight. Allowing your men to run home makes it seem you've no faith in my success."

"Sigfrid took his payment and left after I had dispatched my men."

219

Hrolf flopped back in his chair, crossing his arms with a scowl. Sigfrid had grown so tired of inaction that he had opened negotiations with the Franks and took sixty pounds of silver as payment to leave the fight.

"That is a detail not worth debating," Hrolf said. "Sigfrid is all bluster, but no edge to his sword. We're better off without him and his cowardly followers. I will take Paris alone, and the spoils will be all mine. You were supposed to aid me in this, remember?"

"And every day all I think of is how to breach the walls." Ulfrik inclined his head, hoping to hide the anger rippling into his temper. When Hrolf did not answer, he peered out from under his brow. Hrolf's stony eyes searched him, a sneer twitching to break free on his face.

"My command was to deliver all your men to serve me until dismissed. You broke an oath to me when you sent your men home. Why?"

"I am at war with my neighbors, and in summer they will be certain to attack. Our homes and families must be defended."

"And the men you sent who have no connection to your home?" Hrolf's eyes glittered and the sneer finally escaped. "You have bled away strength I need here, and also signaled that you've no faith in victory."

"Had I no faith, I would have left with my men." Ulfrik stood straight, and held Hrolf's eyes, a sneer of his own threatening to erupt. "I did what I must for the welfare of my people. I cannot ask men to risk their lives here when their homes are in danger."

Hrolf shot up from his chair, roaring in anger. Ulfrik staggered back as the huge man lumbered forward. "Gods, man! You can't be a conqueror if you are going to fret over what Fate has decided for your families back home. You've come this far, but your heart has been left by your hearth. I've no use for a man who can't commit to the task given him."

A fire lit in Ulfrik's belly as Hrolf's rebuke stoked his frustration. "We were to be home by summer, and so I promised my men. My word is my life, and so I sent them home. And so, too, I remain with you. I am committed to the task. I broke through the bridge, if you'll recall."

"A storm did that." Hrolf dismissed the claim, and began pacing with his hands behind his back.

Stunned, Ulfrik fell silent. As he had feared, all the risk he had taken to create a breakthrough remained credited to Fate.

Hrolf took measured steps, as if pacing off a boundary, looking at the ground in silence. Ulfrik's gaze followed him, and he stilled his tongue for fear of worsening the rebuke he knew would come. At last Hrolf paused and turned to him.

"I understand you sent your banner home, and have a new one. A red rag that belonged to the noble you owned as a slave. What does that mean?"

"That I will skin that traitorous bastard alive. He killed an old friend and a good man, and led us ..." Ulfrik bit off the end of his sentence, not wanting to confirm for Hrolf his true doubts about capturing Paris.

"He led you where? Is there more than I know? What are you not telling me?"

"I mean he misled us to believe he was a lowly priest. Had he been honest, I could have ransomed him."

Hrolf gave an apprising smile, as if he had just learned a trader was selling him a nag for a stallion. "As you say, Ulfrik. For now, know that I have been merciful to you. For your defiance I could have called for your death."

"That would be rash, Jarl Hrolf." Ulfrik's gaze did not waver. "You would jeopardize the loyalty of the other men. And I would not lie down to die so easily."

"Ah, a threat!" Hrolf smiled, then chuckled. His stance relaxed and he returned to his chair. "Of course you are right on both counts. The gods have sent you to protect me, after all. So I am inclined to be generous and indulgent with you. Atop all of this, you are a strong war leader. So don't put me in the position of having to punish you."

Ulfrik suddenly felt childish and brash, and his face grew hot with his shame. "Never again, Jarl Hrolf. I swear it."

"Good, now return to your men." Ulfrik bowed and began to leave. Halfway across the hall, Hrolf called his name again. "But do not think this has passed without effect. You have tested my trust, and now I must think carefully about your future with me."

Without looking back, Ulfrik inclined his head then strode out of the hall into the cold twilight.

30

June 5, 886 CE

Thrand crept through the underbrush, hugging the ground and watching the five men seated around the remains of their campfire. Leaves crowned his tangled hair and mud streaked his face. Fate had been kind in leaving him with a green shirt and brown pants, the clothes he had worn the night of his capture. He felt confident no one had spotted him through his camouflage. Mossy, earthy scents clogged his nose as he watched four of the men rise from their log seats and stretch. Only an old man remained, his hair still full and bound with a leather headband. His eyes were closed in blindness as he smiled and spoke with the others who gathered their bows and slung quivers of arrows across their backs.

The men scanned the area, one speaking to the blind man and receiving a dismissive snort in reply. At last, the four men strode into the forest. Thrand's stomach rumbled and though the campers had not prepared anything, he still imagined he could smell the cooking rabbit. Three were strung from a branch in a leather sack, the hunters' catches of the prior day. Thrand waited a while longer before stirring to run for the rabbits. He could seize the sack and flee before the blind man could react.

"You in the bushes, come out. I've sent my sons away so I can learn what you want. The rabbits are what you're after, I guess from listening to your stomach growl." The blind man smiled, his teeth black and crooked. Though his eyes were closed, he faced Thrand directly. "Come on, I know you are there. Let's not pretend any longer."

Rising up, brushing twigs and underbrush from his shirt, he faced the blind man. "What magic allows you to see me?"

"Not magic, but sound and smell. You make more noise than a speared boar and you stink like a seal carcass rotting on the beach. You spent all night circling our camp, trying to find an open approach to the rabbits." The man gestured to the log one of his so-called sons had occupied. "Sit and talk while my sons scout for game. We've got to catch more to feed all of our crews, and with you bumbling around the forest we'll never catch anything. So we decided to find out more about you."

"How long have you known I've been here?" Thrand touched the base of his neck, feeling for the Thor's amulet he had long ago lost. His skin tingled knowing he had not been half as clever as the thought, and closer to becoming prey than he knew.

"A few days ago when you stumbled into our hunting grounds. You leave tracks, clear even to a blind man." The old man laughed again, pointed once more at the log. Thrand finally took the offered seat. "You've got the right ideas, but you'll not sneak up on hunters and scouts like us."

Thrand now surveyed the forest, finding nothing but green and gray half-light between hoary trees and hearing nothing but his own thundering heart. He looked down at his hands, twisted and bony, the hands of a creature he hardly knew. The old man observed him, turned his head to both sides like a raven watching from a high branch. A strange thought chilled Thrand, and he wondered if this man was more than human. He was deep in the forests surrounding the Seine, and he may have found elves or something worse.

"You talk to yourself in the night," the man said. "Nonsense mostly, but at least we knew you were one of us and not a Frank. So if you are a Dane, alone and trying to steal our game, then you must be an outlaw. Am I right? Tell me the truth; give me a good story. If you do, and I like you, you may take a rabbit and leave our hunting grounds."

"What if I take the sack now and flee?" Thrand forced himself to sound commanding, but his voiced was weak and failing.

The blind man rocked in laughter, clapping his hands. When recovered, he wiped his nose with the sleeve of his deerskin shirt. "Well, why not try and find out?"

He shivered again at the man's threat, and the center of his back pricked as if he could feel an arrow point on it already. Slumping forward he put his face in his hands, and trembled. "You want to know my story? I dare not tell it to anyone, much less a stranger I chanced upon in the forest."

"I disagree, the chance meeting with a stranger may be just what you need. I already know you are an outlaw, and you entered our hunting grounds from the wrong side of the battle. So you've been to the Franks, am I right? You are a traitor. We've all guessed this from your first night here. So don't fret, for it we wanted your bounty you'd be strung up beside the rabbits. Give me a good story, and I'll keep my word."

The sack of rabbits swayed from its branch, as if agreeing with the blind man. Thrand sighed. "It is a long tale, and a shameful one. You may yet string me up."

"I wonder if I will. Go on, let these old ears hear your deeds. Leave nothing out."

Thrand omitted nothing, beginning the sordid tale from the death of his brother until Anscharic freed him to help the Franks slip through Danish lines. All the years of his life laid out in simple sentences, naked and unadorned, left Thrand feeling empty. He had wasted his life, fulfilling no purpose other than to drain the generosity of others and drink it away in mead and ale. "All my time in Anscharic's dark pit, and many nights in this forest, spirits have visited me. They have rebuked me for squandering my life. I became a slave to drink and it clouded my mind with foul thoughts. Then Kolbyr put evil into my mind, and I devoured it like a hungry dog. Now I am broken and lost, with no one to take me in."

The blind man bowed his head, listening to each word as if savoring the notes of a song. Once Thrand had spent himself on his confession, the blind man rose his head to face Thrand. "A tale of dishonor and waste. A life of glory turned to ignominy. Now you crawl on your belly like a worm, slithering in the dirt of the forest floor. Valhalla is closed to you and the heroes of that golden hall will never know your name. You are lost not only in body, but in spirit. Where will you wander now?"

"I don't know," Thrand dropped his face into his hands and hot tears began to leak into his palms. "Anscharic promised he would take me into his service were I to retrieve his cloak."

The blind man hissed like a snake, his lips drawn in a snarl. "More treachery, by you and against you. Do not trust the Franks to welcome you, not after your brothers have raped their lands and trapped them behind their walls."

"But Ulfrik would hang me for a traitor." Thrand leaned forward on his log seat, tears mingling with the mud on his face. "My own people despise me, and the Franks won't have me. I tried to find a home among them, but they all fear me. I cannot care for myself, and so I wanted to steal your rabbits. I am worthless and my life is ruined. I am well and truly lost."

The words echoed through the trees, and the blind man sat with his head resting on his fist while he cocked his head back and forth. Again the old man summoned the image of a raven, and Thrand searched the forest for the others. Nothing but woodland stillness greeted him. The blind man at last leaned back, placing his hands on his knees. "You are not lost. You know what must be done, but fear the deed. You fear for your life when your life is not worth having."

The words struck Thrand like a club across his back. He straightened on his seat, again reflexively grasping for the amulet that no longer hung on his neck. "I must redeem myself. I must answer for what I have done and for the oaths I have broken."

The man nodded, certain and confident. "Better to go to death with your debts paid than to die with them pressing on your heart."

Again Thrand found tears in abundance. Starting first as stifled sobs, his sorrow overflowed into uncontrolled spasms. Unlike times past, now he understood the source of his pain. The blind man waited with fatherly patience, until Thrand finally choked out his first words. "I am afraid of death. I am shamed."

"Death is for all mortal men. Do not fear it, for it will find you in the end. Fear only that you cannot embrace it when it arrives. The Fates have not yet tied off the threads of your life. Go find your jarl, listen to his judgment, and live with honor the days remaining to you."

Wiping the snot and slobber from his face with the ripped sleeve of his shirt, he nodded. "Your words are honest counsel. I have only piled shame upon shame trying to decide my next step. This is what I should've done from the beginning. I will find Ulfrik, and accept his judgment. Even if it is death."

"Wisdom at last," the blind man said, rubbing his knees and smiling. "Your tale has moved me, and I believe you will complete this task. Take the sack of rabbits. We will catch plenty more in this forest, now that you will leave."

Thrand sprung to his feet, thanking the blind man who stood and cut the sack from its tether as simply as if he were fully sighted. He placed the bag in Thrand's trembling hands. "Thank you for your kindness and for sparing me when you could've killed me. You are a noble man, the best I have ever met."

Cocking his head, the blind man smiled gently and released the bag. A gnarled finger pointed over Thrand's shoulder. "Travel in that direction and you will come to the Seine before nightfall. Camp on its banks, cook a rabbit, then in the daylight follow the Seine west to where your jarl awaits."

His mouth already salivating at the thought of hot food, Thrand bowed and thanked the blind man repeatedly. He set off straight in the direction the blind man had pointed him. Not until he had walked for a solid hour did he realize he had never learned the blind man's name, nor the name of his sons or his lord. He stopped, turned back on his trail, and called for the blind man. No sound responded, not even the rustle of leaves. His skin tingling with chill, he strode faster for the river bank.

THRAND HAD QUAILED at the sight of Paris, recalling the horrid stench and humid blackness of the pit. The city remained unchanged: smoke streamed away from rooftops; men patrolled the battlements, pennants waved in the breeze; and the walls remained defiantly intact. The stone bridge had been chipped and cracked where Sigfrid's rock-throwers had struck, but it too remained unbroken. The tower supporting it had men patrolling the wooden additions on its roof, clusters of black dots whose mail and helmets flashed in the late morning light. Scores of longships leaned on the river banks or floated at anchor in the brown river. Barracks constructed of fresh cut logs clumped on the cleared fields up from the Seine. Thrand's heart leapt when he saw the dozens of men at their chores. His people, however unwelcoming they would be, were near.

The final approach to the trenches felt like an hour's long journey. Thrand knew he counted his life in moments from this point. The knowledge gave a sharpness to his senses that he had long forgotten. Years of drinking had dulled his world, and now he could finally see and taste his surroundings as they were.

"Start talking or die." Two platinum-haired men stood in their trench, arrows laid across bowstrings drawn to their ears. Thrand tumbled back, hands in the air.

"Peace! I am one of you. I am sworn to Ulfrik Ormsson, and have been a prisoner of the Franks. Take me to him."

The men lowered their bows, reluctantly, Thrand thought. One man disappeared into the trench while the other waved Thrand closer. "I'll take you to him. How long you've been prisoner?"

"Longer than I can count." *And longer than I need ever have been*, he thought.

His escort took him as far as the central field where burnt-out bonfires spread their ashes into the wind. The man pointed at one of the buildings, distinguished only by the banners hanging before their doors. "Jarl Ulfrik's quarters there, though not sure if he's inside. He likes to patrol the trenches. What's your name again?"

"Thrand the Looker." He faced the man, ready to be tackled and beaten, but his escort simply struggled to focus on Thrand's good eye and smiled.

"Welcome back to the shit heap. Ulfrik will probably put you right back into the trenches with the rest of us. We need everyone in the line these days."

Thrand sighed as the obviously new man ambled back to his trench. Summoning his courage with a long breath, Thrand exhaled and approached Ulfrik's barracks. The green standard of Nye Grenner was gone, and Anscharic's cloak hung unmoving in the stiff breeze.

Suddenly his palms began to sweat and his legs trembled. *The cloak is right here*, he thought. *Just grab it and walk off, then join Anscharic in Paris. He promised a fortune, did he not? And the Franks will win this war. I could have all that I dreamed of, all that I killed for!*

Standing before the unmoving cloak, its heavy wool hems still full and tight despite the tears and stains throughout, Thrand stretched a hand toward it. His hand lingered a moment, then he snapped it back as if touching fire. Before he could change his mind, he flung open the barracks doors and thrust himself inside.

In the moments it took for his eyes to adjust to the dimness, he heard surprised voices and saw vague shapes of people standing up from the floor. No one reached for a weapon or reacted with violence. Thrand rubbed his eyes and entered deeper. The hall was unadorned, nothing more than a simple enclosure for a hearth and a berth for men to sleep on the dry earth. Across the hearth pit was a tall chair and a table with benches pushed into a corner. Even at this distance, his blurry eyes locked with Ulfrik's cold gaze. At first, he seemed to not recognize him, but in an instant he was on his feet.

"Seize that man! Don't let him escape!"

Now men grasped at him, each one vying to be the man to fulfill the jarl's orders. Thrand recognized no one, each one a foreign face. Two men threatened to tear Thrand in half as they wrestled him forward. He flopped like a rag, surrendering fully to his fate. To do otherwise would not achieve the redemption he desired. He crashed into the dirt at Ulfrik's feet, and one of the men kicked him in his side. Ulfrik shouted them away, and his familiar hand gripped Thrand by the arm and hauled him to his knees.

"Look at you," he said, lips curled in disgust. "Death has already claimed you, but you still walk."

"I have returned to face your judgment." He raised his face to Ulfrik's, but found he could not hold his eyes. He dropped his head. "I am an oath-breaker and murderer. I deserve death. I have fallen as low as a man can fall, and now land before you to seek redemption."

Thrand stared at the earth, listening to the scandalized murmurs circulating behind him. He could feel the strange men pressing closer to him. Ulfrik stood over him, unmoving and silent. Thrand resolved to say no more, for he could think of nothing worth his breath. Life would come to a sudden end, he expected, and he wanted to savor every breath.

"You planned to kill me once," Ulfrik said. "But you instead protected me."

"No, lord, I feared you could not be defeated, and I killed Kolbyr to buy myself more time. I was not motivated by good intentions."

Several onlookers cursed him, others gasped, but Ulfrik grunted. Thrand closed his eyes, expecting a blow that did not fall.

"You aided Humbert in his escape, and sought to defy me. We both know what motivated you." Thrand nodded, realizing Ulfrik still held his secret of Anscharic's treasure. Even though it was a ruse to bring them to Paris, Ulfrik still apparently believed it existed. "You voluntarily entered the Franks' tower. Why have you been released, if not for more treachery?"

Thrand squeezed his eyes tighter and bowed lower. "My treachery is done. The Franks used me to help slip messengers through your lines. I know not where they went, but it was to seek aid. After this service, I was released to do one final act for Anscharic. He wanted me to capture your standard and return it to him."

"I will wrap his corpse in it. He can have it back in the grave," Ulfrik said. "Now stand up, Thrand. Look at me."

He did as commanded, and Ulfrik's face was no longer disgusted. Instead, he studied Thrand with a strange mixture of curiosity, anger, and pity. Thrand had earned all of it and more, and he did not flinch from it. For his part, Ulfrik appeared more tired and haggard than he had ever known him to be. Yet gold armbands and rings glittered where none had before, showing he had earned the respect of his lord and grown in power.

Though no other face was familiar, Thrand did recognize Einar. The giant man hung in the shadows behind Ulfrik's chair. His face was tight and closed, and he looked through Thrand as if he did not exist. Once they had been close friends, but like everything else, Thrand had destroyed that relationship with his drinking and self-pity.

"Here is my judgment for your crimes." Ulfrik took his chair, uncharacteristically stiff and formal. He scanned the men behind Thrand as he spoke. "You were once a loyal man who protected my wife and son, and risked your life to aid my brother and dearest friend in his time of need. I cannot forget what you have done for me. The law provides the right to claim your life, but I will not. Your life is yours to live, Thrand the Looker. Instead, I banish you from my lands and my people. You may not return to my banner, and to do so will invite death. I assume if I see you again, you will have chosen to end your life."

A clamor of disapproving, bloodthirsty opposition came from Ulfrik's men. Thrand stood, hand reaching for his neck. "But I should die. It is the only way to redeem myself for what I've done."

"You've heard my judgment," Ulfrik shouted. The disapproving crowd hushed as Ulfrik scowled at them. Satisfied at regaining control, he turned a gentler face to Thrand. "Death does not have to be the only way. Find another lord to serve and do so loyally, then your life will be redeemed with meaning again. Now be gone. Einar will escort you to the edge of our camp."

"No one will let me serve, and the Franks will kill me. Lord Ulfrik, you condemn me to death no matter what."

Men jeered him, and one threw the scraps of a meal into Thrand's face. Others began to pelt him with whatever came to hand, until Einar intercepted them and grabbed Thrand's arm. With a withering look, he pushed back the mob, and dragged Thrand from the barracks. Outside, Thrand began to sob. "I wanted to die today. I was ready for it."

"Stop crying," Einar said flatly. "I'll take you to the edge of the camp and then you're on your own."

Thrand stumbled behind Einar as he dragged him like a child across the cleared fields. Men paused to watch them pass. Thrand's mind was ablaze with confusion. He had prepared for death, but now had to live out his days as an enemy of everyone. Once out of sight of most men, Einar stopped.

"This is not the edge of the lands, but it is close enough. Go, and good luck to you."

"You are sending me to death. I will just kill myself, that's what I'll do. It's better than starving or becoming a slave to the Franks."

Einar bowed his head. "If Lord Ulfrik wanted you dead, he'd have done it. Don't be a fool. Listen, you have made bad mistakes and drinking has clouded your mind. I think you are better now. More of the old Thrand I knew. There are many battles ahead, and if you can find a way to serve Lord Ulfrik again he may yet accept you. We both know he is merciful and he has felt grateful to you all these years. Besides, no matter if motivated from greed or good, you did prevent Kolbyr from murdering him."

Thrand scanned the dark line of trees ahead and shuddered. "I cannot serve from that forest. I can't even hunt. I threw away all my rabbits, thinking I'd die today. Now I'll starve."

"Be a scout for us," Einar said, his voice brightening with his idea. "Watch the land for approaching Franks or signs of other trouble. I'll keep you supplied. If you can do this, you might redeem yourself with useful service. It's the best idea I have."

Thrand welcomed any plan that did not end with his death. "I will do it. I will do anything to be who I once was."

Einar's smile faded, and he patted Thrand's shoulder. "Don't think of what was, but what will be. And don't get me in trouble with Lord Ulfrik, or we'll both be scavenging the forests and wishing we were dead."

31

The fields around Ingrid's halls crawled with the black shapes of armored men converging on it. Birds circled in the gray skies above, and Runa studied them. She realized the sea birds had learned that groups of armored men left behind corpses for them to pick apart. She gently shook her head, disgusted that such a scene had happened enough to teach the birds. The mail coat hung heavy on her shoulders, and sagged from being too large. Her helmet, however, fit perfectly, though she had not realized the nose and cheek guards would restrict her vision so severely.

"No resistance yet," Konal said, standing next to her with his sword drawn. "Maybe there's no one here."

"They'll be in the hall," she said with feigned certainty. Her heart told her Ingrid had gone over to Thorod and Skard, but she lacked proof.

"Then we will drag them out." Gunnar drew his small sword and pointed it at the hall. Runa's heart jumped, looking at the childish hand of her son aiming his sword for a death stroke. She pushed the sword down.

"We will storm the hall, but you will remain on the ship." He whirled to protest, but Runa's anger flared. "No arguments! Don't cause me to regret allowing you to follow."

Runa blinked as he offered no resistance and sheathed his sword. Before he turned back for the ship, he hugged her. "Be careful, Mother."

Swallowing hard, she faced the hall. Her life was not in danger.

But Ingrid's was.

Seeing her pale form appear in the doorway, Runa's pulse quickened. Without a word, she charged ahead with Konal following behind. Kell and all the other crew stood in front of Ingrid, spears leveled and weapons drawn. Sweat beaded on Runa's forehead as she forced through the ring of men to stand before Ingrid.

"You have betrayed me," she said, leveling her sword. "In my husband's absence, I come to enforce your oath and have justice for your crimes."

"Runa?" Ingrid's eyes squinted and she leaned forward as if looking out to sea. "By the gods, you're in a mail shirt and helmet. You're wearing pants." Placing a pale hand over her mouth, she began to laugh.

Plowing her fist into Ingrid's soft gut, she let her collapse to the ground as she continued past into the hall.

"Restrain her and follow me," she shouted over her shoulder as she kicked open the hall doors.

Her eyes did not adjust to the dark hall as she swept in, and a momentary panic at her blindness filled her. A few women screamed, and several male voices shouted. The hall smelled like sheep and stale beer. When her vision returned, five men ringed Halla and several other serving women. Runa recognized none of the other faces. A man ran for another exit to Runa's left.

She glided across the pounded dirt floor and intercepted him as Konal and his men flowed into the hall. The man had not drawn his weapons, and pulled up at the sharp edge of Runa's blade. "You're not from here, are you?"

The four men in front of Runa drew their swords. Their trembling hands set the blades glinting in the dull light slanting in from high windows. None of them appeared confident, not with the dozens of scar-faced men flooding the hall.

Runa's opponent glanced at the door, estimating his escape. She already knew he was one of Skard's or Thorod's men. He had the same youthful, cocksure look as the invaders from winter. He flinched toward the exit.

Her blade slashed up and shaved off a hunk of his upper lip and the tip of his nose. He flew back, both hands covering his face as blood streamed onto his chest. She followed through, knocking him to the ground and running him through his gut. She could feel his pulse thrumming up the blade, and she yanked it free. His hands fell away and his breath gurgled blood in death.

Women screamed and Halla began to cry. Runa stared at the man she had killed. She had killed before, but that had been long ago and the man had tried to rape her. Seeing this young man leaking black blood into the dirt at her feet made her stomach lurch. Shaking her head, she stepped over the body with her bloodied sword leading her toward the others.

"Stand down and you will get a clean death. Fight and I will make death last for days."

Konal's men crammed forward, and the men on the stage of the high table glanced at each other. Certain they planned to surrender, she lowered her blade.

"For Skardholmur!" The four men leapt off the stage, slashing at anyone opposing them. One man plowed into Runa, sprawling her out.

Both Ulfrik and Konal had knocked her flat so often, instinct drove her recovery. However, she had never practiced in a mail shirt.

The weight of the mail on her chest pinned her flat. The man above her roared and raised his sword. She kicked into his legs, tripping him.

A spear thrust overhead and impaled the attacker's shoulder. Runa used the moment to scrabble to her feet. In that time, the three others were dead and her opponent tumbled to the ground as the spear lanced in through his neck.

The hall vibrated with screeching women, most of who had crumpled into weeping piles around Halla. She stood with both hands clutching a wooden cross over her chest. Her face was drained of color and her mouth hung slack. Runa hated her sister-in-law for all the trouble she had brought to her family. Smelling the blood and fear, again Runa could blame Halla for more misfortune. For a moment, she envisioned ending her curse, but shook the thought from her mind.

"Five fighting men," she stated flatly. "Who named Skardholmur as they died? We are at war with Skard and Thorod, are we not, Halla?"

"Christ protects me," she said, thrusting the cross in front of her.

Runa removed her helmet, and sneered at her. Throwing the helmet onto the floor, she whirled to view the hall. Dark faces crowded it, making Ingrid's platinum hair stand out like the moon at midnight. "Bring Ingrid forward. I will give my judgment now."

She did not know the proper way to handle a wayward bondsman. As far as she knew, it was within her right to kill Ingrid. No matter what she decided, she needed to appear above worry, fear, or care. She needed to be a powerful and confident leader, so that the men she planned to lead in battle would believe in her. She shoved Halla aside with her bloody hand, leaving a dark red stain on her shoulder, and pulled the bench of the high table forward. Runa stepped onto it, standing high above all others.

"Ingrid, you swore an oath to my husband and now I find you in league with our enemies."

Ingrid hung between two men. Both Konal and Kell emerged from the crowd, standing beneath Runa to lend their presence to the judgment. Behind them, men began dragging the slain enemies from the hall, but not before picking over the corpses for valuables.

"Your husband is dead!" Ingrid raised her head, her face pasty white and contorted with hate. Blue veins stood out on her head and her thinning hair clung to her sweaty cheeks. "I owe nothing to you. I look to the safety of my own people."

"And that safety is harboring my enemies and sending them south to rape and murder."

Ingrid let her head drop, but Runa knew she had revealed the truth. Her hands trembling, she struggled to keep her voice even.

"Over winter, men who looked just like the five we found here invaded my hall. I killed them, as you might have guessed. Before the last one died, he told me how you took them into your hall, how you spoke to them about the easy prey to the south and all the gold awaiting them. He said you promised them anything they could take, as long as you were left alone. You were kin, after all."

"Stop!" Ingrid shouted. Raising her head, her lips quivered and tears streaked from her eyes. Her puffy eyes locked with Runa's, searching them for mercy. "I did as I must, to protect my people."

"You don't deny anything I've said?" Ingrid bowed her head, crying more powerfully. "You thought to protect your people by sending enemies into my hall, to rape me and kill my son? They held my son with a knife to his throat. Shall I show you what that was like?"

Even in her mail shirt, her motions were too fast for anyone to stop. She leapt from the bench and latched onto Halla. With all the strength of her training and anger, Runa yanked her before Ingrid. She clasped one arm about her waist, and with her other hand drew her sax to Halla's neck.

"This is what you sent to me. Do you like it?" Runa jabbed the tip into Halla's chin, drawing blood and a piercing scream. Ingrid refused to watch, so one of the men twisted her head to face Runa.

"Do you like this? Is this how I should protect my family?"

"She had nothing to do with this. Please, leave her alone."

"Neither did my son," Runa said, then shoved Halla to the ground. "Enough. You are worse than an oath-breaker. You are a traitor and an enemy. Do you not wonder who these men are?"

Ingrid stirred, half raising her head to peek at the men around her.

"They are my army. They will sail with me to destroy Skard and Thorod. I promised them blood and plunder from all my enemies. You have sided with them, Ingrid."

"All the men were gone! For years I stood with you, and for years we had less and less. What was I supposed to do? I did not know you had an army."

"Had you known, your loyalty would not have been swayed?" Runa nodded to a man, indicating he should pick Halla from the floor. "My husband has doubted you for years, and I've doubted you from the start. No excuses will save you now."

Ingrid and Halla both stared at her, unblinking eyes locked to hers. Runa let them wonder at their fate, before she gave her decision.

"You should die for your crimes, but I am sure if my husband were here he'd find mercy in his heart. He would forgive you." She stepped down from the stage, and placed her hand on Ingrid's head. "But I am not my husband."

Driving Ingrid's head down, she brought up her knee. Bone crunched and blood sprayed as Ingrid's nose flattened under the blow. Halla screamed and fought to free herself. Still pinned between the two men, Runa grabbed Ingrid by the hair.

"Here's my judgment for you. You will speak no more lies and break no more oaths. I will have your tongue cut out."

"No," she protested through the blood and snot leaking over her mouth. "You can't do that."

"I have men who will do it for me." She whirled to Halla, who shuddered with a mixture of fear and anger. "And you are so innocent? You are the wife of my brother, and yet you allowed your mother to send men to rape me and kill my son? I should throw you from a cliff."

Halla began to shake her head, and the defiant gesture inflamed Runa. Seizing her chin to stop the shaking, she pulled Halla's face closer. "You are the real curse, not Toki. If I truly thought my husband and brother dead, then your life would end today. So thank them for it when you see them again. You will remain my hostage, since even without a tongue your black-hearted mother might still contrive a way to threaten me."

Facing Konal and Kell, both regarded her with passionless faces.

She expected something from Konal, either revulsion or approval, but found only bland patience. She waved her hand dismissively.

"Make sure Ingrid survives the removal of her tongue. Halla returns with us. Everything in this hall, from the servants to the thatch on the roof is for you and your men to take."

She exited as the men began to laugh and tear apart the hall for whatever they could find. She heard Halla screaming, but nothing from Ingrid. Outside, the air felt fresh and cool. The blood on her hand had caked and started to flake. More men waited outside. Looking past them to the ships in the distance, she thought of Gunnar waiting for her to return. She began to stride confidently toward the shore.

Only once she had passed all of Konal's men did she let the tears escape. She did not understand them, and did not welcome them. She was the jarl now, and treachery had to be dealt with violence. She feared her violence had not been enough, and would one day cost her more than she had gained.

32

July 13, 886 CE

Ulfrik surveyed the battlefield. The piles of bodies were mostly Danes, arrows lining their corpses like feathered spines. A light rain fell from the dark sky, plinking into puddles of muddy water and blood. The cheers of the tower's defenders were like the thunder of the storm that threatened to worsen. He spit onto the grass, a foamy mass of saliva and blood. His face still burned where the Frankish spear had raked it.

Men slogged back from the northern tower to retire to their trenches. Banners were limp and sodden in the light but steady rain. Humbert's cloak hung in defeat overhead. Mord had driven the banner pole into the earth, which now grew muddy and caused the pole to list.

"Take the banner down," he said to Mord. "I don't want it to fall into the mud. See to the wounded."

"Not many survived the arrow storm," he said while dragging the pole out of the mud. Einar and several others ambled up, blood and dirt on their faces. "Either you lived or died in that."

"More reinforcements for the Franks," said one of the onlookers. "And more of our own leaving every day."

"Only the worthless fled, and the strong have remained. Never worry, for once we get the Franks to grips, we will slay them to a man." Ulfrik offered courage to his men, who smiled weakly or not at all.

"Ulfrik, come to Hrolf's quarters." Gunther One-Eye's gravelly voice carried across the short stretch of field. He waved toward the quarters, which Hrolf had built for himself and his bodyguards. Only a temporary abode, it was made from the same rough-hewn logs as the other barracks. The pale yellow wood stood out against the black line of trees behind it.

Waving back, he gestured Mord and Einar to follow. As they crossed the field, men bore their injured companions toward the tents where women tended them. Two men carried another with an arrow in his eye, and amazingly the victim still lived—cursing every god he could name.

"He should be thanking the gods," Mord said. "A man can do well with one eye."

Ulfrik chuckled as they continued past. "I know the man you speak of, but I think he sees with three eyes instead of one."

He gave Mord a knowing look. He frowned in confusion, shaking his head.

"I don't know why your father sent you to spy on me, but I hope you have entertained him with good stories. The days have been long and boring."

"Why would you accuse me of spying, Lord Ulfrik?"

"Because it's true." Both he and Einar laughed, while Mord fell quiet.

Men idled outside the hall, chatting in low voices, heads pulled down against the stiffening rain. Gunther waited his turn to enter. The doorway was small and the quarters were not meant to house large groups. Ulfrik approached his old friend.

"You look too fresh to have done any fighting. Were you pissing yourself at the back of the line?" Ulfrik clapped Gunther's back, who laughed at the joke.

"And someone improved your looks." Gunther pointed inside. "Turns out that was no ordinary reinforcement breaking through. We've got a prisoner and he's talking. That was Odo himself returning to Paris."

"He was not already in Paris?" Gunther shrugged.

Each jarl was admitted, but could only take one man. Ulfrik tapped Einar and Mord waited outside. Escaping the drumming rain was a relief, and the snapping hearth fire created a warm dryness in the room. Hrolf sat on a chair looking awkward in what had been built for a shorter man. Two spearmen in full mail flanked him. Ulfrik noted they looked dry and comfortable, while the assembled jarls and their men were sodden and miserable.

The smoke hole was not wide enough, and white haze filled the room as it backed up at the ceiling. Ulfrik and several others coughed. He was about to complain when Hrolf stood.

"Our prisoner has been willing to talk." Ulfrik noted the splotches of blood around Hrolf's knees and boots.

"I bet he's not talking anymore," he whispered to Einar. The comment, which Ulfrik had thought inaudible to others, drew Hrolf's smile.

"He will be sacrificed to the gods at dawn tomorrow. I've got everything I need to know from him, and all are bad tidings."

A murmur circulated through the group, though Ulfrik merely folded his arms and waited. He wondered how this situation could worsen.

"Odo had slipped our lines months ago, and sought aid from his Emperor, Charles the Fat. He has returned successful. Charles is bringing his army from the south, and his brother Henry of Saxony is closing from the east."

Hrolf studied the faces of his assembled men, his eyes flinty and jaw set. When he met Ulfrik's, he nodded.

"We will be outnumbered and surrounded if this happens."

"Then we should meet the fat king's army before he arrives and crush him. We'll take his kingdom," said one of the jarls. A few voices added agreement, but Ulfrik remained mute. The idea of leaving Paris to attack the emperor was foolish, and Hrolf would know it.

"A fine idea, friend, but the emperor's army is three times the size of ours at its peak. Besides, we are here to sack Paris or force a tribute of silver. I've no plans to rule Frankia, for now, at least."

His comment drew the intended laughter, though it was short-lived and uninspired.

"We should make one final attempt on Paris," Ulfrik stated. "Either we break through now or we go home."

Hrolf closed his eyes and silently nodded his agreement. Gunther slapped Ulfrik's back, adding his own encouragement to the idea. Soon all in the room had resolved to make one final push.

"I will have the siege tower repaired." Hrolf joined with the rest of his jarls, moving among them to stop by Ulfrik's side. "Ladders will be built to new heights, and we will be ready for their tricks this time. Before help can reach them, Paris will be a pile of rubble and we will be away."

"How long do we have before the Franks arrive in force?" Ulfrik asked, anxious to have a point in time that he could focus on returning to his family.

"Maybe a month before their emperor arrives, and sooner if he hurries. We can ill afford a delaying attack, but I may send men after Henry of Saxony."

"I will lead the attack," Ulfrik heard Einar suck his breath. Ulfrik's other concern was the lack of plunder and failure to find riches. A rich lord would be a fine ransom.

"Let me consider your offer," Hrolf touched Ulfrik's shoulder, and returned to his chair. Other jarls scowled at Ulfrik, but he ignored them. If they were dull witted and slow, it was not his concern.

Hrolf continued at length on details of their strengths and his plans for the final assault. Ulfrik listened and nodded at the right moments, but his mind traveled back home. Snorri and Toki would have arrived by now, bringing Runa hope as well as protection. He had drilled Runa in basic sword techniques, enough to surprise an unwary man attempting to harm her or their sons. However, it could never be enough in the face of a real attack.

He longed to feel Runa's warm skin under his hand, smell the sweet scent of her hair, and hear the gentle purr of her voice. He wanted to whisk Gunnar into his arms, and carry him on his shoulders as he did years ago, one final time before his son became too old for such frivolity. Hakon would be walking steadily now, and Ulfrik wondered if the boy remembered him. All those desires were so far away, and all that sat between fulfillment and him was Paris. All oaths would resolve when the walls fell.

At last they were dismissed and Ulfrik wandered outside with the others, still lost in thought until Einar broke in.

"Where did your heart go while Hrolf spoke? You were not in the room with us."

He grinned. "It went home, Einar. If we breach these walls, then I can avenge Ander, claim the treasure we came seeking, and be clear to return home."

Outside, the rain slapped Ulfrik's warm face like a cold hand. Mord, now pulled into his cowl, joined them. Completely bedraggled from standing in the rain, he smiled when he saw them.

"All dried off? I've been thinking about what you said, Lord Ulfrik. My father never asked me to spy on you, I just assumed that was my role."

"And have you done well in it?"

"I have." Mord fell in with them as they rushed through the rain for their barracks. "But you've know it all along?"

"Of course."

"My father believes you will become a great jarl under Hrolf, and he wants to know what you stand for."

"And make sure he's always on the winning side. He told me that himself."

"True." They fell silent for the final distance over the muddy field, but as they arrived at the barracks, Mord spoke up again. "Hrolf has no plans to release you once this is done. My father has said so more than once. Do you know that?"

Ulfrik did not answer. He did not want to consider what he had long suspected: even if Paris collapsed today, he might never return home again.

～

ULFRIK WATCHED from the rear ranks with Hrolf and his block of fighting men. After weeks of planning, building, and drilling, hundreds of Danes now scrabbled up the walls of the north tower. Less than half the force remained from eight months before, but the defenders were just as strong. Ulfrik glanced at Mord, who gripped Nye Grenner's standard with a white-knuckled hand. He saw his own worry slashed into the taut lines of his face.

The attack was faltering.

Ropes of fire poured down the tower walls, searing the men below and driving them into the river. Franks shoved away ladder crews, screaming Danes clinging like bugs on a falling branch. The mighty arrow storm from both sides thrummed in the air, shafts snapping on stone walls or clunking into wooden shields. Men cried out in death and fear, frustration and rage. Those who surmounted the top of the tower spent their lives at great cost, hurling Franks out of their defenses to shatter their bodies at the foot of the tower. The air tasted bitter with burnt flesh and spilled blood.

Again the Franks defeated the battering ram, this time with fire arrows and burning pitch. Even after soaking the ram housing in water, it still burned. The iron doors had not even bent before the crew scattered.

"Shall we bring up the attack?" asked an eager-eyed hirdman in Hrolf's command. "The men need inspiration."

Hrolf growled but said nothing. Ulfrik shared his lord's black mood. Lives were being wasted on this tower assault, but there was no other entrance. To directly assail the walls of the city was even more dangerous, giving the defenders a wider berth to fire their bows. As it was, their arrows were deadly enough when shot from the limited space of the tower.

Men streamed away from the tower, covered in blood and fear stretched tight on their faces. It was a scene so often repeated Ulfrik had no need to see it. He closed his eyes against the tide of the vanquished.

Defeat.

He would not be leading a force through the opened tower doors, to push inside and then across the bridge into Paris. Instead, he would wait patiently for Hrolf to admit defeat and conserve his fighting force for another day.

"Sound the withdrawal," Hrolf said after too few men remained to sustain the attack. When his hirdman questioned him, he struck the poor fool in the jaw and screamed his order again. The first notes were weak, the man recovering from the staggering blow, but as his notes strengthened other horns joined. Soon, the riverbank reverberated with the sad call of retreat.

Having never witnessed Hrolf striking his own, Ulfrik regarded his lord. His teeth gnashed in bitter determination, which Ulfrik took as a poor sign. Though he had promised one last attempt before departing Paris, Ulfrik was certain Hrolf would not back down. He would lead them all to their deaths before abandoning his ambition. In his heart, Hrolf was stubborn and driven, and he fostered heavy grudges. His fury was not typical of the Norse people; it was every bit as intense, but slower and steadier and capable of burning far past the point where another man's rage would extinguish.

Ulfrik was tied to this man, who had tied himself to vanquishing Paris. All the while, the defeated army flowed around both of them.

They stood in place, a block of discipline amid a chaos of disorder, each man looking ahead—fixing on nothing but their own thoughts. The Franks cheered, as usual lauding their gods Christ and Saint Denys. Ulfrik wondered if their other god, Saint Denys, was responsible for defying Odin and Thor. To Ulfrik's mind, the gods of the Norsemen had grown bored and abandoned them to the new gods.

"Lord, they have shown a white sheet. What does it mean?" One of the hirdmen pointed at the tower, where a white flag fluttered in the wind while the Franks continued to cheer. Ulfrik did not understand the meaning.

"They want to parley, or surrender." Hrolf's voice did not sound as if he believed they intended surrender. "It's a sign for a temporary peace, like our hazel branch. I will go to hear what they say."

Hrolf took Ulfrik and Gunther along with ten other spearmen, each bearing the siege shields that to Ulfrik appeared more like hall doors. Not even the dirty Franks would attack under the sign of truce, but precaution was always prudent. A translator, a Dane who had long lived in Frankia, accompanied them. They had to step over bodies and slog through bloody pools. A hand grabbed Ulfrik's ankle, a weak and trembling grip of a man not yet dead. Pulling his foot away, he continued forward. Too many suffered like this man, and to save them all would take a half day of labor. Normally, the Franks allowed them to cart away the dead and injured as long as only small parties worked at it.

Halting before the tower, puddles of flame still twisted at the base of the walls. Ulfrik averted his eyes from the smashed corpses, his stomach churning from memories of the sounds of shattering bodies. Gore sprayed the ground along with spent arrows, broken weapons, and blood-soaked clothing. Ulfrik kicked away a busted shield, and squinted up. The flag withdrew and a gray-haired man leaned over the edge, speaking perfect Norse.

"Jarl Hrolf, why have you persisted in this foolish quest? Return to your ships and leave. God forbids you entrance to our city."

"Humbert!" Ulfrik shouted before Hrolf could answer. "I'll pull apart every stone of your walls to get you. I'll dance in your guts!"

"Ah, my old master, Ulfrik. My name is Anscharic and you would do well to learn it. I am bishop now that poor brother Joscelin has passed on to our Lord in Heaven."

"I'll call you a dead man. You killed my hirdman and friend." Ulfrik stepped forward, shaking his fist at the walls. Anscharic spoke to the men beside him, and laughter filtered down.

"I've put a price on your life, Ulfrik. You will not live long."

Ulfrik inhaled to roar back defiance, but Hrolf's long arm yanked him by the hood of his cloak. "Forget your grudges with the old man. Let me talk."

Glaring at the shadowed faces laughing at him atop the tower, he reluctantly stepped back in line. Hrolf cupped his hands to his mouth and shouted.

"Listen, fools, your king has not come and Henry has died on the way to save you. If your god loves your city so much, why has he delayed and killed those who seek to protect you?"

The Franks disappeared back over the edge. Hrolf chuckled, then spoke to his men. "Their wondering if that news is true. I'm glad someone up there is translating for me."

The Danes laughed, but Ulfrik glowered. At this moment, he would trade his life for a bow to shoot Anscharic off the walls.

"Unless you called me here to surrender," Hrolf continued, "you waste your time. For seven hundred pounds of silver, I will be pleased to take my men away. Otherwise, you'd die happier if you jumped from this tower."

Hrolf folded his arms, and the Franks continued to murmur. Their white flag withdrew, and Ulfrik along with the others raised shields expecting an ambush. Only Hrolf did not flinch. Soon, Anscharic leaned over the wall again.

"God will have no mercy on you. Leave before you perish in the mud." Anscharic withdrew along with the defenders.

Hrolf led his group back to the line, stepping over the dead as if they were nothing more than stones in his path. "If we can't defeat these walls, then we will starve them into submission. The Franks are not as confident as they want us to believe. The carry on about their god, but it is empty boasting. Their god is dead, and can't help them. Don't fret, in a few more months they will be starving and ready to open their gates."

Ulfrik swallowed his anger, and glanced at Einar. He shook his head, and Ulfrik agreed with the silent condemnation he read in his face. Months from now, they would be no closer to breaking the

Franks. He closed his eyes and imagined Snorri and Toki arriving to a happy and safe Nye Grenner, where Runa and his sons prospered and received them with joy.

To imagine anything else would inflict more pain than the bite of a Frankish arrow through his heart.

33

Two ships raced across the gray waters, strong winds filling their red sails. Men bristled on the deck, sharpening spears and swords, checking belts and fasteners, or testing the strength of their shields. These were men sailing for war, hearts full of bloodlust and desire for gold. Gulls rode the winds above the ships, squawking encouragement, eager to be led to a feast of flesh and entrails.

Summer had come to the Faereyar Islands, coloring the fields green and the mountains blue. The season of the raider was at hand.

Runa stood with Konal at the tiller. Though the weather was balmy, she swathed herself in a gray woolen cloak. Her pants were loose and comfortable, and her sword and sax carried easily on their baldrics. She would no longer wear mail to battle; its weight was a hindrance and danger to her. Instead, she covered herself with a wolf pelt. Animal skins were almost as much proof against a blade as mail, and less restrictive.

Runa the Bloody would don the armor of the great berserks. She planned to fight like one, as well.

The deck rolled with the waves and sea spray dappled her face in cool pinpoints. Konal guided his ship close to the shores of the islands. Runa did not know the exact location of Thorod's hall, and so they followed instructions given by one of Ingrid's people.

"Mother, I don't want to stay on the ship," Gunnar said, tugging Runa's cloak to draw her eye down to him. "I want to stand with you."

Gazing down on him, he appeared even smaller amid so many strong warriors. She had considered leaving him with the women and his brother, but surrendered to his persistence. He wanted to accompany the men to battle. Though his eyes and hair were hers, Gunnar's heart was all of Ulfrik's. She patted his shoulder, and dismissed him with a faint smile.

"I need a guard for my ship," Konal said. "I've trained you and your friends for that very task."

Shaking his head, he defied his young age by seeing through the trick. "You want me out of the way."

"That too." Konal laughed. "Now if the directions are true, then Thorod's hall should be along that beach."

Runa followed his pointing finger to a dark strip of rocky beach that swept up into hilly grassland. A velvety purple ridge of mountains backed it up. Squinting ahead, she detected delicate twirls of smoke rising amid the hills. "I see their hearth smoke. We have found them."

The crew animated at the news, leaning over the rails to view their landing area. Some began to take their colorful shields off the rails, slinging them over their backs. Konal's second stood in the stern and yelled orders to Kell's ship trailing behind. Once he had their attention, hand signals conveyed his intentions. Watching these ships coordinate their actions bought her mind back to when she had sailed with Ulfrik against Harald Finehair. The battles fought aboard Ulfrik's ships had stained the decks red with blood. She had stood amid fighting and dying men and terror had rendered her useless. Now, nearly a decade later, she would stand at the center of carnage, just as terrified but prepared to fight and kill. She ran her hands along the racked shields until one felt right, then she tugged it free.

Wary of rocks, Konal and Kell dropped their anchor stones in the shallows and the men had to slog to the shore. Gunnar grabbed Runa's arm before she dropped over the rails. She had wanted to avoid seeing him, knowing she might not survive true combat. He looked at her with sober eyes that expressed his realization of the danger. Her neck pulsed and her face was hot. Nothing had prepared her for what to say, and so she remained mute. Gunnar released her, and she splashed into the water.

Stumbling through the cold water, the rocks were sharp against her feet. Konal and Kell organized their men into groups, and looked expectantly at her.

"You're the leader," Konal said, smiling. "Take us to whom you want slain."

"Follow the smoke," she said, not knowing what else she should say. "Drag them out of their homes and do as you will. If they resist, put them down."

They marched up the slope into the shoulders of rocks that concealed Thorod's hall. Kell ordered men ahead to flush out concealed archers, but they found none. The hall emerged amid a thick green field, surrounded by smaller buildings. A horn sounded, and she knew they had been spotted. Behind her, men closed their ranks and raised shields.

"You better get in line with us, if they send men to battle." Konal opened a place to his left.

Runa studied the hall. Distant shouts preceded men and women who rushed toward it. Nothing indicated an organized force intended to meet them.

"If Thorod won't come out, we can break in." She pointed at the hall, and started toward it.

The men scouting ahead now emerged into the open, and escorted the flanks of the main body up the hill until they arrived at the village. Except for a gull perched on a roof ridge, the place was empty. Several buildings had collapsed, and decay had overtaken others. Only the hall appeared in repair, though shattered barrels were strewn around the walls.

"If I didn't see hearth smoke, I'd consider this place abandoned."

Runa scratched the back of her neck. The wolf pelt fur itched her skin wherever it touched.

"They gathered in the hall for protection," Kell said, stepping out from the line. "Unless it's a trap, this is the action of a desperate man."

"We can burn it down and sift the ashes later," Konal suggested. He joined Runa, tapping his shield to hers. "You just want to kill these bastards anyway. Don't need to do it with your bare hands, right?"

Again Runa had no words. She wanted nothing but death for the men who had driven her family to poverty and starvation, and who had sent their sons to murder. Now, standing amid a ruined village that seemed to have suffered the same as her own, she hesitated.

"I want answers. Tear down those doors and let's find what is inside."

"A hall burning is better, and safer for us."

Runa glared at Konal until he snickered and relented. He ordered men to smash open the doors with their two handed axes. Each blow on the door brought a flurry of screams from within the hall. Most of the voices sounded female.

"Feels good to strike terror into your enemy's heart." Konal admired his men at work. "Revenge is a delicious supper."

As the men wrestled their axes free of the sundered door, other men came forward with spears and bows with arrows strung. They kicked apart the wood as carelessly as if it were an ordinary day's work. One even stooped to drag timbers out of the opening. No one attacked.

"I'll go first, and you come behind." Konal barred Runa from stepping through the breach. She did not resist.

Sweeping in behind Konal, she found a hall of women and children and elderly. Six men armed with swords and spears had ranked up at the center of the narrow hall. The light from the smoke hole dropped squarely on their heads, lining them in a bluish-white glow and filling the shallows of their faces with black.

As more men pushed inside, Runa strode the short span to the enemy. Holding her sword low and forward, she kept her shield high on her left. The men responded in kind, shifting into fighting stances.

She searched their gaunt faces for Thorod, but could not identify him. All seemed equally poor.

"If this is all you can muster, you are defeated." Runa filled her voice with all the derision she possessed. "A hundred men surround you."

Her words drew cries and moans from the women. Her eyes did not leave the men arrayed against her, but she stretched her vision so no one might surprise her from the side. No one moved, except for her own warriors. Konal swept the line with his sword, pointing to all of them.

"One of you must be the leader, or you're at least hiding him. You can't be protecting these people, since we've already got them as hostages."

A girl shrieked with horror in time with Konal's words. Runa struggled not to turn behind, leaving herself open to attack. Yet the terrified screaming elicited more from others, until the hall vibrated with terrorized howls and the rough barks of the aggressors. The sounds returned awful memories of her own family hall being raided.

She shook her head. *These are your enemies,* she reminded herself, *these men would rape you and your women, kill your men and take your children as slaves. Don't pity them because they cannot carry out their evil.*

The six men wavered and stole glances at each other. Two of them were not young, gray hair showing at their temples and at the roots of their beards. One finally lowered his sword. "This is all that is left. That last of the hirdmen have joined with Skard."

"Liar!" Runa's sword flickered in the milky light, but one of the other men parried the half-hearted thrust with a spear. He did not counter, so Runa let her blade lower. "You are hiding Thorod here."

The man coughed a dry laugh. "We are hiding his bones under the earth. Thorod died of fever this winter, along with his wife and two sons. Only Gauti, his middle son, lived, and he took the hird to Skard." The man's expression grew distant, and his eyes clouded. "You came too late to defeat us. The fever claimed mostly men. The gods have extracted revenge for you."

That the gods might side with her shocked Runa. She scanned the hall, finding scared and desperate faces. These people were her enemies, but they were too much like her own.

"Better the gods burn you from the inside than me burning you in this hall." She pointed her blade at the man. "Your name?"

"I am Bjornolf, and for lack of anyone else I am who serves as a leader here."

"But Skard has the hird. So you serve him still." The man swallowed, and nodded. "Then you are my enemy. You will climb aboard Skard's ships, sail to my home, and slit my throat. But not before having your way with me. Am I mistaken? Five foolish young men tried that over winter, and I have their heads on poles to show how poor an idea that was. Yet it won't stop you, will it? A whole army at your back, kicking apart my hall and carrying away everything of worth."

Runa's voice intensified as she recounted all the horrors she knew awaited her when Skard finally organized his force. The man shook his head, but he refused to meet her eyes. She knew he lied.

"You have probably been to Nye Grenner to raid. Isn't that so, Bjornolf? Do you know who I am?"

"You are Ulfrik's wife."

"No! I am Runa the Bloody. And I will show you how I earned that name. Konal, bring me one of their children."

Konal did not react, merely regarding her with indifference. She shouted her command again, and he turned to the first child he spotted, grabbing a girl by the leg and dragging her forward. The hall erupted in screams. The six men lurched forward to defend the girl, but a wall of sharp iron warded them off.

Runa twisted her hand into the girl's blond locks. She wondered if the child could feel her arms quivering with fear. Runa hoped someone had the sense to beg for her life, or she would have to follow through on her bluff.

"Men from this place have killed my people for years, either in battle or by raiding our flocks. How many young girls like this one have died because of you?" The girl screeched as Runa yanked her head. "You came in winter, with a knife at my son's throat. Let me return the favor."

Konal's men guarded the six enemy defenders too closely, making interference impossible. She placed the sword edge against girl's white, pulsing neck. Runa's head thundered. She was going to murder an innocent girl. She snarled, and the girl struggled, causing the blade to gash her neck. Bright blood flowed with the girl's cries, though the wound was not mortal.

At last the mother broke through and threw herself on her daughter.

Runa stepped away and released the girl, hoping her relief did not show to the others. The mother cradled her daughter, both sobbing uncontrollably. To maintain a fiction of ruthlessness, she kicked the mother over and dangled her sword at the woman's face.

"How many of your sons did you send to kill my people? I should cut you from gut to neck and drown your daughter in blood."

The woman screamed at the horrid description. Satisfied she had cowed these villagers, Runa returned to Bjornolf.

"Do you have children?"

Bjornolf shook his head, but a woman cowering in the corner of the hall called out, "You have a daughter!"

Runa's smile stretched as she watched Bjornolf glare at the woman. "Be glad, Bjornolf, for you have a chance to do good by your people. I see the gods have struck the hard blow you deserve. I will not waste my time here, but I need to be certain you will not betray my mercy. Give me your daughter."

"No, she is all I have left in the world."

"Konal, make sure Bjornolf dies slowly and without a weapon in his hand. Then take all the children hostage."

No sooner had she uttered the command than Bjornolf's people seized a young girl with blazing copper hair. She fought wildly, screaming for her father. Konal and his men tightened their distance to Bjornolf, who began to weep.

"You are a poor leader to your people." Runa said, watching the girl clawing at the villagers who shoved her into the arms of Konal's warriors. "You cry where you should rejoice. I have spared you, your daughter, and all the people hiding under your protection. But if anyone warns Skard of my coming, or tries to hinder us in any way, your beautiful daughter's head will be returned to you. Her body will be fed to sharks. Understood?"

Bjornolf nodded, and his daughter settled down. She was of an age with Gunnar, thin but possessed of wiry strength. Her hair was strikingly lustrous even in the poor light. "She doesn't look a bit like you. Are you deceiving me?"

"No," was his hoarse reply. "She is the very image of her mother. Dead this winter too."

"Pity," Runa said, turning away. "Everything of value here belongs to me. Konal and Kell, take what you will but leave the people unharmed."

She strode out of the hall, the villagers screaming protest. The men began tearing through the hall, while those outside began to pillage other buildings. Runa returned to the ship, slipping her shield over her back. Her pounding heart began to calm and her ragged breath evened out. She wanted to give Gunnar a hug, and to put the horrible morning behind her.

A SUMMER STORM preceded Runa's approach to Skardholmur. Despite its brief violence, Konal and his crew reveled in it. They screamed glory to Thor every time lightning struck and thunder followed. Black clouds had vanquished the afternoon sun, and winds churned the waters so the ships bobbed and rocked like leaves on a fast running creek. Gunnar and his friends joined the crew, and Runa had to drag him away from the rails as he stepped up to hail the lightning.

"But Thor is with us," he had protested. "We go to destroy our enemies at last, and he celebrates with us."

"No battle is won until you stand in the blood of your enemies." The words sounded like Ulfrik's to Runa's mind, and had the same effect that he had with Gunnar. He allowed her to guide him away from the rails.

For all the fury in the skies, little rain fell. Konal further proclaimed this as a sign of Thor's favor. Wet ground and wet weapons would make combat a misery.

As they neared the island where Skard sheltered his army, the clouds broke up and but for an errant flash of lightning and grumble of thunder, the storm passed. Men on both ships cheered, confident of victory and anticipating glory and spoils. Their looting of Thorod's hall had yielded more than the village would have appeared to possess, but still less than what the men desired. Bjornolf's daughter, whose name Runa still did not know, tucked fearfully into the shadows of the gunwales. Gunnar tried to speak to her, but she dropped her head and refused to answer.

Skard's hall lay within a thin fjord of high cliffs, where Konal spotted men who either were sentries or lucky wanderers. By the time he led his ships to the soft sand beach and disgorged his crews, Skard had been alerted. The warriors on the beach shouted war cries when they heard distant horns blasting in warning.

"Stay on this ship and if evil men come ...," Runa's words faded as she held Gunnar's shoulders. Swallowing, she squeezed his shoulder and turned away. She wanted to wrap her arms about him and promise safety. Yet even Gunnar was not so young to realize if his mother did not return he would be orphaned at best, or killed by the enemy at worst.

"I will protect myself, Mother." He patted the short sword at his side. Runa smiled, admiring his fighting spirit even as she knew Gunnar had little hope in a fight with a man.

"When I return, all evil will be wiped from these islands and we will live in peace. The gods are with us today." Their eyes held, and Runa feared emotion would ruin her ability to lead these men.

Disembarking, she joined Konal and Kell as they assembled with their best warriors. Konal was completing his instructions for the attack. "The land is flat and open, so loop behind and we will have surrounded them. There can't be many of them. It will be butchery today."

The men glanced at Runa as she joined their circle. Konal directed her up a shallow grass slope toward the horizon. Sun shafts poked through black clouds, shining on the dark line of warriors.

"The gods have marked them for us," Runa said. "Skard and his foul kin will be forever wiped from the land today. Let no one live; no one survives."

"What about the villagers?" Kell asked, sharing a look with his brother. "We were promised captives for ransom or slavery."

"Everyone gathered here is my enemy. Do what you will." She had spared the last village, but the men needed spoils and the most valuable spoils would be the ships at dock and the people who crewed them. She could not deny them rewards for risking their lives.

Runa jogged at the front of the group as Konal and Kell lead a swift jaunt toward the defenders. Her thoughts were clear, much to her surprise, though her heart raced and her legs weakened. The heavy shield on her arm covered more of her than a normal man, and her wolf pelt would be proof against most blades. Only her head was exposed, since she had discovered wearing a helmet restricted her vision.

They slowed their approach as they closed on the unflinching line of defenders. A wry smile came to Runa's lips when she realized she could not identify Skard. For a man who had terrorized her home for years, his face remained unknown.

"Looks like maybe twenty-five to thirty spearmen." Konal offered his estimate as they halted. The defenders were like a flock of geese in an open field. "Almost three of ours to one on them."

Kell grunted and ordered both wings of their loose formation to break off the flanks and begin encircling Skard's troops. A ripple of spears and gleams of helmets turning to monitor the attackers were all the reactions from the defenders. They remained unmoved.

"If you want to let them know who you are, do it now." Konal prodded Runa with the side of his shield, then pointed with his chin to the front of the line. "You'll be safe. They're not set up for archers and no one can hide in a field like this."

At last her enemies were gathered into a cluster to be smashed. She had never expected to be the one to do it, standing on the ground where Ulfrik should have stood. She drew her breath, then stepped forward from the line, watching Konal's men complete their envelopment. These were men who knew their deaths had come.

"Skard, you maggot! Nye Grenner has come to burn you out of your holes and lay open your bones. Your war with us has led you all to this doom. What do you say to this?"

Laughter erupted from the surrounded men, and Runa's heart chilled. A half dozen turned and revealed their backsides while others shouted curses. One figure detached from the mass of gray mail and round wood shields. He was indistinguishable from the others beyond the red and white paint on his shield. Those had been Hardar's colors, and identified him as Skard.

"Nye Grenner's bitch has come? Are you a gift to us, that we can each take a turn with you?"

"Surrender now, and your men will have mercy from me."

"My men would rather have you ride them." More laughter flowed, as if the ring of armed invaders around them were only a fanciful dream.

"You had your chance." Skard grabbed his crotch and Runa turned in disgust. Konal's smile showed behind the cheek plates of his helmet.

"Not the reaction you had imagined, I guess. Can we kill these fools and be done?"

Falling in with him, drawing her shield up and sliding her sword from its sheath, she spoke through clenched teeth. "Let's dance in their blood."

Konal and Kell bellowed across the short expanse. All levity from Skard's men vanished, and they roared back. Then the charge launched.

The men behind Runa shoved her forward, one of their shields pushing into her back. Galvanized, she sprinted with speed that astonished her. She felt outside of herself, as if watching another woman running in a pack of wild men. Her face was twisted into an ugly snarl, mimicking the wolf whose pelt wrapped her body. Curly hair flowed over her shoulders and her body bounced and snapped as it pounded toward the wall of shields and lowered spears.

She snapped back into herself.

The collision sounded like a village of houses collapsing at once. Her shield slammed into an enemy's, bouncing her back into her own man, who in turn rammed her forward again. All her training had not prepared her this, feeling like a child's doll flopping between the two shields. Konal had warned her of it, but she had discounted it as an attempt to dissuade her.

Completely pinned, she could only let momentum carry her forward as men grunted, screamed, and cursed. The smell of stale beer and coppery blood bloomed in her nose. The air was hot and foul at the center of the press. A frightful snap of pain in her back flashed white across her vision.

Then she stumbled into the cool, fresh air, tripping over a man lying on his back.

A hand seized her leg, and she slashed it with her sword. Release and warm blood poured over her leg. Kicking to her feet, the man below had lost three fingers to her strike. She drove her sword into his neck, and he flailed in his death throes.

Freed, she assessed the result of the charge. They had flowed through the line, trampling Skard's pitiful resistance. No organized defense remained, only men fighting in scattered clusters.

Training took over and her shield raised to block a strike to her head. The blow was undisciplined, she had already stepped away and now folded up the attacker's sword arm with her shield. He was no taller than Runa and no match for her training. Her sword slid into his gut and pulled away bloody. He crumpled with a whimper.

A foot landed in the small of her back, and she hurled forward, crashing on her shield. Again, all the times Ulfrik or Konal had knocked her flat served her now. Nimble without heavy armor, she rolled into the attacker's legs and tripped him. A stream of curses flowed as he tumbled over her, piling into the ground.

Springing to her feet, another man had already driven a spear into her attacker's back. As Ulfrik had warned her, a man on the ground counted his life in breaths.

Hours seemed to have passed, and she wondered why victory had not arrived. She saw Konal slicing open a man's throat while Kell stood beside him, dragging an attacker by his cloak to the ground. All the other men looked the same to her, and she assumed the prevailing ones were her own. It could not be otherwise, she thought.

The red and white shield emerged from the drab scramble of fighting men. The sky had again darkened, dropping a flat light over the battlefield. Skard's face was more evil than she imagined: scarred, sharp angled, tight skinned, and thin lipped, and midnight black eyes buried under unruly brows. Blood had splattered the white side of his shield and dripped from his face.

"Whore of Nye Grenner! You think yourself a shield maiden? I'll teach you what you are."

Runa lunged at him, striking high but reversing toward his leg. He laughed, and she retracted her arm moments before he slashed at it. They circled amid others who danced the same mortal struggle. Someone bumped into her, and Skard shot out.

She deflected with her sword, and rammed him with her shield. He slid back, cackling as if it was mere play. Her hand numbed from the strike on her blade, but she had bought space to recover.

"Your little boy has joined the battle. Seems the whelp has a death wish."

Her hands froze and her stomach lurched. Instinct overawed her training and she searched for Gunnar.

In the next instant, she was looking at the sky. The pain throbbing in her gut informed her she had been kicked. Her sword hand flexed on empty air.

A man on the ground counts life in breaths. She rolled to the side, then onto her knees and jumped to her feet. Skard had hacked the ground where she had fallen, but recovered swiftly.

He placed his shield before him, the metal rim just below his chin so that his body was completely covered. His sword flashed low and to the side.

"You have no sword, whore." He stepped toward her, his shield denying any chance to tackle him. "Whatever you think you've won today, you have lost your life. And no whore-bitch will go to Valhalla."

Runa skipped forward, pulling her leg back, then kicked the bottom of Shard's shield with all her strength.

Bolts of searing agony rode up her foot to as high as her knee.

The top of the shield plowed into Skard's face with startling force, ramming his nose and sending him stumbling back. Screeching, Runa leapt onto him, tearing the sax at her lap from its scabbard.

Dazed and pinned, Skard did not resist. Runa plunged the blade sideways into his gut, cutting through the links of his mail coat and then into his flesh. Withdrawing the sword, she screamed her anger as she stabbed the sax repeatedly into Skard's torso. He flexed, blood and foam erupting from his mouth, and his black eyes flickered then glazed.

Convinced Skard's words had been a distraction, she allowed a moment to peel herself from his corpse and sit on the grass.

But Skard had not lied.

Gunnar huddled behind a shield three times too big for him, his pitiful blade lancing out at the legs of men still struggling around him. Others ignored him, but Runa screamed his name in horror.

She launched to her feet, only to crumple as soon as she hit the earth. The kick had ruined her foot, which throbbed and swelled in its boot. Still, she scrabbled across the grass, witnessing Gunnar's blade slicing into the leg of an enemy.

The wounded man howled, and having dispatched his attacker, turned his ire on Gunnar.

In one hack, Gunnar's shield spun out of his grip and he tumbled into view. That he was a child appeared to stun the enemy, his next blow suspended overhead. Gunnar's face turned waxy white. Runa screamed his name, hand stretching to snatch him from beneath the sword.

The enemy's shock dissipated and he renewed his strike.

Konal plowed into the enemy, slamming him to the ground and running his blood-caked blade into his leg. Gunnar recovered, his sword ranging to fight off any attack. Konal scooped Gunnar into his shield, and he searched the battlefield.

Tears sprung to Runa's eyes. She forgot the pain in her foot, and fought to stand. All around the battle tide ebbed. Konal appeared calmed, and Runa took it to mean victory.

He spotted her as she rose, and she smiled. His face exploded in fear.

Cold agony bloomed at her back, and she collapsed forward. Her head bounced off a rock that jutted from the ground, then blackness filled her eyes and she knew no more.

34

August 9, 886 CE

"This is the last time I can sneak away before we make contact with Henry and his army." Einar searched the surrounding trees as he handed a sack of bread and venison to Thrand. "Now's the time to make good use of the sword I gave you. Also, here's a shield. Best I could do for you."

Thrand's eyes filled with tears as Einar unslung the plain wooden shield from his back and dropped it to the dirt. His old friend had been true, providing provisions and gear to help him survive on his own. Now he offered Thrand the redemption he desperately sought, the redemption that haunted his sleep and stalked his waking hours. Spirits still followed him in the forest, whispering in his ears and demanding that he do something to make good the evil he had wrought.

"You are a great man, Einar. Your heart is as strong as your body." Thrand scooped up the shield, lacing it through his arm.

The two men stood deep in a forest, morning fog still rolling across the ground. Thrand had grown accustomed to the sounds and smells of the forest, whereas Einar seemed to jump at every cracking branch or blowing leaf. The morning promised a hot day ahead, and sweat beaded on Einar's uncovered head.

"I'm a fool," he said. "Anyway, we are laying a trap for Henry's army. The path of their march will lead them past a wooded hill, where Ulfrik has concealed archers. They will drive Henry's army forward onto us, where we hide in the woods by the road. We've been studying their approach, and they're not scouting ahead. They don't expect us this far out from Paris. They'll pay for that sloppiness."

"Where will Ulfrik be? I want to fight at his side once more." Thrand did not know what he hoped to achieve, other than he craved the camaraderie of battle. If only for a short time, he would again belong with someone.

"With the main force. You know his red banner." He gave Thrand a critical smirk. "I've got to return before I'm missed. Honestly, Lord Ulfrik is fussing over me like I am his child. This isn't my first battle."

Thrand picked the bag of provisions from the grass. "Ulfrik is right to make you his second. If only I had chosen differently, I could've served under you."

Einar grimaced, then shrugged. "Don't be stupid out there. You've not the gear to stand up front like you did before."

Thrand watched Einar leave, the stubborn fog swirling and enveloping him. In moments only black trees and gray rocks peered above the milky haze.

"I will stand with my lord," he said to the forest. "I've years of evil to make amends for, and I cannot do so hiding behind others."

ULFRIK CLUNG to the ground with two hundred other warriors. Cloaks of brown, green, and gray appeared as nothing more than lumps in the earth. Helmets and metal were smeared with mud. White eyes peered out from dirt-darkened faces, all of them scanning the track that wended through the forest. The scent of earth filled Ulfrik's nose, and the dampness wormed through the links of his mail to wet his shirt. He glanced at Einar to his right. Even buried under leaves his bulk was obvious.

"Do you see anything?" Ulfrik hissed at Einar. "Your eyes are better than mine."

"Not yet." Einar's voice barely concealed his irritation, and Ulfrik realized he had asked the question one too many times.

Across the road, atop a tree-studded hill, his archers lurked in the underbrush. Fifty of them waited for the column of Franks to pass, and then would erupt from hiding to shove the Franks sideways into the forest and onto Ulfrik's waiting spears. A blind turn in the road provided excellent cover for his main force. He counted on surprise and confusion to make short work of the Franks. His reputation with Hrolf hung on the outcome of the attack. Hrolf had explicitly stated that a gift of Henry's head would help him overlook Ulfrik's indiscretions.

"The Franks are near," Mord said from Ulfrik's left. He had buried Ulfrik's standard under leaves, and would raise it when the attack began. His hand already sought the pole in preparation of the charge.

The marching of troops vibrated in the ground beneath Ulfrik's chest. He heard a stir of leaves like the wind rushing through the forest, but knew it was his men gathering their weapons for the attack. An ant crawled over Ulfrik's nose. He ignored it as the insect wandered over the crags and peaks of his face. The first of the Franks emerged into view, rounding the blind corner.

He held his breath. All around mounds of leaf-shrouded warriors inched forward. The ant crawled through his beard and bit his cheek.

Franks slouched in their mail hauberks, shouldering spears and axes, shuffled past him. They made dull conversation in bored voices, a rumbling murmur that ran through their column.

Then the thrum of bows followed by shrieks of the injured.

"Hold a moment," Ulfrik commanded, his voice barely louder than normal. "Let their backs turn to us."

Swords hissed from sheaths and arrows slammed into upraised shields. A few shafts sprinkled to the edge of the woods, disturbing the remnants of the morning fog still clinging to the ground. Frankish leaders hollered orders at their men, and the column lined up to face the archers.

"Now! For battle and glory!" Ulfrik sprung and two hundred men shed their camouflage in an explosion of leaves.

They charged the rear lines, spears lowered or swords braced to drive through the backs of the unsuspecting Franks. Ulfrik bolted straight for the first man in his way, and cleaved the Frank at the shoulder hard enough to collapse the man to the ground. Mord followed at this left, the banner of Humbert's cloak swinging wildly overhead. Einar brought up his right, wielding a two-handed ax that chopped an unsuspecting Frank like firewood.

The ambush had been expertly timed and the Frankish column broke and scattered. The archers abandoned their bows and joined the fray, trapping most of the enemy against Ulfrik's force. Screams of terror and curses flowed out of the cleft where the Franks staggered and died. Ulfrik's heart sang with the glory and freedom of battle. His charge carried him through the first man and into the fray. All around he had enemies to strike. Einar's massive ax hooked shields to drag them down and Ulfrik stabbed his blade into the gap. Franks gasped and perished. Mord showed himself as capable as Toki had been with the standard, planting it beside Ulfrik and destroying enemies who sought to batter it down.

After months of inaction or uninspired raids against unworthy foes, Ulfrik was giddy with the thrill of a true battle. His blade flashed white as he slashed right, and his shield slammed left. He cut a swathe of victory through the ranks of the enemy, and Danes swarmed alongside him.

"Kill the bastards," he screamed. "Their blood is ours to spill. For Odin and Thor! For battle eternal!"

The killing song drove him like a madness. Franks scattered at his approach, tripping over one another to escape his wrath. He spit blood into the face of one wide-eyed man and gutted him in the next moment.

Then the thunder.

Ulfrik tumbled back, the sky in his eyes. Dark shapes flying past.

The copper taste of blood filling his mouth. Sounds were muffled and dull. He realized he had been hit in the head, and his helmet knocked away. Someone screamed his name as he felt the thunder throbbing in the earth.

Cavalry.

Out of nowhere horses crashed through Ulfrik's line and scattered the throng of defenders. His standard had fallen. He rolled to the side, away from the approaching sound of hoofs beating the ground. A spear lanced the ground where he had just sprawled out, and the horse and rider sprinted past him.

On his feet, he had little time to consider. The riders rode beneath a standard of some strange beast. A regal man in shining mail and a casque embossed with a gold crown led the group of ten riders, undoubtedly Henry of Saxony. They were turning their horses on the road, hampered by the trees crowding them. They reached for fresh spears carried on the flanks of their mounts as they maneuvered for a second pass.

Ulfrik had lost his sword, and so drew his sax. The short blade was worthless against mounted men, but he had nowhere to turn. Behind him a gap hung open where the cavalry had breached the line. Men were scattered on the ground, dead or dazed. He hoped the horses might trip on the bodies on their second pass.

Henry shouted something in his language, hefted a spear, and kicked the horses to a run. Five went in front with five others behind. Their cloaks of blue or gray fluttered behind them as their horses kicked clods of dirt into the air. Ulfrik and a handful of bloodied men faced them.

"Go on, you Frankish bastards!" he roared at them. "I'll take you and your ponies to the grave."

Henry singled him out, pointing his spear for the others to follow. Ulfrik realized too late he could not escape all five horses. Only one veered off to avoid fallen bodies, and the remaining riders bore down on him.

Shield still lashed to his arm, he ducked behind it. As the first horse reached him, he collapsed on his back and hid beneath his shield. One spear hit him square on the shield, while the others flew wide as the first wave galloped past. Sloughing off his shield, he grabbed one, then flipped it up to face the next wave.

Ulfrik carved out the flank of a horse. It screamed and bucked, sending the rider to the dirt and disrupting the others. In the crash, Ulfrik again sprawled out, horse hooves slamming around him as he covered his head in fear.

Now Mord had raised the standard, and the Danes cheered. They slammed back into the mounted Franks like the tide into rocks. Staggering to his feet and retrieving his shield, Ulfrik bellowed encouragement. "Pull them down and chop them up! Victory is ours."

"Lord Ulfrik, watch out!"

Something hit his back, and he tumbled forward. A man screamed behind him, and fell over his body. Ulfrik spasmed, fearing a killing strike in his helpless position as both friend and enemy converged around him. He shoved the man aside, a shattered spear shaft impaled through the man's thigh and black blood flooding into the dirt beneath him. Over the man's body, a white-eyed Frank was already charging with sword drawn.

Renewed rage strengthened Ulfrik's resolve. He took the Frank's wild blow on his shield, then plunged his sax into the man's groin. The Frank slid to the ground with a howl and Ulfrik left him to writhe in slow death.

The battle churned as the Franks rallied around their trapped leader. Without another thought, Ulfrik dashed for Henry's beast standard that rocked and swayed amid a press of Danes.

"Henry is mine," he shouted. "Move aside."

Henry had already taken several wounds, one hideous gash in his arm glowed brilliant red amid the iron gray surrounding him. He slumped against his bodyguards, and Ulfrik snorted. "You're already dead. Grip your weapon, and go the hall where your god praises his heroes."

Lightning fast, Ulfrik slipped between the bodyguards, deflecting one with his shield and letting another Dane distract the other. Henry's face was old and bruised, defiant and proud, as Ulfrik plunged his sax into Henry's gut. The mail links broke and blood gushed, along with a rush of air from Henry's mouth. His standard bearer fought on, but men clambered over each other to drag him down. Henry fell flat at Ulfrik's feet. The battle was won and he howled victory.

As the standard plummeted to the dirt, Ulfrik's men cheered and the Franks that could not escape pleaded for mercy. As swiftly as the chaos had begun, it had ended.

Mord bore Ulfrik's standard to his side, dirt and blood mingled on his face. "Victory, Lord Ulfrik! Let me plant your standard over Henry's body."

Out of breath, dizzy from the battle and the blows he sustained, Ulfrik nodded. He knelt beside Henry, and tucked the gray-haired warrior's hand over the hilt of his sword. It was all he could think of to honor an enemy leader.

His warriors clamored around him, shouting victory and congratulations. He accepted their adulation, but his thoughts were for the man who had saved his life. He pushed his way through them, back toward the edge of the forest where men lay broken and suffering in scattered heaps. He saw Einar's massive form kneeling in the road, one hand resting on his ax and the other placed atop a body lying before him.

Ulfrik dashed to his side, then leaned down to view the man twitching in the churned earth.

"Thrand!" Ulfrik's heart leapt in his chest. "How did you get here?"

His old hirdman turned traitor was a battered wreck. Blood soaked his pants black and his shirt had ridden up to his neck, revealing bruises and cuts the length of his torso. The spear shaft in his right thigh had stemmed the blood loss, but it leaked from the wound in a steady stream. He would die instantly if the shaft were extracted.

"Lord Ulfrik," Thrand's voice was the hoarse whisper of a man straddling the threshold of death. "You are victorious."

"You saved my life today." Ulfrik glanced at Einar, who stared into

Thrand's eyes. "I don't know how you got here, but I am grateful to the gods for sending you."

"Forgiveness, lord?" Thrand's hand pawed for Ulfrik's sleeve, having no strength to grab it. Ulfrik took the hand and placed his own sax beneath it, then laid both over Thrand's chest.

"Yes, Thrand. You've earned it with your blood."

A smile broke on Thrand's face, his teeth stained red. He closed both eyes, and tightened his grip on the sword. "Thank you."

Ulfrik and Einar lingered over him as his heart pumped its final beats. He sucked his breath, then feebly whispered, "Njal, brother. They have come."

Thrand's last breath exhaled a stillness onto the battlefield. Ulfrik bowed his head and sat back. Thrand's passing stirred so many conflicting emotions: frustration at Thrand's senseless life; anger at not preventing his slide into evil; relief for his redemption; justice for his treachery. He had to force aside all of this else he be swept away.

"What did he mean?" Einar asked, wiping his eye with the back of his hand. "Who has come?"

"The Valkyries," Ulfrik replied, as he struggled to his feet. "We shall see him again. In Valhalla."

35

September 10, 886 CE

Runa awoke with a start, a nightmare vanishing back into the dream world as reality asserted itself. Chill air flowed over her shoulders in the dimness of her bedroom, and she drew the wool blanket to her neck. The place beside her was cold. Konal had already arisen, and the low tones of his voice vibrated through the walls from the hall outside. Sounds of muffled conversation, clacking wood plates, and benches sliding on the floor mingled with Konal's voice. She had overslept, a terrible habit of hers since Konal had begun sharing her bed and Gunnar and Hakon had moved to another room.

Rubbing her face, she tried to recall the dream and was relieved to fail. She slid to the edge of the bed with a sigh and lingered with her injured foot hanging over the side. Even without recollecting the dream, she knew it was of the battle. Ever since that day, the gods sent terrorizing visions of bloodshed and death: her sons decapitated; Ulfrik impaled on a spear, clutching her leg as he bled into the grass; her own legs chopped to stumps as she desperately stemmed the blood pumping from them. She knew the nightmares well. They had all been scenes she had witnessed in the battle with Skard, only the faces were replaced with her loved ones.

Her foot throbbed as she drew her boot over it. She had been lucky not to have broken it. Thor had been with her that day. Not only had Skard's army been killed to a man and her foot spared, but her life as well. In the final moments of battle, a spearman had tried to run her through, but her wolf pelt had protected her. More proof of the gods' favor was that the spear point had caught in the strap buckle that held her sword sheath. In the chaos it had flipped to her back and saved her life.

Each morning she had to ease into standing, but as long as she let her foot accept the stress slowly, she adjusted. In moments, she was able to dress herself, comb her hair, then limp to the hall.

Bright morning light filled the main room. The women were busy preparing breakfast, and Konal sat with Gunnar at the high table. Hakon ran with other children between and around the women's feet. Behind them, she remained unnoticed in the shadowed corner. A smile flickered as she watched Konal leaning into Gunnar's ear to impart some wry observation that set both of them laughing. Ulfrik would have approved, she felt, if he were alive to see this. The thought bought a wince and the threat of tears.

She had cried enough already. Ulfrik had been gone a year with no news and no survivors returned. His final adventure had led him away forever, to Valhalla where he would enjoy the glory and honor he had sought in life. The living remained behind, and had to make their way until Fate cut the threads of their lives.

Konal had been willing to remain with her, and his men were happy to find a land of widows and unwed daughters. Kell had resumed his pursuit of their escaped slave, and had not pressed his brother to join the search.

"At last you've awakened," Konal said, having turned about on his bench. "Come, before I eat your breakfast."

Limping to the table, Gunnar rose and helped her sit. Since the battle, he doted on her. His boyhood had been slain in the battle with Skard. He was no longer carefree, running with the other children. He stayed apart, practiced with his weapons, and frowned often.

"I'm fine," she said as he guided her to the bench. "If you are finished, why not go out and play?"

He shrugged, his dark eyes dodging hers. "I don't feel like it. Those games are not fun anymore."

The silence stretched and Runa studied him as he gazed at the ground. Children squealed outside, and Gunnar twitched at the noise. She shook her head. "All right, but there is work to do. The trading ships will pass here soon. You should play while you have the time."

"We'll practice later today," Konal offered, his mouth full. "I'll show you how to fight spears. How's that?"

Gunnar nodded, then smiled. "It's good. I have to know how to fight everything."

"Yeah," Konal agreed, lifting his bowl to his mouth. "A good spear fighter is a deadly opponent."

Gunnar left them, wandering down to the tables where several of his friends stopped to watch him pass. He ignored them, leaving the hall with hands folded behind his back.

"Looks like he carries the burdens of a jarl." Konal belched and wiped his mouth with the back of his hand.

"He will be jarl here one day." Runa raised a brow at Konal. "And before that, I rule here."

"You mention that every day." Konal belched a second time, then banged his bowl on the table for a refill of the porridge. Elin nodded and sent a girl to collect the bowl.

His dismissive response irked Runa, but she declined to push. Months ago she had realized Konal truly ruled here. The men were his, the ships, the weapons, and the gold. No one could prevent him from claiming every flock and field. To worsen matters, the villagers loved him. He had fed them, brought men for their widows and daughters, restored their honor and defeated their enemies. Some of the more superstitious folk claimed he had walked out of the sea and then summoned his ships with magic.

Whether she wanted it or not, Konal was the new jarl of Nye Grenner.

He smacked his lips as the second bowl slipped onto the table. He grabbed the girl's hand, startling her, then he stroked it and released her. The girl blushed at him, and he winked as she returned to the hearth. Runa's bowl sat cooling beneath her.

"She is only thirteen," Runa said, attempting to keep the edge out of her voice.

"Then she should be married soon. Better she learn how to handle a man now. Her husband will be grateful."

Runa turned away before he could see her grimace. He was becoming the man she had suspected he was. Heat grew on her face, and she bit her lip. She stood to leave, feeling stupid and embarrassed. As she rose, he snared her arm.

"Come now, it was only play. Sit. Eat your breakfast."

Runa hovered, his strong grip tugging at her. Yanking her arm free, she returned to the bench. Konal continued devouring his porridge as if he had not noticed Runa's anger. Ulfrik would have read her in an instant, but then Ulfrik would never have flirted so brazenly with a freeman's daughter. A rumbling stomach forced a surrender of her icy stand-off.

Over the top of the bowl, she glimpsed Halla sneering at her from across the room. Since becoming her hostage, she had spoken only when commanded, otherwise she prayed and glared at everyone around her. Runa regretted not killing her when she had the blood-lust for it. Now, even with Toki dead, she could not bring herself to harm Halla for no reason. Instead, she waited for Halla to give her cause, and suspected that day would be soon.

"Winter is not far off," Runa said, turning to face Konal. "I must know if you intend to stay or return to your family."

Konal's face fell, and he slowly shoved away his bowl. He leaned on his elbows, and studied the few people finishing their meals in the hall.

"You have been gone from your family over a year now. It's time you return to them."

"Don't tell me when it's time for me to do anything." His face pulled into a frown, and his raised voice drew shy glances. "That family is my father's doing, not mine. I've no love for them."

"Your own children?"

"Brats, I've told you. Mad like their mother and grandfather. Kell and I have always been happier at sea than trapped with those madmen."

Runa drank from her bowl again, using the pause to consider Konal's words. Was she a distraction for him, a reason not to return home? Did Kell seek the same excuse, chasing after an escaped slave they had no chance of locating?

"And if you stay with me, will you be satisfied as a farmer? Locked into another winter of darkness on a rock of an island that no willing person visits?"

"You make it sound horrible."

"Isn't it? All my enemies are defeated. Ingrid is old and mute. Skard and Thorod are slain. My riches lie in hay and wool, nothing to bring raiders this far north. What does the great war leader Konal do here besides tend flocks and settle arguments over grazing lands?"

Konal folded his arms, his face collapsing into a thoughtful frown. Runa snorted a laugh, a derisive puff filled with her anger. Taking him to her bed had been a mistake. No man would ever replace Ulfrik. Konal was clearly inferior to him in every regard, and she had contrived to overlook it all.

"I must help Elin and do some good for this hall." She wobbled to her feet, and Konal let her go.

She busied herself with gathering dishes and collecting scraps into a bucket. Elin kept silent but her expression spoke her exasperation. Elin had been a vocal opponent of Konal's men lingering after their need was gone. She called them leeches, and Runa had begun to agree.

After an hour of work, Konal had departed and Runa remained with Elin and the women. As she wiped down the high table, sweeping crumbs into her cupped hand, Konal returned.

"The trading ships have arrived. I thought you said they wouldn't come for another month."

Runa stood straighter, sharing a worried glance with Elin. "You're sure they're traders? They are too early."

Konal nodded. "They're not hostile ships. No beast heads on the prow and shields still on the rack. They're approaching the docks now."

"Thora, keep the children in the hall," Runa said. Dropping her cloth to the table, she and Elin joined Konal. Halla even roused from her murmuring prayers to follow them. From the top of the slope, Runa saw two ships gliding to the docks. A man from the lead ship leapt the rails to land on the dock with a rope to tie off the small boat.

Runa's vision hazed and she nearly fainted. Konal caught her.

"What is it, Runa?"

Halla answered for her as her pale hand pointed at the ship. "It's *Raven's Talon*. That is Toki in the prow."

Konal steadied Runa, but she spared him not even a glance. She limped after the others who had already began running for the arriving ships. Gunnar was in the front, squealing with delight. Men were jumping into the surf, equally delighted at the homecoming. A thin, older man in a ragged gray shirt stood apart from the others, wading ashore on his own. Gunnar charged straight for him, and the old man crouched and threw his arms wide.

Runa also began to run, sharp needles of pain lancing her foot, but she did not care. The old man was swinging Gunnar around in his arms. He was crying and laughing. Gunnar laughed, a sound so sweet and so long unheard that Runa's eyes teared.

She stumbled the final distance, and the old man let Gunnar down, though he remained clutched to his side. Runa stood facing them, the ocean sparkling behind the old man.

"Snorri!"

Collapsing into his arms, he clamped her tight. In that moment, worry and fear flowed out with her tears. She repeated his name, and Gunnar forced his way into their embrace.

"Aye, girl, we're finally home."

NYE GRENNER'S hall had emptied and only Toki and Snorri remained with Runa at the high table. A bonfire outside flickered yellow light between the gaps of covered windows, and low voices of guards seeped through every wall. The night was cold, and many of the guards clustered at the fire burning in the field behind the hall. Runa waited as Toki and Snorri completed their meals. Even after three days, all the returning men still ate as if they would not eat again for weeks. All of them were thinner and more haggard than Runa remembered, especially Toki.

"More ale," Toki said, pushing his mug out without lifting his head from his bowl.

Runa hefted a jug and poured ale until it ran over the sides. She stared at Toki, who hardly acknowledged her since his return. He had become someone else during his time away, more confident and aloof. Even Gunnar, who had spent his childhood at Toki's heels, was held at a distance. Whatever had happened in his time in Frankia had changed him. She knew nothing of the story, but would find out all she desired this night.

"And why are we three sitting here in this dark hall alone and silent?" Runa poured more ale for Snorri, anticipating his need. "If you've nothing to say, Brother, then I will be leaving."

"Stay." Toki still did not pause in devouring his meal, lifting out a lamb bone and gnawing the meat from it. Once he had filled his mouth, he dropped the bone and leaned back. He stared at Runa, who felt as if Toki were looking at her for the first time. Grease glistened on his beard and his dark eyes sparkled with the low hearth light. At last he wiped his mouth with the back of his arm before speaking. "We have family matters to discuss, as well as issues of rulership."

Distant laughter broke into the silence, as if mocking Toki. Within the hall, no one smiled. Snorri armed his bowl aside and looked at Runa with bleary eyes.

"When do you think Konal's brother will return?" Snorri asked.

She shrugged her shoulders. Kell had been gone for weeks, claiming to search for their escaped slave but more likely raiding or trading.

"Konal's men have surrendered their weapons," Runa said, smoothing her skirt across her lap. Toki had demanded she stop wearing pants and carrying a sax after his arrival, and she had complied. "They fought for our home, Toki. Some of them died, and many took wounds. Konal saved Gunnar's life. You're treating them as if they are enemies."

"They are enemies," Toki said, glancing at Snorri. "Of a sort. We only outnumber them until Konal's brother arrives, and then we are evenly matched. I think your new lover wants to make this land his own."

Runa shot to her feet, her body flushing with hot anger. "I have held this land in Ulfrik's name. No one has challenged me in this, nor has Konal ever laid a claim to anything."

"Girl, he wears weapons in this hall and has grown accustomed to sitting in Ulfrik's place." Snorri gave a wincing smile, and rubbed his neck. "He only had to move into Ulfrik's bed to become the ruler here."

"That's untrue!" Runa stamped her foot, and shame immediately filled her. Her face burned at the truth of the accusations, and she sat down with arms crossed. The silence endured until Toki cleared his throat.

"I am ruler here, until Ulfrik relieves me of that duty. See that standard?" A greasy finger pointed at Nye Grenner's standard. It hung wearily from its pole, leaning against the wall. The once deep green was now stained white with sea salt and the cloth ripped and tattered. "Ulfrik bade me to raise it in his hall once more, and to do anything needed to ensure his home and people were protected. Now I've returned to find armed strangers in the land, and my sister running wild with them. I had worried over what I might find upon returning, but never could I have foreseen this. What am I to think?"

Runa could not hold her brother's gaze, but instead slumped forward. Touching her hand to her head, she sighed. "It has been nearly a year with no news. You were to have returned before summer. Konal and Kell were here, and prepared to bring the fight north. What should I have done?"

"It doesn't matter," Toki said as he stood. He patted Snorri's shoulder as he stepped away from the bench. "What do you say, old friend? Is it more important to talk about what was or what must be?"

"We can only look ahead with hope of changing anything," Snorri said.

"No, that's not fair. You have only told me the barest details of what happened while you were gone. I deserve to know, and I am still the wife of your jarl. So respect my demand for answers. Why did Ulfrik send you so late? What happened to change you, Toki?"

Both men stiffened and both glanced aside. Runa waited, her pulse throbbing in her neck but determined to hear their story. Toki finally nodded, then stepped back to the bench and sat again.

"He sent us almost four months ago, and with a third ship full of men. He put all the Nye Grenner men aboard our ships, and then filled another ship's worth of followers who wanted a new land to settle. The journey should've taken no more than a month, but it was the most ill-fated voyage I have ever known. Storms plagued us, set us off course and swept men to ocean graves. We became separated and one ship was lost. Whatever became of the ship and her crew, we will never know. They were good men, eager to return home or to find peace in a distant land. We searched, but the gods have them now."

Toki lowered his eyes and for a moment Runa glimpsed the Toki of old. The edge was gone from his voice as he continued. "My first command and I led my men in circles, wasting supplies and time, getting us lost."

"It was not your fault, lad," Snorri offered in his low, gravelly voice. "We all agreed to search for our brothers."

"Then the pirates found us. They trailed our ships and made us wary of pulling ashore. We did not want to lead them home, and so sailed opposite of our true course. At last they dared a fight, and we were better armed and better skilled. Still, men were killed and time was lost. We were out of supplies for the voyage over open sea and had to trade and resupply. At last, we turned north again and sailed for home. I admit, I have not been more frightened of returning home than I was three days ago. I feared you would all be slain or enslaved."

Again the hall fell silent. The hearth fire popped and the men standing guard outside murmured in tired conversation. Runa's anger quelled and she realized the pressure and responsibility drove her brother to act so differently. She moved to sit beside him on the bench, and draped her arm over his shoulders. "But we are well, and you led your men to the best of your ability. Ulfrik was wise to chose you as his representative, and wiser still to send Snorri as an adviser. I am sorry for my foolishness. What must I do to help you set the land right?"

Toki met her eyes, and the iron returned to them. Yet instead of forcing distance between them, he placed his hand over Runa's at his shoulder. "If Konal and Kell wish to remain, I will not begrudge them. However, they must swear an oath to me, and my oath to Ulfrik ensures the land remains his. I want to claim Thorod's and Skard's estates, to ensure no one rises up there again. I will rule from Ingrid's old hall and you may remain to rule Nye Grenner. There is peace in this land bought with blood, and I want to keep it. Any way you can help with these tasks, I welcome it."

Runa nodded, squeezed her brother's shoulders. "I will do all I can."

"Konal won't swear an oath to anyone," Snorri said, folding his arms over his chest. "Seen his kind a hundred times and he's no one's bondsman. I think it could come to a fight."

"Then we fight," Toki said, dropping his hand from Runa's. "It won't be the first time we've had to repel invaders. Only now they've woven themselves into our homes and hall."

"I know how to make them leave." Runa stood, smiling with excitement at her plan. Both Toki and Snorri exchanged surprised looks.

"Would they not consider taking an oath?" Toki asked.

"I doubt it, but don't fear. Is that slave, Humbert, still with Ulfrik?"

Toki's eyes drew to slits. "He escaped into Paris, but what has this to do with anything?"

"As long as we know where Humbert is, I can get them to follow me. But, I will have one condition for you." Toki looked expectantly, but Runa only laughed. "I will tell you once Konal and Kell have agreed to leave."

~

THE FIELDS behind Nye Grenner were filled with the most warriors Runa had seen in nearly a decade. She stood beside Toki and faced the throng. Daylight grew shorter and the nighttime chill lingered longer each day. The air was filled with puffs of breath from the gathered men's conversations. Kell had returned with his warriors, finding Konal a near-hostage of Toki's. Even stripped of weapons, Konal and Kell's crew had the potential to overtake Toki's force. For now, both groups remained segregated on the field, only a daring few stitched the sides together with amicable conversation.

Konal and Kell stood at the front of their men, both possessing their weapons and accorded respect due their titles. Toki had prepared gifts for their service to Nye Grenner, but he also ensured all his men attended the meeting fully armed. Runa noted the anger on Konal's face. Since she had ejected him from her bed upon Toki's return, he had been cordial but cool to her. Now, facing what he must know would be dismissal, he wore his anger openly. His lip curled in a sneer when Toki called his name.

"Konal Ketilsson, I've gathered us here to express my gratitude for all you've done in service to my sister and the people of this land." He waved Konal forward, and reached his hand back to Halla who stood directly behind him. She placed a gold band into his palm. "For saving the life of my nephew, accept this gold with my thanks."

Konal glanced at Runa as he received the band, inclined his head slightly before speaking. "He is a fine boy and warrior. It has been my pleasure to know him. I accept your gift, but truly I owed my life to both Runa and Gunnar for pulling me from the sea."

Gunnar and Hakon stood behind Runa, and she felt Gunnar tugging at her skirt. She batted his hand away, knowing he wished to speak but not countenancing interruptions.

Men on both sides cheered Konal, and he rotated with the armband held overhead. The pink morning sun blazed on the gold as he fixed it to his arm.

Toki cleared his throat, checked Runa for reassurance before he started his next speech. She offered a slight nod, confident all would turn out well.

"Konal and Kell, your men have been welcomed guests in the lands of my lord, lands given to me to safeguard. But winter is coming, and it's time for you and your men to leave."

The crowd stirred and Runa grimaced at the ill-tuned words. Toki had many things to learn, foremost being diplomacy. She thought of the honeyed words Ulfrik would have employed to ease the tension. A sneer replaced the forced-smile on Konal's face.

"Give me a gift then kick me out, is it?"

"It's not that way," Runa interjected. Toki frowned as if to protest but she flashed her eyes at him and he sensibly tucked his head down. "The men of Nye Grenner have returned, along with all your men here already. There is not enough to sustain so many throughout winter. You know this is true, so don't pretend otherwise."

Konal's flush informed her she had carried her rebuke too far, yet he had to concede to her reasoning. "True as it is, there is still time to send for supplies and to prepare. It is not as impossible as you say."

"Possible or not, there is no other way," Toki said. "We are not prepared for guests, unless you wish to join with us. There are lands to the north that you cleared, and these places need settlement. Swear loyalty to me, and I will grant you that land and their people."

A grumble circulated through the assembled warriors, a mixture of consideration and skepticism. Runa held her eyes on Konal's and she read the mischief twinkling there. He spoke before she could.

"You will grant me the land? It was my men who cleared it of enemies. You've no claim on it at all. In fact, I've a mind to retire there for the winter."

Toki pressed his lips tight, marshaling his temper, and Runa jumped into the gap. She stepped forward to Konal, squaring her shoulders to him.

"I led the men, and you fought under Nye Grenner's banner, even if only in spirit. That land belongs to me."

"It belongs to the ones strong enough to hold it." Konal's growled rebuttal drew angry shouts from both his men and Nye Grenner.

"Forget that land," said Runa. "It means nothing to you. But I have a secret I've long withheld. Bring Kell near, and I will tell you."

Konal stared at her, his face inscrutable, then searched Toki and the others. At last he raised an arm and waved his brother forward. "Kell, there's something you should hear."

Confusion stirred in the gathered men, who wavered like wind-blown grass. Runa ignored them, and focused on Kell as he jogged up to his brother's side. Both of them now looked expectantly at her. She let the moment linger, then finally spoke.

"Ulfrik has the slave you've been seeking. I can prove it to you."

Kell's face dropped but Konal stared at her, appraising her words with hooded eyes. Confident she had his attention, she described Ulfrik's raid, whom he found and the lack of treasure, then of Humbert's capture and his promises. Every moment Konal's face grew more stern and more sober. By the end of her tale, his jaw muscles twitched and his face was taut with anger.

"And you're sure you found no treasure with him, nor any treasure in Paris?"

Runa shook her head, along with Toki who had joined to corroborate the story. "Whatever he stole from you is lost. He had nothing but rags when he arrived here."

Konal and Kell stared at each other as if in conversation only they could hear. The gathering of men had drawn closer, straining to hear Runa's story. Finally, Konal folded his arms and sighed.

"We must still find our slave, if only to learn what he did with our treasure." He glanced at Kell, and shook his head in disgust. "We cannot waste time, and must travel to Frankia. If what you say is true." He raised his chin in challenge and Runa met the gesture.

"I swear before all the gods it is. And you will have the best reassurance of my honesty, since you will be taking me and my sons to meet my husband in Paris."

"And you'll be taking me too," Snorri added. Runa whirled in surprise, but both he and Toki stood calmly awaiting Konal's acceptance. She had expected Snorri to remain to guide Toki. Yet as she regarded her brother standing confidently, hand resting on the pommel of his sword, she realized he would succeed without him.

"It is a dangerous journey, as your brother can attest," Konal said, his voice gentler and a faint smile on his lips. "I cannot guarantee your safety."

"I will be armed," Runa said. "As will my son. We will care for ourselves, and you need only steer your ships. What do you say, Konal Ketilsson?"

"I say it will be a pleasure to reunite you with your husband."

The group laughed, but a chill wind fluttered across them as the Fates gathered loose threads into their bony hands and began to weave.

36

October 17, 886 CE

U lfrik awoke tangled in the furs and blankets of his bed. A still, darkened hall rumbled with the snoring of dozens of men. The hearth had burned low, the man tending it slumped over either drunk of bored into slumber. Tenuous morning light reached in from the smoke hole, and Ulfrik decided to rise before the guards changed for the night. Sitting up, rubbing his face to push the blood into his cheeks, he tried to recall his dreams. Fragmented images of Runa, Gunnar, and Hakon swam through his waking thoughts, but that had been no different from every morning since arriving at Paris.

He roused himself, running a rough comb through hair and beard before throwing his wool cloak across his shoulders. Picking between the people sleeping in the hall, he made for the exit. Einar opened an eye at Ulfrik's passing, but Ulfrik waved him back to his dreams. He wanted to enjoy the dawn alone and without the worries of command. Hrolf had been gone raiding, bored like everyone else, but was expected to return this morning. Ulfrik had served as his commander during that time—his name an honor restored after delivering Henry's head—and he wanted to ensure camp was in order for his arrival.

Outside the fresh scent of cooking fires curled beneath his nose. Hesitant pink light streaked the eastern skies, rising above the golden leaves of autumn trees. Black-and-white feathered magpies hopped along the ground before the longhouse, and leapt into the sky when Ulfrik stepped near. He inhaled and held his breath, exhaling when his eyes dragged across the black walls of Paris. The Seine began to sparkle with yellow light as the sun climbed, and the tops of the towers burned in the dawn. Along the near shore, beached ships leaned like toppled stacks of firewood. The wretched skeleton of Sigfrid's great siege tower had collapsed into timbers pointing skyward. The catapults stood at attention, abandoned and broken. Everything had broken but for the walls of Paris.

The city still squatted in mute defiance. Hrolf's ambition and pride were equal to the size and strength of its walls. Both would resist the other until one collapsed. One more month would mark the anniversary of the siege. This tract of shore had become his entire world. Shaking his head, he strolled from the longhouses across the field to the trenches. Men clambered out as the sun climbed, eager to end their night watch of the tower entrance to Paris.

Gunnar would have loved these trenches, he thought as he walked the edge of one, searching for men who had fallen asleep. Finding an abandoned spear, he picked it up as he patrolled. His son and his friends would speed through the trenches, wooden swords and cloth-covered spear shafts overhead. Runa would have fits searching for him amid the maze of trenches. A smile came to his face and as quickly died. He would not see his family for a long time yet. He had trusted Snorri to safeguard them, and he knew his old friend and mentor would not fail. Besides, something in his heart gave him confidence they were alive and well. He had to believe it, or he could never execute his duties for Hrolf.

It did not take long to find a man curled under a blanket, sleeping on a board at the far end of the trench. Every morning he found shirkers and berated them. The Franks had a canniness for slipping reinforcements into Paris. He had allowed it once, and vowed to never allow it again. Ulfrik kicked dirt from the edge of the trench onto the slumbering man. He ducked his head beneath the dark gray blanket, nothing more than wavy hair showing.

"Hey, get up, the Franks are attacking." Ulfrik jabbed the butt of the spear into the man's leg, but he merely kicked and grumbled.

Licking his lips, Ulfrik searched around. Weary men were shambling away from the trenches, while an equally tired group ambled toward them. He detested these shirkers who slept while good men covered for them. He spun the spear around and pricked the man's side.

"Arrows! Spears! We're overrun!" Ulfrik's false alarm and the jab of the spear sent the man flying to his feet. He wrestled with his blanket, which entwined his legs and set him crashing to the trench wall. Flipping the spear again, Ulfrik clobbered the man across his shoulders. "Too late, you're dead. No weapon in hand, slain with your pants wrapped in a blanket. You'll not see Odin's hall."

The man crumpled and seemed to surrender. He looked up at Ulfrik, the whites of his eyes clear in his dirty face. "Lord Ulfrik! Is it true?"

"No, you fool." He extended the spear shaft again, this time to help the man to his feet. "But if we had been, sleeping half-wits like you would be dead. How long had you been asleep?"

"Only a short time, lord." The man grasped the spear shaft, then hauled himself up. He disentangled from the blanket as he stuttered an explanation. "Nothing has happened in so long, and the Frankish king never came like they said he would. No harm in a little extra rest with them all cornered in Paris."

Ulfrik butted the spear end into the man's face. He howled in pain, white hand clasping over his mouth where the shaft had struck.

"How's that for harm? Could be a lot worse. If the Franks slipped from their walls in the night to put knives to the throats of sleeping men, that'd be harm, wouldn't it? Or if they leapt across this trench, over your sleeping body, to attack the camp, that'd be harm. Do I have to instruct you further?"

In one deft flick, the spear point leveled at the man, who dropped his hand from his mouth and turned his head aside. "No, Lord Ulfrik. I understand. I was a fool, and deserve punishment."

"Every morning I find men sleeping at the bottom of these trenches, and I get less patient each time I find one. You put us all in danger. Now, get out of that trench. For good or for ill, your duty here is done. Tomorrow, you'll give me a better effort or I'll have your eyelids cut off. Understood?"

The man nodded and struggled out of his trench. Ulfrik scowled at him, watching him stumble away as if the Franks pursued him. These new men lacked discipline and feared no consequences. With Hrolf and Gunther away, taking most of the other jarls, too few men in authority remained to enforce discipline. If the Franks pushed on him now, he feared a total collapse.

Turning to find another trench to sweep, a distant light flared. His stomach burned with immediate recognition.

Metal in sunlight.

Another spark, and he located what he feared. To the east, atop the hill where the Franks claimed one of their little gods, Saint Denys, had died, came flashes of mail and weapons in the morning sun.

Between the autumn-thinned treetops, Ulfrik saw the hill crawling with flashing iron. It would not be Hrolf, who was approaching from the west.

A single bell began to toll inside the walls of Paris. Figures on the eastern battlements clumped together, straining like Ulfrik to glimpse that distant hill. Unlike him, they began to cheer, thin voices rising into the clear morning air. Another bell began to chime, and soon another.

Ulfrik swallowed. He did not need his forward scouts to return with their reports. He knew already.

The Holy Roman Emperor, Charles the Fat, had finally come with his army.

And Ulfrik stood alone with half of the Danes to face him.

37

Every bell in Paris clanged and the walls bristled with the dark shapes of men shouting victory and defiance. The flashing iron on the far hill flowed like a river of melting snow, disappearing into the trees.

Ulfrik tightened the strap of his baldric, adjusting his sword on his hip. His arm looped through an iron-rimmed shield. His mail hauberk weighed on his shoulders and his helmet pressed into his hair. Though his heart pounded, he stood beneath his heavily sagging banner of red as if he had nothing more pressing than a review of his troops. Mord, also dressed in war gear, bore the standards next to him, proud and fearless.

"Still no scouts have reported?" Einar asked as he tightened his belt and shouldered his ax.

"You've been with me the whole time, and have you seen any?" Ulfrik observed his men forming into neat columns, their discipline impressive. "Either run off or the Franks killed them. Doesn't matter now. If Hrolf is where scouts last saw him, we've time to join before the Franks reach us."

The camp had responded with unexpected efficiency. Belongings and booty were gathered, war gear donned, ships abandoned, and marching ranks formed within the hour of Ulfrik's alarm. Whatever Charles planned, he was slow in execution. Ulfrik's leaders knew the plan: to locate Hrolf and his men then fight the Frankish army head-on.

At last, a fight he could understand. A fight for glory and honor. Even if he died, it would be as a man and warrior, and not a mash of blood and bone at the foot of a tower.

He raised a horn and blasted an extended note, then shouted the command to march. In reaction, the jeers from Paris grew louder.

The first leg of the retreat into the western woods proceeded in good order. Ulfrik marched at the head, with petty jarls and chieftains leading their columns. Ulfrik never had a true count of the men under his banner, but estimated close to three hundred warriors. They strode the paths through the trees and pushed for the fields where he expected Hrolf to arrive.

As the woods thinned, Ulfrik summoned his scouts, young and small men suited to stealth. Dispatching them ahead, he slowed the march. Several of his leaders complained, but he ignored them. Soon the scouts scurried back through the woods.

"Franks! Scores of them coming through the trees opposite." The breathless scout stumbled to Ulfrik, who caught him.

"Any signs of a battle? Has Hrolf come this way?"

"Not that we could tell, lord."

The column crunched to a halt, and Ulfrik drew his leaders to him, sharing the news.

"We have to out-pace the Frankish scouts. I want men clearing our flanks as the main column pushes west. Beyond this stand of trees is another field, and Hrolf will certainly be there."

"And if he's not?" asked a gray-bearded veteran, his face sharing the same scowls of all the other leaders.

"Then we keep moving west."

"We shouldn't flee. We're not women; we're warriors. We fight no matter the odds!" The veteran and the others agreed, snarling and glaring at the edge of the woods where Franks awaited.

"Fight where victory has a chance. We're outnumbered by their forward patrols, let alone their main army. You've all seen the iron slithering down that hill. Unless it's a ruse, the emperor's army is upon us."

Men flushed in anger, cursed, and growled, but they resumed their march. A detachment of scouts traveled the flanks as the main column laced through the woods as fast as the uneven ground allowed. They stumbled and tripped, but stifled their curses and kept as much silence as an army in mail armor could achieve. Birds scattered ahead of them, betraying their direction but proving no enemies hid along their path.

Scouts from their left flank soon returned with wide eyes and pale faces. "More Franks! They're encircling us."

Ulfrik did not stop, but cursed. "They're funneling us to the ground they have chosen for battle. Curse them to a dog's death. How did they encircle us unnoticed?"

No one replied, as the answer shamed them all. The Franks had been enveloping them while they had grown idle over the long summer of inaction. Had Ulfrik not spotted the movements of the main force, they might have been swallowed like a snake devouring a rat.

Forward scouts returned with better news. Hrolf and his army had formed a shield wall in the field where Ulfrik predicted he would be. The Franks' hesitation to attack Hrolf would give Ulfrik a chance to combine their forces. He redoubled the march, and soon emerged at the edge of the field.

Hrolf's forces were a black clump of glinting mail in a wide field of brown and green grass. Gray trees ringed the clearing, and birds exploded randomly from the red and gold leaves. The Franks were encircling them. The men were unworried, raised their spears and shouted in celebration. Some of Ulfrik's own began to charge from the woods.

"Get your men in line!" Ulfrik commanded. "It could be a trap! Archers in the woods! Quickly, get them back here."

The reasonable leaders immediately grasped the danger and reined in their men. Many still did not heed warnings, impetuously dashing for Hrolf's lines. They arrived without incident, and Ulfrik sighed his relief.

"We have those fools to thank for testing the way. Still, I want shields up all around in case the Franks are smart. They might be waiting for our main body to step into their sight. Careful, we go now."

Under shields, the bulk of the men jogged out of the woods to link with Hrolf and his men. The Franks never fired a shot, if they even had position to do so. Despite the relief, Ulfrik doubted the poor tactical sense the Franks displayed. Would they actually surrender their advantages so easily? Did a greater trap await them?

"Glad you could reach us. Now that you're here, I am assured victory. Stand with me!" Hrolf stood erect at the dead center of his block of warriors. His helmet and mail were no longer gleaming, but stained and dull from weeks on raid. His face creased in a smile behind his cheek plates as Ulfrik arrived before him, with Mord bearing his standard at his left and Einar towering at his right side, where Snorri would have stood in days past.

"There are hundreds of Franks in the woods," he indicated the two points his scouts had located. "So far as I can tell, they're herding us like sheep. Why they did not keep us separated and cut us down is a mystery."

Hrolf laughed, a gusty and careless laugh that infected the men around him. "Franks build strong walls, but that's it. For all the fame of their weapons, they truly don't know how to use them. This King Charles, as I hear it, is a fool. I wonder if the Franks will even ransom him after we capture that bastard today."

"So you know it's the king?"

"We nabbed a few scouts and cut that information out of them. We're surrounded, and I believe they are leading cavalry to us. Good for us, since the horses are bigger targets than men. Easy shooting."

Ulfrik examined Hrolf's face, a placid smile fixed upon it as he scanned the trees. He searched for any sign of fear, a quivering lip, jittering eyelid, a tic of a cheek. Hrolf was as at ease, every line of his body defining confidence in his victory. For his own part, Ulfrik doubted the logic of waiting in an open field for archers and cavalry to destroy them.

"Mord, you stand with me. Einar, line the best warriors with us and the rest integrate with the others."

The new arrivals ordered themselves and waited. Hundreds of men stood in near silence, defiant and bold. Ulfrik took heart from the massive block of fighting strength at his back. Ahead, he watched the Franks flit between trees as if they searched for positions in an elaborate dance. After standing long enough for feet to grow sore, Gunther One-Eye stretched in an exaggerated yawn then shouted. "Anyone who needs sleep can get it now. The Franks need more time to learn which end of the spear to point at us."

Laughter rippled through the front ranks. Ulfrik smiled at his friend down the line, who winked at him.

Ulfrik began to reply when the line tightened and Hrolf drew himself to his full height. Whirling about, he saw the Franks emerging from woods.

"Gods," Toki whispered. "We're doomed."

Rank after rank of soldiers flowed from the trees, encircling them in the field. The morning sun filled their grim faces with black shadow, rendering them in stern contrast to the gray trees behind. Spears parked at their shoulders, men raised their long tear-drop shaped shields, creating a shield wall more massive than any Ulfrik had ever seen. Lightly armored archers formed behind them and placed shafts across their bowstrings.

"Our glory will outshine any who've gone before us." Hrolf shielded his eyes against the eastern sun as he surveyed the serried ranks. "Odin will raise us above all his heroes, for surely none will have faced what we face today."

Ulfrik swallowed, glanced at Mord who had stifled his doubts and straightened his back. At last the Franks halted, and a horn sounded a long note as horses were led through the trees. Their riders had dismounted and guided the beasts, but now climbed onto their backs. Only one man rode, his strong white horse guided by two men.

The massive rider was clad in sparkling mail, a conical helmet topped with a crown sitting crooked on his round head.

"Charles the Fat," Ulfrik said. "The Holy Roman Emperor comes to offer us his blood today. Lord Hrolf, it will be an honor to place his head at your feet."

He offered the words as encouragement to the men around him, and they rewarded him with boasts of their own. Soon, Hrolf had a dozen men clamoring to kill Charles and far more began to growl and curse at the surrounding Franks.

"We are the greatest heroes of all the ages," Hrolf shouted to his men. "No one will be prouder than me to feast with you in Valhalla. The Valkyries will bear us from this field, singing with joy for the death we will bring the Franks. For glorious battle!"

The men shouted and raised their weapons. The Franks responded with a ripple that traveled the ring like mead threatening to overflow a mug. Ulfrik raised his weapon and joined his companions, meeting Mord's eyes as he raised their standard alongside Hrolf's. "Our battles continue until the end of days, Ragnarok! We will fight together as brothers in Valhalla!"

Mord redoubled his roar, bucking Ulfrik with his shield in acknowledgment. Men began to pound weapons on shields and stamp their feet.

Ulfrik's father had been known as the Bellower, and the power of his shout had come through his blood to Ulfrik. His war shout defeated all those around him, drawing gleeful encouragement from Hrolf. *A strong war shout can stop a man as good as a shield wall,* Ulfrik recalled his father's wisdom. Never had the advice felt more appropriate.

The ground shook and the air vibrated with the curses and war cries flowing from the Danes. They drew themselves into a circle, lacing together round shields to offer no gap to the surrounding Franks. Spears lowered over the front ranks and men dared the enemy to charge.

The Franks hesitated, and Ulfrik saw enemy heads turning in confusion as they remained immobile.

Fed up with waiting, Ulfrik stepped out of the shield wall and threw his arms wide. "Fight us or go back to your mothers! Come, fight me! Anyone!"

Whether they understood his words, a gap in the Frankish lines opened. Horses cantered forward, bearing mailed riders with leaf-bladed spears aimed at the Danish lines.

Chastened, Ulfrik jumped back into the shield wall beside Hrolf. The Franks lined up their horses shoulder to shoulder.

Then a horn sounded.

38

The mounted Franks lined up, their horses side-stepping and heads tossing, eyes white with fear. Ulfrik's shield dipped as he watched the warriors dismount and guide their horses away from the center. The huge shape of Charles's white horse emerged, men in yellow and blue surcoats surrounding him as his horse trotted forward.

The emperor drew in his mount, sitting back and staring at the line of Danes from the shadowed depths of his crowned helmet. Taking it as a challenge, Ulfrik pointed his sword at Charles and cursed him. "You come to fight, you fat bastard, then let me be the one to stick you!"

A rush of competing oaths and challenges followed Ulfrik's, and he shared a wry smile with Hrolf. He cared not whether Charles lived or died, but knew challenging the king would inspire the men around him. Outnumbered and surrounded, boldness made the best armor.

A man threw himself on all fours beneath Charles, and the emperor placed his ponderous weight on the man's back as he used him for a stepping stool to dismount. Two other servants assisted him to the ground, where he adjusted his helmet and checked his sword.

"What an oaf," Mord muttered. "Don't ride a horse to battle if you can't get off the damn beast without help."

"No one should ride a horse into battle. Can't be trusted." Ulfrik barely heard his own idle commentary, so focused was he on the unfolding events. Expecting a command for a charge, instead Charles gathered ten spearmen to him and strode out in front of his lines.

"He wants to tell us how he's going to kill us," Hrolf said, a grim smile on his face. "I've no ears for that shit. Let him stand out there like a fool."

The Danes in the front erupted in laughter. It infected the whole troop, who laughed and taunted to mask their fear. Ulfrik joined them. The king gave confused looks to the men beside him, enduring the mockery until he dispatched a single runner toward the Danish line.

"Let him come," Hrolf ordered, stopping several men who had raised throwing spears.

The man was not yet grown into a full beard, thin and pale, to Ulfrik's eyes little more than a boy in poorly fitted mail. Terror showed in his wide eyes and trembling lips as he scanned the shield wall facing him. He did not know where to look, and addressed the crowd in perfect Danish.

"My lord and emperor wishes to speak with the leader of this army. Meet him in the field, but bring no more than ten men."

His message delivered, he wavered as if not knowing what to do next. Hrolf stepped forward, glaring down at the messenger. "A fellow Dane on the losing side once more. Do yourself some good and join us before we hack you to scraps."

More laughter followed Hrolf's taunt, and the messenger stepped back. "Are you the leader? What is your name?"

"I am Hrolf the Strider and I am one of the leaders. Every man here is his own leader. Go ask your lord which one he wants to speak with."

"He wants to speak to the leader in charge of this army." He took three hesitant steps backward then turned to jog back to his lines. Ulfrik and all the Danes in the front ranks hurled insults after him.

"Ulfrik, Gunther, you each take four men and join me. Let's tell the king we are proud to die as warriors and our only sorrow is that it will take all day for his boy soldiers to kill us, and only then if they don't run off first."

Tapping Einar and Mord, Ulfrik pulled in two others from the front ranks and fell in behind Hrolf. Gunther One-Eye smirked at him as they strode toward the enemy. "Maybe they plan to talk us to death instead of blooding their swords."

Ulfrik made to reply, but Hrolf held up his hand for silence as they closed the final distance. Now was the time for the war-face, the impassive, unflinching expression of indifference to death. No Frank would know what fears curled in their guts. Without bluster or curses to fill Ulfrik's mouth, his mind filled with images of Runa and his sons. He had only moments to think of them before the killing would start, and then under the weight of the Frankish numbers he would die with their memories in his heart.

The two lines regarded each other. Up close, Charles was a soft and fair-skinned man, thin-bearded and beady-eyed. Ulfrik counted the shrewd, calculating mind showing in his dark eyes as he swept his gaze across the men, settling on Hrolf. He let the two leaders stand off, and turned his attention to the opposing Franks. They were more encouraging. Their mail was in good repair, but dented and mended from long use. Their faces were flinty and deep-lined, scarred and creased from battles won and lost. They wore the war-face, too, and Ulfrik had to suppress a smile. At least he had worthy opponents to fight and would not cough out his life at the end of some half-man's spear.

"You are the one called Hrolf the Strider?" Charles's voice was rough and shrill, but Ulfrik heard the tiredness in it. Even as the Danish interpreter spoke his words, the emperor covered his yawn with a jewel-covered hand. Several of his guards flicked their eyes at him, though dared not face him.

"Without a doubt, you are Charles the Fat. I am glad you have spared your horse the agony of carrying your worthless body any farther. The beast will be glad to die today, I am sure."

The interpreter froze at Hrolf's insult, his pause drawing an impatient glance from his emperor. He fumbled with his words, and Hrolf snarled at him. "Gods, boy, tell him exactly what I said. Hurry up and get this done so you can go back to sucking your mother's tit."

Ulfrik turned his laugh aside, but Gunther and the others exploded in laughter. Hrolf barked a command for silence.

Finding his voice, the interpreter streamed the bubbling words of the Frankish language to his king, whose face grew darker. His jaw ground, jowls shaking beneath it.

"You are not afraid to die?" The king raised his brow, then wiped his nose with the back of his hand.

"I am more afraid of my mother than I am of you and all these prick-sucking men pretending to be warriors. Death in battle is glory. Glory is everything. We never lose a battle. When we fall, the Valkyries carry us to Valhalla and we fight on in glory until the end of days. Why fear that? We seek it, crave it."

The interpreter streamed Hrolf's words to Charles. When finished, the emperor folded his arms and furrowed his brow. His eyes grew distant and he seemed to not be present with them. The silence grew uncomfortable, and Hrolf's irritation flared.

"Tell your lord to wake up. Tell him we are going to hack his balls off and make him eat them. Then we're going to cut the guts out of every last one of these bastards surrounding us and march off to rape their wives and daughters until their crotches split. Tell them we are his death and the death of his world. Tell him now!"

Hrolf's shouting drew ire from Charles's guards, white-knuckled grips on their trembling spears. Ulfrik admired their discipline, seeing the hate emanating from their faces. Yet Charles had barely stirred. The interpreter said something to him, far too short to be faithful to Hrolf's threats. Then the king held up his hand, a green jeweled ring catching a blaze of light. The interpreter fell silent as Charles spoke. His bodyguards suddenly snapped to him, faces contorted with repugnance and confusion. Several appeared to protest, but the emperor shouted.

Both sides paused at the sudden outburst. Charles surveyed his men, ignoring Ulfrik and all the other Danes around him. He spoke in sharp, clipped words. Several times he looked at the sky and pointed up. Ulfrik and his fellows followed his finger, but saw nothing more than a cluster of white clouds tumbling through a blue sky. Finally, Charles shouted again and commanded his interpreter, who slowly addressed Hrolf.

"What would Hrolf the Strider desire to leave these lands in peace?"

Ulfrik blinked. He looked at Einar, who stared at the interpreter with his mouth open. Hrolf's head inclined slightly, as if he had heard wrong. Even he stole a glance back at Ulfrik, but did not hesitate.

"My demands have been clear since the day I set foot on this wretched land. I want right of passage on the Seine. I want Paris thrown open to me. Most importantly, I want seven hundred pounds of silver. That will keep my sword out of your lord's belly. Go on and tell him."

Words flowed back and forth, one of them, who apparently was more than a bodyguard, pleaded with Charles. The king shook his head, spewed more words over his men.

"The seven hundred pounds of silver was your original demand to leave Paris. You will be paid the silver for abandoning your siege of Paris, but there are conditions."

"No," Hrolf shouted. "No conditions. If your king values his kingdom, he'll give what I ask."

Without need of interpretation, Charles stepped forward to Hrolf and shouted at him. Men on both sides tensed, and Ulfrik dropped his hand to his sword hilt. Behind Charles, the lines of warriors stirred. The interpreter hastened to explain his king's shouting.

"You will have all that you've asked for since arriving. It is more than enough. The conditions I attached will be favorable to you, if you will hear them."

Tensions subsided and Hrolf smiled. "I'll listen."

Mollified, Charles slipped back into his aloof and tired demeanor. He swiped his hand generally to the north as he spoke. "The silver will be delivered in the spring of next year. In the meantime, the lands of Burgundy have revolted against my rule. You have shown an amazing talent for smashing people into submission. On my authority, whip the Burgundians for me. Return them to obedience. Whatever you find there is yours, save anything from the Church. You are not to harm clergymen or destroy churches. If you agree to this, then you have my word on the silver and passage of the Seine."

Ulfrik's legs buckled at the stunning offer and he almost jumped forward to accept for Hrolf. The terms were better than he could have expected, but now Hrolf folded his arms and appeared deep in thought. Of course, Ulfrik realized the performance for what it was and his esteem for Hrolf's canniness increased.

"I will lift the siege of Paris and agree. I give you my oath, and swear it before all the gods. I want to hear you promise in the name of your god."

Charles smiled, pulled out a gold cross hung from his neck and made his promise. The men around him winced as if stuck with needles, but Charles beamed. The expression reminded Ulfrik of a simpleton who had lived in his father's hall. The fool smiled even when slapped or spit on, much like the slap the Danes had just delivered to the Franks.

Promises made, Hrolf led them back to their lines in silence. Ulfrik shared eager smiles with everyone, excited to deliver the news to the rest. As they approached, Hrolf shouted for the men to stand down. "We have reached an agreement, and we are rich. Cheer with me, for you are all lords this day!"

Hesitant at first, the sight the Frankish lines backing down and breaking up convinced them. They burst into delirious celebrations only as men snatched from death could. Ulfrik joined their frenzied rejoicing. He hugged Einar, the two of them slapping each other's backs and laughing. Gunther One-Eye joined them, and soon even Hrolf forced his way to them.

"You've brought me good luck again, Ulfrik. If you hadn't come to me, we couldn't have scared them into a surrender."

"It was the only thing to do, lord."

Hrolf danced with laughter, said more to him that could not be heard above the celebration. Ulfrik let it go, content Hrolf considered him a lucky man.

As the Franks bled away, the Danes continued to dance and celebrate. Finally Hrolf got control of enough people to lead them back to camp. Finding Ulfrik once more, he threw his arm about his shoulders as the two walked from what should have been a raven's feast.

"You and Gunther will help me rule this kingdom. Such a fat fool on this Frankish throne won't last for long. I will stay here and carve out lands for myself. Do well by me and your rewards will be more than you ever dreamed."

Intoxicated with easy success, Hrolf bounced from jarl to jarl and made similar promises. Einar offered Ulfrik congratulations, but as they slipped into the woods from which they had come, Ulfrik had a deeper realization that furrowed his brow.

"Is there something wrong?" Einar asked, his smile fading.

Shaking his head, Ulfrik waved the concern away. "I was just thinking of my family. We're here for another winter, at the least."

Einar frowned, then joined Ulfrik in silence. The two continued to trudge through the woods amid their singing and shouting companions.

Ulfrik thought of his home, of his people, and of his foolishness for chasing after treasures that did not exist. He had led his men to slaughter, tempted a worthy hirdman into betrayal, missed his mentor and friend, and had lost his family. The day's great victory felt more like defeat with every step he took toward Hrolf's camp.

39

Ulfrik emerged from the hall into the morning light. Paris still squatted, sullen and dark, in the center of the Seine. Smoke still rose above its roofs and birds still circled its towers. Its gates remained barred.

Nothing had changed. Three days after Charles conceded all of Hrolf's demands, and the only discernible difference was men no longer filled the trenches surrounding Paris. Count Odo had refused to open his gates and promised to attack Hrolf if he approached the walls. Charles the Fat had departed without even visiting his besieged city. His commands to Odo also failed to breach Paris's walls, much like the Danes' failure.

Morning walks along the trenches had become a nervous habit Ulfrik found difficult to break. Men were still asleep, recovering from nearly three continuous days of drinking and celebration, and the air was crisp and still. To his surprise, he still found men passed out in the trenches, but left them alone.

He rubbed his arms against the chill air. He thought forward to the next phase of this adventure in Frankia, hoping to smash the Burgundians into order and collect their silver by springtime and return home. Even Toki would begin to doubt his survival. He would have to find a trader or traveler willing to carry a message home over winter. Snorting at the impossibility of the thought, he resigned himself to Fate. The Three Norns, spinning the threads of each man's life, would decide what happened next.

His oath to Hrolf came first.

Turning on the muddy grass, he was about to return to the hall when he saw the northern tower doors open and a single man emerge. He carried a white flag with him, its brightness stark against the burn streaks of the tower walls. Instinctively, Ulfrik scanned the walls but found no more men atop them than usual. A small group idly observed the man with his flag, one dark shape pointing to him has he trotted up the banks.

Ulfrik met the flag bearer, who turned out to be a boy, out of bow range from the tower. If any other Dane saw him none were interested enough to learn what he wanted. Only Ulfrik greeted the boy, who was tall but not more than twelve years old and dressed in drab clothes that had been torn in a half dozen places. In one hand he held his flag and in the other a wooden cross.

"You better speak Norse, boy. I can't stand the noise of your Frankish." Ulfrik put one hand on his sword hilt, never underestimating anything the sneaky Parisians might attempt.

"I've come seeking Lord Ulfrik Ormsson. I serve Bishop Anscharic. Could you take me to him?"

"You serve my sworn enemy, did you know that?"

The boy's eyes went wide and he stepped back, mumbling a Frankish prayer.

"Be at ease, boy, I won't harm you under your flag of peace. I am Ulfrik Ormsson, amazing luck for you. Do you have a message from that swine you serve? I would hear it with great interest, though it won't prevent me from gutting him as soon as he's in sword's reach. And your Norse is good, but you can still do better."

A smile flashed at the compliment, but a frown overtook it. "The bishop is a great man. If you are Lord Ulfrik, then he has asked for you to approach the northern tower. He wishes to make a deal with you."

"Deal? He does realize he has been defeated, yes? What could he offer me?"

"He would never tell me such things, lord. But he awaits at the tower. He asks that only you come, as the offer is only for you."

Ulfrik agreed and followed the boy to the tower. The same cluster of lazy guards leaned over the walls, but even at his distance Ulfrik saw the white robes and hair of a man standing beside them. "That's Anscharic, is it? He's the head priest now?"

"Something like that, lord. He is God's chosen, and leads us all in His light."

"That light is probably my people burning one of your villages to the ground."

Stopping in the shadow of the tower, Ulfrik avoided looking at the base. Wreckage of past attacks lapped against it like a tide of death. Bitter scents still lingered in the air, burned bones and charred weapons weathered into a noxious slurry. He craned his neck up the length of the wall, where Anscharic leaned over, waving a bony hand at him.

"You look much older, Humbert, far worse than when you were my slave." Shouting up the tower wall, Anscharic's reply came clearly despite the distance.

"And you look no richer than when you arrived here. You've been given men, and a few armbands. We both know you sought more when you journeyed here."

"I heard your god frowns on lies. You are a master of them."

Anscharic's white-haired head fell back in laughter. "I told you many true things, first among them that God will not allow Paris to fall. It is His city, and His arm bars you and your heathen scum from it. Within these walls is the safety of God's love. Just look at your feet to see what your gods have given to you."

"You have a unique view of victory. Your king granted us everything we demanded. No one cares for this ridiculous city."

"Ah, but you do, don't you? You came here with a lust for treasure in your heart, but never found it."

"That's because you lied about it."

"Indeed I did. A ruse designed for you to take me home. God shepherded me with you as His instrument, and with grave purpose. With poor Joscelin dead, I arrived in time to take up where he left off. I have done well, in fact, where you have only done well in your imagination. In reality you have nothing, not even a place to call home."

Ulfrik's fists balled and his mouth pulled tight. "Well, it's my imaginary army that's keeping you penned in your starving city. I've no time to indulge the ramblings of an old man hiding atop a tower. I am leaving."

"Indulge me one thing, and you may still gain what you originally sought."

Stopping in mid-turn, Ulfrik squinted up into the brightening sky. Anscharic's hair caught the morning light, glowing like white fire. "The time for deals is long past, Humbert. You have killed my friend, and killed scores of my men with your deceit."

"Return my father's cloak to me, and I will repay you in gold. I am an old man now, soon to go to God's glory. When my body is laid to rest, I want to be wrapped in that cloak."

"I will grant you that wish," Ulfrik renewed his walk away. "After I avenge Ander's murder, I will wrap you in that rag and throw you into the Seine."

"Return it to the boy I sent to you," Anscharic called after him. "He will be waiting here. A cross of gold, Ulfrik. It is more than what you have now, with your Lord Hrolf holding all the treasure. You can rebuild your hall with such wealth."

Letting Anscharic's weak voice fade, Ulfrik stalked back toward his camp. Men carried out their duties with more vigor now, at least those who were not still heavy with drink. Banners flew where none had before, jarls vying to bring their standards closer to Hrolf's. Ships were being prepared for portage overland, since Odo's threats made sailing past Paris too dangerous. Pausing at the entrance to the hall, where two men stumbled out with bright smiles on bleary faces, Ulfrik saw more square-sailed ships arriving up the Seine. *Success brings the glory-seekers*, he thought, then ducked inside.

"Still walking the trenches?" Einar asked, shirtless and sleepy-eyed under blankets with a young woman pressed to his side. He recognized her as Toki's former bed-warmer, Bera.

"It's hard to change. If you think I'm bad, men are still sleeping in the trenches."

Einar laughed and disappeared under the covers, where Bera squealed. Ulfrik walked to the banner pole resting against the wall where he had made his bed. He had little to pack beyond war gear. Anscharic had been painfully accurate in describing his poverty. Despite winning honor and status, he had little to show for it. Though he took a larger share of spoils, with so many plundering the land there was not much to claim. He counted on the promised silver to bring him a measure of wealth equal to the suffering he had endured in Frankia.

The ragged red cloak hung limp. Black stains from constant handling smeared it, and flying it so often had torn it in places. It hung heavily, as if it were as tired as Ulfrik.

Taking it into his hands, he yanked the cloak tight, then pulled until it untied from the pole. Anscharic remained hidden behind his stone walls, and Hrolf was leading his army to Burgundia. Justice would have to wait. Bunching the cloak into a ball, he flung it atop his pack and closed his eyes.

"Ander, your vengeance must wait a while longer. Forgive me, old friend. I will bring justice to your memory, only not today."

Pinching the bridge of his nose, he tried to clear his thoughts. Then he heard his name called. Turning to face it, an unfamiliar man in a red cap leaned into the door.

"Lord Ulfrik, ships arrived with men looking for you. A man named Snorri said that he's returned with your family."

40

The three ships that had been observed arriving earlier were now beached on the river bank, a bow shot south of where the mouldering skeleton of Sigfrid's siege tower lay. The morning light clipped across their decks and masts, leaving their hulls in blue shadows. Men worked within the shadows, securing their vessels, receiving sacks thrown down from the decks, performing their duties as if they were only another ship of fortune-seekers joining Hrolf's standard. Men from the camp pointed the newcomers up the slope toward the shoddily built halls and barracks.

Ulfrik studied these arrivals, his heart pounding at the base of his throat. The man in the red cap stopped when he realized Ulfrik no longer followed. He turned, irritation barely concealed. "Those are the ships. You don't need me to show the way. The old man over there is the one who sent for you. Good morning to you, lord."

The man left Ulfrik staring after the group gathered at the edge of the grass. Snorri's grizzled hair had grown whiter and his flesh had shrunk, aging him ten years, but his energy showed as he addressed two men standing with him. He stabbed his finger at the southern bank, toward the ruined abbey. The men followed his gesture, turning to face the south.

As they did, Runa and Gunnar were revealed behind them.

He began to run before he realized it. Gunnar saw him first, hesitated as if he could not believe his eyes, then charged from his mother's side. Ulfrik stopped and threw his arms wide, and Gunnar jumped into his embrace. He lifted his son as easily as if he were still a babe, spinning him around and laughing.

"All along the river people said the Frankish king had killed you and everyone." Gunnar's words were muffled as he buried his face in Ulfrik's shoulder. "But I didn't believe it. No one believed it."

He set Gunnar down, expecting to see tears streaking his smooth skin, yet finding his face dry. His dark eyes shimmered with joy, but Ulfrik saw something different in them. Harder. Stronger. He recognized his son was no more a boy. Doubt crossed Gunnar's face as Ulfrik studied him.

"Bah, the king never drew his sword. He was too afraid of me and ran away. That's the truth of it."

Laughter bubbled up, and Gunnar was a child again. He threw himself back into Ulfrik's arms, but when Ulfrik stood he did not beg to be carried. He took his father's hand and stood at his side.

"Mother has dreamed of you every night. When she sleeps, I hear her speaking to you."

"And I have shared those dreams, this long and lonely year."

Runa approached them, confidently striding across the grass. She no longer wore a skirt, dressing in the deerskin pants of a man. The sax he had given her slapped at her legs, and a sheathed sword bobbed at her hip. Her hair spilled out from the drawn hood of her green wool cloak, and as she closed the distance, she pulled it from her head.

He held his breath. She had changed as well. A streak of gray twined through her curls, rising from her forehead and disappearing into the fullness of hair. Her dark eyes were cooler and her lips thinner. Her beauty had grown fierce, almost cruel. Without pause, she strode directly to him, seized his jaw in a powerful grip and pulled him down to her lips.

They melted together. If the world existed any longer, Ulfrik did not care. For all the hard edges Runa had acquired, her scent was sweeter than he remembered and all the warm softness of a woman remained. They parted enough to speak, Runa's hot breath bathing his face.

"I have dreamed of this moment every night for a year. I imagined all the ways I would hit you, curse you, bite you. Sometimes I thought of killing you for everything you put me through. Now I've failed in all of my plans. I hate you for making me weak."

"We can try the biting later tonight." Runa's eyes met his, and for a moment he feared his awkward humor had gone astray. Then a smile bloomed and Runa began to laugh, tears pooling in her eyes. They fell together again, and Ulfrik remained silent, savoring the moment.

"Lord Ulfrik Ormsson," called a gruff voice. "How did you manage to keep yourself out of trouble without me around, lad?"

Ulfrik greeted Snorri with a rough embrace and a pat on the back. "There must be a good story to tell," Ulfrik said, regarding his old friend. "You look like you swam here from Nye Grenner."

"There are too many stories to tell, but before that you should meet my new master." Snorri turned and beckoned a young woman to approach. Ulfrik recognized her as Thora in the same instant that Hakon appeared from behind her skirts. "Young Hakon has grown since you last saw him, and I admit he has won my loyalty during this long journey."

His son now stood straight and strong, though his face was still round with baby fat his eyes were filled with a soulful wisdom that startled Ulfrik. He clung to his maid's skirts, but as Snorri outstretched his hand, he toddled forward to take it. Snorri chuckled with a grandfatherly pride and guided him forward. "Do you remember your father?"

Hakon shook his head, his yellow hair falling across his face.

Ulfrik swallowed the lump in his throat, and knelt to greet his son. Hakon stepped back, but Ulfrik only smiled. He feared to speak, for his voice might crumble with emotion. Seeing his infant son standing and walking reminded Ulfrik how long he had been absent. As the two got the measure of each other, Ulfrik finally stood. "You are a handsome boy, Hakon. I will have a gift made for you, would you like that?"

His son nodded and Snorri ruffled his hair. Then he spoke more gravely to Ulfrik. "There is one story you will want to hear today." Snorri pointed at the two men he had been addressing earlier. "The two twins, Konal and Kell, have news for you."

"Mother saved Konal's life, and he saved mine," Gunnar added brightly, but Runa shushed him.

"Many stories to tell," Ulfrik said to Runa, his smile growing at the blush forming on Runa's tear-wet cheeks.

The twins joined them, both young and strong, nearly identical to each other in every detail. Ulfrik had never seen twins before, but had heard amazing stories of their powers. Both of them had the weathered skin of long days at sea, though one appeared softer than the other. Their clear eyes struck Ulfrik as shrewdly intelligent. They swept him in simultaneous glances from head to foot, leaving him feeling as if he had been appraised like a gem stone. The one with the softer features focused on Runa, and his gaze lingered enough for Ulfrik to wonder if his look held more meaning than he understood.

"I am Kell Ketilsson," said the harder looking of the twins. "It is a great honor to meet you at last, Lord Ulfrik."

"And I am Konal Ketilsson. I am in your debt, as you will no doubt soon learn." He bowed slightly, his eyes never leaving Ulfrik's.

"These are your ships?" Ulfrik asked, and the twins nodded. "Then your debts will be repaid for delivering my family to me. Though I must ask what has happened to the rest of my men and people?"

"There are many stories to tell, lad. Your people are safe, enemies defeated, and Toki rules the land in your name. Don't worry yourself. Runa wanted to join you, as did I. But the twins have urgent news for you."

Ulfrik looked at Kell and Konal, whose expressions grew grave. Kell folded his arms and explained.

"We are here for the one you've called Humbert. His true name is Anscharic, and he has stolen something of tremendous value from us. We plan to take it back."

"Then you must succeed where Jarl Hrolf and I have failed. He is barricaded inside Paris, and long out of my reach."

Both twins stared impassively past Ulfrik at the walls of Paris. He smirked at the realization blooming on their faces.

"I fear you may have been duped by the same tales of treasure that I believed, fool that I was."

"No." Konal's voice fell like lead into the mud. "I've held it in my hands. It's real."

Ulfrik stiffened, shared a look with Runa who gave no hint of her thoughts. He turned to face Paris again, then recalled Ander and his rune sticks. The gods did not lie, he had claimed.

"Then let us go to my hall, where you may refresh before telling me your tales."

ULFRIK LED KONAL, Kell, and Snorri from his hall. The sun had trekked across the sky and now glowed red in the west, disappearing behind red- and gold-topped trees. Birds raced back to their nests, zooming through the chill autumn air. He scanned Paris, out of habit rather than need, checking for movement, odd lights, or other signs of trouble. It rested at peace, orange points of torches springing up where light no longer shined.

"All private conversations are best held in an open field," Ulfrik explained to his guests, gesturing them to the cleared fields by the makeshift halls. "Inside, we'd have to contend with too many spies. Mord is a good man, but what is said to him is said to his father and Hrolf as well."

"You tolerate spies well," Konal said as they walked across the well-trodden grass. "My father would've hanged the man no matter how much he liked him."

"I have few secrets but the one we discuss tonight." Satisfied that they were out of anyone's hearing, Ulfrik stopped and faced them, eying Konal as he spoke. "Let's be quick. I don't want to appear suspicious, and I want nothing more than to return to my wife's side. She is more beautiful than I remember, and softer that I'd have expected after the tales you shared with me today."

Studying him for any sign of insincerity, Ulfrik saw none. Konal smiled and inclined his head. "Few women can survive such trials and grow more beautiful, but no one can doubt your wife has."

A bonfire roared to life outside of Hrolf's hall, shadows of men flitting before it. Ulfrik wanted to press Konal for more details of his year in Nye Grenner, but Hrolf would soon emerge and attempt to recruit the twins to his army.

"Tell me your stories. Why do you believe Anscharic still has your treasure?"

"We don't know if he still has our treasure, but we guess he does. Even if not, he can tell us what he did with it." Konal paused and regarded his brother, who nodded solemnly. "Forgive me if I hesitate. We've not shared this story outside of our family."

Ulfrik and Snorri shared a glance. "Snorri and I share the same confidence. Don't omit anything from your tale, and we might help you yet."

"We captured Anscharic and all his men off the cost of England. Gave us a terrible fight, and he nearly got away. We had nabbed a fat prize. We'd heard about a Frankish noble traveling with a ship of Christian priests, gone to Wessex on some sort of exchange with the king there."

"King Alfred loves his churches and he'd bestowed a great gift to the Franks," Kell cut in to his brother's talk. He outlined a large cross shape in the air, from his head to chest. "Anscharic was carrying a gold cross as big as my forearm and nearly as thick. Most beautiful thing I'd ever seen. Not sure why Alfred would ever part with it. Maybe Anscharic stole it himself."

"No matter, it was to our gain," Konal renewed his story, idly pulling down Kell's arm from drawing the shape again. "Anscharic loved that cross, and threw himself over it when we found it. Had to beat it out of him, and the bastard could fight well for an old man. We captured a small kingdom in gold that day, and having so much in our holds was frightening. We began to see enemies everywhere, and so sailed back to Ireland with it. Anscharic was going to be ransomed, and all his gold would fill our father's treasure pit."

"So his story about a cross of gold is real," Ulfrik said to Snorri, who scowled and nodded. "Do you know, this morning he summoned me to the walls and tempted me with that cross?"

Both Konal and Kell laughed. "That cross is Loki's work, I say." Konal slapped his brother's shoulder as he explained. "The cross lies in my father's hall, and he can't offer it to you any more than he can offer you the stars rising tonight."

"You're confusing them," Kell chided.

"Sorry, lord, but that cross is how Anscharic slipped us. As you know, his Norse is as good as any foreigner can manage. During our return to Ireland, that tongue of his wagged unceasingly and he found men among our crew who would listen. Not all of those men were happy to return to Ireland. England had been good to us, and some even started families there. Our father, too, is mad. A berserk who never leaves the battlefield, if you understand me. No one was glad to see him again. So Anscharic began to make promises to the crew. You'll recognize them, Lord Ulfrik.

"He claimed his wealth was beyond imaging back in Frankia. If they returned him, not only would his brother pay a fortune in gold but also grant them land and titles. The fools in my crew were too ready to believe. By the time we arrived in Ireland, a full crew of men were eager to betray us. We placed Anscharic and all the other treasures in the hall, where we prepared to reveal everything to our father.

"But when we arrived with our father, Anscharic was gone. The sacks of gold had been carried away and only the gold cross and scattered coins remained. More horrible still, the greatest treasure was gone. The cross was inlaid with gems. Gems the size of fat hailstones. Rubies and emeralds, all manner of gems. Those stones were worth more than the weight of the gold cross."

"Our father banished us from our homes until we can return the treasure Anscharic and our traitorous crew stole." Kell shook his head as he spoke. "We didn't know what had happened at first, and the crew had a strong lead on us. The ocean is wide and trackless, and finding someone in it is a fool's errand. But we had heard news that our traitors had headed to Norway. I suppose they wanted to hide their treasure. We located their hall, but someone had raided and killed them.

"That was you, Lord Ulfrik." Konal peered into Ulfrik's eyes, and again the appraising, shrewd light sparkled within them. "You heard the same news we did, and tracked them down for their treasure. Runa claims you found nothing more than trifling spoils and a mad priest who claimed to have gold hidden in Frankia. I need to know, with all respect and honor due to you, lord, did you find anything more? Did Anscharic carry any gems or try to steer you to a place where the gold might be hidden?"

"Nothing more than you already know." Ulfrik did not hesitate in his answer. He held Konal's scrutiny, then shared a glance with Kell. "He led us here on the promise of ill-gotten gold and a story of revenge upon a bishop. Whatever treasure your crew stole, they did not hide it on the lands we raided, and I made a hard search of that place."

Both Konal and Kell slouched in defeat, Kell rubbing his face and gazing toward Paris. "Is Anscharic so well guarded we cannot reach him?" he asked.

"He is now the bishop of this city. In time Paris may grow lax and allow you inside, but today you will be torn by an arrow storm should you approach the walls. I wish your story could end with more promise, but you at least have your man cornered. For my part, Anscharic led me to ruin."

"Ruin?" Konal's eyes went wide. "Your name is spoken all through this land, in the same breath as Hrolf and Sigfrid. We heard about the bridge and the castle you destroyed. Men say Hrolf believes he cannot die with you at his side and your are high in his esteem. This sounds like success to me."

Ulfrik smiled, and Snorri nudged him. "Lad, Hrolf has come out of his hall, and we better meet him soon. And Konal's right; you've got a lot to be proud of here."

They broke up as the sun stained the bottom of the sky with red and gold. The field was filling with darkness and yellow lights flickered from the open doors of the hall. The twins tried to straighten themselves and appear more cheerful than they actually felt. Yet Ulfrik did not need anything to bring a smile to his face.

He had found Anscharic's treasure.

41

"Do you remember when I claimed only Nye Grenner could be my home?" Ulfrik asked as he walked with one arm looped through Runa's. They had traveled into the woods, not far from where he had been betrayed. Their footsteps crackled on the fallen leaves and underbrush, and birds sang their morning songs in the branches laced above their heads. Runa smiled at him, a wide smile that filled his chest with warmth. He felt the gods could be no kinder to him than delivering him Runa for this day.

"I seem to recall you melting like snow in the spring, so full of despair that Nye Grenner was beneath us but our only choice."

Ulfrik laughed. "I shamed myself with weakness that day."

"It was with me." Runa tugged on his arm. "There is no shame when it is only us."

Nodding, he stopped them at a flat, lichen splattered rock that stood waist high. He scanned the woods, searching for anyone following, and found nothing but black trees hung with russet leaves. He placed the bag he had tucked under his other arm atop the rock.

"I was wrong about Nye Grenner. Toki will hold the land in my name, and expand it to the north. Frankia will be our new home.

Norsemen have already cut out farms and estates along the coast, and the Franks are weak and yielding when not crowded behind stone walls. Hrolf has already promised me lands."

"What of your kingdom?" Runa asked, her eyebrow raised but her smile undiminished. "You did not want to bend a knee to any man?"

"Everyone has a master; even jarls and kings answer to the gods. Besides, I had already sworn myself to Hrolf, and Fate has rewarded me for the loyalty."

Runa's laugh was like the tinkling of bright silver. He drew her under his arm and cherished her a moment longer. Snorri had hinted that she and Konal might have shared a bed. Her stiff and formal manner in Konal's presence confirmed as much for Ulfrik. He did not begrudge her. More than one Frankish slave woman had found herself under his blankets during the long year alone. All that mattered was the future, which he relished like never before.

Ulfrik pressed his lips in a tentative smile. "Have you no curiosity why I've taken you to these woods in secret?"

"You want to build your family, I hope."

Bending back with laughter, he patted the bag on the rock. "That I do, and we will! But let me lay a richer bed for us first. This bag holds our future."

He snatched the deerskin bag by the bottom and tipped out the contents. Anscharic's ragged, dirty red cloak tumbled out and unfolded on the rock.

"What is that?" Runa frowned and lifted the cloak to check if anything was hidden beneath, revealing nothing but stone.

"Humbert claimed it belonged to his father, and that it meant more than anything to him. When I captured him, I nearly threw out the cloak but for his pleading. All throughout his time with me, he clung to this rag. I tore it from him during his escape, and he had to choose freedom or this bit of dyed wool. But he has connived to retrieve the cloak ever since. He sent Thrand after it, then on the morning you arrived he offered a ransom of gold for me to return it. Why?"

"Because it belonged to his father?" Runa prodded the cloak again. "It's just a rag."

"It's just a rag," Ulfrik agreed, drawing a knife from his belt. "After speaking with Konal and Kell last night, I knew it was nothing more than a rag. And the hiding place of Humbert's treasure."

He smoothed out the cloak, felt for the thick and tightly sewn hems and the hard lumps concealed within. Knife point beneath the first stitch, he ripped down the length, his hand quaking and heart pounding.

Gems rolled out from the seam: brilliant stones that sparkled like unearthly eyes, rubies like frozen blood, green and yellow gems that flashed as if rejoicing at being revealed. Cutting along all the edges, more stones popped out, until he had brushed them all into a pile large enough to nearly fill two hands.

Runa covered her mouth and gasped. Ulfrik placed his knife to the side, stepped back and stared at the glittering mound.

"Ander was true. The gods spoke to him. The treasure was hanging over my head all these long months. We are rich beyond imagining, Wife. My hall will be glorious and my men will be adorned with gold armbands. You will dress in the finest linen and wear gold every day. Finally, Runa, we will fulfill our destinies with this treasure."

"But these belong to Konal." Runa's voice was muffled behind her trembling hands.

"No, they belong to Anscharic, who lost them to Konal. Now they belong to me, to us, Wife." Mention of Konal's name galvanized him, and he swept the gems back into the bag and stuffed the cloak over them.

He and Runa stared at the bag for long moments in silence. A bird cawed in the branches above, and Ulfrik spotted a black raven eying them. It cawed again, and fluttered away, flying over their heads.

"Odin has seen this and approves. The gods have been well entertained, and this is the reward. We must keep it secret from everyone, not even Snorri nor Toki will know. In time, we will convert the stones to gold and live in great luxury in this new land."

Turning back toward the camp, neither spoke. Ulfrik continued to hear the raven cawing. The bird, the gods themselves, celebrated his newfound riches.

As they exited the woods, they entered into a future of bright possibilities.

AUTHOR'S NOTE

In 885, Vikings under the leadership of Sigfrid sailed into Frankia (modern day France) and demanded a bribe from the Holy Roman Emperor Charles the Fat to leave. After being rebuffed, Sigfrid raised an army intent on using violence to extract revenge along with the bribe. Cobbling together forces from all over the Viking world, though most were Danish, he led a fleet of seven hundred ships containing 30,000 warriors up the Seine until the bridges at Paris barred his fleet from further progress. This number, while duly recorded by eyewitnesses of the day, is likely a tremendous exaggeration. However, even a force half that size was still a formidable army.

Count Odo was charged with the defense of Paris, which was only an island in the Seine at that time. He could call on no more than two hundred men-at-arms to hold his city against the Vikings. The abbot of St. Germain, Joscelin, bolstered the Franks with his presence and his willingness to fight alongside the men in defense of the city. Desperately outnumbered, the Franks would hold out for an entire year.

Arriving on November 25, 885, Sigfrid tried to negotiate terms. The dialog of that negotiation as written in this novel is a close paraphrasing of what was documented at the time. In essence, the Parisians would not stand down and Sigfrid had to fight. His first attacks opened the following day. Two bridges blockaded the river, one wood and one stone and each with a tower to defend it. Choosing the northern tower, Sigrid had prepared war machines and understood how to besiege a fortress, but the Franks were equally versed in this style of warfare. They repelled the attack, dousing the Vikings with flaming oil. The Vikings attempted several times, but eventually had to retreat. The next day, they discovered the Franks had worked all night to add more levels to their tower. Now Sigfrid's ladders and siege towers were insufficient.

The Vikings dug in all around the city. They terrorized the surrounding countryside, gathering provisions and anything else they could carry away. After two months of siege, they had wearied of delays and tried a different tactic. They shifted to the southern tower and wooden bridge, launching several feints at the tower before assaulting the bridge. They attempted to fill the shallows with debris, ranging from tree trunks to corpses, anything to create a platform for attack. They failed again. On the third day, they sailed three burning ships at the southern bridge. It was an admirable idea, but the ships sank before fire could catch. However, the attack weakened the bridge a great deal.

By February 6, 886, after several days of steady rain, the bridge collapsed as the Seine overflowed its banks. The southern tower was now isolated and the twelve defenders within refused surrender. They sold their lives well, one of the Franks slaying many Danes before being killed. The Vikings were free to continue up the Seine, and left a holding force behind as they attacked other cities.

Odo used this opening to slip messengers through the Viking lines to reach Charles, who was in Italy. During this same period, reinforcements fought their way into Paris. The new men also brought supplies with them, and raised the Parisian's morale. The Vikings, on the other hand, grew ever wearier of the inaction. By mid-April, 886, Sigfrid offered to leave the battle for a mere sixty pounds of silver. Granted his bribe, he took his men and left Hrolf behind.

There is some contention about the identity of Hrolf, but I have chosen him to be Hrolf the Strider. He remained as the sole "leader" of the Viking force, though those who remained considered themselves all jarls and kings of their own men. In any case, all were hopeful of capturing great treasures. By mid-May, the Vikings' confidence renewed after learning Joscelin had died of the plague that tormented Paris at this time.

Finally, in desperation, Odo slipped out of Paris himself to plead with Charles for aid. He returned, fighting his way back into Paris, with news that Charles was on the march along with Henry of Saxony approaching from the east. The Parisians again celebrated their good fortune, only to see it fizzle. Vikings killed Henry on the march and Charles was lethargic in mobilizing his army. Everyone realized no help was coming soon, and in mid-summer Hrolf decided to launch another attempt to take Paris. Again, the attack was driven back.

At last in October, Charles arrived with the imperial army. He camped at the foot of Montmarte, a hill outside of Paris at that time. He surrounded the Viking camp and was ready to crush the invaders in the teeth of his army. However, the Viking indifference to death and defeat shook Charles's faith in the outcome of the impending battle. Instead he negotiated with Hrolf, throwing away victory and making the criminal decision to bestow everything to Hrolf that Odo and the Parisians had so valiantly fought to deny. He promised seven hundred pounds of silver to be delivered in the following spring if the Vikings agreed to withdraw. He also allowed them free passage of the Seine and employed them in suppressing Burgundia, which had risen against Charles.

Odo was understandably furious. He denied the Vikings passage around his island fortress and vowed to continue the battle. The Vikings had to carry their ships overland to another river and sail to Burgundia.

The siege of Paris demonstrated the key strategic value of that island fortress. Prior to this attack, it had never been used for a capitol or regarded with much importance. Whoever controlled Paris could control all of the center of France.

Anscharic was a true historical figure. Also known as Askericus, he served as the bishop of Paris from the time of Joscelin's death until the end of his life. He came from a powerful family in the Isle de France, and was likely a relation of the Counts of Vermandois. His family had an active history of fighting against the Vikings who raided their lands. Everything else I have presented about Anscharic is fiction. Whether he had ever been a prisoner of Vikings is not known, and if he had lost great treasures, that also remains unknown.

Such were the historical circumstances that Ulfrik moved through in his quest to find his treasure. He has arrived in Frankia at a pivotal time in its history. Charles the Fat has weakened his legitimacy after conceding to the Viking invaders. Hrolf is hungry and homeless, and sees Frankia as a ripe fruit for his picking. Some Vikings have become wealthy and famous, and owe it all to their exploits in Frankia. The land will undergo changes in the coming years, and Ulfrik is poised to exploit them. His Fate is far from complete, and more adventure remains ahead.

Printed in Great Britain
by Amazon

79154242R00190